# SUNBURN

ALSO BY DARREN DASH

## *THE EVIL AND THE PURE*

"The book flaunts the grim panache of a London crime saga, and all the characters are engaging, no matter how despicable they are. Not for the faint of heart, but this novel's character studies and ever shifting plot will excite fans of English noir." **Kirkus. Recommended read.**

"*The Evil And The Pure* is a deliciously dark delight; a gritty, realistic look at the depths of human depravity. The twists and turns have you reeling with shock. A glory to read. 5/5 stars." **Matthew R Bell's BookBlogBonanza.**

"A thoughtful and enthralling examination of a society that is seedy, corrupt and painfully uncompromising. Few writers can so easily and powerfully communicate the complexities of people dragged into a world of darkness and despair." **Safie Maken Finlay, author.**

"I found myself brilliantly horrified and captivated as I read and was taken along on a dark journey with a range of dangerous, sick and even innocent characters." **Chase That Horizon.**

## *AN OTHER PLACE*

"This is, by far, the best book of 2016. Possibly the best book of this decade... the bastard love child of Kafka and Rod Serling, throwing in a dash of Ray Bradbury for good measure. 5/5 --brilliant." **Kelly Smith Reviews.**

"Darren Dash has opened a new artery of terror... hints of *The Twilight Zone*, *Pines*, and *Station Eleven*." **The Literary Connoisseur.**

"This book really did blow my mind. Each page turn was both chilling and thrilling in equal measure. The conclusion left me with goosebumps. 5/5!" **Rachel Hobbs, author**

"This story had me hooked from the get go... the feel of *The Twilight Zone* with hints of *Fringe* and *28 Days Later* but yet an entity entirely of it's own... an ending that sent my mind into a spin. 5 stars." **Reviews And Randomness.**

# SUNBURN

DARREN DASH

HOME OF THE DAMNED LTD

*Sunburn*

*by Darren Dash*

*Copyright © 2015 by Home Of The Damned Ltd*

*Cover design by Liam Fitzgerald.* http://www.frequency.ie/

*Proofread by Zoe Markham.* http://markhamcorrect.com/

*First electronic edition published by Home Of The Damned Ltd June 1st 2015*

*Second electronic edition published January 2017*

*First physical edition published by Home Of The Damned Ltd June 1st 2015*

*Second physical edition published January 2017.*

*The right of Darren Dash to be identified as the Author of the Work has been asserted by him in accordance with the Copyright, Designs and Patents Act 1988.*

*All rights reserved. No part of this publication may be reproduced, stored in a retrieval system, or transmitted, in any form or by any means without the prior written permission of the publisher, nor be otherwise circulated in any form of binding or cover other than that in which it is published and without a similar condition being imposed on the subsequent purchaser.*

*All characters in this publication are fictitious and any resemblance to real persons, living or dead is purely coincidental.*

*www.darrendashbooks.com*

*www.homeofthedamned.com*

# PART ONE

*"we're all going on a summer holiday"*

The beast advanced through the forest in search of prey. Despite its great size, it was fleet of foot and made almost no noise as it hunted.

Smaller creatures caught sight of the beast and withdrew into the shadows, sensing menace in the sniffing of its nostrils, the slight twitching of its lips, the heavy scent of blood both old and fresh that clung to it like a caul. The beast spotted some of them as they scurried clear of its path but didn't give chase. It was holding out for richer pickings.

The beast came to a clearing and paused to study a three-quarters full moon. Its mouth opened in a fanged smile and it made a low gurgling sound as it spread its arms and urinated lightly with pleasure. The beast was a creature of the night and the moon was its guiding light. Though its eyesight was weak, it could make out the shape of the heavenly orb, and it was always a welcome sight.

The beast licked its upper lip, teasing dried flakes of blood, remembering other bright nights when it had hunted and killed and wallowed in thick red juices. The beast could manoeuvre in total darkness but preferred nights like this, when it could see the blood dripping from its fingers, the terror in the eyes of its victims, its guts shifting sinuously as it ripped with its fangs and swallowed.

The beast gurgled again and moved on. It never lingered in the open. It knew that there were other hunters, creatures who stood upright like itself, who feared and loathed those who were different. They were many, those others, and clever in ways that the beast was not, with access to tools that more than compensated for their physical frailties. If the beast was spotted by one of them, it would have to flee. There were times when it could engage its loathed foes, places where it was free to stand and fight, but not here, not now.

The beast drifted through the forest, making its own path, no fear of getting lost. It was at home in such terrain, having spent its entire life migrating from one vast wooded expanse to another. It had crossed the continent many times, never stopping in one place for long, always on the move, safety in constant vagrancy.

The beast's stomach rumbled and it paused again, this time in the shadows, waiting for its insides to settle. It scowled, angry that it hadn't snatched a rodent earlier, to keep the first pangs of hunger at bay.

The beast picked up pace, head rotating continuously as it listened and sniffed. It acknowledged the need for patience, yet it was hard to hold itself in check. It wanted to roar and scare up the local animals, send them bolting from their holes, so that it could give chase. But that tactic should only be used as a last resort, if all else had failed and the beast was ravenous. The forest rarely rewarded those who didn't respect the calm, established rules of the hunt.

Although it usually relied on its hearing and scent when hunting, on this night the beast saw its prey first. There must have been a forest fire in this section, because the trees didn't grow so thickly here, letting in moonlight. The beast spotted movement ahead, a large shape, and froze, waiting for the scene to come into focus.

The shape shifted again and the beast realised it was a she-wolf. It was unusual to find a wolf by itself, but the beast could smell no others in the vicinity. The wolf was agitated — she kept pawing the ground and whimpering. If she'd been paying attention, she would have caught the beast's scent and dashed off into the darkness, but she was distracted, unaware of the threat.

The beast backtracked, then slowly circled until it was upwind of the wolf. Digging its hands into the forest floor, it smeared dirt over its arms, legs, chest and face, to mask its smell. It jiggled its stomach around, to work out any rumbles, then closed in for the kill.

The wolf was acting strangely, digging through twigs and leaves with her snout, snarling softly. The beast had no idea why she was distressed and it didn't care. In the forest, in the eternal battle between hunter and prey, you seized any boon that you could.

The beast drew to a halt next to a large, blackened tree. It was only several paces from the wolf now, but it would have to take them in the open, and the wolf would almost certainly spot it coming. It thought about trying to sneak up on her, but decided to rush the canine instead. Flexing its fingers, it readied itself for action, then darted forward.

The wolf's head whipped round and she bared her teeth. She tried to face the onrushing predator, but she didn't have time to straighten, and the beast took her from the side, barrelling across the floor with her, slamming her into the trunk of a tree.

The wolf howled with pain and shock, then snapped at the beast, fangs coming together *with frightening power and speed. But the beast had yanked its arm clear, well used to wolves. As the wolf struggled and sought another angle of attack, the beast's stomach shifted in a way that she had not anticipated. Her eyes widened as she was pressed further back against the tree, suffocating in the embrace of a creature like none she'd faced before.*

*There was a sharp cracking sound as the wolf's spine splintered. The beast knew the duel was over, but held her against the tree a while longer, until she stopped spasming. It had been wounded in the past by animals in their death throes, so it knew better than to relax until the job was definitely done.*

*When the beast was certain that the wolf was dead, it let her corpse drop and licked its lips with anticipation, looking forward to ripping open her stomach and sinking its face into the mess of her hot, delicious guts. Before it could, it was surprised by a frail whimpering sound. Turning away from the slain wolf, the beast retraced its steps and came to the point where the wolf had been sniffing. It saw now why she had abandoned the safety of her pack.*

*A thin, trembling cub lay half-buried in a pile of leaves. The sickly thing must have been the wolf's, and it had obviously been unable to travel any further, either because of illness or hunger. Rather than leave the cub behind, its mother had remained with it, warming it as best she could, hoping it would recover.*

*The cub whined, eyes swimming, wanting to be fed and comforted. The beast stared at the defenceless animal and thought for a moment of feeding it blood from its mother, nurturing it, rearing it as a pet. The beast had never had a pet. It would be nice to have the company of a young, idolising creature.*

*But a pet might attract attention, and it would slow down the beast and maybe render it vulnerable — in a fight-or-flight situation, if the pet got trapped, the beast might feel compelled to duck back to help, end up getting caught as the cub's mother had. No, it was better off without such a companion. You could survive longer in the night if you had no ties to any creatures other than those you were aligned to by blood.*

*As the cub shivered and mewled, the beast stretched out a massive, bloodstained paw. It wrapped its fingers round the cub's head, waited a moment, savouring the feel of the cub's warm breath on its palm. And then it crushed.*

## ONE

Martini was fighting to claim the right to choose where she, Dominic, Curran and Liz went on holiday. The boys had arranged their last few trips abroad. The quartet had hit Brussels, Prague and Ibiza, where they'd drunk themselves cross-eyed and partied till they dropped. Now Martini wanted to try something different.

"But you had a good time in the other places," Dominic reminded her. "You loved Ibiza. I've never seen you dance so much."

"Yeah," Martini sniffed, "but there's more to life than clubbing and getting hammered. That was fine when we were younger, but we'll be twenty-three soon. We need to grow up and broaden our horizons."

Dominic didn't like the sound of that. It was like listening to his mother tell him he had to get a proper job and stop wasting his life working in a bar. He'd been fighting his corner for weeks, since they'd started to discuss destinations. Curran was promoting Amsterdam. Dominic was interested in Corfu or Cyprus. Curran's girlfriend Liz was up for Majorca. But Martini had her heart set on a cultural vacation.

"We've had three booze trips in a row. Enough is enough," she insisted.

Dominic had tried to compromise. He'd made various suggestions, all of which she'd shot down, accusing him of not being adventurous when he mooted the idea of exploring France by rail, or flying to Rome, or pushing the boat out and chancing New York.

"Fine," he finally snapped. "If my ideas are shit, I'll leave it all to you. You can research it, book it, do the whole fucking thing. How does that sound?"

"Perfect," Martini snarled, and there was no pulling back after that.

Curran laughed the next day when Dominic told him. "I'm up for anything, Newt, you know that. If it keeps her sweet, let her off."

Liz wasn't so laid back. She wanted to be included in the planning, and sulked until Martini took her aside and fed her some details of what she had in mind.

Martini spent the next few weeks scouring the web any time she had the flat to herself. She worked in a bar, like Dominic, but different hours. He'd often come in to find her hunched over her laptop (it was his really, as he'd bought it for uni before dropping out, but she'd appropriated it after moving in with him the year before), making notes, checking travel sites. It killed him not to ask any questions, but he kept his mouth shut, figuring a deal was a deal. Besides, this way he'd have a free hand when it came to organising their next trip. He'd book two weeks in Thailand, see how she liked that!

What she *did* tell them, once she'd booked everything, was that they were going somewhere hot. They'd need walking boots for some of it, but there would be days when they could swim and sunbathe as well. They'd be doing a lot of driving, which didn't bother Dominic and Curran, as neither could drive. That meant Martini and Liz would have to share wheel duties. Liz grumbled about that, but Martini swore she'd handle the lion's share.

And that was all she revealed.

A month later, with the trio due to fly out first thing the next morning, she was still giving nothing away. She'd told them it was an early flight, that they'd have to head to Stansted the night before and wait in the airport before they checked in, but nothing more than that.

Despite his grumbling, Dominic was enjoying the mystery, thinking of all the possible places they could visit. Italy, Germany, Croatia, Spain… It couldn't be much further afield, based on the money she'd asked them to fork out.

He could have checked the schedules for Stansted. He didn't know the exact time of departure but Martini wouldn't drag them there last thing at night unless they were on an early flight. But he'd avoided the airport's site, not wanting to rob Martini of her big reveal.

He worked through lunch at the bar, returned to the flat in the afternoon to catch some sleep. Dominic could nap any time.

Martini worked later than him, and turned up after he'd been dead to the world for an hour. She finished her last bit of packing, then slid into bed, cuddled up to him, rubbed her nose over the back of his neck and murmured, "Hey, sexy."

"Mmm," Dominic grunted, eyelids flickering open. "What time is it?"

"Nearly seven."

"Why did you wake me? I told you I wanted to sleep until ten."

"I'm horny," Martini giggled, reaching round to cup his testicles — it was a hot day in July and he was sleeping naked.

"Not now," Dominic said, rolling over to escape her wandering fingers.

"Don't be shy," Martini smirked. "We can have a quickie and you can go back to sleep when we're finished. I'll snooze too."

"No," Dominic snapped. "I'm tired."

Martini's lips thinned. Although she was half Mexican, she most resembled her English mother. It was only when she got angry that her father's genes flared through. At times like that her lips tightened, her eyes narrowed and the fiery Mexican in her woke up and got ready to tear the world a new arsehole. If Dominic had been looking, he'd have spotted the warning signs and let her ravage him for the sake of a quiet life, but he was facing away, eyes closed.

"Seems like you never want to screw me these days," Martini said quietly.

"Don't be stupid," Dominic replied.

"Have you lost interest?" she whispered. "Are you seeing someone else? Are you bored of me?"

"Yeah," Dominic said sourly. "That's it."

She exploded with screams that shocked Dominic fully awake. As he gawped at her, she slapped him and told him she wasn't going on holiday, they were through, he could go with Curran and Liz by himself, he'd probably prefer that.

Sitting up and fending off her blows, he roared back that maybe he would, called her a mad Mexican, a cat in heat, all he wanted was to catch some sleep, they could make love non-stop on holiday, unless they didn't allow fucking in whatever hellhole she'd chosen to take them to.

"Like I'd even notice if you *were* fucking me," she sneered.

"What's that supposed to mean?" he yelled.

She raised the little finger of her right hand and twitched it.

Dominic swore and said that if she wasn't a woman, he'd punch her.

"If I wasn't a woman, you'd be too scared to punch me," she shot back.

Dominic cursed again, knowing he couldn't top that one. He threw off the thin sheet which he'd been huddled beneath, told her he was sick of her, she could choke on her holiday, he was going down the pub to get drunk. Stormed off to the bathroom, slammed the door shut, ran the shower and stepped in, turning it down cold until he was shivering, butting the wall softly with his forehead, eyes closed, wanting to kill her.

He didn't hear her enter the bathroom. The first he knew of her presence was when she laid a soft hand on his back. He turned and angrily stared into her dark brown eyes.

"I'm sorry," she said, blinking back tears.

His stomach flipped. He wanted to carry on the argument, hurt her as she'd hurt him, but he always melted when she turned on the waterworks, especially as he knew they were genuine, Martini never one for crocodile tears. That was the way her temper flowed. After the righteous fury came the contrite calm.

"It's OK," Dominic whispered, pulling her in beside him.

Martini winced when the water struck her. "Cold," she said with surprise.

"Yeah." He reached out to turn it to hot. She stopped him.

"It's OK," she said. "I don't mind."

"You're sure?" He squinted. "You hate the cold. Your Mexican blood."

"I know, but I don't care tonight. Let's turn blue together. Like Smurfs."

"Silly," he smiled, and she smiled too, and they stood there for ages, holding one another, shivering in the chill spray of the water, argument forgotten, freezing but happy.

## TWO

They made love when they returned to the bedroom. They started fast and furious, but Martini slowed things down. "There's no rush," she murmured. "We can sleep at the airport."

"Fuck sleep," Dominic panted, adjusting his pace, letting Martini guide him.

He adored her body. She was short, not much more than five-one, but that was fine as he barely topped the five-seven mark. A bit overweight, but her curves were to die for. Sometimes she dieted, and while he would never say it out loud, he missed her pot and the bulge of her bum when she did. He liked having something to squeeze and hold on to. On occasion he'd playfully sink his teeth into her love handles or her buttocks and mumble, "Mine! All mine!"

Martini had been dieting the last couple of months, to look slim in the holiday snaps, so there wasn't much for Dominic to sink his teeth into tonight, but that was OK. He knew her love of chocolate would restore the curves not long after their return. Holidays were a fallow time, but they wouldn't go anywhere again until Christmas. He'd have his chubby little Mexican back for a long spell after this. (He had never called her that to her face. Dominic wasn't the genius his mother claimed, but he was no moron either.)

Martini came first, beneath the caresses of Dominic's fingers and tongue. As she shook and moaned, he crawled on top and thrust away, climaxing with a soft but prolonged groan while she was still warmly throbbing.

Martini giggled when she felt him come and wrapped her legs round his, drawing him in tight. She ran a hand through his light brown hair. He'd had it cut short a few days earlier. Martini preferred it longer, but Dominic didn't like swimming with long hair, too hard to maintain.

"Good?" she asked, kissing him softly.

"Terrible," he smirked.

Martini raked a fingernail down his back. Dominic yelped, then laughed and kissed her more firmly.

"Careful," she warned him, "or you'll get another boner."

"Wouldn't that be a tragedy?" he smiled.

Dominic rolled off and lay on his back as Martini hurried to the bathroom to clean herself. That annoyed him sometimes, that she could never just lie there and enjoy the afterglow. But not tonight. He felt generous and warm. He would have forgiven her anything right now, even if she'd taken a dump without shutting the door.

They lay on the bed for more than an hour when she returned, cuddling gently. Dominic half dozed but Martini stayed awake, one eye on her watch, thinking about the holiday, hoping the other three would enjoy it, worrying that they might not. She was pretty sure that Liz would have a good time, and Dominic would too under normal circumstances, but he was a different person when Curran was around — *one of the lads*. If Curran was in a foul mood, Dominic would follow him down that bitter road.

*I should have told them*, she thought. *Ran it by them before I booked. Made sure they were all happy with the plan.* But it was too late now. She'd just have to hope Curran was on good form. If not, at least she'd have Liz for support. Worst case scenario, they could leave the boys in a pub and head off for daytrips by themselves.

When it was time to make a move, Martini nudged Dominic. "I'm awake," he grunted, propping himself on an elbow and rubbing his eyelids. He'd been dreaming and thought he had to get up for work. Then he remembered the holiday and relaxed. "How much time do we have?"

"Three-quarters of an hour," Martini said. "I wanted to allow time for us to go through our bags again, in case we forgot anything."

Dominic smiled. "It's hard to be sure when I don't know where we're going. Want to tell me now?"

"Not until we get to the airport," Martini chuckled. "Don't worry, I'll have a look through your stuff, make sure you don't leave anything essential behind."

"I like leaving the decisions to you," Dominic said as she got up and stretched. "I could get used to this."

"Don't," Martini said. "I'm not your mother."

"That's not what I meant," Dominic growled.

"Yes it is," Martini laughed. "Every man is looking for a replacement for his mother. But you won't find her here, Master Newton."

"If I was looking for a mother replacement, I'd have gone for a bird with bigger tits," Dominic said grumpily as she stretched again and her breasts flattened out.

"Let's not start talking about size," Martini murmured, giving her little finger a wiggle, the same gesture that had tipped him over the edge earlier. But this time he laughed. Rising, he bent and kissed her left nipple playfully, then her right. A quick peck on the lips to finish. Then he went to check his bag and get dressed.

## THREE

Their flat was close to Waterloo, so rather than trek to Liverpool Street to catch the Stansted Express, they got the Tube to Tottenham Hale and linked up with the train there.

They sat down at a table opposite one another. It was late, there was hardly anyone on the train, and the seats next to theirs were free, so they stacked the small wheelie cases on them.

Martini was tired, so she dozed. Dominic had downloaded several books on to his Kindle, but he wasn't in a reading mood, so he fished around in his pockets instead. He found an old cinema ticket, a tissue, some fluff.

Bored, he reached into the front pocket of his case and pulled out their passports. Dominic stared at his photo. He'd acquired the passport when he was nineteen. Only three years ago, but he already looked a lot older. He'd been in his second year of uni when this was taken, shortly before he quit. He'd never been interested in psychology, had signed up for the course because he thought it might impress the ladies. (It had certainly impressed his mother.) Vague thoughts of becoming a teacher after he'd graduated. But in truth it had been a stalling tactic while he tried to figure out what the hell he wanted to do for the rest of his life.

Dominic still wasn't sure, and that troubled him as he gazed at his photo. It was one thing not knowing what you wanted from life when you were a nineteen-year-old student, but a man of twenty-two should have a clearer idea, shouldn't he?

Dominic flicked through the passport, looking at all the empty pages waiting to be stamped by stern-faced officials in far-flung lands. He used to think he'd cover the globe and travel to exotic locations. Now he wasn't sure. To date he hadn't ventured far from the standard tourist path, and when he'd gone abroad, he'd spent most of his time getting drunk and sleeping off hangovers.

*Fuck it,* he thought. *There's loads of time to decide. Dad told me to enjoy my twenties, have fun, not tie myself down until I'm thirty and starting to slow up.* He's often said how much he regrets having had me when he was twenty-four.

Dominic chuckled quietly, careful not to disturb Martini. He liked his dad. The old man was easy to chat with over a couple of pints. Even Dominic's mum didn't have much bad to say about him, though things had been hard for the first year or two when they divorced.

Dominic put his passport down and opened Martini's. Hers was less than six months old. She'd lost her other passport when she'd taken it out one night to a club — bouncers sometimes carded her, so she liked to go prepared. Normally she took her driving license, but she'd misplaced that.

He looked at the name on the passport and smiled. *Isabella Martinez.* Her father had named her after his mother and grandmother, but with both women still alive at the time of Isabella III's birth, the baby needed a distinguishing day-to-day name. At first she'd been Izzy. Then, when she was five, one of her mother's cousins stayed with them for a few days and came up with the joke name, Martini Martinez. For a while they'd all called her that, a bit of fun, no intention of sticking with it. But young Isabella loved the name and insisted they continue to address her as Martini long after the cousin had returned home.

Dominic chuckled again, thinking of how the stubborn girl had forced her family to bow to her wishes, and this time Martini stirred. "Wassup?" she mumbled. "Are we there?"

"Not yet," Dominic soothed her. "Go back to sleep."

"What are you chuckling at?" she asked.

"Nothing."

"Dumbass," she yawned, then let her head loll and drifted off to sleep again.

Dominic closed Martini's passport and replaced the two of them. After that he leant back and stared out the window at the darkness for the rest of the journey.

## FOUR

Curran was waiting for them when they got off the train. "My people," he beamed, shaking Dominic's hand and half hugging him, kissing Martini on both cheeks.

He was nearly two years older than Dominic and several centimetres taller. Where Dominic carried no extra weight, Curran had already developed a paunch from his years of drinking and binge-eating when drunk. He had a head of wild, curly, straw-coloured hair. It had started to recede in his mid-teens but that didn't bother Curran. He was looking forward to being fat and bald. *Looking good is a pain,* he often said. *This way there'll be less shit for me to worry about.*

Curran was dressed in knee-length shorts and a T-shirt, the same as Dominic, but where Dominic's shorts were a dark blue colour, Curran's were a psychedelic mix, and his T-shirt sported the cover of a pink-shaded closeup of a man's face from some old album that Dominic had never heard of.

"Who the hell were *Half Man Half Biscuit*?" Dominic laughed.

"Fucked if I know," Curran grinned. "But isn't it a cool cover?"

"No."

"You're just jealous."

Curran had a negligible rucksack slung over one shoulder, the sort you might take if you were going on a hike.

"Is that all you're bringing?" Martini asked disapprovingly.

"Sure," Curran said. "It's got everything I need. A spare pair of shorts, a few T-shirts, Speedos, a toothbrush, a cardigan in case it gets cold, razor, little plastic bag with toothpaste, deodorant, a tiny bottle of shaving oil."

"What about mouthwash?" Dominic asked.

"I keep telling you that stuff will give you throat cancer," Curran tutted.

"And walking boots?" Martini asked more pointedly.

"These will be fine," Curran said, twisting his feet to show off his purple Crocs.

"They look like a woman's," Dominic noted.

"I don't believe in gender stereotyping," Curran shot back.

"I told you we'd be going for long walks," Martini growled, her lips thinning.

"I know," Curran smiled, "but these will be fine. I could walk forever in these."

"You got blisters from the last pair of Crocs you wore, when we were in Ibiza," Dominic reminded him.

"Did I?" Curran shrugged. "Oh well, these are a better fit. I've been wearing them for a couple of hours now, not a whisper of a blister."

Martini glared at him.

"They'll be fine," Curran said, trying to appease her. "I don't like heavy boots. I'll be happier in these. If they cut my feet up, I'll suffer in silence. I won't even bother you for a plaster."

Martini sniffed dismissively. "Doesn't matter to me. Where's Liz?"

Curran puffed out his cheeks. "Can you believe this heat? Let's push through. They'll have air con inside, won't they?"

"You know that they do," Martini huffed. "We flew to Prague from here."

"Yeah?" Curran said, blinking as if that was news to him. "Then what are we waiting for? Do you want me to carry your bag?"

"You don't carry a wheelie case," Martini said, smiling despite herself.

"Typical modern technology," Curran sighed. "Putting a man out of a job. Come on then. Last one to China's a rotten egg."

Martini laughed and trailed Curran to the escalator, rarely able to stay mad at him for long. Dominic followed in troubled silence. He knew Curran far better than Martini did. He'd seen a flicker in his friend's eyes, clocked the slight catch in his voice. Something was wrong. And while Dominic was no Sherlock Holmes, he didn't think it was insignificant that Liz wasn't on the platform. He had a sinking feeling in his stomach that Martini would soon be hitting the roof.

## FIVE

Four minutes later, as Dominic had feared, Martini went apeshit.

"Liz *isn't coming?*" she roared, not caring that people were staring at them.

Curran grinned sheepishly. "I was gonna tell you before but I didn't want to ruin the holiday for you."

"You're too fucking considerate, *Jerome*," Martini snarled, not just looking Mexican now but sounding like her father too. That was bad. Her accent only slipped if she was truly livid.

"What happened?" Dominic asked.

"Yeah, *Jerome*," Martini barked, again using the name that Curran hated. "Did she find another man? Did she get sick of you pissing in the sink when you were drunk? Did she catch you cheating on her?"

Curran blinked, surprised by the venom in Martini's tone. She'd verbally attacked him many times in the past, but usually when he was drunk and immune to her insults. It wasn't often that he found himself at a loss for words, but this was one of those rare occasions. Out of his depth, he looked to Dominic for help.

Dominic shrugged. "Liz was supposed to be the other driver," he said quietly. "This means Martini will have to do all the driving."

"Yeah," Martini snorted, the worst of her anger ebbing away, mollified now that Dominic had taken her side. "Like I've nothing better to do than act as a chauffeur for you two dicks."

Curran cleared his throat and chanced a shaky smile. "It's not what you think."

"No?" Martini said icily, raising an eyebrow.

"She hasn't dumped me."

"Then why the hell isn't she here?" Martini challenged him.

Curran looked away. "Her dad had a heart attack," he mumbled.

There was a moment of dreadful silence.

"Oh God," Martini moaned.

"Two days ago," Curran went on. "She didn't want anyone to know. Her mum is odd like that, wants to keep it secret. Liz had to go be with the family. She didn't even think about the holiday. I was going to mention it but, y'know, I didn't feel it was appropriate."

"Of course not," Martini said. "God, I'm so sorry. I shouldn't have yelled. Poor Liz. I'll phone her to give her our condolences."

"No," Curran said quickly. "I wasn't supposed to tell anyone. If she'd remembered the holiday, she would have told me to feed you some story, but like I said…"

"Poor Liz," Martini said again, tears in her eyes. Then she frowned. "But you can't go away. She needs you."

Curran shook his head. "Her old man hates me. The rest of the family don't like me either, not since Esthergate."

"When you cheated on Liz," Martini scowled. "There have been a few other *gates* too."

"Yeah," Curran conceded, "but they don't know about those. Esther was enough. They don't want me around, even for a funeral. It's good timing actually, me going on holiday like this. If it comes to the worst, I'll be well out of it, and they'll be happily rid of me."

There was another silence, while they all thought about Liz and her father.

"What about you?" Dominic said in the end, touching Martini's elbow. "Do you still want to go? If the driving's going to be too much for you, we can knock it on the head."

"I don't know," Martini said. "It's too late to get our money back." She mulled it over, then sighed. "No, the driving won't be that bad. We can cut a few things out of the itinerary, so that I can have a break and enjoy the sights."

"Brilliant," Curran beamed. "I've been looking forward to this, trying to figure out where we're going. Come on, M, hit us with it. What have you got up your sleeve for Newt and the Curran? Where are you whisking us off to?"

Martini smiled shyly. "It begins with a B."

"Brussels?" Curran said, excited. "Bruges? Belgium?"

"Bruges and Brussels are *in* Belgium, numbnuts," Dominic said.

"Berlin?" Curran pressed. "Budapest? Bilbao? Barcelona?" His eyes lit up. "Say it's Barcelona. I've always wanted to go there. It's meant to be mental."

"No," Martini said, her smile faltering. "It's none of those. It's…" A pause for dramatic effect, then she hit them with it. "Bulgaria!"

Curran's face frosted over. Dominic's eyebrows furrowed.

"*What?*" Martini growled defensively.

"Bulgaria?" Curran said with genuine astonishment. "Why the fuck would anyone –"

"– *not* want to go to lovely Bulgaria?" Dominic cut in, before World War III erupted. He wrapped an arm round Martini and kissed the side of her head, furiously signalling Curran with his eyebrows, warning him not to rile her.

Curran was sulking when Dominic released Martini, but he didn't criticise her. Instead he muttered rather artlessly, "What's in Bulgaria?"

"Mountains," Martini said stiffly. She'd anticipated this reaction but was still disappointed, having secretly hoped to wow them with her choice. "Forests. Lakes. Rivers. Lush lowlands. Spectacular scenery. Beaches too, but we won't be going to those."

"Beer," Dominic improvised. "Bulgaria's well known for its local beers."

Curran stared at him sceptically. "Name me a Bulgarian beer."

Dominic thought hard but came up blank. "Like I said, they're local. Lots of microbreweries. I saw a programme about them."

As Curran's dubious stare lengthened, Dominic flashed on an old geography lesson. "Sofia is the capital, isn't it?"

"Yes," Martini said.

"That's party central," Dominic assured Curran. "Raves everywhere, twenty-four seven, never pauses for breath, I saw all about it on that programme."

"Yeah?" Curran said, showing some enthusiasm at last.

"Absolutely," Dominic lied, smiling as widely as he could.

"We're not going to Sofia," Martini said with a hint of merry malice.

"We aren't?" Dominic said, smile slipping.

"We're going to Plovdiv."

Both men gawped at her.

"It's the second largest city in Bulgaria," she informed them.

Curran glanced wryly at Dominic. "That programme say anything about… what was it?" he asked Martini.

"Plovdiv."

"…Plovdiv?" Curran finished.

"No," Dominic wheezed, unable to carry the lie to that extent.

There was another silence, cool as the air con. Curran finally broke it. "Fuck it," he laughed. "I've never heard of the place, but what does that matter? There are loads of great places I've never heard of. It'll be brilliant. I'm always happy to try different beers. They're bound to have a few nightclubs. It'll be a blast. Nice one, M. Good call. You're a legend."

Martini smiled gratefully and everything was temporarily good between them. Moving on, they set off to find seats where they could rest for the next several hours, until it was time to check in for their flight in the morning.

## SIX

After a quick scout, they chose seats near the car hire kiosks. There were others there too, mostly people their age or younger, booked on to early flights, who couldn't get to the airport at the crack of dawn or pay for a hotel nearby. They were sleeping, chatting quietly, playing cards, reading.

As he was settling down, Dominic spotted someone with a Bulgarian travel guide. "Got one of those for me to have a look at?" he asked Martini.

"No," she said. "I don't like travel guides."

"What are you talking about?" Dominic frowned.

"They give you too much information," she said. "I want us to discover things for ourselves. I did some research online, booked a hotel for when we arrive and the night before we leave, and we'll get a map over there. Apart from that we'll be flying blind."

Martini beamed as if that was a good thing. Dominic thought differently, but this wasn't the time to say so. He'd wait and see how the holiday developed. Keep quiet about his misgivings for now. Save the arguments for later.

"So what's Plovdiv like?" Curran asked, stretching out, taking off one of his Crocs to scratch his toes.

"A lovely old city," Martini said.

"Lots of bars and clubs?" he pushed.

Martini's lips thinned. "I suppose. But we won't be there long. We'll have a look around tomorrow afternoon and the following morning, then we're off."

"Where?" Curran asked.

Martini smirked. "You'll find out when we get there. Let's take it a day at a time. I want to keep you on your toes."

"In that case I'll leave the Crocs off," Curran laughed, wiggling his toes at her.

Martini laughed too, then rooted through her case, making sure she had everything. After a quick check of documents and clothes, she headed for the toilet. Curran waited until she was out of earshot, then sat up and stared accusingly at Dominic.

"I know," Dominic groaned.

"Bulgaria," Curran cried. "What the fuck's in Bulgaria? And don't give me shit about microbreweries. I can tell when you're lying. Your ears go red."

"No they don't," Dominic grunted.

"Had you any idea?" Curran asked, tugging at a lock of his hair.

"No. I knew it wasn't a beach holiday, but I thought we'd be going to Italy or Spain, somewhere we could explore but still hit a big city or two."

"I suppose it can't be that bad," Curran mused. "Everywhere in Europe has cheap beer, doesn't it?"

Dominic nodded. "Except Scandinavia."

"There you go," Curran smiled. "We can get smashed every night."

"But if we're going out driving every day…" Dominic sighed.

"That won't happen," Curran said confidently. "Martini's full of plans, but get a few cocktails down her and she won't want to hit the road any more than we do."

"I wouldn't be too sure of that," Dominic said gloomily. Then he squinted. "That was a load of shit about Liz's dad, wasn't it?"

Curran looked surprised. "How do you know?"

Dominic grinned. "Your ears turned red."

"*Touché!*" Curran laughed, then smiled guiltily. "She caught me trying to get my leg over one of her friends. I guess it was the final straw. She took all her stuff from the flat, a good bit of my gear too. I think it's for real this time."

"Why did you lie about it?" Dominic asked.

"When I saw how pissed Martini was, I didn't dare tell her the truth. It's better this way. She can enjoy the holiday now. She'd have bitched away otherwise."

"You're a real diplomat, aren't you?" Dominic said sarcastically.

"Yeah," Curran replied. "I should be in the Peace Corps, me."

The next few minutes passed by peacefully. Then Martini returned. She was smiling sweetly. *Too* sweetly. "Guess who I just spoke with, Jerome?"

Curran stared at her, worried.

"That's right," Martini purred. "I thought I'd give Liz a quick buzz to sympathise with her."

"Martini," Curran croaked. "Let me explain."

"You son of a whore!" Martini screamed, alarming everyone around them and waking several people who'd been sleeping.

And that was the end of the peace for the rest of the night.

## SEVEN

She almost bailed. For hours she threatened to pull out and leave them to their own devices. It was bad enough that Liz wasn't coming, but to add insult to injury, she thought Curran had been toying with her, that he'd planned the story about Liz's father and set out to make her look foolish.

Curran spent those hours apologising profusely, swearing his innocence, telling her the lie had just popped out of his mouth. He said he was in a bad place mentally, he hated what he'd done to Liz, he was missing her, he was ashamed of himself, he hadn't wanted to admit his indiscretion in front of his friends.

Ultimately it was a threat of Curran's which swung her.

"I'll stay behind," he said stoically. "It's not fair that I spoil your holiday. Go without me. Don't worry about the money. I'm not entitled to a refund. You two go and have the trip of a lifetime. You'll enjoy it more without me."

"Damn right we will," Martini muttered, but she said it beneath her breath, because she'd caught Dominic's expression. He looked miserable at the thought of going on vacation without his friend. That should have angered Martini even more, but instead she found herself feeling sorry for him. He was probably just upset because he was on the verge of losing his drinking partner, but maybe there was more to it than that. Maybe he was concerned that Curran was truly hurting. Maybe Dominic wanted to console Curran in his hour of need.

*As if!* she snorted to herself. But she couldn't be certain, and her love for Dominic made her want to believe the best about him.

"Forget it," she finally sighed. "We'll go as planned and have as good a time as we can. We won't leave you behind."

Curran protested, but weakly, relieved (and surprised) to have won her over. He'd had no intention of staying, but would have split from them once they got there, gone off and had a wild week by himself. But he was happier now that he didn't have to do that. He liked it when Dominic was his wing man. He could get up to more mischief when he had a co-conspirator on board.

They breezed through security in the morning, had breakfast on the other side, just a sandwich and coffee. They were bleary-eyed and out of sorts, though Curran tried to lift the mood by singing lines from various songs and substituting Bulgaria for whatever the key word happened to be. Freddie Mercury's *Barcelona* was given a makeover. John Lennon's classic about a park in Liverpool became *Bulgarian Fields*. And then there was *Bye Bye, Bulgarian Pie*.

"Stop," Martini wept through tears of combined exhaustion and laughter.

"*Stop right now, thank you very much*," Curran sang in response, "*I need somebody with the Bulgarian touch.*"

"You should go on *X Factor*," Dominic grinned.

"No," Curran corrected him. "I should go on *Bulgaria's Got Talent*."

They stumbled on to the plane when their flight was called, chuckling, yawning, smelling as bad as most of the other passengers, who had also been up all night. The cabin crew were the only ones who seemed bright and fresh, smiling as if this was their favourite hour of the day.

"They're sadists," Curran said when Dominic pointed this out. "They know how much we're suffering and they get off on it."

"You think?" Dominic asked.

"They work for Ryanair," Curran reminded him. "That would bring out the vicious streak in anyone."

"Good point," Dominic said.

Martini had booked seats close to the front. She didn't like sitting further back because the turbulence was worse near the tail. Plus you got recycled air as it was pumped down the cabin, carrying germs from those ahead of you. Dominic doubted all of those claims, but she was a nervous flier and he didn't want to argue with her.

Curran slid in by the window without asking if either of the others wanted to sit there. Martini glared at him, but he pretended not to notice, dumped his rucksack between his feet, dug around in it, stuck on a pair of headphones and focused on his iPod, selecting tunes for the flight, putting together an impromptu playlist.

Martini took the middle seat while Dominic went through his case, pulling out the Kindle and his own MP3 player. Martini had already extracted a book of Sudoku puzzles from her luggage and was studying one which she'd started earlier.

Dominic waited for a break in the traffic of passengers boarding the plane, then put up the cases. Sitting down beside Martini, he leant over and kissed her cheek. She smiled at him wearily, then went back to her puzzle. Dominic sighed and started scrolling through his downloads, but then decided he'd wait until they were in the air.

Snapping his seat belt shut, Dominic slid the Kindle and MP3 player between the belt and his stomach, leant back and shut his eyes, hoping he'd be able to snooze. The long, argumentative night caught up with him and he was out flat a minute later. And not only did he sleep through take-off, he also slept through the entire flight to Bulgaria, not even stirring when Martini and Curran clambered over him at various times to go to the toilet.

# PART TWO

*"on the road to God knows where"*

*The beast hovered near the edge of a clearing and stared at a handful of old but carefully maintained cottages. They were clustered round a well that in past times had been the focal point of the settlements. Now they all had piped-in running water, but the owners had kept the well as a scenic feature.*

*The beast knew little of pipes and scenic features. It knew only that its enemies lived in places like this, and it hated them as much it feared them.*

*The beast's foes were everywhere. They bred in huge numbers and had long ago made the world theirs, felling trees, controlling the land, hunting and eradicating anything that posed a threat to their well-ordered lives.*

*The beast didn't blame the creatures for imposing their will on the rest of the natural kingdom. If it could have ruled as they did, it would, but it lacked their guile and inventiveness. It was closer in form and mind to them than any other animal, but their differences meant there could never be a coming together. The beast would always be an envious outsider, and they would always react with aggression if they noted its presence.*

*Not that many ever did. The beast was adept at slipping through the darkness unnoticed, rarely leaving the gloomy shadows of the forests, travelling across unwooded territories only when the weather was fierce and its enemies were sheltering from storms and snow. It hunted slyly, hiding the remains of its kills, leaving little evidence behind. It avoided domesticated animals unless it was starving, knowing from bitter experience that its enemies would search long and hard for predators who targeted what was theirs. And it almost never killed any of the two-legged masters of the world.*

Almost.

*The beast licked its lips as it recalled some of the precious times when it had broken its prime law. Occasionally it was forced to fight and kill, if one of them stumbled across its lair or crossed its path when it was hunting. On those occasions it killed in self-defence, disposed of the corpses as best it could, and moved on swiftly in a panic, fearful of being pursued by a vengeful mob.*

*But there were other, delightful times when the beast killed for pleasure, slowly and malevolently. It didn't allow itself such treats very often, normally just before it was due to migrate to a new area. On those nights it would stake out an isolated house before attacking its unsuspecting resident, or establish watch on a path and ambush the first unfortunate victim to come along.*

*The beast's penis hardened as it thought about ripping open their throats, drinking their blood, devouring their succulent inner organs. It stroked itself softly, longingly, wanting the past to be the present, to add to its store of blood-red memories.*

*The back door of one of the cottages opened and a child stepped out. The beast's breath caught in its throat and its hand stopped moving. It stared, wishing it had better eyesight, as the child crossed to the well and called down into it, listening for echoes.*

*The child was a girl, not much more than an infant. She had light hair and chubby cheeks. She was in her bare feet and a summer dress that exposed her legs and arms. Although it was dusk, it was still hot, and the dress provided all the cover that she required. As the beast watched hungrily, she turned away from the well and skipped towards the trees, singing as she advanced.*

*The beast had only tasted the flesh of a child twice in all its years. Like other animals, the two-legged creatures defended their young fiercely. It was madness to take one that had not matured. Its absence would be noted immediately, and its kin wouldn't rest in search of it.*

*As the child drew closer, the beast remembered the previous two. One had been a girl like this, who lived with an elderly woman. Hardly anyone came to visit them at their home, and the beast had felt safe killing the child along with the old crone. The other had been a boy, even younger than this girl, strapped to his father's chest. They were on a remote path, trekking in the wooded hills a long way from their village. Killing them had been a risk, but one the beast had been unable to resist when it caught the scent of the soft, sweet boy.*

*The child paused to study a flower and the beast leant forward, nostrils flaring, intoxicated by the scent. It looked around at the cottages. No sign of any adults. It could snatch the girl and be gone from here without anyone noticing, perhaps be far from this place before the girl was missed, keep moving, one hand clamped over her mouth to silence her, until it reached a spot where it could stop and relax and commence its grisly work.*

The beast leant further forward and moved its left leg, almost out of the cover of the trees. The girl heard the soft rustling sound and looked up, squinting inquisitively, looking for the source of the sound. She could see the rough shape of the beast, but it was so large that she assumed in her innocence that it was a weird type of tree. The beast's fingers spread wide and it hooked out its arms, still hidden in the shadows. The girl thought the arms and fingers were branches swaying, and paid little attention to them.

The girl took a step closer to the waiting beast, frowning now, determined to find out what had made the noise. The beast gulped and its fingers flexed. It got ready to step out into the clearing and swoop upon the girl. She wouldn't know what was happening until it was too late, until it was running with her through the forest, until she realised she was alone and damned.

A call stopped the would-be kidnapper. It came from inside the girl's cottage. She looked back and replied in a high-pitched voice. The door opened and a woman appeared. She said something scolding to the girl, but laughed at the same time. The girl giggled, then ran towards the woman, forgetting about the strange sound in the forest.

The beast watched with a forlorn expression as the woman picked up the child, kissed her, then retreated inside, leaving the door of the cottage open a crack to let in the fresh evening air.

For a while the beast entertained the thought of crossing the clearing, sneaking in and finishing what it had started, killing the girl's mother as well as the girl. But it was an idle bit of day-dreaming. The beast had more sense than that. In fact, now that it reflected, it was grateful that the woman had come. It would have been a mistake to take the child. It was summer, and the beast planned to rest in the mountains for a while. If it had abducted the girl, it would have had to flee, and it would have been vulnerable.

The beast gurgled accusingly to itself as it withdrew. It needed to be more circumspect. This was a deadly world and it wouldn't last very long if it ignored its years of experience and all that it had been taught growing up.

One of its enemies would fall into its clutches soon enough, on a night and in a place where the taking could be justified. But not tonight. The beast needed to be patient. Its *chance would come again. It always did. The night was generous that way, for those who respected its rules, who didn't take foolish risks, who were prepared to stalk. And hunt. And wait.*

## EIGHT

As the plane hit the runway, Curran leant over, shook Dominic hard and hissed in his ear, "Fire!" Dominic bolted awake and yelped as if a bucket of cold water had been emptied over him. Curran collapsed back in his seat, laughing. Martini was chuckling too, as were most of the people around them.

"Very funny," Dominic grumbled. "Are we there already?"

"Yes," Martini said. "You slept through the whole flight. Like a baby."

"An ugly baby," Curran noted.

"*My* ugly baby," Martini murmured, cuddling up to him.

"Less of the baby shit," Dominic grunted, rubbing sleep from his eyes.

They taxied to their gate and waited for the all-clear to stand and get their bags. The rush to disembark started even before the doors opened, as it usually did on a Ryanair flight. People jostled each other, moaned about the service, complained when they got caught by a stray elbow.

Martini turned on her phone and waited to see what sort of a provider she'd end up with. The boys would be leaving their mobiles in their bags, only to be dug out if there was a problem with Martini's. They could have bought local sim cards, but they were on holiday and didn't want to hear from the mugs back home. The only reason Martini would be leaving hers switched on was to have it on standby in case of an emergency.

They had no problems with customs, though there was a heart stopping moment when Curran couldn't find his passport. But eventually it turned up — he'd stuck it in his back pocket after clearing security in London.

Martini had already converted their holiday money in a post office, so after a quick visit to the toilet they headed straight for the car rental desk. Martini was nervous. She would have been fine if she'd had Liz for support, but neither of the boys had ever driven. They knew nothing about cars and were useless to her, so she had to go through the process by herself.

The lady behind the desk could see that Miss Martinez was apprehensive and handled the customer sweetly, in no rush despite the other customers behind them. She even gave Martini a detailed map of the area, and told her where she could buy a decent road map. Martini was smiling again by the end. She thanked the lady for her help and led the pair of men – both bored by this stage – to the pick-up area, ducking into a shop en route to buy the map.

"That can't be ours," Curran exclaimed when Martini stopped at a bright red Opel Corsa.

"What's wrong with it?" Martini asked.

"It's tiny," Curran said. "How are we supposed to fit in that thing?" Martini turned the full force of her stare on him and he crumpled immediately. "Well, I guess it's not *that* small…"

"It's the cheapest car on the lot," she growled. "I gave you a choice before I booked. Told you what we'd have to pay for the different classes of vehicle. Liz and I didn't care, since we were going to be up front. You were the back seat boys and you chose cheap over spacious. So don't give me any shit, *capisce*?"

Curran gulped. "It's fine. You could fit an elephant in the back of that."

"It *will* be fine," Dominic assured him as Martini was giving the car a once-over, checking for any damages which hadn't been noted on the documents. "Now that Liz isn't with us, you'll be able to stretch out by yourself in the back."

"Yeah, I forgot about that," Curran said, brightening up. "Good thing I made that move on her cousin."

"Cousin?" Dominic snapped. "You said it was one of her friends."

"Well, they were friends too," Curran laughed, then blanched. "Don't tell Martini. Liz didn't mention that on the phone."

Dominic shook his head and grinned. Then Martini gave them the thumbs up. They loaded their bags into the boot and sat in. A few minutes for her to adjust to the car and get the feel of it. And they were off.

## NINE

The drive wasn't as nerve-wracking as Martini had feared. She knew from her research that the quality of the road network in Bulgaria was patchy, but the road in from the airport was fine. The other drivers respected the rules and Dominic navigated sensibly, ignoring Curran as he pointed out anything that caught his interest. "Look at that building. Look at that cow. Look at that car — it's even smaller than ours."

Dominic and Martini shared a smile. For once he had taken her side, treating Curran with disdain, and Martini loved it. She'd never tried to turn Dominic against his oldest friend, but there were times when Curran needed to be put in his place, and she was glad that Dominic had realised it. Maybe this would mark a turning point in their relationship, and Dominic would force Curran to behave like a proper human being over the coming week.

Things got more complicated in Plovdiv. Martini told them it was the oldest city in Europe. That meant the streets were a challenge for those in a car. She would have preferred a simple grid system.

After several wrong turns, Martini and Dominic ended up yelling at one another. Curran kept quiet in the back, sensing it wasn't the time to make a quip.

"It's the map that's wrong," Dominic insisted. "It has different names for the streets."

"Don't be stupid," Martini snapped. "It can't have."

"It does," he insisted, thrusting the map at her.

"Keep it out of my face!" she screamed, almost running over an old man who was crossing the road.

Eventually they found their way to the hotel and parked. As they were getting out, Dominic noticed that the hotel offered their own rental car service, meaning they could have got public transport in from the airport and rented a car here. He thought about mentioning that to Martini, saw how stressed she was, and thought again.

The Metropol was a small hotel, modern and clean, in a good location. They checked in without any difficulties and headed to their rooms.

Curran was impressed. "Sweet," he nodded. "A bit 1980s, but for what it cost, I was expecting a dump."

"Bulgaria's great value," Martini smiled. "We could have gone more upmarket, but we're only here for one night, so I didn't see the point. But we're heading into the countryside after this, so the other places probably won't be as nice."

"I have faith in you," Curran said, then started to follow them.

"Where are you going?" Martini stopped him.

"I want to see what your room's like."

"You can have a look later. I want to settle in first."

"OK," Curran shrugged. "When are we heading out? Five minutes? Ten?"

"Men," Martini snorted. "You don't understand us at all, do you?"

"What are you talking about?"

"I want to relax, take my time unpacking, have a shower, make myself up."

"But it's a lovely day," Curran protested. "We'll miss the best of it if we hang around here all afternoon."

"It won't be *all* afternoon," Martini sniffed. "But it's boiling out there now, mid-thirties. We'd melt if we went trekking in that heat."

"I was only gonna trek to the nearest pub," Curran said.

Martini stiffened. "I told you, this is a day for sightseeing. Tomorrow will be a day for sightseeing too. And the next day. And the next. And…"

"OK," Curran laughed. "Don't bite me. So when are we stepping out?"

"We'll call for you," Martini said. "An hour, maybe more."

"OK," Curran said again. "A shower won't hurt me either. Then I'll nip down to the lobby and ask the receptionist if she can recommend any sights." By *sights*, he meant *pubs*. "She was giving me the eye when we checked in."

"Seriously?" Dominic was unimpressed. "She had to be at least fifty."

Curran winked. "You can learn a lot from an older woman."

Martini led Dominic away before he could get into a debate with Curran about the merits of mature women. It was a recurring topic of conversation for them, one she'd tired of long ago.

Their room was similar to Curran's, clean and spacious, with a good-sized bed.

"I love the colours," Dominic deadpanned. "Pink walls. Green tiles."

"Since when did you become a critic?" Martini asked.

"I wasn't being critical," he protested. "It's sweet, in a retro sort of way."

"You should write a book about it," Martini huffed, then dragged him over to the bed and pulled his head down to kiss him.

"I thought you wanted to unpack and have a shower," Dominic said with a grin as Martini released him and fumbled at his belt.

"Later," she said, sliding down his trousers and boxer shorts.

"I'm sweaty after the flight," Dominic warned her.

"I don't care," she said, sinking to her knees and moving in on him.

Dominic smiled, looked around at the pink walls and draped curtains, and murmured happily, "Welcome to Bulgaria."

## TEN

They hit the street a little before three in the afternoon. It was still a lot hotter than it had been in London and they were sweating within minutes. They ducked into a few local churches, more to escape from the heat than anything else. Then they wound their way down to Old Town and visited the Roman Theatre, which Martini said was one of the country's most famous sights.

Dominic and Curran were sticky and irritable, and neither wanted to be dragged across town to look at a load of ruins. Martini might have forced them to pay attention, but she was tired and wilting in the heat. As impressive as the ruins were, they didn't linger long.

Plovdiv was full of archaeological sites, a mecca for travellers in the know. Martini had planned to spend all afternoon and evening exploring the city, weaving in and out of churches, mosques, Ottoman baths and more. But she hadn't counted on two things — the heat and Curran's thirst.

"Come on," he pleaded as they wandered the streets of Old Town, drawing to a halt outside a pub that didn't look like it had changed much over the last few centuries. "Just one."

"You never stop at one," Martini growled.

"It's hot," he whined. "We'll get sunstroke if we don't have a rest in the shade. And we need to keep hydrated."

"Then let's get a bottle of water and sit beneath a tree," she suggested.

"Newt," Curran groaned, turning to Dominic beseechingly.

"A beer would be nice," Dominic said guardedly. "And it looks like a cool old pub. I'd love to have a look inside."

"To check out the architecture?" Martini said archly.

"Over a pint, yeah," he smiled. "It's been a long day. We haven't had much sleep. We're hot and bothered. An ice-cold pint, sitting in a corner of a pub, will do us the world of good."

Martini sighed. She wanted to keep going, but she was tired, it was hotter than she'd imagined, and yes, she was tempted by the thought of a refreshing pint.

"OK," she gave in. "But just one."

"Sure thing, boss," Curran whooped and trotted in.

Dominic smiled at Martini and held the door open, the perfect gentleman, only spoiling it slightly when he slapped her bum as she went past.

It was dark inside. Curran bought drinks and they sat at a thick table, natural timber, stained with time and spillages. "Cheers," he grinned and downed his beer in one. "That was *good*," he beamed, then hurried to the bar for another before Dominic and Martini had even touched theirs.

"Dominic…" Martini said warningly.

"He's just excited," Dominic said. "He'll calm down after another beer. Do you have any sun cream?" This was a diverting tactic. Martini had stressed the need for lots of cream before they left the room, especially with his pale skin.

"Are you burnt?" she asked, instantly concerned.

"No, but I want to give it time to soak in before we go walking again."

Martini nodded, pleased that he was being so sensible. She searched in her bag for the miniature bottle which she'd packed. She didn't spot him gesturing to Curran, telling him to get two more drinks in for them, quick!

Martini found the sun cream and passed it across. "Thanks," Dominic said. "I'll rub it on in a minute. But first…" He picked up his drink. She smiled, raised her glass, chinked it against his, and they both said at the same time, before taking a long, cold draught, "Cheers."

## ELEVEN

Dominic didn't use the sun cream in the end. Martini protested when Curran returned with two more drinks, but since the beer had been paid for, and it was so hot outside, and the beer was so temptingly cold, it would have been churlish to refuse. By the time she got to the bottom of the second glass, it never crossed her thoughts to complain when Dominic nipped to the bar and returned with a third round.

As Martini would acknowledge afterwards, they had a whale of a night. They stayed in the bar for a few hours, got chatting to some locals, old men whose grasp of English was poor but who warmed to Curran when he started chanting the names of Bulgarian footballers. "Berbatov! Stoichkov! Petrov!"

The old men beamed and nodded, then told Curran the names of other great players, carrying on a faltering conversation that ran for the better part of an hour and moved on to embrace politics – "Fuck Thatcher! Fuck Bush!" – the country's gravitation towards sources of renewable energy – "Fuck coal! Nuclear! Wind! Solar!" – and the quality of British comedians – "Benny Hill very funny!" – among other subjects.

"How did you know the names of those footballers?" Dominic chuckled as they staggered out of the pub to go grab something to eat. "You hate football."

"Hate's a strong word," Curran tutted. "I've no interest in the game, but lots of people do, so I make it my business to pick up the basics. You can always start a conversation with a few footballing nuggets, no matter where in the world you are."

"You're a man of hidden depths," Dominic laughed, giving Martini a hug and asking what she was in the mood for.

"Don't care," she mumbled, glassy-eyed. "As long as it's not kebab."

They wound up eating in a restaurant that served decent local dishes.

Their waiter spoke English and was keen to practice, so they spent as much time talking with him as they did eating. Curran bought him a couple of drinks, which he downed swiftly — staff drinking on duty didn't seem to be an issue here, which impressed Curran. "We could learn a lot from these Bulgarians," he noted.

Martini was happy to carry on drinking after dinner, but she didn't try to keep up with the boys, having the occasional glass of water, conscious of all the sights she wanted to see the following day.

"Don't get too hammered," she warned Dominic a few times. "We've an early start."

He nodded soberly when she said that. Part of him believed it too. That part could visualise himself rising early, checking out fabulous Roman ruins, seeing what else this fascinating old city had to offer. But the greater part of him knew he was in the middle of a serious session and doubted he'd be able to get up before midday, probably considerably later.

Curran proved a hit in the handful of pubs that they crawled to over the coming hours. The locals liked his bright shorts and T-shirt, his winning smile, his willingness to buy a round and engage in heartfelt talks about anything, growing more loquacious as the night progressed, willing to tackle everything from the agricultural economy to Bulgaria's burgeoning arts scene.

Dominic loved it when his friend was in full flow. At his best, Curran was as captivating as a skilled politician, the focus of gazes in the room. Some people eyed him resentfully, as they always did when an individual hogged the limelight, but most smiled and listened politely as he soared and sang and speculated.

Martini chatted with a succession of serious young men. Dominic felt protective at first – he assumed they were making moves on her – but came to realise that they just wanted to talk, to complain or enthuse about famous people and the powers-that-were. They wanted to tell her about their writers, poets and singers. They couldn't understand why people in England were disinterested in Bulgaria. Why didn't more tourists come? They recommended many places to go, things to see and do. When Dominic saw that their intentions were innocent, he left her to it, focusing again on Curran and doing his best to join in.

Martini was in her element. *This* was why she hadn't bought a travel guide. She was experiencing the *real* Bulgaria, not following some well-worn tourist trail and gathering with the other foreigners in Western-themed pubs and hotels. This was authentic in a way she hadn't experienced before.

There was a point in the night, on her way back from the toilet, when Martini looked around, took in the noise, the music, the throb of voices, the clink of glasses, the accents and difference of it all, the delight with which Curran was interacting with the locals, the dopey smile on Dominic's face, and noted smugly to herself, *This is going to be the best holiday ever.*

Then she returned to her table to hold court and discuss the state of affairs with the earnest young men, long into the hot, beer-chilled night.

## TWELVE

Martini got up at nine, somewhat later than planned. She felt better than she'd feared, especially once she'd had a shower. She chuckled as she dried herself, recalling the young men and all that they'd talked about, dancing on a table at one point while a small band of folk musicians played a high-tempo version of *Macarena*.

Pulling the curtains aside when she returned to the bedroom, Martini peered out to check the weather. The glare of sunlight shocked her and she let the curtains swish shut with a yelp. It was going to be another scorcher. She made a mental note to wear the strongest of the four pairs of sunglasses that she'd packed, and to lather on the sun cream.

"Come on, Romeo," she called to Dominic, tweaking his exposed left foot.

"*Mhrfuff*," he mumbled.

"That's not what you said when we got back," she laughed, flashing on a memory of him trying to seduce her, then falling asleep in the middle of it. "Come on. Move it. We've a full day ahead."

Dominic rolled over on to his back. His eyes slowly opened and he groggily stared at her. He tried to say something. Failed. Licked his lips and tried again. "Water," he croaked.

Martini tutted, but fetched a bottle and fed the water to him slowly, picking his head up so that it didn't dribble over his chin.

"Time?" Dominic wheezed.

"Almost ten," Martini exaggerated.

"Too early," Dominic groaned.

"I told you that today would be busy," Martini scowled.

"I know." Dominic smiled weakly. "I'll be fine. We'll see everything you… want to see. Just give me… a bit longer… in bed."

He rolled over again and was snoring moments later. Martini thought about kicking him awake, but decided an extra half hour of kip would do him no harm. Besides, if he was this bad, Curran would be worse, since he'd drunk even more.

Once she'd dressed and slapped on sun cream, she strolled downstairs and out in search of a cafe where she could eat whatever the locals had for breakfast. She found a small place on the corner of an intersection, with a table and chair outside, and settled back to have a light snack, a drink, and watch the world rumble by.

Martini felt incredibly relaxed as she enjoyed the morning show. She was particularly delighted when a few of the locals nodded to her when passing, as if she was one of their own. She tried to recall some of the Bulgarian phrases which the young men had taught her the night before, but her mind was a blank.

She went for a walk after breakfast, taking turns at random, loving the freedom of being in a strange city with nothing to do and nowhere to go. She considered staying out all day, drifting through the streets like a bohemian wanderer. Dominic and Curran wouldn't mind. They'd be happy to lie in bed. But she felt it was her job to rouse them. She didn't want them to miss out on such a special experience. Besides, she'd only booked the rooms for one night. The staff would turf them out soon. She'd gently wake the boys, help them clear their heads and pack, then shepherd them to the car for the start of their adventure into the unknown.

Martini smiled warmly as she imagined sharing this splendour with the man she loved and his best friend. They'd been dubious when she told them where they were going, but she was sure they could already see why she'd chosen Bulgaria over the more obvious options. They'd be full of praise once their heads had cleared and they were on the road. Martini would have to be careful not to puff up when they applauded. She didn't want them thinking she was smug or conceited. There was no place for self-conscious vanity in dreamy Bulgaria.

## THIRTEEN

It quickly became clear upon her return that neither Dominic nor Curran would be singing her praises any time soon. Dominic was sound asleep and it took a minute of brutal shaking to wake him.

"What's happening?" he gasped, eyelids fluttering open.

"We have to check out," Martini told him.

"No," he groaned. "Too early. Can't move."

But Martini kept on at him until he lurched from the bed and stumbled to the toilet. She tried getting him into the shower but he said it was too much effort. Instead he hung his head over the sink and splashed cold water over his face and neck, moaning pitifully.

When he came back to the room, Martini made him throw on some clothes and they went to wake Curran. His door was open a crack and his snores were echoing through the corridor. Martini knocked but there was no response. She checked with Dominic but he was unresponsive, so she seized the initiative and pushed in.

A young woman had accompanied Curran back to the hotel, but there was no sign of her now. One whiff explained why. The air was noxious. Curran must have been farting all night.

"That's so gross," Martini squealed, hurrying to the window to open it.

"What's the smell?" Dominic muttered, eyes watering. "Did something die?"

"Only if it got trapped up Curran's arse," Martini snapped, opening and shutting the window over and over, trying to fan out the fumes.

Curran registered the light even in the depths of his sleep and turned facedown into his pillows, shivering as he did so — the air con was set to its lowest level.

"Pull the covers off him," Martini told Dominic. "That might wake him up."

"Why don't you pull them off?" Dominic asked.

"In case he shat himself during the night," she said.

Dominic almost threw up at the thought of that. "I'm not going anywhere near him," he protested.

"He's *your* friend," Martini reminded him.

"Yeah, but there are limits."

"Just wake him up, Dominic," she said tightly, and he could tell by her tone that this wasn't the time to argue.

Sighing, Dominic pinched his nose shut and edged closer to the bed. He reached for the covers. Paused. Changed his mind. Slapped the back of Curran's head and roared, "Fire!"

Curran screamed and shot up. Dominic fell over, laughing with delight — revenge was sweet. Curran caught sight of Martini and screamed again. She was so surprised that she screamed too. When he heard that, he raised a fist and half-fell out of bed towards her.

"He's naked," Martini screeched. "Dominic! I do *not* want to see *that*!"

"Curran!" Dominic bellowed, also not wanting Martini to see him naked — he knew his friend had a long penis and didn't want her to draw any unwelcome comparisons. "Curran! Wake up! Jerome!"

Curran automatically scowled when his real name was called. His gaze cleared and he refocused on Martini. "Oh," he muttered weakly, crawling back beneath the covers. "It's you. I thought it was Idi Amin."

"Excuse me?" Martini replied, too baffled to be insulted.

"Caught a documentary a few weeks ago, late one night when I was channel surfing," Curran explained, sounding remarkably lucid for a man with bloodshot eyes and smears of dried vomit running down his chin. "I've had nightmares about him since." He looked around, frowning. "Why's it so cold?"

"You must have turned the air con down," Martini told him.

He nodded. "That makes sense. What happened to the girl?"

"Have a whiff, take three guesses," Martini growled.

Curran sniffed the air and stared at her blankly. "I don't smell anything."

"Are you kidding?" she gasped. "It's toxic in here."

Curran sniffed the air again and shrugged. "If you say so. I never did have the best nose in the world." He grinned at Dominic. "Some night, eh?"

"Yeah," Dominic said, returning the grin. "But I feel wrecked now."

"Me too," Curran said. "I have vague memories of crawling to the toilet in the early hours. My legs wouldn't support me."

"Well, I hope they're better now," Martini said. "We're leaving."

"Leaving?" Curran echoed.

"We only booked the rooms for one night. We have to check out."

Curran shook his head. "No way."

"We have to," Martini growled.

"They'll have to drag me out kicking and screaming," Curran said stubbornly.

"Not if I stab you to death first," Martini snapped.

"Dominic?" Curran turned to his friend as he always did whenever he was having an argument with Martini.

"I feel rough as hell, M," Dominic mumbled. "Could we get a late checkout?"

"Late my arse," Curran snorted. "Pay them for another night. It's chickenfeed in the grand scheme of things. We can afford it."

"It's not about what we can afford," Martini barked. "We're on tour. We have to move on. There are places I want to see."

Curran smiled like a salesman. "You told us there wasn't a fixed schedule, that we were free to make it up as we went, day by day."

"Well, yes, but –" Martini began.

"Then I vote we stay here," Curran interrupted. "All in favour?" He stuck a hand up and nodded at Dominic.

Dominic gulped as Martini glared at him. "I want to push on," he said, "but there's no way I can check out. I'll need two or three hours at least. And if we're going to stay that long, we should stay the rest of the day too. I don't want you to have to drive in the dark."

"Very considerate of you," Martini snarled.

Dominic winced. He knew he'd catch hell for this later, but he felt like the walking dead at the moment and the weariness of the present took precedence over whatever the future might bring.

"Doesn't matter what Newt says anyway," Curran said, deciding to take one for the team. "I'm not budging. End of."

"Then we'll leave you here," Martini shouted, truly losing her temper.

"That's your prerogative," Curran said, pulling out a phrase that he often used in situations like this. "If you want to dump me, fine, I'll find my own way around. I made lots of new friends last night. You don't need to worry about me. If you and the Newt want to shoot off and explore, go with my blessing. But I can't move today. I'm shattered. If you're determined to press on, it will have to be without me."

"Martini…" Dominic pleaded, not wanting to abandon his friend.

Martini hesitated. They'd probably have a better time without Curran, a sweet, interesting, romantic holiday. He'd been on fire last night but this was the flipside and she wasn't sure that the highs compensated for the lows.

But Dominic was blinking at her like a puppy who'd been scared by a loud blast, and although she was sure that Curran would get on fine without them, she'd feel lousy if she walked out on him. His absence would hang over them like a cloud (like the foul-smelling cloud in the room) and they'd end up coming back to rescue him, maybe lose more than half a day doing so.

"You're a pain in the arse, Jerome," she snapped.

"I know I am, Isabella," he grinned.

"You should have stayed in London if you didn't want to join in."

"But I *do* want to join in," he assured her. "Just not this afternoon."

Martini stared out the window at the beautiful blue sky. There was a lot still to see in Plovdiv. "*If* we stay another day," she said stiffly, "it's on the condition that we leave first thing tomorrow, eight o'clock, no excuses, *capisce?*"

"You love that word, don't you?" Curran giggled.

"I mean it," she said hotly. "Eight on the dot, or else."

Curran nodded sombrely. "Eight. Not a second later, whether I'm hungover or dead. You have my word."

"I'd better have," Martini said, wiping a hand across her cheeks as if brushing away angry tears, not wanting them to see that she was secretly pleased to get to spend another day in Plovdiv. Huffing dramatically, she spun on her heels and stormed out, leaving Dominic to follow.

"Sorry," Dominic said miserably.

"It's fine," Curran smiled. "She's right. We were out of order."

"Yeah," Dominic said glumly.

Then Curran winked. "Let's do our best to get out of order again tonight."

And although Dominic laughed, he caught the smell of trouble in the air — the only scent in the room that couldn't be traced directly to his best friend's arse.

## FOURTEEN

Martini didn't enjoy the afternoon as much as the morning. It was boiling, the temperature hitting the high thirties, and the heat sapped much of her energy. She tried to concentrate and recapture the sense of calm which had made the earlier hours so special, but she felt hot and irritable.

She was damp with sweat when she returned to the Metropol in the evening, her feet ached from all the walking, and despite reapplying sun cream a couple of times, she'd caught the sun on her shoulders and the back of her legs. She wanted to collapse on her bed and have a long weep, but when she got to her room it was being serviced by housekeeping.

Martini stood in the doorway, blinking at the Bulgarian maid who was stripping the bed. There was no sign of Dominic. "Where's my boyfriend?" Martini asked.

The maid shook her head and said something in Bulgarian.

Martini pointed at some of Dominic's clothes and said slowly, "Boyfriend?"

The maid's face lit up. She pointed at the floor and said something that Martini couldn't understand. Then she crooked her fingers as if gripping a glass and tilted them at her mouth. "Beer?"

Martini's features darkened. "Thank you," she snapped and set off.

She found Dominic sitting at a table in the bar with Curran. Both were talking softly, smiling as they tried to piece together the events of the previous night.

"Hey, gorgeous," Dominic beamed as Martini swept forward. "We were just –"

"Bastards," Martini hissed, stopping him short.

"M?" Dominic said nervously.

"I've been out there in the sweltering heat, hauling my arse around, worried about you, and you've been sitting here drinking all day?"

"No," Dominic said quickly. "You've got it wrong. I've been in bed. I got up an hour ago, maybe less. Then a maid knocked on the door. I let her in, fetched Curran and we came down here. This is our first pint."

"It's true," Curran assured her. "We didn't want to start the party without you."

"There'll be no fucking party," Martini snapped. "You promised me you'd be ready to leave at eight."

"In the morning," Curran said uneasily, wondering if he'd got his facts wrong.

"How will you do that if you go out on the piss tonight?" she snarled.

"You'd be surprised what I can do when I put my mind to it," he laughed.

"Well, you couldn't crawl out of bed this morning, could you?" she raged.

"That was different," he said, smile fading. "I won't drink as much tonight."

"It looks to me like you're making a good fucking start."

"It's after five," Curran growled. "Do you want me to drink water all night?"

"Easy," Dominic said, trying to calm things down. "What's wrong, M?"

"You are," she spat, starting to cry. "You and your fucking friend. This was supposed to be a magical holiday. Then that arsehole comes without Liz, meaning I have to do all the driving, and you go and get pissed the first night, and we have to scratch an entire day and… and… it's fucked!"

"You're overreacting," Curran tutted, and Dominic groaned.

Martini whirled on the gangly man and thought about scratching out his eyes.

"Ignore him," Dominic said, getting up to step between them. "You know what he's like."

"What's that supposed to mean?" Curran grunted.

"We'll stop after this one," Dominic promised. "I'll come up to the room with you, we'll rest for an hour or two, then go for a really lovely meal. Just the two of us if you want."

"You're hurting my feelings," Curran pouted.

"And we won't get drunk," Dominic said. "We'll have a few to keep our spirits up, no more. In bed by midnight."

"New York time," Curran muttered, but both Dominic and Martini blanked him.

"Honestly?" Martini sniffed, dabbing at her cheeks with the back of her hand.

"Yes," Dominic said.

She smiled at him weakly, then scowled at Curran. "OK, but we're bringing him with us. I don't trust him. If we let him off by himself, he'll get rat-arsed."

"Oh, the injustice," Curran cried, wringing his hands theatrically.

Martini flipped him the finger, then turned her scowl on Dominic. "I'm going up by myself. Stay and have another drink. I want some time alone to cool down. But only one more."

"Whatever you say," Dominic agreed.

Martini nodded, glared at Curran again, then returned to their room, where she waited in the corridor until the maid was finished.

In the bar, Curran arched an eyebrow at Dominic, who was still on his feet, looking worried. "Women," Curran snorted.

Dominic frowned. "Drink your drink and shut the fuck up," he said quietly.

Curran's expression flatlined. He almost snapped back. But then he recalled the tears. Dominic wasn't able to handle it when a girl turned on the waterworks. Such drama never bothered Curran, but Dominic was made of softer stuff. His lovers could twist him round their little finger with nothing more than a sniff and the glint of a tear. Martini, to be fair, rarely exploited him that way, but some of his earlier girlfriends had been more calculating.

"Forget about it," Curran said. "I'll say sorry to her later. It'll be fine."

Dominic smiled gratefully, sat, sipped his drink, and tried not to brood. Beside him, Curran resumed the conversation about the night before as if all was the same as it had been, but inside he was seething.

## FIFTEEN

Nobody enjoyed the meal. Martini and Curran exchanged barely a few words throughout dinner. Dominic kept trying to bridge the gap between them, but both were out of sorts, feeling that they'd been unfairly treated by the other.

They went for a few drinks afterwards, and things thawed slightly, but Martini switched to soft drinks after a couple of cocktails, while Curran's beer sent him into a rare gloomy state.

They were back in the hotel before eleven. Curran hit the sack immediately. Martini stayed up for half an hour, preparing for the morning, then lay down and fell asleep within minutes.

Dominic lingered before retiring. He sat by the window, listening to Martini breathing, staring out at the city and its twinkling lights. He felt bad about what had happened. Martini had worked hard to arrange this holiday and he and Curran should have paid her more respect.

On the other hand, what had they done so wrong? Last night had been a blast. Today was a write-off, and should have been from the start. Martini knew what Curran was like, Dominic too when it came to that. She should have figured that the excitement of being on holiday would get the better of them the first night, and worked in a fallow day, not organised the road trip until the day after.

Indeed, did they need to hit the road at all? There was lots for them still to see in Plovdiv. Would it be such a bad holiday if they stayed here, lived it up every night, slept in late, explored the city for a few hours in the afternoons? That sounded like a good mix to him, better than spending hours on end crammed into their tiny car, trying to find their way around a strange country's roads.

Dominic thought about proposing a change of plan to Martini, but he knew it would be the signal for Armageddon if he did. She was already on the edge, what with the Liz debacle and having to scrap a day of the tour. It wouldn't take a lot to push her over. Better to play along, enjoy it as best he could, maybe go away on a lads' break with Curran and a few of their mates in the autumn.

He decided to put that proposal to Curran in the morning. Ask him to take this holiday for what it was, not go overboard on the drinking, save it for when they could cut loose in one of Europe's hotspots.

*Besides*, he told himself as he continued to stare out into the night, *it's not that bad. There'll be plenty to see and do. We'll have a nice time. I mean, as long as we keep Martini sweet, how much can go wrong?*

## SIXTEEN

They didn't manage to check out at eight, but weren't too far behind schedule and were on the road by twenty past. Curran was still in a sour mood and he stretched out indolently across the back seat, barely grunting at Dominic or Martini.

That didn't matter much to begin with, as they focused on clearing the city centre. It was a straight run to the main road to Haskovo, the first stop on Martini's list, and they navigated it without incident. Soon they were bombing along through the countryside and Dominic felt relaxed enough to ask Martini where they were bound for.

"We're heading for the mountains, which is where we'll spend most of the rest of the trip, but we'll stop in Haskovo for lunch," she said. "If we hadn't wasted yesterday we could have spent longer working our way across, exploring the area off the main road."

"I don't think we missed much," Curran said. "It looks boring as shit."

Martini bristled and shot Dominic an angry glance. He cleared his throat and glanced back at Curran. "You sleep OK?"

"Yeah," Curran sniffed.

"Didn't see you at breakfast."

"I didn't dare eat," Curran said. "Didn't want to hold you guys up."

Dominic sighed. He'd hoped that Curran would have wiped yesterday's quarrel from his thoughts. He wasn't normally one to hold a grudge, but he was prickly as a hedgehog wrapped in barbed wire today. Dominic cast an eye over his friend, looking for something to chat with him about. He spotted his opening gambit on the middle finger of Curran's left hand. "What's that?" he asked.

Curran had been waiting for Dominic to enquire. In fact he'd been stroking his cheek with the finger since getting into the car. But he feigned ignorance. "What?" he said innocently.

"The thing on your finger," Dominic said.

Curran looked down. "Oh, just something I picked up the other night." He slipped it off and passed it up front. "Cool, isn't it?"

*It* was a heavy silver ring, with a long curved spike sticking out of it. The spike must have been five centimetres long. It was broad and flat along the top, with a blunted tip, but the underside was sharp.

Dominic slipped on the unusual ring and admired it as he flexed his fingers. Martini stared at it suspiciously. "Looks like a weapon to me," she said.

"You couldn't be more wrong," Curran said. "I bought it from a guy in one of the pubs. Apparently it was an old-fashioned tool for cutting up strips of cloth or leather. He showed me how it would have been handled in the past. Here, I'll demonstrate."

Dominic slid off the ring and handed it back. Curran put it on, the spike pointing in the same direction as his finger. "Sometimes they'd use it like this and run their hand along a length of cloth or whatever." He curled his fingers into a fist and made a slow, forward movement, the spike of the ring slicing smoothly through the air where the imaginary cloth was hanging.

"But usually they'd do it the other way," he said, taking off the ring and turning it around before putting it back on, so the spike was pointing towards his wrist. "They'd pull their hand back along the cloth," he explained. "That way they could exercise more control."

"How much did it cost?" Dominic asked.

"Not much," Curran said, unable to remember, or even if money had exchanged hands — he had a vague idea that he might have simply forgotten to give it back.

"It looks dangerous," Martini said. "You'll take an eye out with that."

Curran almost snapped, *Hopefully yours*. But he caught himself and forced a chuckle. "It's fine. The tip has been dulled."

"You'll never sneak it through customs," Martini warned him.

"I'll put it in the hold," Curran said.

"We don't have any hold luggage," she sneered.

"Oh yeah," he frowned, then shrugged. "I'll buy a cheap case."

"It'll cost a small fortune to check in a case at the airport," Martini said.

"I don't care," he said obstinately.

"Let me try it again," Dominic said, testing it on the finger of his other hand this time. He ran the blunt side down his cheek, then picked at the sharp side with a fingernail. "I like it. I might try and find one for myself."

"But you don't wear rings," Martini said.

"I could start."

Martini shook her head. "You'd catch it every time you stuck your hand in a pocket. And you couldn't wear it to work — you'd scratch all the glasses."

"As if I'd be dumb enough to wear it while working," Dominic huffed.

"You couldn't wear it clubbing either," she continued. "You'd blind someone if you waved your hand around and caught them."

Dominic glared at her, forgetting yesterday's tears, how wretched he'd felt, his determination to keep her sweet for the rest of the holiday. "I'll wear whatever the hell I want," he snarled.

"Not when I'm around," she retorted.

"Curran," Dominic barked. "How much do you want for it?"

"Not for sale," Curran said. "It has sentimental attachment."

"But you only just bought it," Dominic said.

"I know, but I like it." He beckoned for the ring and Dominic reluctantly returned it. "But I'll let you play with it sometimes," Curran said, enjoying the way Martini's shoulders stiffened, relishing the icy silence which followed as Dominic deliberately folded the map shut, leaving Martini to navigate using just the road signs. *Normal service has been resumed*, he purred inwardly, and he was back to his bright, natural, smugly annoying best after that.

## SEVENTEEN

It was too early for lunch when they arrived in Haskovo, so they found a spot to park and went for a stroll. It was a nice place, with some interesting buildings, but it lacked Plovdiv's character.

"It's a dump," Curran said as they were eating lunch, sitting outside a restaurant on a quiet city centre street.

"No, it's not," Martini reacted. "It's sweeter than a lot of towns in England."

"Yeah," Curran said, "but I don't go on holiday to those places either."

"He's got a point," Dominic chipped in. "It's hardly spectacular."

"I never said it would be," Martini growled defensively. "It was meant to be a stopover, nothing more."

"I hope the rest of the holiday's better than this," Curran said.

Martini quivered. "As I explained in the car, we'll be spending most of our time in the mountains. The scenery's amazing."

"Yeah, well, it better be."

Martini turned away from them to pointedly stare at the street. Curran rolled his eyes at Dominic, who nodded glumly in reply. In the silence that followed, Curran tried scratching his initials into the table with his new ring, but stopped when a passing waitress gave him the evil eye.

"It's like a furnace here," Dominic finally said, running the rim of his glass round his forehead and cheeks after he'd drained it.

"Yeah," Martini admitted. "How's your skin?"

"Fine," he said. "The sun cream's doing its job."

"You'll have to be extra careful in the mountains," she warned him. "It will be cooler up there but the sun's as strong as it is here. We'll be trekking through forests a lot, so it will be shaded, but you'll need to apply regularly."

"Yes, Mum," Dominic grinned, and Martini slapped him playfully. She raised an eyebrow at Curran. "Let me have a look at that ring." She studied it carefully, tried it on for size – it was far too big, even for her thumb – and tested the sharp curve of the spike. "I think the guy in the pub was pulling your leg."

"What do you mean?" Curran asked.

"This isn't as useful as a knife or a pair of scissors. You'd have a hard time slicing through cloth with it. It looks more like an ornamental ring."

"Why would he lie about it?" Curran frowned.

Martini shrugged. "To drive up the price?"

"But I didn't…" Curran stopped short of saying he hadn't paid for it. He was pretty sure, having thought about it some more, that he'd stolen the ring, but he didn't want to admit that.

"What the hell," Curran said, changing tack. "It's a cool ring, no matter what. And if that's not what it was used for in the past… well, maybe I'll open my own fabric shop and start using the ring as my main work tool."

Dominic and Martini shared a smile. Then Martini handed back the ring, they settled the bill, went to the toilet, and returned to the car for the next leg of their road trip.

## EIGHTEEN

The plan was to stay in Kardzhali for the night, a city less than an hour's drive from Haskovo, but Martini had been told by one of the young, serious men in Plovdiv that they should stop along the way and see a place called Peri-Peri.

"You've got to be joking," Dominic laughed.

Martini laughed too. "That might not be the actual name, but it's something like that."

"I hope it *is* Peri-Peri," Curran enthused. "Maybe that's where the sauce comes from. Even if it isn't, I want a picture of me beside a sign with the name on it."

When they saw the signs for Perperikon, Martini chuckled ruefully. Curran was disappointed but sanguine. "I knew it was too much to hope for," he said, as if he'd missed out on fulfilling a lifelong dream.

Martini took a left turn when prompted, followed the road and began to climb one of the hills which had been a feature of the landscape on the way down.

"I hope the car can handle this," Dominic said with a worried frown.

"It's fine," Martini assured him. "We'll be going higher than this later in the holiday."

"My ears will pop like buggery," Curran muttered.

"That's a shame," Martini murmured, making a mental note to take them as high as she could whenever possible.

Perperikon turned out to be the ruins of an ancient city. It was like stepping into the past and even Curran was impressed. They spent a good chunk of time wandering the ruins, then lay down in a quiet spot to admire the spectacular view. It was cooler up here, a pleasant wind taking the sting out of the sun.

"I wonder how many battles have been fought here over the centuries,"

Curran mused aloud as he perched on a wall and gazed at the neighbouring hills.

"Trust you to think about that," Martini snorted.

"Warfare is history," he said earnestly. "Everything else slots in around wars. Without a strong defending army, culture never has a chance to develop. Societies have to fight before they can flourish."

Martini squinted. "Sometimes you sound halfway intelligent."

Curran laughed. "I could have gone to uni. I was a lot smarter than my teachers realised. But I was careful not to score highly in my exams. Why heap pressure on yourself? Life's a cruise if no one expects you to achieve."

"Some would call that a waste of a brain," Martini noted.

Curran shrugged. "We're all worm fodder at the end of our days. I plan on having as much fun as I can before that happens. I want to die with a carefree smile on my lips, not go skeletal worrying about my mortgage repayments and how much tax my heirs owe on their inheritance."

"The man makes a good point," Dominic smiled.

Martini shook her head, exasperated. Curran was a bad influence on Dominic. He started thinking he was Peter Pan when they were together. She thought about berating him but didn't want to anger her smiling boyfriend. Let him enjoy his fantasies for now. She could work on him when they returned home. They were both young. There was plenty of time for her to nag him into growing up to be a man.

## NINETEEN

They were all much more relaxed when they drove into Kardzhali in the evening. They parked and went looking for sleeping quarters. Martini had warned them that they might have to settle for B&Bs after Haskovo, but it was a bigger town than she'd anticipated, with quite a few hotels to choose from.

They liked the look of Hotel Perperikon, especially as it was named after the hillside ruins, but they got a better deal at the Arpezos, an older, more faded hotel, but with good-sized rooms, a nice bar, a sauna and more.

Curran headed straight for the bar once he'd dumped his gear in his room. Dominic would have joined him, but Martini wanted to test the bed before they went out to explore.

"You're insatiable," Dominic faux-whimpered as she climbed on top.

"Have you a problem with that?" she growled, tightening her grip on him.

"No, mistress," he squealed, and they laughed. Dominic pulled her head down and kissed her. "I love you, M," he mumbled.

She only smiled in response, cuddled in to him, let him get his breath back, then picked up the pace again.

"What the hell kept you so long?" Curran snapped when they finally turned up.

"I was keeping my woman happy," Dominic declared.

"I'll be walking bow-legged all night," Martini simpered.

Curran winced. "Too much information."

They had a few drinks in the bar, Martini as grateful for them as the boys, having been stuck behind the wheel for so much of the day. Then they went for something to eat, roaming the streets at random, choosing a little restaurant with seats outside, where they could sit and feel like part of the night.

They tried to order beer with their food but the waiter insisted they have wine. It wasn't that wine was more expensive, he just believed that you couldn't enjoy food without wine to accompany it.

They ate slowly, relishing the wine, savouring the warmth, the sounds of the city, the clothes and accents of the people around them. Curran was back on form, telling jokes, making wild plans, chatting away to the waiter and an elderly couple at the table next to theirs. It promised to be another great night, like Plovdiv all over again, and that was when the trouble began.

"I don't want to go to a pub," Martini scowled. They were nearing the end of the meal and the boys were keen to move on. "Why can't we stay here, have a few more glasses of wine, then call it a night?"

"Don't be a spoilsport," Curran cried. "The night is young. It's our duty to give the tourist trade a boost. The publicans need us."

Dominic laughed but Martini didn't see the funny side. "I want to set off early," she said. "We'll be hitting the mountains tomorrow. The road won't be easy. There's lots to see and do along the way. We need to have clear heads."

"Bollocks to that," Curran said.

Martini's lips thinned and Dominic groaned. "Come on, M, don't make a scene. We were good for you today, weren't we?"

"*Good for me?*" she echoed icily.

"We didn't go crazy last night, got up early, went to see the sights with you."

"The sights are for all of us," she said. "I didn't mean to force them on you. If you were that miserable, you should have said."

Dominic sighed. "Don't twist my words. I had fun today. Curran did too."

"Absolutely," Curran nodded.

"But that doesn't mean we can't have fun at night as well," Dominic pushed on. "We're happy to do the tourist thing, but don't deny us a few drinks at the end of the day. There's got to be a compromise."

"What do you call this?" Martini said stiffly, waving her wine glass at him.

"A good start," Dominic and Curran said at the same time, and laughed.

"Seriously," Dominic smiled, "what's wrong with hitting a few bars?"

"That's not what we're here for," Martini said.

"Yes, it is," Dominic said, then added quickly before she could snap at him, "I mean, not predominantly, but it's part of the holiday. An added bonus."

Martini crossed her arms and glared at them. "What if I go back to the hotel and let you off by yourselves?"

Dominic crossed his arms, angrily mimicking her pose. "I won't stop you."

"You'd go without me?" Martini said quietly.

"If we have to," Dominic said, not wavering.

Martini scowled. "OK, Mr Romantic, if that's the way you feel, I'll leave you to it. Don't wake me up when you come home."

And she got up and left.

Dominic gulped and rose to go after her.

"Hold firm, man," Curran said.

"I didn't think she'd really go," Dominic muttered.

"I did," Curran grinned. "She had to, having made such an issue of it. But she'll calm down in her room. We'll give it a couple of drinks, then swing by and pick her up. It'll be fine after that."

"You think so?" Dominic asked.

"Of course," Curran beamed. "We'll be laughing back to our ears about this in the morning. Trust me."

## TWENTY

Dominic meant to return to the hotel for Martini after they'd had a couple of drinks, he truly did, but the night didn't quite work out that way.

The pair stumbled across a group of students in the first pub they visited. One was celebrating her twenty-first birthday. It didn't take Curran long to ingratiate himself with the crowd and they were invited to stay for the festivities, which mostly consisted of drinking a lot of beer and shots very quickly.

The students wanted to know all about London, what life was like there, where the visitors had been in Bulgaria, what they thought of the country. Dominic kept saying that he had to go fetch his girlfriend, but the more he drank, the less important that seemed, until he forgot about Martini for a while.

When the students moved on, Dominic and Curran trailed along. In the open air, Dominic recalled his earlier plan to return to the hotel for Martini, but he knew he'd left it too late. He was drunk and she was sober. He'd only catch hell if he went back now.

"I'm in so much shit," he moaned to Curran.

"What are you talking about?" Curran replied.

"Martini will kill me when I get back."

Curran thought about that, then nodded. "Yeah, she will." He slapped Dominic's back. "So you might as well make the most of the night while you can."

That made sense to the sozzled Dominic, so he pushed on stoutly, like someone on his way to the guillotine, determined to show no fear along the way.

Late in the night, Curran fell into a deep conversation with two of the girls. He withdrew to a corner of the pub and waved away Dominic when he tried to join them. Dominic wasn't sure what was happening until he spotted

Curran on his way to the door, an arm around each of the young ladies. Curran caught Dominic's eye, beamed wolfishly, and mouthed, "The dream come true!"

Dominic laughed and shook his head. Curran had been chasing a threesome for most of his life, and it looked as if he'd finally nailed it. Dominic checked his watch and was stunned to see that it was only just gone eleven. Maybe it wasn't too late to patch up things with Martini. If he left now, walked around for half an hour, drank lots of water, threw up… The situation could be recovered.

He decided to leave, but he had an almost full pitcher of beer, and a pretty young woman was telling him about her plans to move to London. It would be rude to withdraw straight away. He'd finish the drink, excuse himself by saying he was going to the toilet, slip out on the sly, no harm done.

Dominic had about a third of the pitcher to go when Curran barged back into the pub and made a beeline for him.

"That was quick," Dominic said, surprised.

"Never happened," Curran growled.

"Why?" Dominic asked, starting to smile.

"One of them got cold feet," Curran said, tears of frustration glittering in his eyes. "I tried to convince the other one to come with me anyway, but she didn't want to abandon her friend, so the pair fucked off and left me with a burning hard-on and the detritus of a shattered dream."

Dominic howled with laughter. Only Curran could have phrased it that way, no small feat after all the beer he'd swilled. "Never mind," he chuckled. "It wasn't meant to be."

"It fucking was," Curran shouted. "Tonight was the night. I felt it in my bones."

"You mean in your boner," Dominic corrected him, spluttering at his wittiness.

"Very funny," Curran sneered, unimpressed.

Dominic tried to console him. "They weren't very good looking anyway."

"One wasn't," Curran agreed. "The other was OK. The strange thing was, it was the uglier one who chickened out." He looked at Dominic glumly. "They broke my heart, Newt."

"I doubt that," Dominic smiled. "Let me get you a beer. It'll all seem better after a few pints." And since he couldn't leave his friend in the lurch when he was emotionally vulnerable, Dominic had to stay and drink with him, so the plan to beat a retreat and console Martini was scrapped, and the chance to repair the damage was squandered.

## TWENTY-ONE

The pair of worse-for-wear friends found themselves staggering back to the hotel at one in the morning. They'd stopped to grab something to eat, judging by the stains running down their T-shirts, but neither could remember that. Their eyes were unfocused and they had to lean on one another for support. They were still talking about the aborted threesome. Curran was disconsolate.

"It'll happen one day," Dominic muttered.

"No," Curran moaned. "This was my chance. I blew it. I'll never have another."

"You can't think that way," Dominic told him. "You've got to believe. There's no telling what's around the corner, or where… when…" He drew to a halt and blinked at the walls of the buildings around them. "Are we going the right way?"

"Yeah," Curran said.

"This doesn't look familiar."

"No," Curran agreed, "but we'll get there. My radar never lets me down. This must be a short cut."

Dominic was dubious, but Curran had exhibited the homing instincts of a pigeon on many a drunken night, so he let him lead. A few minutes later they rounded a bend and there was the Arpezos.

"Told you," Curran said.

"Scientists should study you," Dominic said earnestly. "It's uncanny."

"Maybe when I'm dead," Curran laughed as they spilled into the hotel lobby.

"Night," Dominic whispered, heading for his room.

"Do you want to come sleep with me?" Curran called him back.

Dominic frowned. "Curran… I like you… but…"

Curran laughed. "You're sweet, Newt, but not *that* sweet. I was thinking about Martini. You might not want to stagger in and wake her."

Dominic sighed and shook his head. "She won't be asleep."

Curran checked his watch. "This late?"

"Trust me," Dominic said bitterly. "She'll be sitting up in bed, face like a slapped arse, waiting for an argument."

Curran winced. "All the more reason to kip in my room."

"No," Dominic said. "Better to face the music now. She'll hopefully keep her voice down because it's late, so as not to wake everyone around us."

"Good luck with that," Curran giggled, then waved goodnight and sloped off to hit the sack and dream of his elusive threesome.

Dominic saw a sign for the toilet and relieved himself, cleaning up as best he could, wiping brown smears – what the hell had they eaten? – from around his lips and chin, running his fingers through his hair to pat it into shape. He wet a finger and ran it over his gums, then gargled with tap water and spat it out into the sink. In his intoxicated state, he thought he'd done a tip-top job, and he saluted his reflection in the mirror.

His smile faded as he climbed the stairs. This was going to be ugly. Martini would tear into him like a harpy. He'd be lucky if he saw the dawn.

"Man up," he grunted. "It won't be *that* bad. And she should have come with us. It was her choice to bail, not mine."

Mumbling away, he found the key to their room, paused to take a steadying breath, then opened the door and stepped inside.

Martini was sitting up in bed as he'd predicted, her face black with rage, brows furrowed, cheeks stained with dried tears, lips trembling with anger, hurt and self-pity. Dominic knew that his next words were crucial. He wanted to say something comforting and apologetic, admit he'd made a mistake, tell her how sorry he was, start trying his hardest to put things right. But in his drunken state what he ended up doing was spreading his arms, grinning at her like a monkey, and bellowing in a poor Jesse Pinkman impression, "Yo, bitch, I'm home!"

## TWENTY-TWO

Martini wouldn't talk to him in the morning. They'd been a couple for almost two years, but this was the first time she'd properly subjected Dominic to the silent treatment, so he wasn't sure how to respond. After lobbing a few questions her way and having them completely ignored, he decided to keep his mouth shut and wait for her to direct him.

They'd argued for more than an hour the night before. There had been tears, bitter accusations, curses. Martini had said repeatedly that she never wanted to see him again when they got back to London, that he'd have to move out. Dominic had reminded her that the apartment was in his name, so if one of them had to go, it would be her. In retrospect, he wished he'd thought a bit more about it before coming out with that one.

Martini had kept her voice down for the duration of the fight, but that had made it worse. The threats had sounded more serious when hissed, and it meant she had to keep her face close to his in order to be heard. She would have been easier to deal with at a distance. It would also have made it harder for her to hit him.

Dominic rubbed his jaw and his eyes watered. He could have handled the slaps, but at one point she'd made a fist and punched him. The force of the blow had knocked him backwards on the bed, and his chin still stung.

Martini might have carried on fighting all night, but exhaustion took over and he fell asleep, nodding off in the middle of another of her verbal broadsides. She would have woken him, but she was tired too and couldn't think of anything new to say, so she left him snoring and slept on the floor.

Dominic didn't hear the alarm when it went off at eight. Martini let it ring, getting louder and louder, but when Dominic didn't stir, she reset it and treated herself to another hour of slumber.

Even at nine, Dominic was dead to the world, but Martini shook him awake. She was tempted to slap him again, but her fingers were still sore from the punch.

"What's up?" Dominic groaned, opening an eye. Martini flashed her watch at him in answer. "I don't… what?" Dominic started to sit up. Then he remembered the night before and groaned. "What time is it?"

Martini shoved her hand up close to his face, forcing him to focus on her watch.

"Nine?" Dominic yawned. "God, it must have been two at least before we fell asleep. Can't we nap for another couple of hours?"

In response, Martini stormed to the bathroom and slammed the door shut. Dominic fell back and moaned. He wanted to sleep off his hangover, but he could sense that there was no point arguing with her.

He tried to make the peace when she came back, but quickly realised that she wasn't going to reply to any of his gambits. He endured the silence for a while, then crawled out of bed the next time she went to the bathroom, threw on some clothes and went to call Curran.

"I'm not moving for God, man or beast," Curran declared.

"Please," Dominic croaked as Curran pulled the covers over his head.

"Not until midday at the earliest," Curran said, his voice muffled.

"Martini punched me," Dominic said, and Curran stuck his head out. "Here, on the jaw. You can see the bruise."

Curran squinted. "Doesn't look like much of a bruise to me."

"It hurts like hell," Dominic said miserably.

"You never could take a punch," Curran grunted. He noted Dominic's slumped shoulders and trembling lower lip. "How bad is it?"

"The worst ever. She's not talking to me."

"It's not all bad news then," Curran chuckled.

Dominic's features hardened. "This isn't the time to wind me up."

"Sorry," Curran sighed, scratching his chest. "Give me half an hour to wash and shave. I'll meet you in reception."

Dominic didn't have time to shave when he got back. Martini was hogging the bathroom, and he was only just able to squeeze in a quick shower and a piss. Then she was marching him downstairs to check out, not a word to either him or Curran.

The silent treatment continued in the car. Dominic tried to sit up front. One glare from Martini let him know that he'd been banished. He slid in beside Curran without a word, shushing him when he frowned and started to complain.

"Do you want me to navigate?" Dominic asked.

Martini ignored him and studied the map. She spent ten minutes poring over it while the pair on the back seat shivered. Finally she put the map away and took off.

She drove northwest, circling back towards Plovdiv, not that the boys had any idea. The road climbed as they cut through the hills and mountains. It wound a lot, but wasn't as difficult to negotiate as she'd feared. She stopped in a few villages to explore briefly. Each time she scowled at Dominic and Curran, letting them know that she expected them to stay in the car.

"I need to piss," Curran said in one village, while they were waiting for her.

"Go at the side of the car," Dominic said dully.

Curran was incredulous. "You're joking, right?"

Dominic shook his head. "If she comes back and you're not here, she won't wait."

"She wouldn't drive off and leave me," Curran protested.

"You want to chance it?"

Curran looked around. It would have been easy to get a bus to Plovdiv, less than a two-hour journey, but he didn't know that. As far as he was aware they were in the middle of nowhere. Grumbling darkly, he opened the door, crouched beside it, and pissed while squatting. *From the promise of a threesome to this*, he brooded as he shuffled his feet and tried to avoid the splash of yellow spray.

They pulled into a large town called Asenovgrad for lunch. Dominic chanced a few comments while they were sitting at a table in a rudimentary restaurant, but Martini didn't reply. She was busy texting friends back home. It would cost a lot but she didn't care, and Dominic figured this wasn't the time to advise caution.

"This is the worst meal we've had," Curran whispered when Martini went to the toilet.

"I know," Dominic said. "She chose the lousiest restaurant she could find, to punish us."

"This is over the top, isn't it?" Curran ventured. "You should sort her out."

"How?" Dominic snorted.

Curran frowned. "It's a tricky one, her being the only driver. I suppose we have to keep her sweet, at least until we shore up for the night. We can look into our options then, find an internet cafe, hatch an escape plan."

"Escape?" Dominic said blankly.

"We can't go on like this," Curran said. "I'm not going to spend the rest of our holiday pissing by the side of the car while Martini treats us like mannequins."

"What can we do about it?" Dominic asked.

"Get a bus or train to Plovdiv."

"Leave her?" Dominic said quietly.

"If we have to."

"It would be over for real if we did that," Dominic noted.

"I thought it was anyway."

Dominic sighed. "We've been together a long time. I don't want it to end like this, over something so stupid."

"Then you need to get her talking," Curran said. "Because as things stand, your relationship is dead and buried."

"When did you become such a pessimist?" Dominic growled.

"That's realist, baby," Curran smirked. "Realist."

Then the pair lapsed back into ruminative silence and waited for the glowering Martini to return.

## TWENTY-THREE

Once they'd paid the bill, Martini set off to explore Asenovgrad on foot. Dominic and Curran trailed along behind, Martini not even acknowledging their presence.

It was a lovely old town, packed with monasteries and churches. Martini visited a few of the attractions and shopped for souvenirs. She seemed to be on better form, so Dominic tried breaking the ice a few times. She responded with stern silence, although she did grunt at him once, which he took as an encouraging sign.

It was Curran who eventually breached Martini's mute defences. "This is a cool place," he said to Dominic. "We'll have a great time here tonight."

Martini stopped and glanced back at him. "Who said we were staying?"

"Well, I assumed..."

Martini smiled thinly.

Curran frowned. "We're not staying?"

Martini hesitated. She'd actually planned to stay in Asenovgrad. She thought it was a charming town and had been looking forward to spending the night here. But when she heard Curran raving about the place, she wanted to spite him.

"How about you?" Martini asked Dominic. "Do you want to stay?"

Dominic smiled. "Yeah, it seems like a nice spot."

That decided Martini. "Too bad. I've somewhere else lined up."

"Where?" Curran asked.

Martini touched the side of her nose.

"What if we want to stay?" Curran challenged her.

Martini shrugged. "You're free to come and go as you please."

Curran looked to Dominic for support. This was their chance to ditch her. She'd carried this too far. If she wanted to play with the big boys, this was when they'd stick it to her and leave her with a clear choice — cut the dramatics and continue with them, or hold the moral high ground and piss off by herself. He was hoping it would be the latter.

But Dominic didn't want to lose Martini without a fight. "I don't mind where we stay," he said sullenly. "I'll go wherever you go, M."

Martini almost melted. She was sorry she'd taken the argument so far. She wanted to hug him, have a little weep, put the last twenty-four hours behind them. But it was hard to back down and not look like she was caving in. Curran had a face like thunder. If she threw herself into Dominic's arms, Curran would feel like he had a license to carry on acting however he pleased.

"We're moving on," Martini said, deciding to give ground gradually. "But we might come back tomorrow or the day after, depending on how things work out."

"Great," Dominic beamed.

"You mean we can come back if we're good little boys?" Curran grunted.

"Yeah," Martini said, her upper lip curling.

And then, because his tone had annoyed her, she marched them back to the car, cutting short their tour of the town. *That'll teach them*, she was thinking as she sat in, pleased with herself for not buckling under pressure.

Getting into the back, Curran was smirking and thinking, *The cow has dug a hole that she'll never climb out of. She'll be dumped and ditched by twilight.*

Next to Curran, Dominic wasn't thinking much of anything, except how sweet Martini's neck looked as a drop of sweat slowly trickled down it, and how happy he would be if he could lean forward and kiss her there and have her smile in the mirror at him and tell him to do that again.

## TWENTY-FOUR

Martini studied the map as casually as she could, as if to confirm her route out of Asenovgrad. In fact she was looking for a place where they could hole up, which the boys would believe had always been her goal.

A small town – or large village – to the south caught her eye. It was called Laki and it seemed to be out of the way of where she imagined most tourists visited. Also, it was nestled among the mountains, and she'd told Dominic and Curran that they'd be spending a lot of time up high. So south she set.

After a few kilometres they stopped at a place called Asen's Fortress, a popular destination for daytrippers. Built on a high, rocky ridge, it offered a similar experience to the ruins of Perperikon, but it wasn't as rundown, with a functioning church perched among the fortified walls.

The sun beat down on them as they strolled around. Martini glanced at Dominic disapprovingly. She could tell he hadn't rubbed in enough sun cream that morning. She didn't want to remind him – that would show she cared – but she hated the thought of him getting burnt. In the end she reached into her bag, produced a small tube, rubbed some cream into her face, then offered it to Dominic. "Want this?"

"Thanks," he said, ecstatic to have been addressed directly.

"You need more," Martini said as he tried to hand back the tube.

"I don't want to use it all up," Dominic said.

"I can replace it later."

"What about me?" Curran asked as Dominic set to work.

"Burn, baby, burn," Martini said with sweet viciousness.

"Be nice," Curran growled.

"Why?" she shot back.

Curran held her stare a moment, then spat – to his left, not at her – and turned to leave.

"Where are you going?" Dominic asked.

"To find sun cream," Curran said.

"Where?" Dominic called.

"I'll beg the other tourists for some."

As Curran stomped away, Dominic looked to Martini appealingly. She rolled her eyes, then tossed him the car keys. He shouted at Curran to stop, but Curran ignored him. Dominic looked to Martini again. "Go on," she sighed. "I don't want him bothering anyone."

"Wait here," Dominic said. "I'll be back in a minute."

"No," she said. "I'm carrying on with the tour."

Dominic stared at her longingly as she swivelled away. He looked from her to Curran, trying to choose. In the end he decided that Curran needed him more. "I'll come find you," he shouted, then set off after his friend.

"I won't hold my breath," Martini whispered, then went to check out the murals in the church, feeling a lot glummer than she had a few minutes before.

Curran was hiding a smile when Dominic caught up with him. He sniffed when Dominic jangled the keys, followed his old friend to the car and stood gazing off at the view as Dominic rooted around for sun cream.

"Where's Martini?" Curran asked.

"Still looking round the ruins. I told her I'd join her when I was done here."

"Do you want me to come?" Curran asked.

"Of course. Why wouldn't I?"

Curran pulled a face. "I'm in her bad books. You are too, but she might be thawing on that front. Maybe you need some time alone."

"Don't be stupid," Dominic said. "We're on holiday together. We have to make an effort to get along." He grinned and sang, "Did you think I would leave you crying when there's room on my horse for two?"

Curran laughed. *Two Little Boys* was their favourite song. They'd sung it the first time they'd ever got drunk, and it often resurfaced on long, booze-fuelled nights. "The trouble is," he said, "it's two little boys and a pissed-off little girl. Maybe the horse won't hold all three of us."

"It'll have to," Dominic said firmly.

Curran smiled and focused on the sun cream. He paid more attention than he normally did, taking his time, squinting at the sun as if worried. He didn't go so slowly as to arouse Dominic's suspicions, but he knew exactly what he was doing, stretching it out as long as he could, sure that every minute would be like a nail being driven into Martini's skull. He didn't normally try to cause trouble between Dominic and his girlfriends, but he could only be pushed so far, and Martini had shoved him way past that point. If he could turn Dominic against her, he would.

Finally he stopped, handed Dominic the tube and stretched. "Let me have a quick drink, then we're off," he said, opening the back door and fishing out a bottle of water which he'd been sipping from the last couple of days — Curran wasn't a fan of water and could get by on very little, even in temperatures as sizzling as these.

When he was done, he smiled at Dominic, waited for him to lock the car, then shot off, yelling, "Last one to find Martini is a rotten egg."

"What are you — ten years old?" Dominic shouted, not rising to the bait.

Curran looked back, grinning, and started to slow. Then his foot caught on a stone – or that was what it looked like from where Dominic was standing – and he went sprawling. Dominic raced after him. "Are you OK?" he asked as he drew level with Curran, who was sitting up and nursing his ankle.

"I think so." Curran winced. "Should have been looking where I was going." With Dominic's assistance he got up and took a step forward. "Fuck!" he yelped.

"What's wrong?"

"Must have sprained it," Curran said, raising his left foot and flexing his toes.

"Nothing more serious than that?"

"I don't think so." He set the foot down and took a few wobbly steps forward. Shook his head glumly. "It's not bad, but I'd better go back to the car and rest."

"I'll help you," Dominic said, wrapping an arm round him.

"Don't be stupid," Curran grunted. "Martini's waiting for you."

"Did you think…" Dominic started to sing again.

Curran laughed and fluttered his eyelashes. "My hero," he cooed.

Dominic helped the wounded soldier to the car, opened the back doors and squatted as Curran lay across the seats and groaned softly. Curran again urged Dominic to go find Martini, but Dominic brushed that aside and stood watch over his friend, in case his ankle swelled.

They chatted away as normal, about their school days, other holidays they'd been on, favourite movies and bands, memorable nights on the razz. Dominic was soon smiling, cares of the morning forgotten. In fact he was enjoying himself so much that he also forgot about Martini and his promise to find her. To Dominic, in those soft, relaxing moments, nothing in the world was lost, so nothing needed to be found.

## TWENTY-FIVE

Martini wasn't angry when she returned, just disappointed. She looked at Dominic questioningly. He coughed and pointed to Curran. "He twisted his ankle."

"Oh?" Martini stared at Curran with unconcealed suspicion.

"Nothing serious," Curran said cheerfully. "I told him to leave me but he was determined to play Florence Nightingale."

"What was the church like?" Dominic asked.

Martini shrugged. She almost snapped at him that if he was that interested, he would have come see for himself, but she didn't want to rear up in case Curran had suffered a genuine injury. Instead she treated herself to a long drink. "Are you really OK?" she asked Curran when she was done.

"Yeah, I just went over awkwardly on it."

"Because if you need a hospital, now's the time to tell me," she pressed.

"God, no, it's nowhere near as bad as that. I kept telling the big lug that I was fine, but he wouldn't leave my side."

Dominic smiled at Martini. "So, are you ready to tell us where we're going?"

She shrugged again. "It's a place called Laki. Just a small town I spotted on the map, but it's in a nice location." Martini picked the map out of the car and showed them the spot, then said, "I got chatting to someone in the church. He's local. His daughter married an Irishman. The husband's parents are here on holiday, so Hristo is showing them the sights."

"Give a woman five minutes with someone and she can tell you their life history," Curran commented wryly.

"I asked Hristo about accommodation in Laki," Martini went on. "I was sure we'd have to settle for a B&B, because it's such a small place, but he said there's a nice hotel, assuming they have availability."

"Sounds like a winner," Dominic nodded.

"He also said it's not the most scenic of places," Martini warned them. "It's a mining town – lead and zinc – so it's industrial. That put me off, but then he told me what the name means in English and I knew it was the place for us." She stared solemnly at the puzzled boys for a few seconds, then smiled warmly for the first time that day. "It means *lucky*."

At that, all three of them, having by coincidence been to a live performance of *The Rocky Horror Picture Show* only a few weeks earlier, cried out, "I'm lucky! You're lucky! We're *all* lucky!"

"Except Eddie," Martini piped up.

"Sshhh!" Dominic and Curran both hissed in character, then all three were laughing and singing and doing impressions of Dr Frank-N-Furter, and all was copacetic again for a short, sweet while as they buckled up, backed out of the parking lot and wound their way leisurely to the unlikely promised land of Laki.

# PART THREE

*"hail, hail, the gang's all here"*

*The beast circled the shack, sniffing the air. It had used this place as a base several times before. It had its favoured spots in most areas, usually caves or abandoned mines, but also a scattering of rundown, deserted old buildings like this. It always felt a pang of comfort when it came to one of its hideaways, but it never took its safety for granted. The world could change overnight. Its enemies could reclaim a ruin at any point. The beast always approached such dwellings cautiously, ready to turn tail and slip away if there was any hint that they'd been used by others recently.*

*The beast never disputed territorial rights. It was easier to move on if one of its boltholes had been taken over. There was no profit in fighting over something so trivial. Fights drew attention, and secrecy was the key to the beast's survival.*

*Discerning no troubling scents, the beast advanced into the clearing and moved closer to the shack. It peered in one of the windows, waiting for its weak eyes to adjust. The room looked much as the beast recalled. No signs that anyone had been using it since the beast last passed this way.*

*Gurgling happily, it pushed the door open and stepped inside. Once it was in the middle of the room it took a long, deep sniff, turning its head as it inhaled.*

*Nothing. The shack was secure.*

*The beast urinated lightly, marking its spot, then spread the piss around with a foot. It was smiling. It liked this shack. It was one of the beast's more luxurious sleeping quarters. And it had a hidden secret, a horde of sharp-fanged, permanent residents.*

*The beast recalled the she-wolf, how it had considered letting her cub live and keeping it as a pet. It had decided against that in the end, since a pet might prove more trouble than it was worth, but it would have a pet-like substitute during its stay here.* Lots *of them.*

*Chuckling darkly, the beast stepped outside and went around the side of the shack, to where a pair of doors was closed over the entrance to a cellar. Pulling one of the doors open, it lowered an arm and felt for the tree trunks which it had left here a long time ago. They were still in place, and the beast could even smell the acrid stench of its urine, from where it had pissed frequently round the base of the trunks during previous stays.*

*The beast made a high-pitched hissing noise, then beamed when it was answered by hundreds of squeals. The tiny creatures wouldn't remember it — they didn't live very long, and those who'd been here last time would have been replaced by a new generation — but they'd adapt to its presence swiftly, especially when it treated them to the off-cuts of its kills.*

*The beast had always enjoyed its visits here, and felt sure that this one would prove no different. While it had no real home, vagrancy being integral to its continued existence, this place felt more like a home than most. It wouldn't stay here longer than anywhere else, no more than a few weeks, maybe a month at a stretch, but it would relish its days spent resting in the shack and the cellar, and look forward to returning every night when it had finished hunting.*

*Opening the second door, the beast crawled in and started to climb down the trunks, feet first, pissing as it went, frightening off the creatures on the floor, pulling the doors shut after it, immersing itself in the unbroken darkness of the undulating and sweetly stinking underground world.*

## TWENTY-SIX

It was late evening by the time they parked outside Hotel Akvareli in the remote town of Laki. The town was more scenic than Martini had been led to expect, situated in a high valley in the Rhodope Mountains, the houses rising up the slopes of the surrounding peaks. The hotel had been recently built, and boasted views that would have cost a fortune in a more touristy area.

"The name of our hotel means watercolours in your language," the receptionist told them as they checked in. A slim man in his forties, he was pleased to be able to practise his English. "We open for business in 2008. We have twenty rooms. Six are available. I will put you in the best of what we have, no extra charge. I am not expecting more guests to check in at this late." He laughed as if he had cracked a joke and the others obligingly laughed too.

Dominic carried Curran's rucksack to his room, even though Curran protested that he could manage it himself, and left him there to settle. Once they'd closed the door of their own room, he pulled Martini in tight and kissed her deeply.

"Nice to be back on smooching terms," she giggled, rubbing her nose over his.

"Even nicer to be back on other terms," Dominic murmured, sliding a hand up between her legs.

"Not now," she stopped him. "I'm exhausted. I didn't get much sleep last night, it was an upsetting time, we've done a lot today, I'm not in the mood."

"That's fine," he smiled. "But later…?"

"I'm sure I'll recover swiftly," she smirked.

He kissed her again, before unpacking his toiletries and placing them around the bathroom. Martini took a long shower, then Dominic slipped in and had a quick one, to wash off the sun cream. He hated the oily residue which it left behind. It was always a relief when he could suds-up and scrub it all away.

Martini was lying face down on their bed when he came out, leafing through a magazine, yawning. Dominic tiptoed over, leant across and kissed her neck, as he had wanted to do earlier in the car.

"Nice," Martini said.

Dominic kissed her there again, then stopped before he got too aroused. "So, what's the plan?" he asked, sitting down and drying between his toes.

"Get something to eat," Martini said lazily. "Stroll around. Grab a few drinks. Come back."

"You don't mind us drinking?"

"One or two will be fine, but no more than that, OK?"

"I promise," Dominic said. "A quiet, boring night."

"I think they have a lot of those here," Martini sighed.

"Do you wish we'd stayed in Asenovgrad?"

She shook her head. "It'll be nice to see what life is like in the more out-of-the-way places."

"I guess you can't get much more out-of-the-way than this," Dominic laughed. He kissed the top of her head, then finished drying himself, got dressed, and they went to collect Curran.

## TWENTY-SEVEN

There wasn't an abundance of eating and drinking options, but they found a busy little restaurant that served up tasty food and the best beer they'd yet to sample.

"This must be from one of those famous Bulgarian microbreweries," Curran commented.

"Ha bloody ha," Dominic replied drily.

Setting his beer down, Curran licked his lips. "I can't wait to sink my teeth into a burger."

"I thought you liked the local grub."

"I do, but there comes a point in every holiday where I get a McDonalds Moment."

"You'll struggle to find a McDonalds here," Martini smiled.

Curran shrugged. "They'll have their own version. I'll track down a burger bar later, sink my teeth into something thick and juicy and dripping with grease."

"Actually, we're going to have an early one tonight," Dominic told him.

"No problem," Curran said.

"We're tired," Dominic continued, feeling that he had to justify himself.

"Fine. Doesn't matter to me."

"What about you?" Martini asked. "Coming back with us?"

"Nah, I'll go cruising, see what I can find. There's got to be action going down somewhere. Miners party hard. I've seen *Priscilla*."

"That was Australia, not Bulgaria," Dominic reminded him.

Curran sniffed. "Geography changes. People don't."

"Just don't get plastered," Martini warned him. "We've another early start."

Curran stared at her, his left eyelid twitching. He almost exploded, but caught himself, forced a smile and muttered, "Yes, ma'am." Inside he seethed, *That's it. I was ready to play nice. Not now. She wants a quiet night in with the Newt? In your fucking dreams, lady.*

They'd each had a glass of beer and were almost done with their second. Curran had bumped into the proprietor on his way to the toilet earlier and enquired about the delicious beer. Turned out it was stronger than the regular brews back home, almost 11%. He'd planned to tell Dominic and Martini, but now, as he raised a hand to attract a waiter's attention, he decided to keep the information to himself.

"Are you calling for the bill?" Martini asked.

"No," Curran said, then smiled at the waiter and requested three more beers.

Martini frowned. "I'm not sure…"

"Why not?" Curran boomed. "If you're going to love me and leave me, at least have a few drinks with me before you head off."

"One won't hurt, M," Dominic said.

"Of course it won't," Curran smiled. "It's only beer."

Martini hesitated. If she hadn't drunk the second glass, she would have insisted Dominic return to the hotel with her, as he'd promised. But the unexpectedly strong second helping had left her feeling warm and fuzzy inside. She couldn't understand why she was light-headed – it should take four or five pints before her head started spinning – and while a nagging voice at the back of her mind was telling her to stop, she wanted another. It would help her sleep soundly.

"OK," Martini said as the waiter arrived with three freshly poured glasses of the tempting beer. "But we're out of here after this one, agreed?"

"Absolutely," Dominic said, crossing his heart.

"Whatever the lady wants," Curran said with a sinister little smile.

Martini lifted the glass and stared into its amber depths, feeling for a moment that she was teetering on the edge of a cliff. Then she shook her head, scowled and took a sip. She was being silly. There was nothing to be afraid of. As Curran had noted, it was only beer. How could you possibly go astray on that?

## TWENTY-EIGHT

They all wobbled when they got up after their third glass of beer. "Woah!" Martini cried, grabbing the back of her chair to steady herself. "What the hell?"

"You OK?" Dominic asked, reaching for her and missing. He frowned and glanced at Curran. "You didn't add anything to the drinks, did you?"

Curran snorted. "Yeah, didn't you see all the dealers out back? Wise up, Newt. Where the hell could I score anything up here? Let's go for a walk. The fresh air will clear our heads in no time."

"Look at me," Martini laughed, letting go of the chair and sticking her arms out as if balancing on a tightrope.

Dominic and Curran laughed, but Dominic cast another suspicious look at his friend. Curran was right, there could be no one selling drugs to tourists in this remote spot. Besides, he would have seen Curran fiddling with the beers. But he could tell by the twitch in his old compatriot's lips that he knew more than he was letting on. Dominic just couldn't figure out what that might be.

They spilled out of the restaurant, giggling and wobbling, then went on a tour of the small town. Martini's face was flushed and she was smiling, but Dominic doubted she'd be grinning about this in the morning. "Maybe we should head back to the hotel," he said.

"So soon?" Curran replied.

"Like M said, we've an early start."

Curran shrugged. "I'm nicely wired. I don't mind pushing on by myself. But are you sure you don't want one more before you call it a night?"

Dominic looked to Martini. She burped and declared, "I'm up for another."

"You're sure?" he asked.

"Yeah," she said, then remembered her earlier pledge. "But only the one."

"Your wish is my command," Dominic smiled, and waved a hand at Curran. "Lead on, my man, and root out Laki's finest pub."

"Yes, boss," Curran laughed, then let his instincts guide him.

He spurned the first two pubs, even though one was busy and looked like a fun place. Busy and fun weren't enough. Curran was searching for a young person's establishment, where he could hook up with like-minded drinking partners, not just for company but because Dominic always found it hard to walk away from the allure of a group.

Curran finally spotted what he was looking for on a dimly lit side-street. It was a dark, grotty pub, one that most people would have passed without noticing. But with a quick glance Curran clocked the bartender with tattoos running up both burly arms, and the youths sitting huddled in a corner, their jeans and leathers, slicked-back hair, lots of drained glasses and bottles strewn across their table.

"This is us," Curran said, drawing to a halt.

Martini peered into the gloom. "Really?"

"Trust me, this is where the action's at."

"But we're not looking for action, are we?" she said uncertainly.

"You two aren't," Curran said, "but I am. This is where I'll spend the rest of the night. We can go somewhere else and I can come back by myself later, but does it make any difference to you since you're only staying for one?"

Martini hesitated, studying the dusty tables, the fierce-looking barman, the kids – no more than eighteen or nineteen years old – who were smiling tightly and trying hard to look cool. It was a dive. But they hadn't been in any dives yet. It might be fun to sample the seedier side of Bulgaria before focusing on the forested mountains brimming over with waterfalls, lakes and wildlife.

"Come on then," Martini giggled. "Maybe it'll be fun."

And with a woozy, crooked smile, she led them in.

## TWENTY-NINE

Curran bought the drinks but didn't linger at the bar. He wandered over to the young people in the corner and introduced himself, effortlessly slotting into their conversation, despite the fact that they were speaking Bulgarian.

There were four boys and two girls. The younger girl didn't look more than fifteen or sixteen to Dominic, the rest maybe a few years older. Dominic watched with fascination as the teenagers stared at Curran, wary at first. Then, as Curran kept babbling, they began to relax. One of the boys replied to him in good English, then the older girl chipped in, and another of the boys, not as fluent as the first, but with enough words to make himself understood.

A minute later Curran was sitting at the table, and Dominic and Martini had pulled up chairs beside him. The teenagers were chatting away rapidly, a mix of Bulgarian and English. The young girl and one of the boys spoke no English at all, but the others were at least partly bilingual and happy to translate for them.

They began revealing their names, though it took a while before Dominic was able to memorise them. The oldest boy was Iliya. He was beefy, with long, dark hair and a few tattoos on his forearms. He had a loud, abrasive laugh, and a habit of slamming his fist on the table when he found something especially amusing.

The boy with dirty blond hair was Kaloyan. He was thin but muscular, with a sharp look. He was the one who knew no English. Through the others he explained that he wasn't stupid or bad at languages, he just didn't want to learn the lingo of the Americans, since he saw them as global terrorists.

They had a passionate rant about Americans. Martini argued that they weren't that bad, they'd done a lot of good for the world too, and Dominic pointed out the fact that they'd made loads of great films.

"Bullshit to their films," Zdravko cried. He was the smallest of the boys and the ugliest, with a birthmark running across his forehead and left cheek. Unlike the others, he didn't slick back his hair, but let it grow long over his face, to hide as much of the mark as he could.

"Yankee films shit," Zdravko elaborated. "Fellini, Kurosawa, Bunuel... great. World once full directors like them. Now only Yankee shit. They..." He frowned and said something to the older girl.

"Corner market," the girl said.

"Yes," Zdravko nodded firmly. "They corner fucking market."

Boyka laughed. She had the darkest hair of any of them, with silver highlights running in a line along one side. She wasn't beautiful, but pretty in a punkish way. While her clothes were similar to everyone else's — jeans, T-shirt, a leather jacket — she wore them with more style.

"Have you always lived here?" Dominic asked.

"No," Boyka said. "Used live Sofia, Plovdiv, other places. Father moves a lot. But been here three years, a long time for me."

The fourth boy, Valko, was the quietest in the group. He was also the tallest, though he hunched his shoulders to mask his height. He had brown hair and an alarmingly crooked nose. Curran had started to ask about that, but Valko had frowned and made it clear that he didn't want to discuss it. To Dominic he seemed the most hostile of the teenagers, saying little, even though his English was good.

The young girl, Nevena, didn't say much either, but she smiled a lot and nodded as the others were chatting. She had fair hair, bad acne, and was overweight. She wore a short skirt — too short, Dominic thought, with chubby thighs like those — and kept swinging her legs back and forth.

"How old is Nevena?" Dominic whispered to Boyka.

"Nearly fifteen," Boyka whispered back.

"The barman doesn't care?" he asked.

She shrugged. "In small town, parents know when children drink. If they

OK, barman OK."

"I like it," Dominic chuckled. "I wish I'd lived here when I was her age."

Martini, on the other hand, saw nothing that she liked. She hadn't engaged much with the locals, except for when talk turned to Americans and their manners. She found the Laki gang loud, opinionated and boring. She had barely touched the glass of beer which Curran had bought for her. She was angry at herself for coming here, and angry at Dominic for not heading back to the hotel with her after dinner. (She'd forgotten that he'd offered. As she remembered it, they'd forced her to come with them.)

"Hurry up," she snapped at Dominic, tugging his arm.

Dominic had almost finished his drink and had intended to leave once he'd downed the last dregs. But he didn't like being ordered about like a dog in front of the smirking teenagers. "What's your problem?" he snapped back.

"We said we'd have just one," she growled.

"Sure," he nodded. "But we didn't put a time limit on it."

The Bulgarians laughed. "Dominic under thumb," Iliya guffawed, pounding the table. "Home, little boy, to be tucked in by Mummy."

"Fuck you," Dominic grunted, and Iliya laughed even louder. He leant across and thumped Dominic's arm.

"You OK for English," Iliya boomed.

"And you're not too bad for a Bulgarian," Dominic grinned.

Iliya laughed again, then shouted at Zdravko, "More drink. For our new friends too."

"No," Martini said immediately. "We've had enough. We're going."

"I'm not," Curran said.

"I didn't mean you," she sniffed. "But Dominic and I are done."

"No," Iliya protested. "One more. You can't go now. It would be rude."

"I don't care," Martini said, getting to her feet. "Dominic?"

Dominic stared at his girlfriend with something close to loathing. She had no right to treat him this way, or to act so discourteously towards their hosts. This was what they'd come here for, to mix with the locals and experience the real Bulgaria. So why was she acting like a spoilt bitch?

"Sit down," Dominic said stiffly. "Have another drink. We'll go after that."

"No," Martini barked. "We had the one that we said we'd have. Now we're leaving. We have an early start. You promised."

"I know," Dominic said slowly, "but I'm enjoying myself, these people have been nice to us, and it won't matter if we have one more to be respectful."

"Maybe you should go," Boyka said, casting a worried glance at Martini.

"No," Iliya shouted. He turned to face Martini. "If you want go, go, we don't give shit. But don't make him go too. Are you afraid we... what you say... bad influence?"

Martini wilted as Iliya glowered at her. He had been in many fights over the years and knew how to intimidate his opponents, puffing himself up, turning his arms to flash his tattoos, narrowing his eyes. She'd stood up to tougher men than him at home, confident that they were all bluster and wouldn't dare strike a woman in public. But this was a different country, and a remote part of it. She didn't know the rules.

"Iliya," Boyka tutted, and said something harsh in Bulgarian.

Iliya sighed. "OK, go if you want," he said to Dominic. "Not our business." He sneered and made the sign of the cross at Martini. "Peace."

Martini was shaking. "Dominic?" she said again, quietly this time. Normally he would have seen that she was upset, understood that she'd felt threatened, and offered her his arm without a second thought. But in his anger he'd missed Iliya's posturing and wasn't registering Martini's nervousness. All he saw was his girlfriend standing over him, belittling him in front of Curran and the others.

"I'm going nowhere," Dominic said. "I'll finish my drink, have another, and maybe another after that."

Martini stared at him, stunned. She shouldn't have snapped at him – she already regretted that – but the Bulgarian boy had squared up to her aggressively. She thought Dominic was siding with Iliya against her. Her jaw tightened.

"OK," Martini said frostily. "Have it your way. Just don't be surprised if you wake up in the morning and I'm gone."

Dominic blinked as she stormed off.

Curran leant across. "Want me to go after her?" he said softly, voicing the thought before Dominic had it himself.

Dominic shook his head meekly, not wanting to admit in front of the others that he was concerned that Martini might abandon them.

"Don't worry," Curran said, giving his knee a squeeze. "She was only blowing off steam. She won't leave us. Who'd navigate?"

Dominic smiled shakily and focused on the remains of his pint, trying not to show his confusion or fear. Curran studied him covertly, saw that he was going to stay, and smirked as he crowed silently to himself, *The night is ours.*

## THIRTY

Dominic didn't enjoy his next drink. It left a bitter taste in his mouth. He thought about stopping and following Martini back to the hotel, but Curran was on high form, talking with the teenagers about their lives, their dreams, what it was like to live in such an out-of-the-way town. He did it artfully, making them feel as if their answers were important to him, nodding seriously, smiling sympathetically, encouraging them to open up.

Dominic began to warm to the conversation. Boyka asked him about London, what he did, where he lived, what he got up to in his spare time. He felt flattered by the pretty girl's interest and told her about going to uni, quitting because he wasn't interested, working in pubs, the club scene. He didn't notice when Curran slipped to the bar and ordered another round, and this drink went down a lot easier.

Through Boyka, Nevena asked Dominic what bands he liked and if he'd been to many live shows. He told her about the various venues he frequented and she pumped him for more information, wanting to know how often bands played there, what their capacities were, how they were decorated.

"If she annoy you, tell me and I send her home," Iliya said.

"She's fine," Dominic laughed as Nevena scowled, understanding what Iliya had said even though it had been in English. "Is she your girlfriend?"

Iliya frowned. "You think I fuck jail bait?"

"No," Dominic said quickly. "I just meant... the way you said it... it sounded like she had to do what you say."

"She do." Iliya nodded heavily, then laughed and thumped the table. "She my sister."

Dominic laughed, relieved that Iliya hadn't taken the unintentional slight more seriously.

Kaloyan said something in Bulgarian and smiled when Iliya responded. "I tell him what you say," Iliya explained.

Valko sneered and made a comment. Iliya scowled and barked in Bulgarian. Valko shrugged and looked away.

"What was that about?" Dominic whispered to Boyka.

"Nothing important," she said with an uneasy smile. "Valko like to talk nasty. Just an act."

Dominic figured it was his turn to buy a round, so he headed to the bar and bought the drinks from the tattooed barman, who started pouring as soon as Dominic stood up. He passed the first beer to Valko and smiled, hoping to make a connection, but Valko blanked him.

"Cheers," Nevena giggled when Dominic handed her a drink.

"See?" Iliya boomed. "She speak perfect English."

Nevena giggled again and said something cheeky. Iliya shook his finger from side to side, then blew her a kiss.

Zdravko tried to talk politics with Dominic, but it was difficult since Dominic knew nothing about Bulgarian politicians. They agreed that the Middle East was fucked, the British and Americans should never have invaded Iraq, and Nelson Mandela had been a saint.

Curran was talking with Kaloyan, Boyka translating for them. "It's amazing," he said to Dominic. "Kaloyan has never been further than Asenovgrad. He has no interest in travel. Isn't that insane?"

"Doesn't he get bored?" Dominic asked.

Kaloyan shook his head when the question was put to him, and this time Valko translated when he replied. "I love this place, family, friends. Beside, what's great about the rest of world? What you do in London so different to what we do? You have bigger buildings, more pubs. Who cares? More isn't better." Kaloyan raised his glass, saying something short and sharp. "Beer is beer," Valko finished.

"That should be our motto," Curran laughed. "*Beer is beer!* Cheers." He clinked his glass against Kaloyan's and Valko's.

Valko stared at Curran coldly. Then he shrugged and said softly, "Cheers."

"Cheers," Nevena echoed, the only word of English that she seemed prepared to volunteer. The others laughed, yelled "Cheers!" back at her, then they were swamping their pints and calling in another amber round.

## THIRTY-ONE

A couple of hours later, Dominic was wasted. They'd drunk at a furious rate, he and Curran paying for most of the rounds, men of wealth compared to the teenagers, happy to splash the cash around. He'd long lost track of the number of pints they'd chugged. And there had been shots strewn among them too, demanded by Iliya, who insisted they couldn't leave Laki without trying the local firewater.

Curran had spent a lot of time talking with Boyka, in pursuit of her, but she merely laughed at his passes and pushed him away whenever he leant in too close. She was evasive when Curran asked if she was in a relationship. Dominic got the impression that she'd dated a couple of the guys but wasn't with anyone at the moment. But he could have been wrong about that. It was hard to tell with a brain that felt as if it had been pounded with a mallet all night.

Nevena was asking questions about his favourite bands again. She'd taken to tapping his shin with her foot and smiling shyly at him whenever Iliya wasn't looking. Dominic had to keep warning himself to be careful. He didn't think the bulldog-like Iliya would see the funny side if Dominic made a move on his sister.

Valko was on his way to the bar for another round when he paused, glanced at his watch, then said something in Bulgarian. Iliya had been listening to Curran, but he turned and replied to Valko. The pair spoke quickly, then Valko said something that made Boyka sit up and squeal, "Yes. The lake. Perfect."

"What's going on?" Curran asked, smiling lazily, eyes unfocused.

"We have enough of bar," Valko answered. "Time move on."

"There's a club up here?" Dominic asked.

"We don't need club, asshole," Valko snorted. "Lake!"

As Curran and Dominic stared at Valko ignorantly, Iliya explained. "Lots of lakes, some hard get to, not much visited. We know great lake, nobody go there. Used be road, but swept away, forest grow, people forget. Kaloyan and Zdravko hiking one day, find path. We go up sometimes. Want come?"

"You want to go swimming instead of drinking?" Curran asked.

"Both, fucknuts," Valko huffed.

"Stop being rude," Boyka yelled, then smiled at Curran. "Yes, both. We take beer, vodka, get *really* drunk. Maybe swim, maybe not, depend how cold water is. A great place if swim or not. Big moon tonight. Beach has lovely view of sky."

"There's a beach?" Curran gawped.

"Not beach," Boyka giggled. "What you call it?" She frowned, then shrugged. "I don't know. Land round lake where we can lie. Sunbathe there sometimes."

"What do you think, Newt?" Curran asked. Dominic could tell by his beam that he was sold on the idea.

"How far away is it?" Dominic asked.

"Half hour drive, then half hour walk," Valko said.

Dominic checked his watch. Close to midnight. If they went now, stayed up there a couple of hours, it would be four in the morning before he crawled back to the hotel. Martini would be furious. "I dunno. We've sightseeing again tomorrow."

"Fuck that," Curran laughed. "We'll do our sightseeing tonight."

"Martini…" Dominic whispered.

"She'll be pissed at us no matter what," Curran pressed. "Might as well make the best of things, eh?"

Dominic frowned. He wanted to go but knew he shouldn't.

"Come," Nevena murmured. "Fun. Cheers."

Dominic chuckled but shook his head, still undecided.

Kaloyan said something and all of the Bulgarians laughed.

"What did he say?" Dominic asked.

"You need get OK from your girlfriend," Zdravko translated. "He say you not just under thumb, you under arse."

Dominic gave Kaloyan the finger. Kaloyan smirked and shot it back at him.

"Come," Boyka said. "Nevena right. It be fun. You like swim?"

"In the daytime, yeah, but at night…" Dominic was dubious.

Boyka shrugged and stretched her arms over her head. "Might be too cold, but if not and we swim, we swim with no clothes."

Curran's eyes boggled and he looked at Dominic with delight.

"Bullshit," Dominic wheezed.

"Maybe," Boyka said, then wiggled her breasts at him. "But if you not come, you not find out."

"I get naked for you too," Iliya said, flexing his pecs, and everyone laughed.

Dominic hesitated, then imagined Boyka in the buff and threw up his hands. "OK. I'm outvoted. I'll come."

The others cheered and surged to the bar, dragging Curran and Dominic with them. The locals ordered the booze, Iliya passing round the beer, Kaloyan choosing a few bottles of vodka with care. When the barman told them the total, Iliya translated for Dominic and Curran. "OK with that? Want us pay some?"

"No," Dominic said. "We're fine."

"Yeah," Curran smiled. "The booze is on us, the lake's on you."

Iliya nodded happily. "A fair deal."

"But how will we get there?" Dominic asked. "We won't all fit in a car."

"Fuck car," Iliya boomed. "We got better way." He winked at the pair of glassy-eyed tourists and said, "We get lift with Whore of Babylon."

## THIRTY-TWO

The Whore of Babylon was a battered old van with peeling green paint, deserts of rust everywhere, a series of webby cracks in the windshield, and a German license plate. One of the wing mirrors was held on with masking tape. The tyres were different makes. The front seats were covered with rugs. There was a hole in the driver's door that you had to reach through to unlock it from within, the handle having fallen off long ago.

"What you think?" Zdravko beamed. "She a beauty, right?"

"What the hell is it?" Curran asked, examining the van as if he was afraid it was going to come to life and bite him.

"Love of my life," Zdravko chuckled.

"German campers dump it here couple years ago," Valko explained, sneering at the Germans as he seemed to sneer at anyone who wasn't Bulgarian. "They on holiday. Van broke down. Decide it too expensive to repair, so left it, flew back or got train or who the fuck knows."

"I find," Iliya said, "but I not need van."

"He wanted to burn her out," Zdravko tutted, running a loving hand over the van's roof. "I stop him. We roll it to safe place. I study online. Ask mechanics in Laki for advice. Fix her myself. My van now. Whore of Babylon."

"Why the name?" Curran asked.

"Because all the fucking we do in it," Iliya said, then roared with laughter and made a fist to slam the side of the van.

"No!" Zdravko cried. "Rust."

"Wheels," Valko bellowed.

"Mirrors," Boyka shrieked.

"Fuck you all," Zdravko grunted sourly.

"No," Boyka said in answer to Curran's question. "I name it. Nothing to do with fucking. Just like."

"The name suits," Curran said. "But does the rust bucket work?"

"Of course," Zdravko said indignantly. "My love. My baby."

"Long as you don't hit pothole," Valko said, but he was smiling.

"Better than it looks," Iliya assured them. "It run fine."

"Better than fine," Zdravko insisted. "Fucking dream."

As Zdravko reached in to open the driver's door, Iliya opened the side door. The floor in the back was covered with rugs, the same as the seats up front. "Planks to cover holes," he said. "But all OK. You not fall through."

"That's a relief," Dominic said sceptically, then glanced at Curran. "This thing looks like a death trap."

Curran shrugged. "We've all got to go sometime," he said and crawled in. Kaloyan, Valko and Nevena followed him, while Iliya and Boyka got in up front.

Iliya rolled down his window halfway — it wouldn't go any further. "Come or not?" he called to Dominic, who was standing there hesitantly.

"What if it breaks down?" Dominic asked.

Iliya reached into his pocket and pulled out a mobile phone. "Signal not great up there, but OK. We break down, we call help."

"Not first time," Valko said pointedly.

"Hey," Zdravko winced. "Only once."

"Twice," Valko corrected him.

Zdravko thought about it and shrugged. "OK. Twice."

"Worse thing, we sleep side of road and walk back in morning," Boyka said.

Dominic debated it internally for another few seconds, then sighed and climbed in. "Fuck it. You only live once."

With a cheer, Curran tried to slam the door shut. He couldn't manage it, so Kaloyan had to lean over and help. As the others laughed, Zdravko fired up the engine. The van shuddered forward with a volley of farting noises, then lurched down the road, the teenagers drinking and singing as they went.

## THIRTY-THREE

They coasted along a main road for twenty minutes without any problems, then turned on to a dirt track just past a village. Every light in the village had been switched off, except for a couple in what looked like the local pub.

Their speed dropped alarmingly as they bumped along the dirt track, making slow progress in the juddering Whore of Babylon, Zdravko whimpering every time they hit a hole or bump, the others jeering at him, winding him up.

"I get out and walk," Iliya laughed. "Quicker."

"Fuck you," Zdravko snapped, focusing on the track ahead as best he could, but it was difficult since only one of the headlights worked, and the trees on either side grew thickly overhead, cutting out most of the natural light.

Dominic checked his watch. They'd already been gone for three-quarters of an hour. "How much further is it?" he asked. "You said half an hour in the pub."

"Not driven there at night before," Zdravko muttered. He was sweating, and not just from the heat. "Fucking hard. Should have wait till morning."

"No point going back now," Iliya said calmly. "Nearly there."

"Whore hurting," Zdravko said. "This not good for her."

"She be fine," Iliya assured him. "This shake her up and... how they say?" He babbled something at Valko.

"Iron out kinks," Valko translated.

"*We'll* need ironing out after this," Dominic said, his teeth chattering as they were thrown around.

"Stop complaining," Curran grinned. "It'll make a man of you. If you can survive this, you can tackle anything the world throws at you."

They bounced along, everyone holding on tightly to whatever they could grab. *At least we can't drink anything,* Dominic mused. He was glad of the break. It was giving his head a chance to clear. With all the bumping, he should have felt sick, but oddly he didn't, just dizzy from the beer and shots.

Eventually they stuttered to a halt. As Zdravko wiped sweat from his forehead and patted the steering wheel, whispering to the van like a parent congratulating a child who'd come through an ordeal, the rest of the group spilled out, stretching and groaning, then ducked back inside to make sure they didn't leave any of the alcohol behind.

Dominic rubbed the small of his back and looked around. It was a clear sky with a bright moon, but being a city-boy, it took his eyes a while to adjust. As things swam into focus, he saw the dirt track running ahead of them, snaking through the trees. He turned and looked behind — it was a mirror image of the view ahead. "You're sure this is the right place?" he asked.

"Sure as shit," Iliya beamed.

"But it looks the same as everywhere else," Dominic noted.

"That why nobody know it," Iliya said, then led them into the bushes, many of them taller than the men. "This old road."

Dominic couldn't see anything, but he could feel rubble underfoot. "So we follow this?" he asked.

"Do we fuck," Iliya snorted.

"Blocked off," Boyka reminded him. "Can't get past. Wall of trees and rocks."

"Beside, dangerous in dark," Valko said. "Snap ankles if we try walking on it."

Kaloyan said something and Boyka translated. "But path near. We not sure who made it. Maybe hunters or miners. Run same way as road, but bend a bit, bring you to lake at different spot."

"Will we be able to follow it in the dark?" Dominic was starting to wish he'd gone back to the hotel to patch up things with Martini.

"Easy," Iliya said confidently and started ahead into the undergrowth.

"It *is* easy," Boyka said softly as Dominic stalled. "Path just there. Bushes on sides all way. Can't get lost." She took hold of Dominic's hand and gave it a squeeze. "I not do it if I think we might go wrong. Mountain bad place to get lost, even in summer."

Dominic thought of Martini, livid or crying or both. He was sorry that he hadn't gone after her. But the others were dead set on advancing. He'd gain nothing if he waited for them in the van. "OK," he sighed.

Boyka smiled, gave his hand another squeeze, then led him forward into the forest-defined dark.

## THIRTY-FOUR

The path was nothing more than a thin foot trail through the bushes and trees. Weeds had grown over it since the teenagers had last passed this way, but it was still easy enough to follow. As Boyka had said, the bushes grew in close around it. You couldn't veer from the path unless you forced your way through the thick, bushy barriers on either side.

"How long do you think this path has been here?" Curran asked.

"No way know," Iliya said. "Maybe few years. Maybe hundreds."

"Hundreds?" Curran was sceptical.

Iliya nodded. "Old forest. Might be path people use before road built. Maybe not use for long while, then hunter or miner find and open up again. Or maybe it new. Can't tell."

They made swift progress. The locals had come this way many times, and even though it had been months since they'd last been up here, they rarely stumbled, warning Dominic and Curran about roots or low-hanging branches.

Every so often Dominic caught sight of the moon through a break in the trees. He paused each time to smile at it dreamily. He was starting to feel romantic. It was a shame Martini wasn't with them. She would have adored this. Maybe Dominic would bring her here the next night, if she was still talking to him.

"Any houses up here?" Curran asked.

"Joking?" Valko snorted. "We in the middle of nowhere, man."

"Then does anyone mind if I sing? It's chilly. A song would take my mind off the cold."

"Go on," Iliya chuckled. "You start, we join."

Curran tried an old Thin Lizzy song, but the Bulgarians hadn't heard of it, so he launched into *Hey Jude*. They all knew that one, or bits of it, and sang along heartily to the chorus.

Dominic was glad to be singing. Curran was right. There was a chill up here. He would have brought a jacket if he'd known.

"OK at lake," Boyka told him when she spotted him rubbing his hands up and down his arms. "Warm. Hot in day, catch sun and hold heat. Nice. Trust me."

"I thought you said you hadn't driven up here at night before."

"No, but sometimes come evening and stay night. Should do more often. Don't know why don't. Getting old and lazy." She laughed and Dominic laughed too. Then they sang more of *Hey Jude* and pressed on.

## THIRTY-FIVE

It took them less than half an hour to reach the end of the path. Iliya was first to step into the glade. He gave a shout of triumph, then fell quiet. The others were quiet too when they stepped out into the open. When Dominic joined them, he saw why.

The scene was like something from a postcard. A small, irregularly shaped lake, the surface completely still, surrounded by trees which pressed close to the water's edge except in the grassy area where they were standing. It would have been impressive any time, but it was particularly beautiful now, reflecting the three-quarters full moon and some of the many stars glittering unobstructed by clouds.

"Wow," Curran said softly, genuinely moved.

They advanced, nobody saying a word. Nevena had taken Dominic's hand. He thought about breaking contact, but when he looked at her, she was fixated on the lake, smiling warmly, a child who wasn't thinking about anything sexual, who just felt compelled to grip the hand of the person closest to her.

Kaloyan crouched by the water's edge and dipped a few fingers into the lake. When he brought them up, he flicked drops to his left, then his right, then touched the damp fingertips to his forehead and muttered something under his breath.

"What's he doing?" Dominic asked Nevena in a whisper. Then, remembering that she couldn't speak English, he directed the same question to Boyka.

"Like prayer," Boyka whispered back. "Kaloyan believe in forest spirits. He spend lots of time in mountains. Likes to honour spirits."

"For real?" Dominic asked.

"Real," she nodded.

Kaloyan stood and turned. He called to Iliya softly, and Iliya translated for Dominic and Curran. "He say water spirits pleased to see us."

"Tell them we're delighted to be here," Curran said. Kaloyan frowned and Curran raised his hands. "No bullshit. I mean it."

Iliya translated and Kaloyan relaxed. He pulled a bottle of beer out of the rucksack which he was carrying, opened it with a twist of his hand, and poured a good measure of beer into the lake. Then he toasted the lake and drank.

"We all need do that," Zdravko said, moving forward and opening his own bottle. The others followed suit, quietly, not making a fuss of it. Dominic expected to feel strange when it was his turn, but he didn't. Up here, with the teenagers, it felt like the most natural thing in the world.

The only problem was he couldn't twist off the top on his bottle. "How the hell…" he grumbled, fingers slipping and the cap biting into his flesh.

"Give here," Iliya said, and opened it for him. "Lots practise." He reached for Curran's bottle.

"Nuh-uh," Curran said. "I won't be bested." He struggled with the cap, grunted, tried again, winced, then yanked it off with a small cry.

"You OK?" Dominic asked as the others cheered.

"Yeah," Curran said, but he was bleeding from a cut in the soft flesh at the side of his palm. He raised it to his mouth to lick clean.

Kaloyan reached out to stop him. As Curran stared, the blond teenager guided his injured hand out over the lake and held it there while a few drops of blood dripped into the water and dispersed. He spoke as the blood dripped and Boyka translated for him this time.

"Beer good," she said. "Blood better."

Curran didn't know how to react. Eventually he smiled shakily and said, "I could open a vein if you like."

Kaloyan grinned when that was translated. He pressed his thumb over the cut, spread the blood around, then released Curran and nodded approvingly.

"Wash now," Zdravko said as Kaloyan moved away. "Not want it get infected."

"The water's safe?" Curran asked.

"Safest in world," Zdravko assured him.

Curran stared at the blood on his palm, then shrugged, knelt and immersed his hand. He shivered at the coolness of the water, then wriggled his fingers and smiled happily.

"Now must give lake what it demands most," Valko said seriously.

"What's that?" Dominic asked, chuckling uneasily at Valko's grim expression.

For a long moment Valko said nothing, his eyes glinting in the moonlight, the rest of the teenagers staring at him solemnly. Then Valko's lips split into a grin. He raised his bottle of beer high over his head and yelled with a rare display of enthusiasm, "Time to fucking party!"

## THIRTY-SIX

Dominic had struggled to keep up with the teenagers in the pub, but it was even harder here. They seemed to be draining their bottles with two or three swigs, even little Nevena, though big brother Iliya insisted she limit herself to one bottle for every two that the rest of them drank.

They were soon passing round the first bottle of vodka, taking long gulps from that as well. Dominic blanched when he caught the scent. He tried to pass it on without drinking, but Curran chanted, "Newt! Newt!" The others took up the chant and Dominic caved in to peer pressure. With a resigned groan he shut his eyes, put the bottle to his lips and took a deep swallow.

There was a huge cheer when he finished, but Dominic could only smile weakly. He knew he was going to be sick, but he wanted to wait a while, so that he could slip away and pretend he was going for a piss.

Kaloyan started singing a Bulgarian song. His friends joined in and Curran gave it a go too, sounding halfway like a local, albeit a step or two behind everyone else as he echoed what they were singing. But Dominic didn't dare test his voice, afraid that he'd projectile vomit if he opened his mouth, so he just swayed from side to side, grinning sickly, almost as green as the grass.

Boyka started a new song as Kaloyan finished his. This was more familiar, though at first Dominic couldn't place it. Then he realised it was the old European Song Contest winner, *99 Red Balloons*, and he swayed more swiftly. This had been one of his favourite songs when he was a child, and he still liked to dance to it if it came on when he was clubbing.

"Boyka! Boyka!" Curran crowed, the same way he'd chanted Dominic's name. Then he got up to dance. Boyka and Nevena joined him and they performed as a trio for the hooting, whistling boys.

Zdravko led them in another Bulgarian song when Curran collapsed in a fit of laughter towards the end of his act. This was a heavy, fist-thumping song, and Iliya and Kaloyan pounded the earth in time with it, while Valko clapped slowly and solidly, proudly jerking his head to the rhythm.

"Gotta... go," Dominic mumbled, getting to his feet and tugging at his flies to fool anyone who might be paying attention. Nobody was, and he stumbled away, forcing his way through a couple of bushes until he was out of sight. He started to throw up before he'd stopped walking, turning his head to one side so as not to splash his trousers or sandals.

He kept expecting someone to shout after him, to ask if he was OK, but the song must have masked the sounds. Either that or they didn't give a damn.

As the heaves eased, Dominic bent over and forced himself to hurl up the last of his stomach's contents. He waited until he was sure that he was done, wiped his mouth clean with the back of his hand, wiped the hand clean on the grass, then stood and had a piss, figuring he might as well while he was there.

A few deep breaths later and he almost felt human again. He stumbled back into the clearing and took his place by the rest of the gang, who were singing another song, this one a crazy mix of a Bulgarian ballad and *Twist And Shout*.

Nevena touched Dominic's arm and looked at him, worried. "OK?" she asked.

"Yeah," he said with a shaky smile.

She studied him, saw that he was suffering, then urged him to his feet and led him to the lake, where she made him crouch. Dipping her hand into the water, she held out a cupped palm. Dominic glanced round and saw Iliya scowling at them. He smiled again at Nevena, then made his own palmed cup and drank from that instead. Nevena shrugged, but he could tell that she was disappointed. He didn't mind. He'd rather a disappointed Nevena than an angry Iliya.

Dominic drank until the acidic taste had been washed from his mouth. The water was fresh, clear and cold. For a few seconds he entertained hazy thoughts of buying a license to bottle it, setting himself up as a water magnate.

Then Curran called, "Hey, Newt. More vodka."

Nevena frowned and shook her head at him.

Dominic chuckled weakly. "It's fine. Can't let the team down."

With something between a moan and a roar, he dragged himself back to where a smirking Curran was holding out the bottle. Dominic stared at it half lovingly, half loathingly. Then, putting his dreams of dominating the world of water behind him, he took the bottle, smiled as the gang egged him on, upended it and gulped it down until he felt that his stomach was as round and glowing as the soul-warming moon above.

## THIRTY-SEVEN

They drank and sang and danced for what felt like hours but which Dominic, when he checked his watch, realised was actually no more than thirty or forty minutes. They were all light-headed from the beer and vodka by this stage. Kaloyan was smiling vacantly at the moon, whispering a song or old poem. Valko was reeling off a list of the atrocities the super powers had inflicted on the world, darting from the Americans to the Germans to the British to the Romans to the Spanish to the Chinese. The way he was rambling, all of them had been operative at the same time, temporal boundaries blurring in his head.

The rest of them ignored Kaloyan and Valko. They were huddled together close to the lake, stretched out, talking about the future, friends, nights like this that they'd enjoyed in the past.

Nevena was asking lots of questions through the others, not just about music now, but what boys in their country were like, if they thought boys here were the same, how she should deal with them. She was getting teary. She'd recently broken up with her boyfriend. They'd been together for nearly four months, and to her that was a lifetime. She wasn't sure if she could make things work with a new guy, and was worried that she might never find true love.

The locals switched into Bulgarian as Boyka, Iliya and Zdravko assured Nevena that she was too young and pretty to worry about such matters. Curran listened for a while as if he understood everything they were saying. Then he turned to Dominic and said, "Women are the same everywhere."

"Be nice," Dominic tutted.

"I'm nice as pie," Curran whispered, "but c'mon, fifteen and worrying about her long-term love life? When we were that age we didn't give a fuck about the future. No fifteen-year-old bloke ever does."

"Some twenty-something blokes don't either," Dominic smiled.

Curran frowned. "I should be offended by that, but I'm too drunk."

The friends laughed. Then a thought struck Curran and a crafty look crossed his face. He stood, shifted his feet around until he was steady, then stared at the lake. "Hey," he said, interrupting the earnest-looking teenagers, "what about that swim we were promised?"

The Bulgarians paused and blinked at Curran. Nevena hadn't understood him. Zdravko looked uncertain. But Boyka and Iliya both smiled.

"Cold," Boyka warned him.

"We've survived the Atlantic Ocean off the coast of Ireland," Curran boasted. "Remember Ballybunion, Newt, when we went on that holiday with your dad?"

"How could I ever forget?" Dominic said sourly, recalling the day in March when Curran had dared him to go swimming in the sea. He shivered at the memory.

Iliya stood, then Boyka, then Zdravko, who still looked nervous. Nevena asked a question which Boyka answered. When she realised what they were planning, she leapt to her feet and clapped with delight.

Iliya tugged off his T-shirt. There was a tattoo on his chest but Dominic couldn't make out the design in the dim light. He had the physique of a male model and Dominic eyed his muscular torso jealously.

Curran tore off his own T-shirt. He looked a lot less butch than Iliya, but he flexed his meagre muscles like a body-builder, making a joke of it.

"My turn," Boyka murmured, removing her top. She wasn't wearing a bra, which astonished Dominic, who couldn't believe he had only noticed that now.

Curran's smile faded. He gulped and stared at Boyka's breasts. She ran a hand through her hair, watching his eyes as he watched her, all too aware of the effect she was having on him and Dominic. Iliya didn't seem too excited, as if he'd seen Boyka topless many times before.

Zdravko started to take off his top. Then he glanced at the lake, pulled a face, shook his head and sat down again. "Too cold. I stay and drink."

Iliya laughed, unbuckled his belt and slid off his trousers and boxers. He had a semi-erection and Dominic was unhappy to note that even in this half-alert state the teenager's penis was longer and wider than his. "In or out?" Iliya said to him challengingly.

"I don't..." Dominic looked to Curran for support.

"Fuck it," Curran grinned and slid down his own trousers and boxers in one quick movement. He stepped forward into the moonlight, fully erect. He flung his arms out and said, "Tah-dah!"

Boyka applauded, then took off the rest of her clothes, slowly, teasing the boys, all of whom were staring, even Iliya, who was getting harder now. When she was naked, she posed as Curran had. Dominic stared at her pubic hair. It was neatly trimmed, like Martini's. There seemed to be a line of blond running through it, to match the streak above her ear, but that might have been a trick of the light.

"OK," Dominic sighed. He undressed clumsily, almost falling over as he climbed out of his trousers, and stood with his hands crossed in front of his groin when he was done, blushing and shivering, his flesh prickling with goose bumps. Unlike the other two men, he wasn't erect, not even the beginnings of a semi.

"Gay?" Boyka asked him with surprise.

"Of course not," he snapped, his blush deepening. "I've got a girlfriend."

"But..." She waved at his sleeping penis.

"You're not *that* good-looking," Dominic said petulantly, then grimaced when her features hardened. "Sorry. I didn't mean that. Of course you are. I'd have a raging hard-on any other time, but I'm drunk and embarrassed."

Everyone laughed and Boyka smiled again. "OK," she said, giving one of her nipples a playful tweak. "I hate to think I lose charms."

Nevena said something that Dominic figured would play in English as, "Only me left now." And she started to pull at her shirt buttons.

"No!" Iliya barked. Nevena pouted, but Iliya said something sharply. Nevena's eyes filled with tears and Boyka leant across to wrap an arm round her. She whispered to the younger girl rapidly, warmly, trying to cheer her up.

Iliya glared at Dominic and Curran. "Sister underage. She not get naked. Got problem with that?"

"Hell no," Dominic said immediately.

"What do you think we are?" Curran sniffed. "If she took those clothes off, we'd be out of here faster than you could fart. I'm having a great holiday. I don't plan for it to end with me bunged up in prison on child molesting charges."

Iliya frowned, not having caught all that. But he saw that neither man was trying to make a move on Nevena and that mollified him. He nodded heavily and said, "OK. We clear."

Nevena had stopped crying and was staring spitefully at Iliya. She snapped at him but he only laughed. "When older, do what want, but now do what I say." When she stared at him blankly, he repeated himself in Bulgarian. Nevena shot him the finger and turned her back on them all, sitting down in a huff.

Dominic looked around. Valko and Kaloyan weren't interested. Zdravko was gazing at them curiously. Boyka stretched again. She was loving this, a born exhibitionist. "OK," she said. "Let's show we have balls."

With that she ran to the edge of the lake and waded in, diving under as soon as the water was deep enough, emerging with a delighted shriek. Iliya roared, "Fuck yeah!" and surged in after her, wading out further than she had before he dived.

Curran and Dominic shared a bemused look. This was a surreal situation and they weren't sure how to react. Then Curran grinned. "Last one in's a rotten egg."

"Not that lame old line again," Dominic snorted. "When are you going to grow up?"

"No time soon, I hope," Curran cackled.

They laughed, whooped and raced forward, yelping when they hit the cold water, screeching when it struck the undersides of their testicles, then evaporating into temporary silence as they dived and went under and surrendered to the chilly encompassing of the anthracitic, nocturnal lake.

## THIRTY-EIGHT

The water wasn't that cold once they'd adjusted. They were soon swimming leisurely, splashing one another, floating on their backs and gazing at the moon. Boyka kept darting beneath the water, disappearing for up to a minute at a time. When she emerged, it was often to grab one of the others and pull them under. When that first happened to Dominic, he thought a monster from the deep had snatched him, and swallowed a load of water trying to scream as he was dragged down.

"That wasn't funny," he shouted when he had his breath back, but Iliya and Curran just laughed at him, and he didn't mind when she did it again. In fact he started to hope that she'd do more than grab him, that she'd slide a hand between his legs and take things to another level. Dominic wasn't a born cheater, but the night was full of illicit promise and he was deliberately driving thoughts of Martini from his mind. If this turned into an orgy, he'd prove a willing participant, and he'd deal with the guilt in the morning.

But it was all innocent fun as far as Boyka was concerned. She enjoyed teasing the boys, but did so in a light-hearted fashion. When she leapt up and flashed her breasts, she laughed, and if Curran or Dominic tried to grab her, she swam away.

If he'd been more sober, Dominic might have been frustrated, but he was in too light a mood to care. Like Curran, he just shook his head, swam some more, half-heartedly grabbed at her again the next time she swung by.

Only at one point did things look like they might ramp up. Iliya had swum in close to shore and was standing, the water just above his knees. His penis was hard again and he was studying Boyka as she splashed around. His right hand went to his erection and Dominic's throat tightened as scenes from a thousand porn movies zipped through his head. But then Iliya looked over his shoulder and saw Nevena sitting on the bank.

When he saw his sister, Iliya sank to his haunches, hiding his hard-on and waiting for it to pass. Dominic knew then that this was not to be a night for orgies. But maybe Boyka would lead him or Curran off into the bushes by herself. All hope was not yet entirely lost.

Eventually Boyka tired of the water and hauled herself on to the bank, where she sprawled on the grass beside Nevena to dry. That was the signal for the boys and they climbed out after her, lying down close to where they'd left their clothes. Dominic picked up his watch to check the time, but it was too dark, and he gave up trying after a few seconds.

"Sleepy boys," Boyka giggled, looking at their now flaccid penises.

"We can wake up quickly when we have to," Curran joked.

Boyka shook her head. "Stay sleep." She opened a bottle of beer and passed it to Curran, then did the same for Dominic, before getting one for herself.

"Are you a naturist?" Dominic asked.

Boyka's forehead wrinkled. "No. Why?"

"You seem very at home in the nude."

She laughed. "So you."

Dominic chuckled. "Yeah, I suppose I do."

"Naked good," Iliya said. "When with friends, no one else, why the fuck not?"

A silence fell over them. It was a moment of pure happiness. Dominic knew it couldn't last – no such moment ever could – but he never expected it to end as disastrously as it did.

Nevena got up to stretch her legs, and glanced at the naked foreigners, fascinated by their unfamiliar bodies. She had been looking at them a lot since they undressed. They'd acclimatised to it and paid no notice. But something suddenly switched in Curran as the teenager stared at him. Forgetting her age and her brother – maybe he forgot that there was anybody else there at all – he stood and faced her. His smile faded and so did Nevena's.

"Hey," Dominic said uneasily as Iliya sat up, fingers tightening into fists.

"Nevena," Curran murmured, taking a step forward. Dominic was horrified to note his friend's penis rising and hardening.

"Hey!" Dominic barked and tried to get up, to step between them, but he slipped and fell back.

"Want to come with me into the woods?" Curran whispered, extending a hand towards the wide-eyed girl, who tentatively reached out in response.

Before their fingers met, Iliya roared, "Bastard!" Then he was on his feet, storming towards Curran. A fist flew, Curran's head snapped back, and the moment of peace and perfection was lost to the world forever.

## THIRTY-NINE

Curran hit the ground with a cry of pain. Iliya moved in on him as he tried to get up.

"No," Dominic yelled, forcing himself between them, having risen at the second attempt. "It's OK, he didn't mean anything, he's just drunk."

"That fucker try fuck sister," Iliya bellowed.

"No," Dominic said again, grabbing one of Iliya's arms. "He's drunk. He got carried away. It was a mistake. He's sorry. He didn't mean it. He won't –"

He was cut short by a roar. Curran was up now, and swinging for the muscular Iliya. One of his blows hit Dominic on the shoulder as he turned towards his furious friend.

"Easy," Dominic panted, wrapping his arms round Curran, trying to calm him down.

"Hit me when I wasn't looking," Curran shouted. "I'll fuck the fucker. Come on, you Bulgarian bastard."

Dominic pushed Curran backwards and glanced at Iliya. The teenager was still angry but he'd lowered his fists. A sobbing Nevena was screeching something at her brother, and her words were having an effect. He took a step away. Dominic saw that this could be fixed. They were drunk and had over-reacted. Another drink, a sit-down, a powwow, and all would be fine.

But as he was focusing on Curran, trying to coax him out of his fury, Valko threw himself at them, hitting them both, screaming like a wildman.

As Dominic desperately fended off blows, Zdravko and Kaloyan started after their friend, to pull him off, and Dominic knew the situation was still not beyond repair. If he could repel their assailant for a few more seconds, Zdravko and Kaloyan would subdue Valko, Dominic would soothe Curran, and peace could be thrashed out.

But while Dominic was struggling with the writhing Curran and trying to pull clear of Valko, his right arm jerked and accidentally connected with Valko's jaw. His elbow caught Valko cleanly, knocking him back, knocking him down, knocking him out.

As the teenager slumped, everyone paused, stunned by the unlikely twist. Dominic and Curran knew it was a freak blow, but the others started to think that they'd underestimated the Englishman.

Dominic saw the teenagers readjust and knew he was in trouble. He opened his mouth to protest his innocence, to convince them that it had been an accident, but before he could, Boyka screamed, "He hurt Valko. Kill the fuckers!"

Dominic was shocked. He gawped at the naked girl, her face now filled with violent hatred, and his tongue froze. He forgot what he'd meant to say. And before he could compose himself, Iliya, Kaloyan and Zdravko launched themselves at the outsiders, pulled them apart, pinned them down, and tore into them like a trio of savage dogs.

## FORTY

At first the teenagers punched Dominic and Curran, but it was difficult to connect since they had to bend, and they kept knocking into one another, so they quickly switched to kicking the downed pair. If they'd been wearing the heavy boots which they'd had on back in the pub, they would have caused serious damage, but they were all barefoot by this stage, so while the blows hurt, no bones were broken or internal organs damaged.

Curran tried to fight back. He tugged at the ring which he'd picked up earlier in their trip, planning to turn it round so that the sharp tip was pointing outwards, meaning to use it as a weapon. When that proved too delicate a manoeuvre under the circumstances, he roared and slapped at the Bulgarians instead. Dominic just lay there, curled into a ball, hands clasped over his head.

The naked Boyka joined in the attack, throwing a few carefully judged kicks at them, laughing manically. Her foot struck Dominic's chin, the most direct blow of the assault, and his head snapped back. But it hurt Boyka too, and she limped away, cursing, to sit and rub the top of her foot.

Nevena was screaming at the boys, begging them to stop. When they ignored her, she darted forward, grabbed Iliya and tried to haul him away. He turned on her angrily, almost pushed her to the floor, then clocked her tears, remembered she was his sister, and pulled her in close for a hug instead.

Iliya stared at Kaloyan and Zdravko as they carried on kicking Curran and Dominic, lashing out wildly. His head cleared and he considered the situation. Boyka hadn't meant it when she roared at them to kill the Englishmen, but if they carried on, there was a chance that one of them might do more harm than intended.

"Enough," Iliya barked in Bulgarian, and the other two instantly stopped. As Dominic and Curran writhed on the ground, groaning, Iliya turned his attention to Valko. His eyelids were fluttering open. Iliya helped him sit up and checked that he was OK.

"What happened?" Valko asked in his own tongue.

"One of them hit you," Iliya said. "I think it was an accident, but we beat them up anyway. Had to teach them a lesson, right?"

Valko focused on the whimpering Dominic and Curran. His expression hardened and he tried to rise and go after them.

"No," Iliya stopped him. "We took care of them. It's enough."

"But I want to –"

"I know," Iliya calmed him, "but there's nothing more you can do. We've punished them. They're in agony but they'll recover. If you wade in now, maybe you'll break a neck or snap a bone that ruptures their lungs. Let it go."

Dominic and Curran weren't able to follow any of that. For all they knew, Iliya was telling Valko that the others would hold them down while he slit their throats. Curran wanted to grab Dominic and run, but he couldn't, his legs felt too heavy, he'd been cut over one eye, his vision was obscured with blood, he was panting heavily.

Valko sighed and nodded, and Iliya released him. Valko stretched, rubbed his jaw where Dominic had hit him, and grunted. "Come on," he said. "Let's go."

"And the English?" Iliya asked.

Valko grinned. "Let the fuckers walk."

Iliya laughed and turned to face the moaning Dominic and Curran. "We leave you fucks here," he snarled in English. "Walk back yourselfs."

"No," Dominic groaned. "Please…"

"Fuck *please*," Iliya sneered. "Be glad we not drown you." He looked around at the rest of his gang and asked if they were ready to go. When they nodded, he told them to gather their belongings, then went to fetch his gear.

Boyka was getting dressed when she paused, catching sight of Curran's shorts. With an evil smirk, she told Kaloyan to help her pick up the clothes.

"What are you going to do with them?" Nevena asked, wiping tears away.

"Take them with us," Boyka chuckled. "Empty the wallets, dump the shorts and T-shirts along the way. Make them walk back naked and penniless."

"That's too harsh," Nevena murmured. "All he did was ask me if I wanted to go with him."

"And they knocked out Valko," Boyka reminded her. But when she saw that Nevena was worried, she sighed. "OK, we won't throw the clothes away. We'll leave them at the road sign outside Laki, so they can find them when they come back. And we'll only take cash from the wallets, leave the credit cards."

Nevena decided that was the best she could hope for and nodded glumly. She glanced at the sprawled Dominic and Curran and thought of saying something to them, but one of the others would have had to translate. In the end she waved half-heartedly at the pitiful pair, picked up her shoes and headed for the path.

The boys were laughing and joking, viewing the fight as the perfect end to the night. Valko hooted when Boyka told him they were taking the clothes, and he insisted on pulling on Curran's T-shirt, wearing it as a war prize.

They paused before exiting the glade and looked back at Dominic and Curran, who were still lying there, Dominic curled up, Curran flat on his back and gasping. Their smiles faded and they shared an uncertain look, wondering if they were doing the right thing.

Then Valko glanced at the clear sky, checked his watch and said, "They'll be fine. It'll be morning in a few hours. They can't miss the path — it's the only way in or out of here."

"Maybe we should leave their sandals," Zdravko muttered.

"No," Kaloyan said. "It will toughen their soles. They'll be real mountain folk by the time they get back to Laki."

The others laughed at that and relaxed. Valko was right, the outsiders would be fine, there was nothing for them to fear up here, unless they stumbled into the lake and drowned, but if they did that, more fool them.

"Bye-bye lovebirds," Boyka called out, blowing each of them a sarcastic kiss.

"Come look for us in Laki," Valko joked. "We have breakfast together."

"Not me," Iliya snorted. "I breakfast with Martini. I fuck her good, *Newt*. She not be waiting for you. She my girlfriend now." He was so delighted with his parting quip that he slammed his fist into a tree and almost crushed every finger.

The others laughed, slapped Iliya on the back as he whimpered and flexed his fingers, then staggered off down the path, leaving the bruised, groaning, bleeding foreigners alone in the glade with nothing but the moonlight and their pain for company.

## FORTY-ONE

Dominic was first to his feet, several minutes after the teenagers had deserted them. He swayed from side to side, then leant over and threw up what little was left in his stomach.

"You OK?" Curran groaned.

"Think so," Dominic muttered, squinting at the vomit. "No blood in it. I think. Hard to tell when it's this dark."

Curran sat up and touched the cut above his eye. He yelped, but when he checked his fingers there was only a thin smear of blood. "What a bunch of shits," he snarled, slowly standing, gritting his teeth against the pain.

"Why did you have to make a pass at Nevena?" Dominic growled.

"I wanted to fuck her," Curran snapped.

"She's underage," Dominic reminded him.

"Yeah, well, that didn't stop her getting drunk," Curran sniffed. "I bet I wouldn't have been her first. Anyway, I asked. I didn't try to force her."

"No," Dominic said, "but you shouldn't have asked in front of her brother. When you were naked. With a hard-on."

Curran laughed, then moaned. "At least they didn't kick me between the legs. How about you?"

"Caught me there a few times," Dominic said. "But not cleanly."

The pair studied one another, counting bruises and cuts. Dominic sat again and shook his head glumly. "It'll take us hours to walk back to Laki."

"We'll get a lift if we're lucky," Curran said.

"Like this?" Dominic waved a hand at his naked body.

"Hey, look on the bright side," Curran smiled. "If our thumbs get tired, we can hitch with our cocks."

Dominic laughed out loud at that, then groaned. "I feel like hell."

"Me too," Curran said, "but it could have been worse. When Boyka told them to kill us..."

"Yeah," Dominic nodded. "What a bitch."

"Typical woman," Curran noted. "When they get the scent of blood, nature kicks in and they want to see fur fly. Guys always get blamed for wars. *If women ruled the world*... But every warmonger is egged on by the little ladies back home. It's instinct. They want to pit us against each other, survival of the fittest, so they can mate with the winner and produce big, strong children."

"How the fuck can you be speaking like that when you're so drunk?" Dominic asked.

"You don't sound too dopey yourself," Curran said. "The beating sobered us up. We'll have the mother of all hangovers when we wake, but right now I feel fit as..." He stopped to examine something on the ground.

"What is it?" Dominic asked.

Curran bent and picked up whatever he had spied. He was grinning when he turned back towards Dominic. "It's not all bad news, Newt. Look what they left." He held out a bottle of almost-full vodka.

Dominic blanched. "You've got to be kidding. I don't ever want to touch that stuff again."

"Don't be stupid," Curran said, opening the bottle to take a swig. "It'll numb us to the pain."

"I don't think..." Dominic said weakly, but his heart wasn't in the protest. "What about Martini?" he tried again.

Curran shrugged. "Like you said, it'll take us hours to walk back. Chances are she'll have taken off long before we get there."

"You really think she'll abandon us?" Dominic asked.

"Nah," Curran winked. "She likes me too much."

"Fuck you," Dominic wheezed, then eyed the vodka nervously.

Curran limped across and sat beside his friend. He took another swig, then passed Dominic the bottle. "Best thing we can do is get hammered, sleep it off, head back to the village when it's sunny, when there'll be traffic on the road and a chance of a lift. I don't want to walk in the dark, and we'll be cold without our clothes. The vodka will warm us up."

"You make it sound like a cure-all," Dominic mumbled.

"Hey," Curran said, "it's all we have."

Dominic considered that. He stared at the lake, the moon, the path. For a moment he thought he heard noises, the locals coming back to take them home. But it was just a breeze rustling the trees.

"Fuck it," Dominic sighed, lifting the bottle to his lips. "Here's to better times."

The first mouthful made him gasp and shiver, but then a rosy glow spread through him, quenching the pain and igniting a fire in his soul, and the subsequent draughts went down smoothly and swiftly after that.

## FORTY-TWO

Dominic wouldn't remember much of those last few hours the next day, even if they *were* hours — they were knocking back the vodka as if it was beer, so it was possible they might have finished it off quicker than he assumed. He would dimly recall sitting there, chatting, singing. He had an image of Curran howling at the moon, but he couldn't be sure if that actually happened or if he imagined it.

One clear memory would be of his first piss after the beating. It hurt, but not as much as he'd feared, and he couldn't see any traces of blood in the urine, although as he had already noted, it was difficult to be sure in the moonlight. "All good," he belched, and Curran cheered in response, downing more of the vodka.

It might even have been the last of the bottle, since Dominic's next recollection would be of the pair of them in the lake, not swimming, just standing in the water, splashing each other and laughing hysterically. He didn't feel cold, but he was thirsty, so he buried his head in the lake and drank deep. Curran decided that was a fine idea and he drank too.

They staggered out not long after that and collapsed, giggling and shivering, close to the water's edge.

"We'll catch pneumonia," Dominic groaned.

"It's summer," Curran said.

"But we're in the mountains," Dominic reminded him.

"It's not fucking Everest," Curran grunted.

For some reason that tickled Dominic's funny bone. He started laughing and couldn't stop. Curran asked him what was so funny, but Dominic could only shake his head and splutter.

"Arsehole," Curran growled, but he was grinning. He beamed at his friend like a proud father. "Are you really OK?"

Dominic mumbled something.

"What was that?" Curran asked.

Dominic shook his head. "Shut up," he wheezed. "Tired."

"We should make a bed in the bushes," Curran said, forcing himself to his feet with a groan.

"Who you think… you are?" Dominic yawned. "Robin… fucking… Coosoe?"

"You're slurring your words, my good man," Curran said imperiously.

Dominic worked his jaw left then right, tried to form a response, decided it was too much effort, shot Curran a shaky finger instead. Then, as Curran talked about his plans to build a shelter, Dominic lay his head down, twisted from side to side until he was comfortable, and passed out. He stayed like that, spreadeagled in the open glade, knowing nothing, dead to the world, unconscious and unmoving, as the moon saw out its last few hours and the sun started to rise. And shine.

## PART FOUR

*"if you go down to the woods today you're sure of a big surprise"*

*The beast waited in the shack impatiently. There were candles, part of a supply that had been left behind many years ago, before the beast had first stumbled upon the place. Matches too. The beast wasn't a master of fire, and preferred to dwell in darkness more often than not, but it knew how to strike a match and had treated itself to light tonight, feeling safe in this secluded, familiar spot.*

*It had watched the flickering flames for a long time, fascinated by their eternal dance, but its interest eventually waned. Standing, it stamped the floor and grinned at the squealing noises in the cellar. It thought about going down to play with its makeshift pets, but it craved more action than that. It was a clear night, the moon three-quarters full, and the beast didn't want to be stuck inside.*

*Boredom rarely troubled the beast. It was happy with its natural lot, content to hunt and kill, feed and relax. But it occasionally craved distraction. Some nights, when it was stationary like this, time dragged and it itched to be active.*

*The beast shuffled to the doorway, pushed open the door and stared out forlornly. This wasn't fair. It shouldn't have to spend this night cooped up, when the moon was so bright and tempting, when hunting would be a delight. The beast had been looking forward to its stay in the shack, but so far it had been no fun at all.*

*Snarling, the beast pounded the wall either side of the door with the palms of its hands. As much as it wanted to venture forth and assert its independence, it knew it needed to stay where it was. This wouldn't last forever. Another few nights and it would be free to roam again. It just had to be patient, accept its restrictions, then…*

*The beast had been turning away from the door to return to the candles, but now it paused. It had sniffed something in the air, carried on a breeze from far away, the smell of one of its enemies.*

*The aroma was distant and faint, and few other animals would have noticed it, but the beast's nostrils were attuned to such scents, and it was always testing the air for them, wary of the weapons-bearing creatures.*

*The beast stepped into the doorway and took a deep sniff. It couldn't discern the scent this time, but was certain it had been there before.*

The beast stared at the moon, then at the trees around the glade. There was no way of telling if the creature was a lone member or part of a pack. The safest thing would be to ignore the smell and stay where it was, maybe even bolt and seek shelter deeper in the forest if the smell strengthened.

But the beast remembered the girl. It had been dreaming of its foes since then, wanting to taste that soft, sweet flesh, to drink the salty blood again, not the nicest that the beast had ever enjoyed, but always a vicious pleasure.

The beast hesitated, torn between holding firm and wanting to track and kill if the circumstances played into its favour. It flexed its fingers and pondered its dilemma. There would be repercussions if it strayed, and stinging punishments if it killed, but the joy of the hunt would compensate for those.

One last look at the moon. A final moment of indecision. Then the beast hissed, threw caution to the wind, and slipped out of the shack to go in search of the source of the elusive, mouthwatering scent.

## FORTY-THREE

Dominic woke and yawned, and the pain kicked in immediately.

He felt as if he was on fire. For a horrified moment he thought that Iliya and co. had returned, splashed him with petrol and set him alight. With a shocked gasp he staggered to his feet and looked for the lake, meaning to plunge in and douse the flames. But the sudden movement set off flares inside his head as his hangover exploded. Dominic cried out and collapsed on his arse.

"What the fuck?" he whimpered.

Blinking away tears, he shaded his eyes with a hand and closed them for a few seconds. He opened them slowly and brought up his other hand for more shade. The world began to come into focus.

The first thing Dominic noted was that he wasn't on fire. He gave silent thanks, then stole a look at the area around him. No sign of Curran, but the empty bottle of vodka lay nearby, pointing at him accusingly.

Dominic began to recall his boozy night, all the beer he'd drank, polishing off the vodka with Curran. As he sat staring at the bottle, other details clicked into place. The row with Martini. Making friends in the pub. Coming up here. Skinny dipping. The locals turning on him and Curran, kicking the shit out of them.

"Curran," Dominic croaked, and his throat stung with the effort. He grimaced and didn't try calling again. It hurt too much.

Dominic's gaze switched to the lake. He needed to drink. Water would help soothe his parched throat. It might help clear his head too, although he could tell even in this early stage that it was going to be a long-suffering hangover. But he knew from experience that you had to start somewhere, and a good drink of water was always the best starting point. Flush out your system, fill your stomach with liquid, have a piss, get your system working again.

Dominic set his right hand on the ground, to push himself to his feet, but the movement caused him to cry out with pain.

"What the fuck?" he mumbled again, staring at his hand. The boys had hit him hard the night before, but he hadn't clocked any serious damage. He bunched his fingers and tiny tsunamis of pain raced up and down his arms.

The glare of the sun was combining with Dominic's tears to sap the world of its colour. It was like he was staring across an endless sea of sand dunes in a desert.

He closed his eyes again, and this time left them closed for a minute. When he opened them, he kept them slitted, head bowed, shading them with his left arm. He focused on his hand and waited for his vision to adjust.

For a long, confusing period he thought his eyes weren't working properly. No matter how much he stared, his skin failed to regain its natural colour. There was a red sheen to everything, as if he was looking through a crimson filter.

It was only when his gaze slid to the green grass framing his hand that he realised there was nothing wrong with his eyes. The red wasn't a result of faulty wiring between his eyeballs and his brain. It was the colour of his skin.

"Fuck me," Dominic whispered, gingerly raising the hand to stare at the devil-red fingers. "*Sunburn.*"

## FORTY-FOUR

With his pale skin and lack of an appetite for outdoor activities, Dominic had been susceptible to sunburn all his life. He'd often been singed as a child, when his parents had dragged him off to one British beach or another and forced him to *have fun* swimming in the chilly sea and running around on the sand like a maniac when he would have been much happier playing video games in the gloom of the arcades.

His experiences of sunburn had diminished during his teenage years, once he'd been given the liberty to do what he liked with his free time, though he occasionally caught the sun on his neck and arms when he was drinking in a beer garden in the summer.

But even as a child, when he'd spent an entire day out in the open, with only the occasional dab of sun cream to protect him from the piercing rays, he'd never been burnt anywhere near as severely as this.

The red didn't stop with his fingers. It crept over the back of both hands and all the way up his arms. His chest was radioactive, as was his stomach. Apart from a small stretch of white down the sides, his legs were just as roasted, and his feet were like a pair of lobster's claws. Even his penis had taken the full force of the sun, although only along the top — the underneath had escaped.

As Dominic incredulously surveyed the damage, he turned his arms over and bent his legs aside, to discover that he was red all round, broken only in a few places by spreading purple bruises. He must have turned in his sleep, maybe a few times, and been evenly cooked like a pig on a spit.

"No," Dominic moaned, touching the head of his penis, which jerked away from his finger in protest. He then pressed the finger deep into his thigh, gritting his teeth against the pain, held it there a moment and released it. He recalled from childhood lessons that if a white spot remained, you'd been seriously burnt. If the spot swiftly faded back to red, the damage wasn't so great.

The white spot on Dominic's thigh when he took his finger away could have been the moon, and it seemed to linger for a full lunar cycle.

Dominic licked his lower lip, cringing as it stung. The slightest movement caused him to flinch. Now that he was paying attention, he realised that it even hurt when he blinked.

"This is bad," he whispered, and cringed again. He made a mental note to keep his observations to himself from this point on, but his brain was swimming and he soon forgot that silence was golden.

Dominic stretched out a leg and it was as if somebody had jammed dozens of needles into his calf and thigh at the same time. Tears came to his eyes and he let them roll down his cheeks — it would have hurt too much to wipe them away.

"Martini," Dominic wept, wanting her to magically appear. She'd always guarded him against the sun, warning him to be careful every time they went out. He'd sometimes complained, accused her of mothering him, but now he would have given anything to have her here. She'd have fished the world's most effective aftersun lotion out of her bag, smeared it on with loving care, brought relief within seconds.

But Martini wasn't here and Dominic knew he'd have to get through this with only the help of Curran.

He frowned as he thought about his friend. There was no sign of him. Where had he got to?

Ever so slowly, Dominic turned his head and glanced towards the trees. His face creased with a pathetic, pleading expression. Why couldn't he have fallen asleep in the shade? He was in the middle of a forest. This might be the only exposed section for kilometres in either direction. Trust him to pick the worst possible spot to black out.

He vaguely remembered Curran talking about making a bed in the bushes. Dominic figured he'd gone ahead with that, or at least crawled in there to rest up and shelter from the sun.

He was angry that Curran had left him behind. Maybe he thought it would be fun to let Dominic stew in the open. Or perhaps he'd only meant to leave him for a while, let him get slightly burnt, before waking him and leading him to safety. Maybe he'd fallen asleep while watching over the snoozing Dominic and would be mortified when he saw the consequences of his lack of attention.

Dominic wanted to shout for Curran, but he was dehydrated and needed to hold fast until he'd wet his whistle. He wasn't thinking clearly — the sunburn and hangover had wrought havoc inside his head — but he wasn't delirious either. (Not yet anyway.) Instinct had kicked in and his first priority was water. Get to the lake, drink deeply, maybe immerse himself and seek solace in the coolness.

"Yes," he murmured, seeing hope for relief from the worst of the pain. He could sink into the lake up to his nostrils. The water would soothe him. Not as effective as aftersun, but it was all he had, so it would have to do.

The difficult bit would be getting to the lake. He wasn't far removed, nothing more than a few short hops. Any other time he'd have jogged across in a matter of seconds. But this was going to hurt. Just stretching his leg had been a torment. He imagined the whole of his body rising, the explosions such a coordinated move would ignite, and shivered at the thought.

Dominic had never been especially brave. He didn't like challenges and rarely sought them out. Martini had cited that as his main problem countless times, the reason why he was coasting along purposelessly in life. She'd often urged him to set himself a goal and work hard towards it. But it was so much easier to cruise.

As he lay there, considering the alternatives, all Dominic wanted to do was hold his position, not twitch a muscle, endure the constant throb and do nothing to exacerbate it. If it had been night when he'd awoken, perhaps he would have sat there indefinitely, delaying the moment when he must rise for as long as he could.

But the sun was still beating down on him. He had no idea what the time was, but felt sure from the heat that dusk was a good way off. If he stayed out in the open, he'd continue to burn, and as bad as he felt, he knew things had the potential to get worse. He'd heard horror stories of people who'd been hospitalised with extreme sunburn, whose skin had split open with blisters, bones exposed, a mess of blood and pus.

Dominic winced. Although he was red from foot to head, he couldn't see any blisters (unless his back was bursting with them), so he had to believe that the damage wasn't as severe as it felt. There was hope that he could get out of this with his skin intact, and that was a literal concern.

Dominic turned his head back towards the lake, again very slowly. Fresh tears flowed down his cheeks but he ignored them. He scrunched his fingers up into fists, gasping with agony, then focusing all of his senses on it, trying to make the pain in his hands the over-riding pain, so that he wouldn't feel it elsewhere.

Loosening his fingers, he rested a moment, then bunched them up into fists again, tighter this time, nails digging into the flesh of his palms. The pain brought a scream to his lips, but as he screamed, he rose with it, forcing himself up, rising and screaming in one swift motion, until he was standing, trembling and weaving, but secure on his feet, Promethean man come to defiant, red-skinned life.

## FORTY-FIVE

Dominic had often tried to imagine what real pain might feel like. Not the sort of pain associated with toothache or twisting an ankle, but the kind endured by martyred saints or soldiers caught in the crossfire on the killing fields. He didn't think it could be that bad. He figured there was only so much that anyone could consciously endure, and that once you passed that point, the body must start to adjust. For instance, if your leg was cut off, how much worse could you feel if someone chopped off your arm as well?

Now he could see what an idiot he'd been. He had only taken a few short, halting steps, but already he could tell that the body didn't shut down when it was wounded, but reacted to every fresh assault. No matter how much pain you might be suffering, if you stepped on a thorn, your foot sent out a distress signal that your brain processed, regardless of what else might be going on.

Dominic paused and drew breath, but slowly, trying to make it as painless as he could. He looked down, unable to believe that he could have turned such a deep red colour. It was as if he'd been boiled alive. When he held the palm of his hand close to his thigh or stomach, he could feel the heat radiating out. If he'd had a slice of bread, he might have been able to toast it.

He chuckled weakly, then stopped. Laughter was a bad idea right now. Any sort of movement was a no-no. But he had to keep going. The water was drawing him on. If he could make it to the lake, everything would be fine. Or so he told himself.

Dominic started walking again. Every step was a torment. The soles of his feet stung when he pressed down. His calves screamed as his legs bent and straightened. His buttocks thundered as they bunched up and relaxed. His back prickled as if he was being lashed with nettles. His shoulders felt as if he was carrying a load of heated branding irons. Steam seemed to rise from his cheeks and obscure his vision. His ears were two burnt stubs that had been stapled to the side of his head.

It would have been nightmarish any time but the hangover made it worse. He felt sick, and would have surely thrown up if there had been anything left in his stomach to expel. A headache was tearing through his skull, more like a hurricane than a migraine. It hurt to breathe, to look, to think.

Dominic shivered, and the sensation was similar to barbed wire being dragged over his flesh. He wanted to scream again but his throat was raw. He told himself to wait until he'd drunk his fill in the lake. Everything would be fine once he made it to the water. All of his problems would fade away. He'd drink and think and come up with a plan. Just a few more steps and normality would be his again.

He took the first of those steps mincingly, then the next few in a rush, unable to hold back any longer. Suddenly he was at the edge of the lake. He almost threw himself forward, face first, then recalled that it was shallow. He'd need to wade out.

In a hurry now, Dominic stepped in with his right foot and lifted his left to take a giant stride forward.

"Mother of fuck!" he shrieked, freezing in that position, his left foot mid-air.

It was as if he'd stepped into a tub of acid. His right foot was on fire from the shin down. More tears flowed as he perched on one foot, arms windmilling to maintain his balance.

His first instinct was to leap out of the acid-like liquid, to recover on the safety of dry land, but an old memory kicked in. Water had stung like this when he was a kid and his mother had forced him into a bath after he'd been sunburnt. He remembered crying and fighting with her, trying to wriggle free. She'd held him under, and shortly afterwards the pain had faded.

Clinging to that dim memory, Dominic held firm, and moments later the worst of the pain died away and he began to feel the benefit of the cool mountain water.

Dominic's eyes closed and he said a silent prayer of thanks. He wasn't sure why he was praying, since he didn't believe in God, but it felt like the right thing to do. Some situations demanded a religious response, even from a die-hard atheist.

Dominic opened his eyes again. He smiled weakly at the lake, then frowned as he thought about all the steps he'd have to take before he was submerged. He pictured the water creeping up his flesh as he glided forward, burning every inch of the way, biting into his shins, his knees, his thighs, his…

"Oh no," Dominic moaned, staring at his unnaturally red penis. He gulped, contemplated retreat, then steeled himself. Scowling, he clenched his fingers into fists again and started ahead into the cold, burning depths.

## FORTY-SIX

Dominic felt like one of those Japanese monkeys he had occasionally seen in travel programmes, who sought the sanctuary of hot springs in the middle of winter, fully immersed in the pools except for their hairy heads and pink, pained-looking faces. He hoped he didn't look as foolish, but suspected that with his red cheeks, he probably did.

Wading out had taken forever. In retrospect he wished he'd pushed on swiftly, but at the time he hadn't been able to force himself to go fast. Instead he'd taken it one slow, agonising step at a time, waiting for each newly submerged section of his body to acclimatise before subjecting himself to the torture all over again.

Lowering his torso into the water had been the worst. While wading forward, his steps had taken him several centimetres further in each time. But when he had to crouch, he couldn't bear to sink in more than a centimetre or so per movement. He knew it was stupid, that he should dunk himself and have done with it, but his body resisted.

Still, it was all behind him now. He'd finally sunk in up to his chin, the back of his head turned towards the sun in order to afford his face some protection. The feel of the water was delicious. He was still in a lot of pain, but nowhere near as nerve-chewing as it had been in the clearing, especially if he didn't move.

Tears came to his eyes again, but this time they were tears of relief. Maybe he could stay in the lake for three or four days, until the sunburn had faded to a tan, emerge like a Greek god, leaving his aquatic kingdom to walk for a while on land.

Dominic smiled at the crazy thought, then leant forward and sipped, ignoring the bruises to his face that he could see in his reflection — those injuries meant nothing to him at the moment. The water stung his throat. He coughed, hissed at the pain, then drank again. This time it went down smoothly and he carried on sipping, breathing through his nostrils, stopping only when he felt that he could drink no more.

Raising his chin, Dominic did nothing for a few minutes, only squatted in the water, smiling blissfully, swaying softly from side to side. Then he had a thought. He was loath to duck beneath the water, because he knew his face would sting, but that didn't mean he had to ignore his head entirely.

Making a fist of his right hand, Dominic lifted it up out of the lake, water cupped within, and poured it over the top of his head. He sighed with delight as the liquid soaked into his short brown hair, then cupped more of it and kept pouring it on until his head was damp all over. A few drops trickled down his cheeks but they didn't hurt as much as he'd feared, his tears having already led the way in that area.

"This is the life," he muttered, and it didn't hurt so much to speak now.

He grimaced. How quickly the universe could change a man. Yesterday he'd needed beautiful countryside, fabulous ruins, the love of a good woman and an endless supply of beer to feel at one with the world. Now all he needed was water and plenty of it.

Dominic studied his forearms, lifting them, not all of the way out of the lake, but close to the surface. They seemed to have turned an even redder shade since he'd last examined them, but maybe that was a trick of the light on the water. At least there were no signs of any blisters.

His eyes started to swim while he was focused on his arms. Dominic shook his head, alarmed, then groaned as his vision steadied. His brain was pounding. It had been baking in the sun all day, and he'd assaulted it with alcohol the night before. He hadn't often blacked out in his life, but it had happened a few times when he was severely hungover and dehydrated, so he recognised the warning signs.

Dominic leant forward and drank more water, but he couldn't force a lot of it down. Spluttering out a mouthful that he was unable to swallow, he considered his options through the jackhammering thrum of his headache.

He wanted to stay in the lake, to cool off and replenish all of the moisture that he'd lost. But if he fainted, he'd drown. It would be different if he had someone to look out for him, but on his own…

Dominic frowned. "Hang on," he growled. "I'm *not* on my own. Where the fuck is Curran?" He looked around, spotted the pathway into the clearing and yelled, "Curran!"

His voice bounced off the trees and mountain and echoed back to him. It was as if someone had struck a gong next to his head. He moaned, waited for the echoes to die away, then listened for a reply. He assumed his friend was lying out of sight, in the bushes or the shade of a tree. The booming echoes would have roused most people, but Curran was a deep sleeper, especially when hungover.

"I'll murder that fucker," Dominic snarled, but he knew that Curran wasn't to blame. Dominic was a big boy, as Martini often noted, more than capable of looking after himself. He was responsible for this mess and he would have to deal with it. As a grown man, you couldn't count on your friends to help you out of problems of your own making, especially if those friends were as unreliable as Jerome Curran.

As Dominic tried to decide how to proceed, his eyes swam again, and this time he vomited up some of the water that he'd swallowed. That made up his mind for him. He was facing a double threat now. If he fainted and didn't fall face down and drown, he might float on his back and choke to death on his own vomit. That was a noble way for a rock star to check out, but a pitiful way if you were an ordinary loser who worked in a bar.

He shouted for Curran one last time. When there was no answer, he shook his head glumly, then lowered his face and drank again, replacing the water that he'd lost. Wiping flecks of vomit from his lips, he gazed around at the still surface of the lake, as if he was parting from a loved one. He almost said something mushy but caught himself. As bad as things were, he wasn't going to declare his undying love for a lake. What if Curran was loitering closer than he suspected and heard? Dominic would never be able to live it down.

"Fuck this shit," he grunted, trying to sound like a hero in an action film, but sounding more like a squeaky-voiced yet shockingly foul-mouthed character in a Disney cartoon.

Gritting his teeth against what he felt sure would be a soul-destroying wave of pain, he began to rise and took his first stride back towards the agonies of dry land.

## FORTY-SEVEN

By the position of the sun, Dominic reckoned it was evening, and that he'd been lying in the open most of the day. But despite the hour, the sun was still incredibly strong, so once out of the water, Dominic staggered towards the trees before his skin dried and the last comforting traces of the lake were lost.

When he reached the point where the path started, he paused before stepping into the shade. He suddenly felt sure that the teenagers from Laki had returned, or had never left at all. He could sense them waiting for him, weapons in hand, ready to pounce as soon as he abandoned the light.

Or maybe they didn't need weapons. Maybe they were vampires, sheltering from the sun, willing him forward. Perhaps they'd already dealt with Curran and had been patiently biding their time in the safety of the gloom, watching him sizzle, knowing he'd eventually stir and come to them, unsuspecting, easy prey.

Dominic wavered. In his bruised, reddened, bewildered state he was ready to give credence to his superstitious fears, turn and run, find another way out. He almost took a step back, but halted before he did.

"This is ridiculous," he muttered. The gang from Laki might have come back, and he'd be in trouble if they had, but there were no vampires waiting for him in the shade.

Straightening as best he could – which still left him looking like a hunchback – Dominic took the final few steps forward, into the dark cover of the trees.

## FORTY-EIGHT

He started to shiver once he was out of the sunlight. Partly it was with fear that he might be attacked, but mostly it was a reaction to the change in temperature. Having felt on fire up to this point, he now felt cold. He wanted to run his hands up and down his arms to generate warmth, but that would cause more pain than it alleviated.

"Curran?" he called out piteously. When there was no answer, he cleared his throat and called for the Laki teenagers instead. "Iliya? Nevena? Are you there?"

Silence.

He tried to recall the names of the others but couldn't. "Nevena?" he groaned. "I'm sorry that Curran made a pass, but you've hurt us enough. Look at me — I'm ruined. Take us back with you, please. I need help. Curran might too."

There was no change in the timbre of the silence.

"Anybody there?" Dominic screamed.

The trees and bushes swallowed his cry, no echoes this time.

Dominic cursed, then decided he was calling to a non-existent audience. The boys and girls were at home in Laki, sleeping off their hangovers or tucking into a late breakfast. Maybe Martini would come looking for the men, demand their whereabouts from the sneering teenagers, drive up here herself to collect them.

Dominic daydreamed about that, smiling softly as he pictured their reunion, the row forgotten, Martini filled with concern. She wouldn't hold a grudge, not when she saw the state that he was in. She'd bundle him into the car, find a hospital, make sure he received the best treatment that Bulgaria could offer. Maybe she'd report Iliya and the others to the police, have them rounded up and tried for crimes against Very Important Visitors.

He chuckled at the thought of a stern-faced judge sentencing Iliya to ten years hard labour. Then he frowned as he considered another option. Maybe Martini would come looking for them, and the boys would offer to drive her up here, only to pin her down and rape her when they got her away from Laki and any witnesses.

"Martini," he whimpered, shivering worse than ever, imagining her screams as she was gang-raped. Despite the chill in his bones, his brain was heating up again, and in his deluded state he was inclined to believe the very worst.

"Curran," he roared. "We have to get out of here. Martini needs us. Wake up, you useless piece of shit."

There was a groaning noise and he thought Curran was stirring. He took a few quick, hopeful steps forward, but then the sound came again, from overhead, and he realised it was just a tree creaking.

"Not good," Dominic whispered, his head clearing, seeing his rape fears in the same light now as his worries about vampires. The boys from the village weren't animals. Things got out of control last night, but they hadn't tried to kill the sister-seducing outsiders. They were quick-to-flip teenagers, but he'd seen nothing to suggest they were rapists.

Yet for a brief while he had considered them a threat, just as he'd thought that vampires might be real. That was a bad sign. It meant he couldn't trust his brain. He was thinking clearly right now, but might succumb to fantasy again at any moment. He needed to find Curran ASAP, or rest up and wait until he was better.

But how long might that be? He knew from his previous roastings that sunburn could take hours to manifest fully. As a child he'd often left a beach with a light pink glow, which had deepened into a dark red hue by bedtime.

While he wanted to believe that a few hours of sleep would do him a world of good, he had to accept that he might be at his mental peak as far as the next few days were concerned, that he could slip into a heat-induced fugue that would leave him a gibbering, useless wreck.

"Got to find Curran," Dominic whispered. "He won't be as bad as me. Wasn't out in the sun. When he sees what I'm like, he'll know it's serious, he'll look out for me, bring me water, keep me warm when it gets cold later, help me get back to Laki. Can't do it by myself. Need Curran."

Dominic nodded weakly. He was too feeble to contemplate any other plan. He had to keep things simple. Finding Curran was an achievable goal. If he could do that, all else would follow. The lake had been one crucial step forward. This was the next.

"OK," he said, facing the gloom of the forest path. "He's got to be along here somewhere. Need to go slowly, check every bush, listen for snores."

Dominic nodded affirmatively, tried to stop shivering, then set off down the path, shuffling slowly, feeling lost and alone, fighting not to imagine any demons lurking in the shadows.

## FORTY-NINE

He didn't get far down the path before he was confronted with a dilemma.

He was enjoying an extended lucid period, focused on finding Curran and placing himself in his friend's hands, no delusions of vampires or anything else. He didn't dare believe this would last, sure that his senses would start to swim again in the near future, so he was determined to make the most of it, calling vigorously for Curran as he limped along, shaking bushes, stooping to peer beneath low-hanging branches.

He mumbled away to himself when he wasn't calling Curran's name, hoping that it would help him stay focused. Silence was his enemy. He would imagine sounds if he wasn't making any, and those dark thoughts might be enough to set his mind adrift again.

The pain was coming back worse than before, and he was noticing wounds that he'd been previously ignorant of. His jaw was throbbing, a hard lump sticking out of it where he'd been kicked. And the limp wasn't just because of the sunburn — his knee was almost black beneath the red sheen, where one of the gang must have connected hard.

Then he spotted another path and for a few moments forgot about the pain and everything else.

It wasn't obvious, the start of the path just a gap between a couple of otherwise solid bushes, but the gap had been recently widened, the bushes pushed back, several branches snapped and hanging loose. Dominic hadn't noticed the gap when coming along the path last night, and doubted he would have seen it in the daylight either if he hadn't been looking so carefully.

"Curran?" he called again, warily, some of his fears creeping back in. Something about the snapped branches sent a shiver down his spine.

Dominic stared at the gap for a long time before taking a cautious step towards it, to examine the smaller path. It wasn't as well defined as the path up from the road. Indeed this only barely looked like a path, and might not be — Dominic couldn't see far down it and for all he knew it dead-ended a few metres further on.

He was wary of the path-that-might-not-be-a-path, and would have pressed on down the more familiar route to the road. But there was a patch of damp earth a short way past the gap in the bushes, and an indentation in it that might have been nothing, but might also have been the mark of somebody's foot.

Dominic edged forward, turning sideways to avoid being scraped by the bushes, then bent to study the mark in the earth. He groaned as he went down, then again when he considered the fact that it would hurt even more when he stood up.

Sighing miserably, Dominic reached out and ran a finger round the mark. Hard to tell if it had been made by a person. It might have been an animal, or simply the earth shifting in an unusual way. But it certainly looked like a footprint.

"Robinson Crusoe," he snorted. He'd never read the book, but he remembered a friend talking about the footprint in the sand and how ludicrous a literary scene it was — a person walking along a beach would have left more than a single print.

(Dominic might have smiled if he'd recalled trying to mention Robinson Crusoe to Curran early that morning, when he'd been talking of making a bed in the bushes. But that section of the night was a blank.)

Dominic kept close to the ground as he stared at the maybe path. His eyes had adjusted to the gloom, but it was impossible to tell how far the track went, just as it was impossible to tell if this was truly a footprint.

After a long pause, Dominic rose – it was every bit as painful as he'd feared – and stepped back on to the definite path. It would be a long walk to the road in his condition, but an even longer walk back if he got there and found no trace of Curran. What if his friend had wandered down this side-path and collapsed? Maybe he was lying around a bend, unconscious, injured, helpless.

"Curran," Dominic yelled, but he expected no answer this time. He was sure it was his brain over-reacting again, but he had a sudden, horrible image of Curran impaled on a stake-like tree stump, dying slowly, whimpering for help, wondering in his final moments why he had been so cruelly abandoned.

Dominic considered his options, which wasn't easy given the pounding inside his head. He was safe on the path to the road, and would almost certainly find Curran along the way, or waiting for him where the path ended. But if Curran *had* taken this turning, and *was* lying somewhere along the secondary path, dead to the world and in need of aid, it would be a lot easier to look for him now, when he was here and in command of his senses, than trek all the way back up when he was weaker and maybe hallucinatory with sunstroke.

"Damn you to hell, Jerome," Dominic growled. And then, making a snap call, he stepped off the main path and advanced into the menacing-looking undergrowth.

## FIFTY

It soon became apparent that this was an actual path. It had been used even less than the path up from the road, and bushes grew in tightly most of the way along it, but people or animals had passed through here occasionally enough over the years to establish a route of passage through the dense forest.

The protruding branches of the bushes were a real problem. If he even brushed against them it was like being stung by wasps. He had to ease along, using his fingers to lever back the larger branches. But even that was uncomfortable, since his fingers had been burnt too.

He was making slow progress and his thoughts started to wander again. He began to think that the branches were the bones of dead people or the twisted claws of some hideous forest creature. He stiffened every time there was a noise, heart beating fast, peering into the gloom, sure he was about to be attacked.

He was thirsty, despite all the water he'd drunk, and he had stopped calling Curran's name, since it hurt to shout.

His skin had continued to darken and areas were beginning to blister, bumps rising like the undead crawling out of their graves. His face was particularly bad – his cheeks looked as if fat beads of sweat had been frozen in place on them – but his shins had also suffered, along with the backs of his legs. His arms and sweeping sections of his back were giving birth to boils too.

Dominic was unaware of his worsening condition. It was darker here than it had been on the main path, so he would have struggled to assess the full extent of the spreading damage in the dim light. But he wasn't even looking. His brain was buzzing in and out of rationality. He was more concerned about the fantastical monsters cavorting in the bushes than he was with his all-too-real burns. At times he even forgot that he'd been sunburnt, and was confused when a branch scraped his back and brought a yelp to his lips and tears to his eyes.

"Their fingers must be soaked in acid," he croaked. "Mustn't let them touch me. Got to suck in my stomach. Shimmy like a dancer. Dancing Dominic." He cackled madly, lips twisting into a pained grin as he thought of himself whirling along the path, dancing his way to safety, a magical ballerina repelling the forces of darkness through the power of his pirouettes.

"No tights though," he muttered with a scowl. "Won't wear tights."

Dominic had lost track of time. On those rare moments when his senses clicked into place he wasn't sure if he'd been on this path for ten minutes or several hours. It was still day, so he figured it couldn't have been hours, unless this was the next day and he'd missed the coming and passing of night.

He froze when he considered that. Maybe he'd been on this path for *days*. It might be a path without end, one that he was doomed to follow until the last of his strength deserted him and he collapsed among the roots of the bushes to die.

"No," he growled as his limbs trembled. "Pull yourself together. It's been minutes, not days. I can turn around any time and..."

He drew to a terrified halt. What if he'd already turned? He looked left then right, up and down the path. It was the same in both directions. Maybe he had unconsciously about-faced and was heading back the way he'd come. If that was the case, and he turned again, he'd end up wandering even deeper into the forest.

Was he lost? He wouldn't have thought that he could be, given that he was on a path with no junctions. But with his brain flickering in and out of consciousness, anything was possible.

"No," he said again. "I wouldn't have turned for no good reason. I've got to trust myself. I'm still going forward. I can go back if I want to, any time."

He nodded firmly and almost turned to test his theory, planning to return to the original path to prove that he could. But if he did that, he wouldn't find the strength to set off this way a second time, and he'd have to abandon his quest to find Curran.

"Stay focused," he snarled, pinching the flesh of his left arm to draw a gasp and snap his mind into shape. "Eyes on the prize. Give it a quarter of an hour, search for Curran as thoroughly as I can. If I don't find him, I can get the fuck out of here and head back to the road with a clear conscience. Fifteen minutes of clear-headed searching. I can do that much, can't I?"

And because he believed he could, he took a deep breath and carried on down the path, as slowly as before, but alert this time, with a cut-off point in mind.

## FIFTY-ONE

That cut-off point was discarded unceremoniously approximately ten minutes later.

The light was starting to fade and Dominic knew he'd have to give up the search for Curran whether he wanted to or not. He'd be able to see very little on the path once night fell, so he'd have nothing to gain by pushing ahead.

But before he could draw the search to a halt, he came to a clearing in the path and everything changed.

He stopped before he realised why. His eyes had clocked something but it took his brain a while to catch up with them.

The bushes grew thickly here, but they'd been flattened back on both sides. The floor was dusty with dry earth, and the dust had been recently disturbed. There were sweeping gouges through it, as if someone had come through with a broom and given it a fast and furious once-over.

Dominic reached out and put the palm of his right hand to one of the bushes. The branches hadn't been broken as they had been at the gap where the path began, merely pushed in, as if something heavy had pressed against them. They were already starting to spring back into place.

By themselves the bushes and dust patterns wouldn't have bothered him, but there was something else, a disturbance he had registered but was reluctant to focus on, fearful of what it might portend.

For a long time Dominic swayed on his feet, staring at a spot on the path, not wanting to move closer to it, telling himself it was a trick of the shadows, maybe even a trick of his brain, his senses spinning off the wires again.

But if it was his imagination run havoc, he needed to prove that to himself. If it was a delusional projection, it would be better to confront it, so that he could dismiss it, chuckle at how easily he'd been spooked, then move on or retreat.

"Easy does it," Dominic wheezed, then slid forward and crouched.

There was a small puddle of what looked like chocolate sauce in the middle of the path. Not very wide or deep, a few drops scattered around it, some streaks where it had been scraped through the grass and dust.

Dominic stared at the puddle, then looked further down the path. In spite of the dusky conditions he spotted more flecks and dashes, picked out by some of the dwindling rays of the sun which had pierced the covering of trees and bushes.

Dominic stretched out a trembling finger, paused, said a silent prayer, then dipped his finger into the puddle. He hoped the pool would disappear, revealed as nothing more than a mirage, but his finger sank into the liquid, which was cooler than he'd expected, pleasant on his dried-out, sunburnt, blistering skin.

This liquid was thicker than water but not as thick as chocolate sauce. He almost shied away from testing it, but he couldn't rest easy unless he confirmed it one way or the other. So, having taken another deep breath, he lifted his finger and slowly brought it towards his parched, cracked lips.

Some of the liquid dripped off along the way, but there was plenty still smeared to the tip as he opened his mouth, fought off the dry heaves, then pressed the finger to his tongue and closed his lips around it.

For a few seconds he couldn't taste anything. There was very little moisture in his mouth and his taste buds weren't functioning normally. But as he waggled his finger around, his tongue salivated, and the taste of the liquid seeped in.

Dominic spat out his finger, retched wretchedly, then sank to his arse and stared at the puddle with horror. There was no longer any doubting what it was. Even if his eyes had been fooled, he could trust his sense of touch and taste. It wasn't a trick of the shadows. It wasn't water. It wasn't chocolate sauce. It was…

"*Blood*," Dominic wheezed, and as he said the word his eyes fluttered in their sockets, his brain spasmed, and he fainted into the blood-spattered dust.

## FIFTY-TWO

It was night when Dominic recovered and sat up with a weary, agonised groan. He had been lying on his front, and it tingled like crazy as he swayed from side to side and stared at the smeared blood, but he ignored the pain. He knew upon waking that he wasn't on fire, just as he knew that the blood was real. There had been no slowly swimming back to consciousness. He remembered everything the instant his eyelids flickered open.

Dominic frowned as he squinted at the blood. It was obvious that the sun had set, so why was he able to see the blood at all?

Looking up, he saw that an almost-full moon had risen. The sky was clear of clouds, and he was perched high above the glow from any city or town, so the night was brighter than almost any he had ever experienced.

There was more than enough light for Dominic to study his sunburnt, blistering skin, but at that moment he was fully concentrated on the blood.

He had no reason to suspect that it was Curran's. It was more likely that this was the result of a clash of animals, a larger beast targeting a smaller creature, a brief fight, the lesser specimen ripped apart. That sort of encounter must happen all the time in a forest like this. It was probably pitted with countless pools of blood, the way the streets in a city were pitted with dog shit in countries where pet owners weren't obliged by law to bag and bin it.

But he was convinced that the blood had been shed by his friend. He felt the same way he'd felt when staring at his grandmother's corpse as a teenager, or his dog Prince when he was nine years old, after it had run out into the road and been hit by a car. He could smell the death of a loved one in the air tonight, just as he'd smelled it then and at other times.

"Imagining it," Dominic moaned, but without conviction.

Tears came again, but this time he wept the way he had when his father had kicked Prince's remains into a plastic bag, cursing the driver who hadn't even stopped to apologise. He wept the way he'd wanted to but hadn't been able to at his grandmother's funeral, dry-eyed on that occasion, incapable of expressing his grief.

As Dominic cried for the friend he felt sure he'd lost, he recalled his first day at secondary school, and for a while his senses meandered and it was as if he was a child again, re-living his entry into a brave, exciting, frightening new world.

He'd started at a younger age than most boys. A bright child, he'd failed to hide his intelligence from his teachers. As a result, he'd been pried away from his friends and cast into the hellish pit of secondary school a year earlier than scheduled, with no one to watch his back.

His parents had been delighted. Their *gifted son* had leapt ahead of the crowd. They were thinking of university when he was seventeen, maybe even younger. A doctor or lawyer if his mother had her way, an entrepreneurial investment broker if his father had anything to say about it.

All Dominic had been thinking about was how he was smaller than all the other boys. He'd never been one of the biggest, even among those his own age. Now he felt like a sparrow surrounded by hawks, though he didn't phrase it that way to himself. What he *had* thought, as he'd wandered the yard of his new school and glanced at the taller, broader, more muscular boys, was, *I'm fucked.*

That feeling had persisted through his first few classes, as he'd staggered around in a daze, bumped into and shrugged aside by classmates who hadn't yet bothered to note him as a target. It was their first day too. They were settling in, getting the lay of the new and hostile land, scared and uncertain like Dominic. But they were older than him. More experienced. Bigger. They'd swiftly find their feet and instinctively look for boys who were vulnerable. And like vultures swooping on road kill, they would spot him, circle him, pick him apart and feed.

One boy stood out. He was taller and older than everyone else in the class, with a mop of curly, straw-coloured hair. He strutted around confidently as if he owned the place, joking with those he was choosing for friends, establishing himself as a kingpin. By what a couple of groaning teachers said when they saw him, Dominic gathered that the older boy had been forced to repeat his first year. To Dominic that would have felt like a disgrace above any other, but the wild-haired, gangly boy seemed proud of his demotion, and boasted to his new friends that he could show them the ropes. "All old hat to me," he sneered. "I could do this shit in my sleep. In fact I did. That's why I failed so many of my tests."

Dominic wouldn't have dreamt of approaching the alpha male, any more than he'd have tried to make a move on the best-looking girl if he'd gone to a mixed school. He wasn't sure of his exact place on the totem pole, but he knew it wasn't at the top with the cool kids.

That first lunchtime, as Dominic was wending through the corridors, trying to find his way from his locker to the yard, fate threw him the sort of bone that it only rarely tosses in the direction of out-of-their-depth adolescents. The straw-haired boy came tearing round a corner and barged into Dominic. He looked scared but thrilled, his eyes wild with fear, his lips twisted into an ecstatic grin.

As Dominic bounced off the bigger boy and slammed into the lockers, the boy thrust a rolled-up magazine in his direction. "Hide that," he panted.

Then he was off, whooping with terror and delight.

Dominic stared after the taller boy. He almost unrolled the magazine, but then he heard others approaching and jammed it behind his back just before they turned the corner, in hot pursuit. They were the same sort of size as Dominic's classmate, and he figured they were in the year above.

Dominic thrust his head down as the group cast a quick look at him. When they realised he wasn't the one they were after, they blanked him and carried on down the corridor, leaving Dominic to resume his search for the exit.

Later, as a lonely Dominic was lingering close to one of the yard walls, trying to work up the courage to join in a game of football, the tall boy from his class sauntered up to him and stared off into space, as if unaware of the smaller boy's existence. "Have you got it?" he whispered.

"Yeah," Dominic squeaked. It was tucked down the back of his trousers.

"Did you look at it?" the boy asked.

Dominic blushed. "Yeah." He had opened it in a cubicle in the toilets. It was a pornographic magazine. Most boys his age would have considered it softcore, but Dominic had enjoyed a sheltered upbringing. His parents had zealously protected him from the more lurid areas of the internet and he'd never seen anything as graphic as the pictures in the magazine before.

"Good, isn't it?" the boy sniffed.

"Yeah," Dominic said, assuming that was the correct response.

"I nicked it from Simon Naylor," the boy growled. "I could tell that bastard was going to go for me, so I struck first, bashed him up, went through his bag, found the mag and took it. His mates chased after me to steal it back."

"Did they catch you?" Dominic asked.

"Yeah." The boy shrugged. "Couldn't do much to me though. We were close to the staff room."

"Won't they get you later?" Dominic asked.

"Nah," the boy said. "They don't like Naylor much. Nobody does. They were only chasing me for fun, a bit of excitement on the first day back. They'll have forgotten all about it by close of business this afternoon."

"What if they don't forget?" Dominic pushed.

"Then I'll take my beating like a man and chew one of the bastard's legs off while they're laying into me." The boy laughed, then looked at Dominic at last. "You're in my class, aren't you?"

"I think so, yeah," Dominic said, as if he wasn't sure.

"Slip the mag back to me during geography. Mrs Abulhoul writes up so many notes that she never sees what's going on behind her back." He paused. "Unless you want to keep it for a night or two?"

"No, that's OK," Dominic said quickly, blanching at the thought of his mother finding such a thing in his bag.

The boy shrugged again, then said, "I'm Curran. Who are you?"

"Dominic Newton," Dominic said.

"Newt," Curran nodded, off-handedly giving Dominic the nickname that he would bear for the duration of his secondary years. He cocked his head. "Did you get a boner looking at the pictures?"

"What's a boner?" Dominic asked innocently.

Curran burst out laughing, then smiled at Dominic's bewildered expression. "You've got a lot to learn, young one, but stick with me and you'll go far."

## FIFTY-THREE

As the school scene faded, others flooded in, snapshots of their years together, not in order, or as detailed as that first recollection. He replayed the night when Curran lost his virginity at a party, Dominic delighted for him but jealous at the same time, then disgusted when Curran forced his fingers into Dominic's mouth to "give you a taste of what you're missing."

Curran explaining the facts of life to him not long after their first meeting. Wading in to pull him to safety when a fight erupted at a party some months ago. Consoling him in his own unique way when a heartbroken Dominic was dumped by his first girlfriend at the age of fourteen — "It was always going to happen. She was too high class. You need a minger who's more on your low level."

Lots of memories of getting drunk, laughing, dancing, chatting up birds. They'd had a few arguments over the years, usually when they were both trying to get in the knickers of the same girl, but had never fallen out. Other friends came and went, but Curran had been constant.

He remembered their first proper concert, getting drunk, staying out all night in a kebab shop because they couldn't afford the fare home. The one time that he'd seen Curran cry for real, when a friend of theirs had been killed in a motorcycle crash a few days before his nineteenth birthday, Curran distraught, talking about life and death and his fears of what would happen to his soul when his own day of reckoning came.

Playing football, a nothing lunchtime game, Dominic scoring a hat-trick, Curran lifting him into the air as if he was Pelé and had just won the World Cup, Dominic laughing with alarm and roaring at Curran to set him down. His first kiss at a friend's thirteenth birthday party, Curran interrupting the sweet moment to ask if Dominic could smell her bad breath while he was kissing her.

So many memories. Dominic could have spent the whole night reliving them, and would have liked to. But after a while they began to dissipate and the present dragged him back into focus. He realised he was rocking back and forth, moaning softly. He made himself stop, wiped tears from his cheeks – wincing as he brushed his hand over the blisters – and studied the blood again.

"It's not his," Dominic said. "It's an animal's. He probably didn't even come this way. Waiting for me on the road. Or maybe he woke up and is at the lake. He might be looking for me, the same way I'm looking for him. Worried about me, afraid I drowned."

Dominic paused as a new thought struck. Perhaps Curran had waded out into the lake earlier in the morning when Dominic was dead to the world, fainted and gone under. That might be why he hadn't responded when Dominic hailed him.

The more he thought about that horrific possibility, the more credible it seemed. Would Curran really leave him to sleep off his hangover in the middle of nowhere? It wouldn't be the first time that he'd left Dominic to his own devices, but usually he only did that if he was in pursuit of a hot bit of skirt. Much more likely that he'd crawled into the lake to drink or soak, blacked out and...

Dominic shuddered. He thought about returning to the lake, dredging it, pulling up Curran's bloated, lifeless form. Maybe fish would have already set to work on his face and stripped it of its flesh.

"Fish my arse," Dominic grunted. "This isn't the Amazon. There aren't any piranha in Bulgaria."

He tried to laugh away his fears. Curran was going to get a kick out of this. "Let me get this straight," Dominic imagined him crowing. "First you thought I'd been ripped to pieces by a savage Bulgarian animal. Then you thought I'd drowned and been eaten to the bone by ravenous fish. Fuck me, Newt, you make the prophet of doom look like a fucking clown."

"Got to stop thinking this way," Dominic muttered. "It's the sunburn. I'm not seeing things as they are. Imagining all sorts of dark shit. He's lying in a bush, snoring. Or he made it to the road and hitched a lift back to Laki. Or he might be searching for me, up at the lake or along the path."

Dominic raised his head and roared at the moon, "Curran!"

For a second he thought he heard an answer, but it was just his voice echoing back to him. When it died away there was silence.

Dominic sighed and stared glumly at the blood. He wanted to retrace his steps, return to the lake, look for Curran. If there was still no sign of him, he'd follow the path to the road, walk or catch a ride to Laki. Find Martini, ask her to do a quick sweep in case Curran was holed up in a pub. If not, they'd summon the police, leave it to them to organise a search party. Dominic could tell them about this secret path, the blood he'd found, let the experts test it and explore further.

That was the best plan. It would be madness to do anything else. Nodding solidly, he got to his feet – the pain was monumental – and turned to take his first step back towards the lake.

Then he paused.

But what if the blood *was* Curran's? What if he'd stumbled along this path and been attacked? Dominic had no idea what sort of creatures might be loose up here. Wolves? Bears? Wildcats?

He glanced down at the blood again, then at the dried bloodstains on his chest where he'd fallen in the liquid. If Curran had been killed, it would be a tragedy which Dominic would struggle to deal with for the rest of his life. But if he was dead, there was nothing Dominic could do to help him. It would be for the best in that case if he was discovered by others — Dominic didn't want to be the one to stumble across his best friend's mauled corpse.

But what if he was alive, lying against a tree further down the path, blood pumping from his wounds, gasping for breath, staring at the glorious moon, eyes wide, sure he was beyond hope, saying his final prayers?

Dominic imagined sitting down with a solemn police officer or medic. The man – or maybe it would be a woman – would look aside, clear their throat, mutter, "It wasn't your fault. There was nothing anyone could have done."

But Dominic would be searching for the lie. He'd see the shifty look in the man's – or woman's – eyes. He'd insist they tell him the truth, then crumple when they said, "He was still alive when you abandoned the search. If you'd only carried on for a few more minutes, a few more turns, you would have found him, you could have helped him, he'd be sitting here now, alive and well."

Dominic cursed softly and shut his eyes. This was too much for him. He didn't want to think. Was in no fit shape to reason. He should stick to the plan, leave the decisions to somebody else. But if he retreated when there was a chance that Curran might be out there, barely alive, in need of assistance...

"Did you think I would leave you dying?" Dominic sang croakily, a line from *Two Little Boys*. Then he sighed, readied himself for the pain that he would have to endure, turned, stepped over the blood and continued down the path into the shadows.

## FIFTY-FOUR

The sun was no longer beating down on him, but there was little comfort to be found in the coolness of the night. Dominic was stinging all over. His head wasn't spinning as wildly as it had been – the sleep had done him at least that much good – but otherwise he was caught in the same physical nightmare, where he almost wanted to chop off his limbs rather than endure the ever-present pain.

He paused at one point to wipe his chest clean of blood with the leaves of a large plant. He was tempted to chew on a leaf, to quench the dreadful thirst that had befallen him, but was wary of trying a plant that might be poisonous.

A short time later that problem was solved when a small stream cut across the path. Dominic eased himself on to his knees and tried to cup a handful of the mountain water. When the stream proved too shallow, he leant and supped from it directly, even licking the pebbles that lined its base.

It was a slow process, and he was eager to keep drinking until full, but he forced himself to stop after a minute and rest. He let the water settle in his stomach before drinking again, then rested, drank, rested and drank.

He needed to go to the toilet when he was finished, but walked a safe distance from the stream before pissing, not wanting to contaminate the water in case he had to drink from it again.

Dominic felt better after his drink, and when he came to a clearing along the path, where the light from the moon intensified, he paused and studied his scalded flesh. At last he saw the raised blisters, like crops of mini mushrooms. They troubled him, especially since he figured there were more that he couldn't see. He wondered if he should rub them with a dock leaf, or cake them in damp earth. But he was no survival expert and he feared doing more harm than good.

"Should have watched those wildlife programmes with Dad," he mumbled bitterly. His father spent most of his spare time watching documentaries about the natural world, but Dominic had always considered them a waste of time.

Something rustled in the trees overhead, maybe an owl or some rodent on the prowl. As Dominic listened, he thought for the first time of the danger he might be in if the blood had been Curran's. If the forest was home to a creature capable of disabling his taller, stronger friend, why shouldn't it target Dominic too?

He couldn't believe he hadn't taken that into consideration before. He was normally very quick to focus on his own needs, something he had in common with Curran. What would he do if a wolf came barrelling down the path towards him, or if a bear sprang out of the bushes?

"Shit myself and die," he cackled, but he couldn't raise a smile.

Another good reason to go back. He was crazy to press on. What was he trying to prove? Nobody would blame him if he abandoned this string of a path. Dominic had done more than most people in his position would have dared. The officials in Laki would commend him for coming this far, not condemn him for going no further.

Besides, he no longer thought that the blood was Curran's. If Curran had been assaulted by a bear or wolf, there would have been more signs further along the path, marks in the dust if the creature had dragged his body away, pools of blood if he'd repelled it and staggered off under his own steam.

"So why don't I quit and head back?" he sighed.

The answer was that a stubborn streak was forcing him on. He felt as if the path was challenging him. To turn back now would be an admission of failure. He'd invested so much time and effort (and fear) in the path that he felt compelled to find out where it led. Most probably it would peter out nowhere special, but at least if he tracked it to its end he would have the satisfaction of proving that.

So on he ploughed. He tripped occasionally on an exposed root, and branches often snagged an arm or leg or jabbed into his side, but he barely noticed such annoyances any more. He expected the scrapes and stings, and when they came he shrugged them off, sometimes literally, as when a branch from a tree fell on his shoulders, scaring the life out of him.

He grew so accustomed to the path that he stopped focusing on it and didn't actually notice when it opened into a glade. He shuffled on for a few metres, humming softly, walking in an odd, hunched-over way which had become the norm.

Then a wind blew and he shivered and stopped. There had been no breezes on the path, where the bushes grew tightly around it.

Dominic lifted his head, groaning at the effort, then blinked stupidly. Ahead of him, in the middle of the glade, as if it had materialised out of a fairy tale, stood a small, ancient cottage in poor repair.

There were two stained, cracked windows in the front. The cracks looked like spider webs, and Dominic might have been wary of them any other time. But right now they struck him as the most beautiful windows in the world, not because of their design, but because he could see a light shining inside. Somebody was home.

Dominic wanted to sink to his knees or raise his fists and shake them at the moon, but either gesture would have hurt too much, so he simply smiled and shuffled forward, slightly faster than before, offering up a silent prayer to the God who had looked down favourably upon him, slipping gratefully (if not gracefully) out of the darkness and into the light.

## FIFTY-FIVE

The cottage was constructed out of logs, but with a small stone wall running around the base, no more than half a metre high. Dominic guessed the stones had been put in place to give the structure a sturdy foundation. It was roofed with black slates, many of which were cracked or missing, and moss grew thickly over it as if eating the building alive. A chimney jutted out of one end, but no smoke drifted from the flue. It wasn't the time of year for fires.

There was a boxed section to the left of the cottage that looked to Dominic like it might be used to store logs for the fire. It was covered by two doors, one of which was open, but Dominic ignored that and focused on the front door. It was a battered, pitiful-looking thing that had often been repaired over the years with nailed-on bits of wood and even slates taken from the roof. There was no knocker or doorbell, but Dominic supposed there wasn't much need for them out here, where visitors were surely in scant supply.

There had once been a small porch, but it had rotted away long ago. The three steps up to it still remained, however, and a couple of short planks connected the top step to the doorway.

Dominic climbed the steps, wincing and groaning, then carefully edged along the planks, worried in case he slipped and fell into the pitch-black pit beneath.

When he came to the door he paused, not sure how to continue. In the end he rapped on it a couple of times and called out, "Hello?"

There was no answer.

Dominic knocked again. Still no response. He was reaching up to try for a third time when he saw the bolt that kept the door shut. It was a rudimentary lock, just a bit of metal stuck in a fist-sized hole in the door, that you could slide back and forth with your fingers from either side.

He stared at the bolt for a few seconds, not sure if he would be making a mistake if he slid it open. He'd seen films about hillbillies, *Deliverance* being the classic example, which a gleeful Curran had introduced him to when he was an impressionable thirteen-year-old. It had given him nightmares for a week.

Of course he was in Bulgaria, not the Deep South USA, but maybe they had their own version here, mountain-dwellers who liked peace and quiet, who objected to outsiders knocking on their doors and disturbing them. If he entered such an abode without permission, there was no telling where it might end.

"Squeal, piggy, squeal," he whispered, lips twitching at the memory of those long-ago, *Deliverance*-spawned dark dreams.

He stood on the step, pondering his course of action. Then he caught sight of the blisters on his right forearm, which was half-outstretched towards the bolt. Surely even the gruffest of hillbillies would take pity on him when they saw what a sorry state he was in.

Dominic knocked on the door again, louder this time, and bent to shout through the gap around the bolt, "Hello? Anybody home?"

When there was no answer, he straightened as best he could, covered his genitals with his left hand (in case there was a sweet little grandmother sitting inside in a rocking chair), slid the bolt back with his free fingers, pushed the door open and entered.

## FIFTY-SIX

It was a dump inside. If there had been inner walls, they'd been torn down long ago, leaving one large room in their place. In terms of access, there was the door he'd come through, the pair of windows at the front and one at the rear, which was in better condition than the other two.

There wasn't much in the way of furniture or appliances, apart from bedding on the floor to his left, a large wicker basket set against the wall to his right, and six buckets in the far-off corner beyond the bedding, which had been arranged in a cluster and turned upside down, a tall, thick candle set on top of each.

The light was coming from the candles, two of which were burning. Dominic stared at them, momentarily mesmerised by their flickering flames. He wanted to go over and sink to his knees, press close and watch the dancing lights. He took a step towards the buckets, then blinked and frowned. There would be time for that later. First he had to find whoever had lit the wicks, seek help, ask if they could dress his wounds and look for Curran.

"Hello?" Dominic called, but again there was no answer.

He studied the rest of the room. The floorboards were warped and stained with dark smears. It was hard to tell in the candlelight, but some of the stains looked like blood, others like excrement.

The stains made Dominic uneasy, but he figured this was a hunting lodge. The bedding, now that he studied it, was little more than a pile of grass and leaves spread over old, reclaimed floorboards.

This didn't feel like a home. Even the poorest of hillbillies would have turned up their noses at such a hovel. Dominic thought it more likely that the cottage had been converted into a base for hunters, a place to rest up when they were weary, or to gut and skin their catches.

That would explain the blood and feces. A few hours ago, in his delirium, he would have assumed that he'd wandered into a serial killer's charnel house, that the blood was Curran's, that a large man in a butcher's apron and a mask stitched together from human flesh would barge in on him at any moment, swinging an axe.

But he was in control of his senses now. He wasn't going to panic and tear off into the night, heart racing, screaming like a leggy blond victim in a slasher flick. This was a den for hunters. They'd be back soon – they wouldn't have left the candles burning otherwise – and if Dominic sat here and bided his time, all would be well.

He considered the bedding – he was tired and fancied the idea of grabbing some shuteye – but was worried about his blisters. If they popped in his sleep, on such a dirty base, the wounds might get infected. Besides, he wasn't sure that the bedding was what he'd first assumed. Instead of being a place to rest, maybe the hunters stacked animal corpses on the bed of grass and leaves, to let the blood trickle out.

Dominic had had enough of blood for one night. The last thing he wanted was to lie down and find himself floating in a mess of crimson gore.

He turned towards the wicker basket and limped across. It didn't fit in with the rest of the room. It was old and stained like the floorboards, but if you gave it a quick once-over with a mop it wouldn't have looked out of place in a rustic home.

The basket was large enough to accommodate a good-sized animal, probably not a bear, but maybe a small deer. Dominic decided to look inside before he sat down, to set his mind at rest, so that he wouldn't get a shock if the lid collapsed and he found himself eyeball-to-eyeball with a glassy-eyed, death-snarling buck.

The lid was heavier than he'd assumed and he struggled to lift it. He winced at the fresh pain in his arms and back as he heaved, then bent and snuck a look inside. It was empty, although by the multitude of stains on the floor, he was certain it had been used to store bodies or hides in the past.

Dominic let the lid slam shut. Before he sat, he patted the cheeks of his arse, checking for blisters. He found quite a few, but they were firm to the touch and he didn't think they'd pop.

"What a world," he sighed pathetically. This hadn't been part of the holiday plan, worrying about pustules on his bum exploding.

Dominic managed a weak chuckle, able to see the light side of his torment now that the end was hopefully within sight. The sunburn wasn't going to fade away by magic. There were days, maybe weeks of agony ahead of him. And that was even before he began to peel.

But doctors would be able to ease his pain. Lotions and drugs would numb him to the worst of the suffering. Nurses could bandage him if pus seeped out of the blisters, cool him down if he was overheating. Give it a couple of weeks and he'd be back to normal, laughing about this with Curran and Martini in a pub in London, swearing over a pint never to stray from his home shores again.

"Fuck Bulgaria," he muttered. "Fuck Iliya and his scummy crew. Fuck the sun. And fuck this fucking forest."

Sniffing righteously, he turned and sat on the wicker basket. He drew in a sharp intake of breath — it was like several daggers had been jammed into his arse — then settled until the worst of the pain had passed. Fixing his gaze on the front door, he twisted his lips into a smile of welcome for when the hunters returned, and waited.

## FIFTY-SEVEN

He felt sleepy, sitting on the wicker basket, lulled by the flickering candles. He would have worried about falling asleep and toppling from his perch, but the pain in his jaw flared every time his head drooped, jolting him back to life. He might faint in this position, but there was no way he could doze off, not unless he leant against the wall, but then some of the blisters on his back would pop, which would fire him wide awake.

Dominic was concerned about the blisters. Sunburn was a nuisance, but a minor inconvenience when put in context. On the other hand, if the blisters burst and he got infected, poisons could seep into his bloodstream. He might lose one or more of his limbs, or even suffer an excruciating death.

Perhaps he should wait for the hunters outside. Take a candle, find a clean patch of grass, make himself comfortable. But it was cold out there and getting chillier. Far cosier in here. And what if a bear or wolf wandered by? Or ants and bugs might target him. He thought about his blisters popping, insects being attracted to the pus and blood, crawling into his wounds.

Dominic shivered and decided he was perfectly happy where he was.

As he was shivering, a high-pitched keening noise cut through the silence of the cottage. It was like the cry of an old-style kettle, the sort he'd seen in movies set in the distant past of the 1960s or 70s, before electric kettles became the norm.

Dominic held his breath, eyes widening.

"What the hell was that?" he finally whispered.

He got to his feet and stared at the floor. While he had no idea what had made the noise, he was pretty sure it had come from somewhere beneath the warped, stained boards.

"Hello?" Dominic called, but softly this time, not really wanting an answer.

He knelt and found a large crack between a couple of boards. There were other boards below them, running horizontally to those on the upper level, but when he cupped his hands together and pressed an eye to the space, he could make out a dim glow seeping through.

"A cellar," Dominic sighed, pulling back from the boards and squinting at them. He recalled the boxed section outside. He'd assumed it was a storage area for logs, but it could just as easily be the entrance to an underground room.

And one of the doors had been open.

Dominic stood and stared at the floorboards. His legs shook as he replayed the keening noise inside his head. He thought of all the horror films he'd seen over the years, where foolish young people strayed where they shouldn't. He'd always mocked the celluloid victims, saying that anybody with half a brain would run for the hills if they found themselves in a creepy old house, not push through a creaking door into a room filled with the buzzing sounds of a chainsaw.

Curran had often challenged him about that. "Nobody expects to run into a serial killer in real life," he'd claim with the air of a professor delivering a lecture. "If you were brave enough to enter a deserted house, you'd explore it thoroughly. Why wouldn't you? It's ninety-nine point nine-nine percent certain you won't find anything amiss.

"Besides," he'd continue, "we don't think of ourselves as fodder. In our heads, each of us is a star. Even if you felt there was a chance you'd wandered into a killer's lair, you'd still open that door, because you'd be thinking you were the hero who was going to stop the villain. If you turned and ran, you'd have to accept that you're a scared, small-time nobody. Who wants to own up to that? You'd push that door open every time, Newt, and so would everybody else."

And at that point he'd usually burp or fart. Curran didn't like it when things got too serious. That wasn't his thing.

Dominic made his slow, pained way to the front door, slid back the bolt and stepped out on to the planks where a porch had once stood. He thought about taking a candle with him, but the area was lit by the moon and he didn't want to risk dripping hot wax on his sunburnt hand. Besides, the glow from the candle might give his position away, and he wasn't sure he wanted to do that. If he didn't like the look of things and made up his mind to get the hell out of Dodge, darkness would be his ally.

Crossing the planks, he limped down the three steps to the ground, then edged to the corner of the house and stared at the box with the open door. This time he saw light coming out of it which he'd missed before.

He was certain now that this was the entrance to a cellar. And he was just as certain that somebody was down there.

He almost turned and retreated, to be able to prove to Curran that his theory held no water. That would drive Curran mad. He hated being wrong.

But Curran was sharper than most people credited. As selfish, lazy and carefree as he was, he could see things in human nature that Dominic never would. He was a sound judge of people, which was how he was able to make friends no matter where he went.

As nervous as Dominic was, he knew his fears were ill-founded. He'd be a fool if he turned his back on this opportunity and crawled off into the forest. His sunburn and blisters were real. His need for help was real. All else was morbid fantasy.

So, as ninety-nine point nine-nine percent of people would have done in his position (assuming Curran's statistics were on the nose), Dominic ignored the chance to slip away like a coward, and instead staggered towards the open entrance of the almost certainly threat-free cellar.

## FIFTY-EIGHT

When Dominic got to the box and looked down the opening, he expected to see stairs. But while there probably had been steps at one point, they'd been replaced with a couple of tree trunks, long and slender, with many stubs where branches had once grown.

He couldn't see much of the floor from here. The light was coming from one or more candles somewhere else in the cellar, and the area directly beneath him was only dimly illuminated.

Dominic opened his mouth to call out, then closed it, not having uttered a word.

He could hear noises.

They were similar to the high-pitched keening sound he'd heard a few minutes earlier, but far softer. There were scurrying noises too, as if someone was scraping a rake through dry earth.

Dominic had a bad feeling about this. He thought again of all the horror films. If this was a scene in one of them, the character in his position would climb down, no doubt about it. The plot would demand it.

Unlike his movie counterparts, Dominic had a choice. He could head back into the cottage or return to the path. He wasn't tied to a script. His destiny was his own to decide.

But Curran, if he'd been on hand, would have argued that we're all creatures of fate, that specific situations call for specific responses, and very few of us can break the chains of our destined futures. If a person spots a baby in the middle of a burning room, crying and waving its chubby arms over its head, that person will feel compelled to dive through the flames and risk all for the helpless child.

There was no baby in the cellar (at least not that Curran could see) but he was obliged to descend regardless. From the moment he'd heard that strange sound, he had been drawn to this. He was caught in a string of events, and while in theory he could sever that string at any moment and turn his back on whatever destiny was holding in store for him, in reality that was never going to happen.

Dominic gulped, glanced at the moon and cast a bitter look of blame in its direction — if it hadn't been such a bright night he wouldn't have spotted the gap in the bushes and started down the path or chanced upon this creepy cottage.

Then, since he had no real choice, like a puppet obeying the pull of its master he stepped into the box, careful not to bump his burnt legs against the door which was lying flat in place — he considered lifting it out of the way, but was worried it would creak. He turned round, backed on to one of the trunks, found a couple of footholds, then swung down into the gloom.

## FIFTY-NINE

Dominic clung to the trunk a moment, ready to leap from it and grab on to the box if he felt it was going to collapse, but the trunk easily supported his weight.

He stretched out a foot, searching for another stub. When he found one, he moved a hand down, then his other foot, then his other hand. He went slowly, testing each hold carefully, determined not to lose his grip and spill off the trunk. He wasn't very high up and would probably suffer no worse than an ankle sprain if he fell, but he didn't want to chance it, especially as there was as yet no way of telling what awaited him below.

His eyes were adjusting all the time, especially with the aid of the candlelight once he cleared the cottage floor. He paused and turned his face towards the light. As he did, the cellar came into focus, and he froze as if glued to the trunk.

The first thing he saw was a rat. He was conscious even as he stared at it that it wasn't the only rat in the cellar. Far from it. They were legion, which he duly noted, but on a deeper, less immediate level. For several long seconds he was only consciously aware of one of the rodents.

It was a long, dark, vicious-looking predator, with cruel black eyes. It was standing on its back legs, nibbling at something, face cocked towards the ceiling. He felt for one long, terrifying moment that the rat was looking at him, that it had clocked his presence and was figuring out a way to attack. Then it finished chewing on whatever it had been holding, dropped to all fours and faded into the crowd. Dominic felt relief, until he blinked and realised that the fact it had faded into a crowd wasn't a positive thing, as it meant there were lots more of its kind.

That was when Dominic's brain kicked in and confirmed that the cellar floor was swarming with rats. There must be thousands of them. Dark, bulky pockets of furry shadows with fangs, malevolent-looking eyes glinting when they caught the flicker of the candlelight, tails swishing menacingly.

They moved as a single mass, one body flowing into that of another. It was like staring at an undulating picture. While individuals moved at different speeds, as an entity they swayed slowly, a grim cloud drifting across the cellar floor.

Dominic had no inbuilt fear of rats. In fact he had once considered buying one, but he'd spent his money on a CD instead and given up on the idea, figuring it would be more hassle than it was worth. He didn't want to feel tied to a pet, having to feed and clean up after it.

But while Dominic wasn't afraid of rats in general, seeing so many together in one spot struck terror into him. There was something horrifying about them when they were bunched up, snapping irritably at one another, scrabbling through the dirt, sniffing the air, squeaking softly.

Most of the rats were grouped round a cross on the floor. It was a life-size crucifix, and while it was difficult to tell for sure, given the swarm of rats, Dominic thought there was a body attached to it. He wanted it to be an animal, and maybe it was, but he'd never heard of animals being crucified, only humans.

Dominic stared at the cross for a long time, watching the rats wash over it, chewing at whatever unfortunate creature was strapped to the intersecting planks. He thought he caught an occasional glimpse of flesh, but that might have been his mind playing tricks.

He wasn't sure how much time had passed. Maybe he'd hung there a minute. Maybe five. He hadn't moved a muscle, except his eyelids when he blinked. He was clutching the trunk tightly, the white of his knuckles showing through even the thick red shade of his skin. His feet hadn't budged from the stumps on which he was standing. He barely even breathed, lips open a merest fraction, drawing in air through his nostrils rather than through his mouth.

It wasn't the healthiest air. There was a foul, acidic stench, one that reminded him of piss, but sharper. He felt as if his sinuses were going to melt. He wanted to pinch his nose shut, but that would have meant releasing his hold on the trunk, and no smell in the world could have compelled him to do that.

Part of him thought he would cling to the trunk for the rest of his life, staring out over the tide of rats, ensnared in a web of fear. But eventually his fingers tingled and the more clinical part of his brain told him that he needed to pull himself together and haul himself back up the trunk to the world above. He wasn't paralysed. He didn't need to stay here. He had the power to put this behind him and get on with his life.

He almost scurried for safety straight away, but that sensible voice murmured to him to relax and take his time. The rats were on the floor, oblivious to his presence. Even if they spotted him and gave chase, he had too great a start on them. He could scamper to the top, slam shut the door of the box, and be halfway back to the lake before they could chew through.

"*No need to panic,*" that voice said. "*Don't do anything you'll regret. Take your time. Be sure of your handholds. There's no rush.*"

He smiled. The voice was right. He wasn't in any trouble. The rats had freaked him, but he was out of their reach. He'd climb back up in a minute, no drama, hand after hand, foot after foot. First he wanted to take a closer look at the form on the cross.

He had no plans to descend any further – perish the thought – but if he waited a few minutes, and watched closely but calmly, he was sure the rats around the crucifix would part, affording him a clear view of whatever was strapped to the wood. He was confident it wasn't a person – that had just been his terrified subconscious supplying dark images – but he'd rest easier if he could confirm that. One good look was all he craved. Then he could climb out of here, chuckle at how he'd reacted, return to the cottage and wait for the hunters, or retrace his route back along the…

A high-pitched keening sound stopped his thoughts dead. It was the same sound he'd heard while sitting on the wicker basket, but it cut through him down here in the confines of the cellar. He winced at the unexpected noise, shook his head to clear it, then looked up from the rats and the crucifix, stared across the room to where a single candle was shining, and saw a monster.

## SIXTY

Dominic knew instantly that this was a literal monster, and to his surprise he had no problem accepting it. He'd been told all his life that monsters didn't exist, but here was proof that they did, and that was enough for him.

The creature was massive, maybe two and a half metres tall. It was broad, with muscular arms like a silverback gorilla's, although ending in oddly small, slender fingers. Its legs were unusually short, but stout enough to support the rest of its body, with a pair of huge, knobbly feet.

Its flesh was transparent, revealing its network of veins, arteries, muscles, sinews and more. It had a bulging, low-hanging stomach, its looping, twisting guts pressing tightly against the restraining flesh. He couldn't see much of the creature's organs behind the intestines, though he caught a glimpse of the top of its lungs and heart, which was the size of a small football.

The beast was hairless from foot to head, and it was the head that convinced Dominic beyond all shadow of a doubt that he was staring at a true monster. It was almost double the size of his own. Its skull housed the creature's brain and was flat on top. A thick chunk of bone jutted out of its forehead and arched forward between the creature's eyes, like a horn, curving down towards its nose but stopping a few centimetres short.

Its ears were mammoth, flapping shreds of skin on either side of its head. Its eyes were oval-shaped like a human's and roughly the same size, but ran vertically down its face, as if a person's eyes had been flipped ninety degrees. There was a cloudy white film over them and two freaky red pupils in the centre.

The monster's mouth was set in a snout that grew out of the lower half of its face. When its lips opened wide – you could fit a baby's head in there – Dominic saw two or three rows of fangs, small and sharp, stained red with blood.

The monster had picked up a rat and bitten its head off. It was spitting the head at the other rats when Dominic laid eyes on it. The rodents tore into the severed morsel, excited by the blood, ripping it apart with no consideration for the fact that it had been one of their own. The monster made a soft grunting noise that Dominic translated as laughter. Then it bent and turned the rat's corpse over in its palm. It raised its other hand and Dominic glimpsed short but sharp nails sticking out of the end of each thin finger. The monster used one of those nails to carefully slit open the rat's stomach. As guts oozed out, it turned its hand and held the corpse close to the floor, guts dangling just above the heads of the dead rat's kin.

When the rats sniffed the guts, they went wild. They launched themselves at the tidbit hanging from the monster's fingers, snapping at the extended coils, standing on their hind legs to try and reach. Guts were obviously nectar to them.

The monster teased them, keeping the corpse just out of reach. It would lower its hand a fraction, let the rats on the floor get close, then whip it back up, all the time making that weird little grunting sound.

Finally one of the rats snagged a loop of intestine and the rest of the guts began to spool out as it scurried away, teeth dug in, barrelling through the others. As the guts spilled from their resting place, more rats grabbed hold, and within seconds the dead rat's insides seemed to explode out of it, showering the floor and its snapping, hungry companions.

The monster relaxed its fingers and the rest of the rat followed after its guts, instantly lost to the crush. The beast watched the rats feed, then lowered its head and licked its palm clean with a rough, red tongue. It made the high-pitched noise again, raising its head towards the ceiling, a look of what must have been pleasure on its face, although it was hard for Dominic to judge, not being accustomed to the facial expressions of monsters.

Several rats swept over the monster's feet as it was shrieking with delight.

It growled, then leant back, so that its enormous round stomach lifted. Dominic spotted a long, thin penis, allowing him to finally peg the beast's gender. The lack of breasts – it didn't even have nipples, which he only now noted – had suggested to him that the monster was male, but the penis confirmed it.

When the monster's penis was free of its stomach, it pissed. The piss hit the rats on their backs and they span away, screeching with outrage. The stream splashed over the monster's feet, but it only made the chuckling noise, wriggling its chunky toes as if amused. When the rats sniffed the piss-smeared feet, they scurried clear, hissing and choking.

Dominic now knew why the smell of urine had been so unfamiliar. A quick glance at the base of the trunks also helped him realise why the rats hadn't strayed from the cellar floor. There were dark, dried-in circles of piss around each of them, and he figured the monster had pissed there so often that it had become a permanent barrier for the scent-sensitive rodents.

A shuffling noise drew his attention back to the monster. He watched with numb horror and fascination as the beast nudged forward, sniffing the air – its nose didn't look much different to a person's, just a bit flatter, with slightly larger nostrils – and studying the rats for another victim.

By the way the monster kept ducking its head to stare at the rats up close, Dominic assumed the creature's eyes weren't the strongest. That was probably why it hadn't spotted the naked human hanging overhead, an oversight for which Dominic would have offered up a silent prayer of thanks if he had been able to think clearly.

Dominic was in shock, yet in a strange way he'd been more scared of the rats than he was of this stumbling, pissing, exceedingly ugly monstrosity. Having spent most of his life denying the existence of monsters, he wasn't able to look upon it as a genuine threat in the way that the rats were.

This was a creature of unknown qualities. For all Dominic knew, it could be a benevolent giant. Sure, it was ripping apart rats, but he could empathise with the monster on that score — he'd have ripped them apart too if he'd found himself stranded among them. That didn't mean the beast would view Dominic the same way as the rodents. Maybe he had nothing to fear from it. If anything, the monster might be more scared of him. It had likely been hunted by humans in the past, fearful of its appearance. He could well be more a threat to the monster than it had ever been to one of his kind.

But then the beast revealed its true nature, leaving Dominic in no doubt about where he stood.

Losing interest in the rats, the monster lumbered to the cross, which Dominic had momentarily forgotten about. Pissing again to drive the rats back, it leant down, grabbed the crossplank, and lifted the crucifix up into a standing position. There was a slot in the floor, revealed now that the majority of rats had withdrawn, and the monster rammed the base of the cross down into it, so that the crucifix would stand upright.

The figure attached to the cross now faced towards Dominic, and the possibility that it was an animal vanished with a single glance. It was definitely human, probably a man, although much of the person's flesh had been stripped away, so it was hard to tell for sure.

Rats were still clinging to the corpse, although several dropped while a horrified Dominic was watching. Bones had been exposed all over, and most of the guts had been torn out. Strands poked through the holes in the corpse's stomach, and Dominic could see rats inside, moving through the remains of his intestines, treating his body as if it was an extended nest.

The man's eyes were gone, dark liquid staining the now empty sockets. His nose had been chewed away, along with his ears and much of the flesh of his cheeks. His own mother would have struggled to identify him, but Dominic had an idea who it might be, and he looked for evidence to confirm his worst fears.

He found it on the middle finger of the man's right hand. There was a silver ring with a strange spike sticking out of it. The spike was pointing back towards the man's wrist, as it had been the last time Dominic had noticed it, when its bearer had been fighting with the teenagers from Laki, struggling to turn the ring round, so that he could use the spike as a weapon.

Most of the flesh had been stripped from the finger, but the ring was lodged tight, gleaming in the middle of the bloodied shreds of skin, veins and tendons. It wasn't much of a memorial marker, but enough to provide the corpse with a name, and Dominic instinctively moaned it aloud, unable to hold in the cry.

"*Curran!*"

## SIXTY-ONE

The monster's head shot up. It stared at Dominic with shock, immediately pinning his position, pupils widening as it tried to see more of the figure on the trunk. Next to it, Curran's corpse shook as rats dug around inside whatever was left of his guts.

"You bastard," Dominic wheezed, starting to cry.

The monster cocked its head and frowned. Then it leered and leant backwards, as it had when pissing. But Dominic could see that it didn't plan to piss again. Instead its penis was hardening.

"Fucking *Deliverance*!" Dominic screamed, flashing on an image of being raped by the beast, almost losing his grip on the trunk as he shuddered with repulsion.

The monster winced and covered its ears. Then, as the echo of the scream died away, it lowered its hands, its eyes went dead, and it charged, making the same high-pitched sound it had made before biting off the rat's head.

Dominic didn't wait to be dragged down from his perch. He knew he had mere seconds to play with and he had no intention of wasting them. Grief could come later. Right now he had to forget everything else and focus on saving himself.

As the monster crashed across the room, Dominic scrambled up the trunk. His feet slipped, and for a sickening moment he thought he was going to fall, but then his left foot struck a stump and he thrust forward.

The monster grabbed the base of the trunk and heaved, ripped it out of the hole where it was anchored, then retreated with it, meaning to bring the human down with the pole.

Dominic felt the trunk dropping beneath him and lunged for the edge of the hole round which the box had been built. If he missed, he was done for — he was no match for a creature that could drag around a trunk that size. Dominic probably wouldn't have been able to budge the length of tree.

As Dominic lashed out with his arms, his head connected with the door on the box that had been swung closed. He yelled with shock and almost fell after the trunk, but then his elbows caught on the earth round the hole and he leant forward, shifting his centre of balance. His legs were still dangling, but he had a purchase on solid ground and would be able to drag himself to safety.

In the cellar, the monster saw what was happening. Letting go of the trunk, it hissed and jumped after Dominic. It was tall enough, with a long enough reach, to grab him, and it grinned savagely as its right hand tore through the air. But it hadn't checked before jumping, and one of its feet caught on a jagged stump of the downed trunk. Its leap was cut short and it fell heavily, squealing with surprise.

Dominic didn't glance down at the monster. He thought its cry of pain was one of triumph, that it was about to clasp its fingers round his ankles and haul him back into its pit. Screaming with horror, he grabbed hold of the edge of the box and pulled himself out of the hole in one swift movement, ignoring the agony as his red-raw stomach scraped across the stone rim of the hole and then the sharp edge of the wooden box, blisters popping wildly and smearing his flesh with hot, sticky fluid.

Below, the monster was back on its feet, hobbling but otherwise unharmed. Scowling, it bounded over to where the remaining trunk stood and started to pull itself up.

Dominic looked for something to lob at the advancing monster, but there was nothing to hand. With a curse, he turned to run. Then he forced himself to stop. Stepping out of the creature's line of sight, he turned, bent and took hold of the door that was hanging open.

He couldn't believe he was doing this, taking on the monster instead of fleeing, but he had to buy time for himself, otherwise he was damned. So, taking a deep breath, he listened and watched.

As the monster neared the top of the trunk, it reached up with one of its hands and took hold of the edge of the box, the way Dominic had moments earlier. It was what he'd been waiting for. Roaring hatefully, he slammed the door down on the creature's outstretched fingers.

The monster hadn't expected the terrified human to make such a bold move. It bellowed with shock as well as pain, then squealed with panic as it lost its grip on the trunk and toppled backwards, fingers tearing free, blood spurting from them as the flesh ripped away, hitting the floor with a resounding thump, causing the cross with the corpse on it to shudder and the rats to break away in a worried flurry.

Dominic didn't wait for the monster to regain its composure. He'd bought the time he needed. Now he had to make the most of it. Turning his back on the box and the cellar, he faced the forest and ran.

## SIXTY-TWO

He got no more than a few paces before he stopped. He could hear the monster caterwauling in the cellar, a piercing cry of pain and fury. By the sound of things, the beast was already back on its feet. It wouldn't be long before it crawled up the trunk and burst through the doors.

Dominic had no idea how fast the monster could run, but doubted he could out-pace it in his current shambolic condition. If he had more time he could try to hide, and hope that with its poor eyesight it couldn't find him. But it would make the open before he could slip from sight and find a place to lay low.

Dominic turned and stared at the cottage. The last thing he wanted was to trap himself, but that looked like his best bet. The windows were surely too small for the creature to crawl through, so if he could find a way to bar the door, maybe he could keep it at bay.

"*And how exactly are you going to do that, Sherlock?*" he asked himself witheringly.

But this wasn't the time to hold an internal debate. The choice was simple — flight or the cottage.

He decided to make a stand. If he couldn't block the door, and the monster gained entrance, he could dive through one of the windows and take his chances in a race with the beast. At least that way he had a Plan B. And something else might crop up in the meantime that could work to his advantage.

"*Yeah,*" a sarcastic part of him grunted. "*The monster might drop dead of a heart attack.*"

Unhappy with his choice, but feeling tied to it, Dominic limped towards the steps that led to the front door. He hurried up them and started across the planks. As he was crossing, the monster slammed open the doors of the box and dragged itself out into the night, howling keenly.

The volume of the high-pitched noise unnerved Dominic. He flinched and missed his footing. Next thing he knew, he was falling into the pit where the porch had once stood.

He yelled with alarm as he fell, not sure how deep the pit might be, but his yell was cut short when he hit the floor and realised with relief that it was nothing more than a shallow ditch.

As Dominic turned over wildly, to climb back on to the planks, his right elbow struck something metallic. The shadows were thick down here, but he paused and forced himself to focus. For a second or two he couldn't see anything. Then, as he moved his head, the object glinted and he saw... a knife!

Dominic's heart leapt as if he'd discovered a cache of lost gold. He snatched for the knife, grabbed its handle and pulled it in close. It was a dull old blade, covered in what was either rust or dried blood. Hardly a sword to slay dragons with, but at least he now had a weapon. It probably wouldn't be much good when faced with a beast this size, but anything was better than nothing.

Dominic got to his knees and reached for the planks, meaning to drag himself on to them. But he could hear the monster pounding closer. It would round the corner any second now. There was no time to crawl out of the pit. The monster would catch him before he could open the door and slip inside.

Making a snap call just before the monster lumbered into sight, Dominic threw himself to the floor and slid beneath the boards, trying desperately to disappear into the dirt of the ditch as the monster bounced across the last few strides and mounted the steps, casting its thick, murderous shadow directly across him.

## SIXTY-THREE

Dominic couldn't recall closing the door when he left the cottage, but he must have, because the monster now pounded on it with its uninjured hand, screeching hatefully. Blood dripped from its injured fingers, splashing in the dirt beside Dominic's head. He couldn't tell in the darkness whether the creature's blood was the same colour as his — for some odd reason that seemed to matter.

The monster stopped hammering the door and began to fiddle with the bolt. Dominic swiftly played through his options. He could wait for the monster to step inside, then try to sneak off into the forest. Or he could leap to his feet as it entered and try to stab it while its back was turned to him. Or...

The planks linking the top step to the doorway had been roughly set in place. There were wide gaps between them. Dominic could see the monster's feet, filthy with dirt, blood and rat shit. As he stared, a dry fleck of shit was knocked loose and fell on Dominic's lips. He quickly spat it away, coughing with disgust. Then, acting instinctively and angrily, he slid the blade of the knife between two of the planks and drove it up and into the monster's foot.

There was a howl of stunned pain. The monster wheeled away, tearing its foot free. The knife was wrenched from Dominic's grip, but the handle wouldn't fit through the planks, so it bounced off and fell back into his welcoming grasp.

He could see the monster's arms flailing as it tried to regain its balance. Snarling, he struck at its foot again with his knife. This time he only scraped a couple of toes but the jab was enough to send the monster over the edge. Literally.

It fell to Dominic's left, crying out with alarm, another of its high whistling noises. It landed hard on its back in the pit, arms and legs thrashing crazily.

Dominic dragged himself away from the monster, clear of the boards, and staggered to his feet. If the planks hadn't been between them, he might have leapt upon the monster and continued stabbing — his strikes against the creature had excited him and he sensed victory. But by the time he pulled himself on to the planks and stood, the monster was already sitting up and shaking its head.

Dominic stared at the beast's inhuman head, the rows of fangs in its snout, its massive arms and translucent, barrel-like stomach. The reality of the situation reasserted itself. He was David up against Goliath, but since this wasn't a Biblical tale, the chances were that the giant would squash him like an ant if it caught hold of him.

"No fucking way," Dominic moaned, rejecting the image of him leaping on to the monster. This might be his best chance of defeating it in a fair fight, but Dominic didn't want to fight such a monstrous opponent, fairly or otherwise, not when the option of running away and hiding was still on the table.

"Fuck you, you fucker!" Dominic bellowed, remembering the way the monster had reacted to loud noises in the cellar.

To his delight, the beast shrieked and jammed its hands over its oversized ears, giving him another few seconds to exploit. Instead of striking while the beast was temporarily vulnerable, he turned towards the door, slid the bolt, lurched into the cottage, then slammed the bolt back into place, locking himself in, all but issuing a written invite to the monster to launch an assault on the poorly barricaded fortress.

## SIXTY-FOUR

Dominic cursed his cowardice as soon as the door was shut. He should have struck. The momentum had been his. The beast was wounded and confused. He'd taken the high ground. So why hadn't he seized the initiative?

"Because it's a fucking monster," he sobbed, crying again now that there was a lull. "How the fuck am I supposed to take on a fucking…?"

He stopped. There were scrabbling sounds outside. Then wheezing sounds. Then creaking sounds.

Dominic pieced together the scene. The monster had risen and climbed back on to the planks. It must be standing there, taking a few calming breaths, analysing its options as Dominic had analysed his when lying on his back in the ditch.

He adjusted his grip on the knife and waited. His hands were trembling. He felt both incredibly cold and unbearably hot. Sweat mixed with tears on his cheeks. He thought about Curran hanging lifelessly on the cross, the rats chowing down on his pitiful remains.

He moaned softly, wanting to mourn his lost friend but knowing that he had to stay focused on his own deadly plight.

As soon as it heard the moan, the beast slammed a fist into the door, which shook wildly. Dominic screeched and took an impulsive step backwards.

The monster must have anticipated his reaction, because suddenly it was scrabbling at the bolt, trying to force it open. It should have been a simple manoeuvre, but the creature was agitated, stinging from its wounds and irate that its prey had twice got the better of it. Its hand was trembling and it fumbled with the bolt, trying to work all of its fingers around the piece of metal, rather than just use a couple to slide it back.

With a panicked moan, Dominic lunged at the monster's fingers and slashed the knife across them. It screamed and released its hold. Blood spurted from the wound as it jerked the fingers away and Dominic distantly noted that it was red like his, but a few shades darker.

On the planks, the monster was making a short, livid whistling noise over and over. It reached for the bolt again, with a single finger, trying to slyly slip it underneath without Dominic seeing. But he spied the moving shadow and jabbed the tip of the knife into the hole beneath the bolt.

This time the monster was too quick from him and it yanked back its finger before he drew blood. Dominic stood there, knife poised, blinking to keep his eyes clear, waiting to strike again.

There was a pause while the monster assessed the situation. Dominic gulped and offered up a quick prayer, hoping his attacker would abandon its position and take off, deciding he wasn't worth the effort, that he'd fought back too fiercely.

But he knew, even while he prayed, that it was a futile hope, and seconds later the monster started banging on the door with its fists and feet. The door shook and parts of it began to snap. The hinges danced madly, beginning to jolt free.

He had a minute, maybe less, before the door would tear loose or shatter. Then there'd be nothing between them. The monster could simply step inside, knock the knife from Dominic's hand and rip into him. Game over.

## SIXTY-FIVE

"No," Dominic groaned. He wasn't going to let it end this way. The monster wasn't some unstoppable behemoth. As startled as he'd been, as puny as he was in comparison, as clumsily as he'd fought, he had already hurt it. The creature's skin was no tougher than his. It bled the same way he did. And if it could be injured like a human, it could be killed like one too.

But he wasn't interested in killing. Sure, it would be sweet to take revenge for what it had done to Curran, but he would rather out-run than out-fight it. His main goal was to make it out of this forest alive. He was all in favour of whatever gave him the best chance of doing that.

As the door buckled beneath the monster's onslaught, Dominic decided it was time to flee. If he could evade the creature, find a spot to hide, wait for daybreak, make his way back to the lake and then the road…

Turning away from the door, Dominic staggered across the room to the rear window. The monster was making so much noise that it wouldn't be able to hear him. He'd let himself out, slip away, make the most of his head start, hope the stab wound he'd inflicted on the monster's foot would slow it down. Hell, maybe the fucker would catch fast-acting gangrene and drop dead during pursuit.

Dominic got ready to smash the glass. He cocked his elbow and prepared to bite down against the pain. Then he paused, flicked the latch open and tried to slide up the lower pane of glass. To his astonished delight, it slid like a dream. Luck seemed to be coming his way at last.

He had his right foot through the open window when he stopped and looked back.

One of the hinges had come flying off and gone clattering across the floor. The others wouldn't hold much longer. The monster would break through within seconds, spot the open window, duck back out, circle the cottage and come straight after him. He'd have a narrow lead, but he could manage nothing more than a quickish hobble. If the damage to the monster's foot was minimal, it would run him down long before he could find a place to hide.

"*You don't have a choice,*" his brain hissed. "*Get out of here, fool. Now.*"

But the bitch of it was, he *did* have a choice.

The wicker basket.

Dominic stared at the basket with a curious blend of misery and hope. When the monster saw the open window, it would assume he had run. It wouldn't expect him to corner himself. What sort of crazy coward would curl up into a ball and wait for death rather than take off like the wind when the chance presented itself?

The sort of crazy coward, Dominic reflected, who *couldn't* run like the wind, who had been sunburnt so severely that he could barely walk. But the monster didn't know that. It had only glimpsed him, and it had lousy eyesight. It had no reason to think that he was wounded, that he hadn't the energy to push on.

Dominic hesitated, desperate to hit the path and take his chances, so at least he could die in the open, trying to escape. Maybe the monster would kill him cleanly, a single swipe to the back of his head. He might not even realise he'd been killed. No pain. No torment. No drawn-out dread.

But he didn't want to die. He wanted to live. So, hating himself for having had the idea in the first place, he drew back his foot, limped to the wicker basket, opened it and climbed in, lowering the lid over his head no more than a few seconds before the monster finally kicked the door loose of its frame and barged into the room.

## SIXTY-SIX

The monster screeched with triumph, swinging its arms like a pair of scythes, eagerly looking for its foe. Inside the basket Dominic tried not to tremble, not wanting to give away his position. He could see out between a few of the strands, but only vaguely.

When the monster saw no sign of the human, it stopped, bewildered. It turned in a slow circle, studying all four corners of the room, then glanced up at the ceiling. It made a soft squeaking noise that Dominic translated as, "What the fuck?"

Next, the monster bent and picked up the door, as if it expected to find a squashed human underneath. In the basket, Dominic struggled to suppress a chuckle.

With a frustrated grunt, the monster spun the door across the room. It smashed into the bedding and hit the wall with a muffled *whumph*. One of the hinges, which was still attached to the door, broke free and rolled across the floor, coming to rest in front of the wicker basket and a horrified Dominic.

The monster's gaze followed the hinge and flicked idly over the basket. Then it paused, cocked its head and took a step forward. Dominic gripped his knife firmly and readied himself to fight. He bit down on his lip to cut short a whimper. The monster took another step towards the wicker basket, then...

...spotted the open window, bared its fangs and made a furious hissing sound. Abandoning interest in the basket, it hurried to the window and sniffed the air. Roaring furiously, it stuck its arms and head outside and tried to pull the rest of its body through.

Dominic couldn't believe the beast could be that dumb. There was no way it could slip through so small an opening. It was going to get stuck. He'd be able to climb out, walk up behind the monster and carve his name in its hideous flesh before driving his knife into its heart and paying it back for killing Curran.

Eager to seek retribution, Dominic poked up the lid of the basket. Then he stopped, eyes widening, barely able to comprehend what he was seeing.

The monster made a choking sound, and as it did, its stomach seemed to cave in. The beast shuffled its feet further away from the window and a bulge developed above its arse as its insides shifted.

Dominic knew he should stay down, but he couldn't help himself. He prodded the lid up another fraction with the top of his head so that he could see clearly. From this angle, he was able to watch as the monster's chest, free from the bulk of its stomach, slipped easily through the window.

There was now a sizeable gap between the monster's midriff and the window sill. As an almost hypnotised Dominic stared with astonishment, the beast's guts-packed stomach oozed forward a roll at a time, slipping through the hole like a string of condoms filled with jelly being fed through the slot of a letterbox.

Within a few seconds the monster had worked its stomach out of the room and was able to drag its legs after itself. Now clear of the window, it took off with a vicious cry of intent, to hunt for its prey among the moonlight-bathed trees.

Back inside the cottage, Dominic wheezed, "Unbe-fucking-lievable." Then, with no idea how long the monster might be gone, he made up his mind to act swiftly and take off in the opposite direction. His plan had succeeded so far. Now he had to make the monster's confusion work in his favour.

Pushing the lid all the way open, Dominic stood up quickly, to step out of the basket and take to the forest. But the sudden rush of blood to his brain threw him off-balance. He felt his stomach lurch. Familiar warning flares went off inside his head. He had time to say "Oh," but before he could finish it with "no," he had fainted and collapsed back into the basket, almost as dead to the world as the corpse in the cellar beneath.

## SIXTY-SEVEN

The cottage was silent when Dominic came to. For a while he thought he was in bed at home. He'd had some strange dream about Curran, a monster and lots of rats. He wasn't normally an exotic dreamer, so he reached over to wake Martini, to tell her what his brain had conjured up.

When his hand hit a panel that shouldn't have been there, he frowned and sleepily explored with his fingers. His head was leaning against what felt like stiff rope. There was a similar panel on the other side, and overhead as well. Finding himself boxed in, and still uneasy from his dream, he blinked himself properly awake and focused.

That was when the memories kicked in and the pain returned.

Groaning, Dominic put the pleasant diversion of dreamland behind him and checked through the slats in the basket. No sign of the all-too-real monster. Prodding the top of the basket open with his head, he crawled out, arms and legs stinging as he moved. Some of the blisters on his back had popped while he'd been comatose, and his torso was now covered in a sticky, yellow film. He deliberately didn't look down at the congealed pus and blood. He was afraid he might faint again if he did.

He couldn't believe he'd fainted. Everything had been playing his way. If he could have just kept his damn eyes open for a few more minutes he would have been out of here.

Then again, as he leant against the basket and woozily reflected, he guessed he should be thankful that he hadn't fainted in the cellar. He could just as easily have passed out there, and if he had, it would have been lights out forever.

Dominic's brain was pounding, due to sunstroke and dehydration, so it was hard for him to focus, but he forced himself to take stock. There was no telling if or when he might black out again, so he needed to act while he was in control.

He couldn't see or hear the monster, so hopefully it was off deep in the woods, hunting for him. But he had no idea how much time had passed. It might have been a few minutes or it might have been hours. Maybe the monster had abandoned the hunt and was on its way back.

"*Move your arse, Newt,*" he croaked, sounding like Curran. He winced as he recalled his crucified, rat-infested friend, but this wasn't the time to dwell on that. Get out, get safe, get back to civilisation. If he achieved those goals, there would be all the time in the world for mourning. Until then, every other concern had to be put on hold.

His legs were stiff and tingling with pins and needles. He gave them a shake and worked his arms, moaning with the pain that caused, then lumbered towards the doorway, heading for the great outdoors and its promise of freedom.

He was almost at the opening when he stopped and frowned. He was missing something. He weaved from side to side, trying to work out what it might be. Not clothes or shoes — he remembered that long, naked trek from the lake. No bottles of water either. So what was it? Why did he feel uneasy and unpro…

"…tected," he sighed. The knife. It must have slipped from his grip while he was unconscious.

Dominic glanced back at the wicker basket, then at the doorway. Speed was of the essence, but the knife might come in handy. Even if the monster didn't track him down, there might be other threats to contend with, wolves or whatever. He could slice his way through bushes with it, cut and sharpen branches if he needed a walking stick or spear, maybe stab a rabbit or squirrel if he was hungry. It would be foolish to leave the weapon behind when it would only take him a few seconds to retrieve it.

Muttering darkly, Dominic limped back to the basket, grimacing every painful step of the way. More blisters popped on his back and he could feel the slimy pus oozing down his flesh.

He spotted the knife immediately, lying on the wicker floor. He was lucky it hadn't dug into him while he was unconscious and added to his woes.

He started to lean into the basket, then thought better of it. Another rush of blood might knock him out again. Better to minimise his movements. Holding tight to the side of the basket, he bent slowly and knelt beside it. Then, keeping his head upright, he reached in, cast around for the knife and picked it up.

"There," Dominic smiled, studying the knife in his hand. "Now I'm ready for anything this stinking forest throws at…"

He stopped. He thought he'd caught a glimpse of something in the knife's blade. It was probably his imagination but he turned the blade slowly back towards him.

The knife was an old, stained thing, rusted and bloodied, but there was enough metal on show to reflect Dominic's sunburnt, blistered features. And when he turned it another few degrees, the blade reflected the bedding on the floor, then the discarded door, and finally the gaping doorway…

…which was filled with the bulk of the obese monster, standing in the middle of the opening, gawping at the knelt-over human, hardly able to believe its stroke of luck.

## SIXTY-EIGHT

Dominic moved first and started to rise. The monster responded with a gleeful shriek and came lurching across the room. Dominic swept his hand up, hoping to stab the monster in the chest, but the beast saw the glinting blade and slashed at the human's limb with a beefy forearm.

As the blade was knocked from his grasp, Dominic cried out with fear. He tried to run, but the monster clubbed his back with an elbow and he collapsed with a roar of pain, feeling even more of the blisters explode.

If the monster had fallen on him and dug in with its nails and fangs, Dominic would have been unable to fight back, as he was momentarily dazed. But the creature was intrigued by the sticky stains where it had hit the human. It hadn't seen anything like them before and knew nothing of sunburn or its associated blisters. So instead of finishing off the feebly struggling figure on the floor, it studied its arm with fascination, then extended its tongue and licked exploratively. Liking what it tasted, it proceeded to lick further, running its long, red tongue over the translucent skin.

Dominic couldn't see what the monster was doing, but his head was clearing and he frantically looked around, seeking a way out. He spotted the knife close by. Not pausing to think, he grabbed it, half-turned and jammed the blade into one of the monster's legs.

The monster howled and kicked Dominic. He was withdrawing the blade to strike again. When the monster kicked him, it only succeeded in driving its leg further down on the knife. Blood gushed from the wound, striking Dominic between the eyes.

The monster howled again, in real pain now. Half-blind from the blood, but clutching the knife tightly, Dominic tried to get up and take the fight to his opponent. The monster grabbed him as he was rising. Its nails dug into his stomach and it was Dominic's turn to scream. But his scream was cut short when the monster hurled him across the room, to smash into the wall that it had thrown the door against earlier.

The wind exploded out of Dominic, the knife went flying from his hand across the floorboards, blisters on his back popped like crazy, and he collapsed in an agonised huddle on the bedding. Stars danced along his field of vision and he expected to faint again, but somehow he stayed conscious.

Over by the basket, the monster was hopping on one foot, making a miserable squealing noise. Dark blood pumped from the wound in its leg. Its stomach lifted and fell repeatedly. Then the monster leant over and vomited. There were bits of human flesh mixed in with the bile but Dominic failed to notice that, which was probably for the best.

As he sat up, choking and wheezing, the monster screeched and closed in on him, determined to make him pay for what he'd done.

Dominic blinked blood from his eyes and looked for the knife. It was too far away. He'd never reach it in time.

Then he spotted one of the reclaimed floorboards beneath the disturbed bedding of leaves and grass. The end that he could see was splintered. With nothing else to defend himself with, he grabbed the plank and swung it up towards the monster, gurgling defiantly as it launched itself at him.

The monster saw the human point the board, but it had already thrown itself forward, so it was too late to halt or turn aside. Screaming with panic now, it tried to knock the board aside, but it was a fraction too slow and the splintered end sliced into the creature's stomach. The other end dug sharply into Dominic's chest, bringing another pained cry to his cracked lips. But that end of the board was blunt and didn't cut through his flesh.

As the board was stopped short by Dominic's sternum, the monster's momentum drove it forward and it was impaled on the makeshift stake. Its bulging stomach slid along the length of the board until it pressed into Dominic's face and came to an agonising halt.

Dominic turned his head away from the monster's sweaty folds of flesh and gasped for air. The monster was gasping too, but with a wretched rasp.

For several seconds they lay joined in that strange fashion, like lovers after the moment of climax. Then the monster staggered backwards, blinking dumbly, blood dripping from its snout and flowing from the hole in its stomach, down the board – still lodged in its guts – to splash on the floor.

The monster backed across the room and finished up sitting on the wicker basket, the lid of which had swung closed again. It stared at the board jutting out of its stomach. Raised a hand to touch it. Decided not to and let the hand drop.

Across the way, Dominic forced himself to his feet. He felt as if he'd been assaulted by a burly lunatic with a sledgehammer. He'd been bruised by the locals from Laki, but that beating was nothing compared with this. His back would be black and blue for weeks to come. He'd be lucky if ribs weren't broken. There was a good chance that he was bleeding internally.

But he couldn't worry about that. The tide of battle had improbably turned his way and he had to end this while he had the advantage. The monster's wound looked fatal, but Dominic had seen how it could shift its stomach. Maybe it would pull that trick again, bunch its guts and inner organs clear of the damaged area, then carry on as normal.

He could have run, but if the monster recovered and chased him, it would surely make no mistake the next time. It was strike now and secure victory, or hobble off like a coward and maybe pay the price further down the line.

Gritting his teeth against the pain, as he had so many times this mad and grisly night, Dominic shuffled over to where the knife had come to a rest. He picked it up, paused while fireworks went off inside his head, then warily edged towards the stricken monster.

The beast watched him as he drew towards it. It was making a soft mewling noise, the lips at the end of its snout quivering pathetically, blood smeared across its jaw, flowing down its nippleless chest to merge with the blood pooling around the area of its stomach where the board was imbedded.

With a small choking sound, the monster weakly extended a hand in Dominic's direction, pleading for help.

"You've got to be fucking joking," Dominic snarled.

Then he fell upon the monster and stabbed wildly. He wept as he drove his knife into the soft, barely resisting walls of the creature's stomach, hot tears rolling down his cheeks, moaning with horror, never having killed anything larger than an insect before. This was the most horrific thing he'd ever attempted, and it hardly mattered that the beast had killed Curran and tried to kill Dominic too. That didn't make the sickening execution any easier.

But this was a duel to the death and mercy wasn't an option, so he ignored the monster's shrieks of torment, its gurgling moans for mercy and the way its hands slapped weakly against his arms, and kept on stabbing, knife sinking in deeper each time, widening existing holes, slicing through guts, organs, lungs, heart. He cried out as he stabbed, "Die, you bastard, die!" And he kept moaning that over and over, weeping at the same time, until it became more of a plea than a command.

The monster stiffened then slumped, and life drained from its eyes, but Dominic didn't stop, stabbing repeatedly, wailing like a frightened child, his arm a piston, the knife his only ally in the world, continuing until there was almost nothing left of the stomach wall, until he was absolutely certain.

And at that final point he pushed himself off, threw the knife away with a cry of triumph and self-hatred, then huddled up in a ball on the floor, where he lay in a pool of blood, shreds of flesh and tears, and trembled like a baby as he wept.

## SIXTY-NINE

Dominic lay on the floor for a long time. He was crying so hard that his whole body was shaking. Every so often, as the tears began to subside, he'd look at the corpse spreadeagled across the top of the basket, and that would set him off again.

He felt wretched and mean. It had been self-defence, but he still found it hard to excuse what he'd done. Deformed monster and killer that it was, until a short while ago it had been a living creature. Now it was a pile of rotting meat. And Dominic had been its executioner.

Maybe he should have run, left it huffing and puffing, impaled on the piece of wood. It might have survived, crawled free, licked its wounds, shuffled off to…

"What?" he snorted. "Kill another innocent like Curran?"

Anger flared in his heart and he stopped crying for a moment to glare at the monster's corpse.

"Fuck it," he snarled. "It got what it had coming. It killed Curran and I bet there are other bones in that cellar. It might have killed dozens… hundreds…"

Tears filled his eyes again as he recalled his butchered friend. He would have to come back with the police when he told them about this. They'd want him to show them the way, maybe lead them down into the cellar.

He hunched over and wept some more, dreading having to tell Martini that he was a killer, having to tell Curran's parents that their son was dead, having to tell this story for the rest of his life. It would be easier if he could slink out of here and forget about this, never mention it to anyone.

But that wasn't an option. If he'd come to this forest by himself, he could have left the monster to steam in its juices, slipped away, returned home and resumed his normal life. But Curran's body had to be retrieved and laid to rest. He couldn't just abandon it.

Curran had never spoken of his final wishes. While he'd often waxed lyrical about death, he'd never said what he would like done with his remains. Dominic figured it was too late to ask him now. Curran's parents would have to decide.

Eventually, when he had no tears left to shed, Dominic pushed himself to his feet with a moan and stood, weaving in the dim candlelight – one of the candles had quenched and there wasn't much life left in the other – waiting to see if he would faint. When he didn't, he shuffled across to survey his handiwork.

The monster's mouth was open, blood drying on its cheeks, gaze fixed lifelessly on the ceiling. Dominic stared at the bone curving out of its head, its snout and fangs, its massive frame, its see-through skin, and wondered where such a creature had hailed from.

He would have heard of a beast like this if its existence was common knowledge. He occasionally read a magazine called Fortean Times, which focused on frogs falling from the sky, people spontaneously combusting, that sort of thing. Its reporters had often written about the search to find a Yeti, Bigfoot, Abominable Snowman or whatever you wanted to call it.

Had he found proof that such beings were real? Was this a parallel version of humanity, its ancestors having developed in tandem with his over the millennia, hidden away from the prying eyes of the world until now? Or was it a more recent genetic mutation, the result of inbreeding, radioactive spillage or mad chemical experiments?

In truth, Dominic didn't care about the monster's origins. It had tried to kill him, they'd fought, and he'd defeated it. That was all that really mattered.

"Thought you were a big guy," he sniffed. "Thought you could rip me apart and pick my bones clean, easy as you please." He shook his head. "You shouldn't have fucked with me." He didn't say it mockingly, but miserably. He truly wished the monster had left him alone, that he hadn't been forced to slaughter such a unique creature. For all he knew it was a one-off and he'd robbed the world of a singular specimen, as guilty in the species-ending table of shame as the guy who'd killed the last dodo.

"I'm sorry," Dominic whispered, and stretched out a hand, planning to shut the monster's oddly aligned eyes, to afford it at least that much dignity.

A high-pitched noise tore through the air.

Dominic flinched and took a startled step backwards, sure for a moment that the monster wasn't dead, that it had only been injured, that it was about to leap to its feet and…

"No," he chuckled edgily. The monster was finished. There could be no doubt about that. He had imagined the whistling noise. Not surprising really. As freaked out as he was, he was surprised he wasn't hallucinating all sorts of crazy stuff.

Then the noise pierced the air again. Only this time he realised it was coming from outside, and it was slightly different to the sound the monster had made, and he knew for sure that it was real.

Wheeling away from the cooling corpse, Dominic limped over to one of the windows at the front of the cottage and stared out at the moonlit glade. His heart was beating quickly again, and the dryness in his mouth had nothing to do with dehydration.

For several long, blissful seconds he couldn't see anything and was able to start believing again that he had imagined the noise.

Then the bushes on the path into the clearing rustled and a monster stepped out into the open. This beast was the same shape as the one lying dead on the wicker basket, only broader and bigger, over three metres tall.

As Dominic stared, appalled, the beast paused, leant back and scratched a lower section of its stomach, revealing a penis even longer and thicker than the dead monster's. And Dominic knew in that instant, beyond a shadow of a doubt, what their relationship had been, and he found himself whispering, awestruck and horrified in equal measures…

*"Daddy's home."*

## PART FIVE

*"run, run as fast as you can"*

*The elder beast had spent the night hunting by itself. It often hunted apart from its son, now that its offspring was old enough to operate solo. That was part of its training. It had to learn to fend for itself. This was a hard world, and the beasts had to toughen up at a young age if they were to successfully negotiate it.*

*The beast had been troubled the night before when its son had come back with one of their two-legged enemies. They never killed many of this breed, knowing the problems it could generate, and the beast was worried that others would come looking for their missing companion. It had spent most of the day on watch in the trees around the shack, ready to pull out at the first whiff of danger, snoozing fitfully while its child played with its catch, killing the man slowly, teasingly.*

*When night fell again, the beast relaxed. Their enemies were more naturally suited to the day world. If others were to come, they would have done so when the sun was shining. It felt safe now, though it would remain on alert, and they'd have to move on sooner than planned.*

*The beast considered abandoning the shack when the sun set, but it wanted to punish its son first. The younger beast shouldn't have abducted the creature without its father's permission. It needed to be taught a lesson.*

*As the young beast tried to follow its father out of the cellar, having wrung the last of the life out of its plaything, the beast growled and pushed it back. Shaking its head, it made it clear that its son was to spend the night in the cellar with the rats. The young beast had whined and made threatening growls of its own, but obeyed its father and stayed as ordered.*

*The beast knew its commands wouldn't be respected forever. Its son would turn on it eventually, as it had turned on its father during its own coming of age. There would be a direct challenge, a fight for dominance. If the beast won, the child would continue to serve under its parent's watchful eye until it was ready to make another attempt to assert its authority. When it finally triumphed and stood victor over its sire, the elder beast would limp away and that would be the end of their relationship. They would probably never see one another again after that, and if they did, it would be as equals and competitors, and one of them would very likely kill the other.*

*The beast paused and thought about the night when its son would cast it aside. It wasn't much given to looking ahead, but occasionally it contemplated the future, the loneliness it would experience, the death it would have to face at some point.*

*It had been a quiet night in the forest. The beast had hunted half-heartedly, still wary of other men coming to search for the one who'd been taken. It had spent much of its time checking various paths in the forest, making sure they were clear.*

*Now, thinking of its growing son and the time when they would have to part, it grew maudlin. The child wouldn't be ready to challenge it for another few years, but that was not a long period and the months would fly by. These nights were precious. The beast should be spending as much time as it could with its beloved son, because soon enough they would become rivals and strangers.*

*The beast made a low-pitched whining noise and decided to return earlier than usual. It had been harsh on the child. It would go back to the shack, invite its son out to hunt, and then they'd move on together, ahead of any posse, to set up base in another dark, rarely disturbed area of the forest, where they could rest easily, enjoy one another's company, and bask in the love that would soon be nothing but a distant memory.*

## SEVENTY

As the larger monster started towards the cottage, Dominic drew away from the window and bit back a whimpering cry. This beast was taller and stronger than the one he had killed. In fact the monster he'd so valiantly defeated was probably still a child. When *Daddy* hit the scene and saw what the human had done, Dominic was fucked.

He set off for the rear window but he could barely walk. He was a severely sunburnt cripple after his experiences of the last twenty-four hours. He doubted he'd be able to climb out of the window, never mind race away from the cottage.

His terrified gaze settled on the corpse on the wicker basket and he paused. "No," he croaked, seeing what he must do, but dreading it even more than he had earlier in the night. But he'd no other realistic option. If he was to stand even a slim chance of getting out of here alive, he'd have to hide before he could flee.

He couldn't act quickly, but the monster was dawdling outside. Dominic didn't know what was keeping it. Maybe it had stopped to scratch its balls. If he hadn't been in a rush, he might have giggled at that notion, but there was precious little time to play with and he was determined not to waste a second of it.

Stumbling to where the younger monster lay sprawled across the top of the basket, Dominic grabbed its elephant-like ears and pulled. It wasn't as heavy as he'd feared, but it was by no means a light load. It slid forward a few centimetres, then he had to stop, take a breath, gather his strength and try again.

It took him four attempts to move the monster far enough for gravity to take hold. As it started to roll to the floor, Dominic suddenly considered the noise it might make. A satisfied smile had been forming on his lips. That disappeared in an instant and he thrust his knees forward, bending at the same time, like a limbo dancer.

The corpse landed on Dominic, whose legs buckled, and he ended up being pinned. He had muffled the sound as planned, but now he lay trapped beneath the dead monster. As blisters popped and agony wracked his body, he had to grind his teeth to hold in a cry of pain, not wanting to alert the slain beast's father.

Rolling his eyes wildly, Dominic arched his back and pulled with his hands, terror granting him the ability to temporarily ignore the pain. The monster's body started to slide down his chest, leaving a bloody, slimy trail. He thought he was going to suffocate when it got stuck while passing over his face, but then he tore his nose sideways and it jerked free.

When he had enough space to wriggle out, he hauled himself to his knees, cast one distraught glance at the door – no sign of the elder creature – then pushed up the lid of the basket.

He paused before getting in, abruptly remembering the knife, his only means of defending himself. There was no sign of it, so he figured it must be lying beneath the monster's remains. He thought of digging around for it, but there was no time.

Cursing silently, the knifeless, hapless Dominic slid into the basket, pulled the lid closed and lay down in the gloom. Closing his eyes, he said a quick prayer, then waited for all unholy hell to break loose.

## SEVENTY-ONE

He heard the steps outside creak as the monster mounted them. Then a pause as it stopped to stare at the open doorway and wonder what had happened to the door. Then a sharper creak as it stepped on to the boards. Another pause when it caught sight of the scene inside. Then...

The monster howled with disbelief and grief. It was more piercing than any sound the younger beast had managed, like the scream of a steam train's whistle.

Dominic's eyes snapped open and he jammed his hands over his ears, hissing with discomfort. The cry of the monster continued, slicing through his head the way his knife had sliced through its son's innards.

Unable to help himself, Dominic leant closer to the wall of the wicker basket, to peer at the wailing monster. It was still standing on the planks. It had caught hold of its ears and was tugging them, clearly distressed.

A sickened Dominic numbly studied the father of the slain beast. Its arms rippled with muscles and its fingers were thicker than its son's, although still out of place with the rest of its massive body. Its guts were darker than the child's. The bone jutting out of its forehead was longer, actually touching the tip of its nose. Its feet were so big that it could have squashed Dominic's head with one of them.

He shivered as he thought of the monster stamping on his head, squishing it underfoot, grinding it into the dirt.

Then the monster's cry ended and it tried to barge into the room. It was too wide to fit through the doorway and it got stuck for a moment, the way its son had in the window. But like its child, the beast juggled its guts, so that its stomach oozed through, making way for the rest of its body to follow.

When it was inside, it ducked to avoid hitting its head on the ceiling – Dominic re-estimated and reckoned the monster might be three and a half metres tall – then hurried to where its child had been dumped on the floor.

The monster sank beside its butchered son. Even through the limiting veil of the wicker strands, Dominic could see the horror and pain in the monster's eyes. It made a short quivering sound, and Dominic was sure that it was calling to the youngster.

The sound came again, curtly this time, and Dominic was reminded of all the times his parents had called after him when he was a child and running off to play when he was supposed to stay with them. "Dominic?" one or other of them would sing. Then, when he failed to respond, they'd snap, "Dominic!"

This was what the monster was doing, and in a weird way it was heartbreaking, even for the bloodied, battered human in the basket.

The stricken monster had landed on its side. Its father turned the beast on to its back and stared at the ruined mess of its stomach. It reached out towards the holes, but stopped before it touched the jagged strands of flesh.

Switching its attention to the dead creature's head, the monster lovingly lifted it and slid a massive arm underneath. It made a cooing noise as it turned the beast's face one way then the other, vainly searching for signs of life. With its free hand it stroked the bone curving down the front of the youth's face. Then it leant over and pressed its own arched bone to the child's, like an elephant nuzzling its calf.

For a long time it stayed that way, hunched over, making sad little noises. It didn't cry, which made Dominic suspect that these creatures were incapable of producing tears.

Then, without warning, the monster thrust the dead beast's head aside and slammed a fist into the floor. It screeched wildly, hatefully, and Dominic thought his ears were going to burst.

The monster pushed itself to its feet and screamed again. Then it grabbed the door which its son had torn free, picked it up and started slamming it into the wall, not stopping until it had shattered into pieces in its hands.

When it had no more door to vent its rage on, it punched the wall, using its elbows rather than its fists. It knocked holes in the crumbling logs, and a couple of them shifted alarmingly. Dominic was worried that they might tear free and bring the roof crashing down.

But the logs held and the monster moved on, transferring its attention to the windows. It went from one to another, smashing every pane of glass, shrieking out into the night through the holes, challenging the world to send a champion its way, something for the beast to grapple with and kill.

When it came to the last window, the one at the rear, the monster smashed it as it had the others, then paused. With the front two, it had swept a hand around the frame to knock out every last shard of glass. But this time it didn't do that. Instead it snapped off one of the longer remaining shards with its left hand, stared at it a while, then deliberately dragged the pointed tip down its right arm, from elbow to wrist, carving a shallow gulley in its own flesh, from which blood began to seep.

The blood calmed the monster. Its shoulders slumped and it moaned piteously, shuffling its feet. Letting the piece of glass drop, it licked the wound in its arm, then cradled it to its chest, as it had cradled its dead son's head.

And then, as Dominic's heart went out to it, the beast turned, looked around the room with an angry glint in its eyes, and set its sights on the basket.

## SEVENTY-TWO

Dominic was certain that the monster had spotted him or caught his scent, that it knew he was hiding in the basket. It stood, staring across the room, chest heaving as it took deep, ragged breaths. Dominic noted dully that the father, like the son, had no nipples.

Then the beast was walking slowly towards him. Dominic would have shot out of the basket and made a break for freedom, but his limbs were lifeless. He could only lie in the shade, eyes wide, watching his executioner close in for the kill.

The monster stopped when it drew abreast of its murdered child. It gazed at the corpse, an unreadable expression on its face. One of its hands slowly snaked out and came to rest on the lid of the basket. Its fingers drummed softly, nerve-wrackingly, Dominic flinching at every tap, expecting the monster to rip open the basket and yank him out.

Careful not to tread on its dead son, the monster slid between the body and the basket. It stopped drumming. Dominic knew it would happen now. The monster would open the lid, grin viciously at its trapped prey, maybe screech its equivalent of "Peekaboo!" And then the bloodletting would commence.

The moment stretched out. The waiting was torment. Dominic wanted to stick his head up and shout, "Here I am!" Just to get it over and done with.

But then, to his confusion, the monster turned. Looking up, he caught a glimpse of a hairless arse, lower intestine disgustingly visible through the translucent skin of its cheeks, a smooth ball sack wedged between the folds of flesh, thick penis dangling over it.

As he gawped, the monster sat and leant against the wall. And then, disproving Dominic's earlier theory about tears, it started to weep.

It wept softly, a low keening noise. Dominic couldn't see the tears, but could picture them by the sounds it was making and the way its body shook desolately. He imagined that he had cut a similar figure not that long ago, when he'd wept freely in the middle of the room.

After a while the monster leant forward and pulled the corpse closer. Sliding its hands beneath the dead child's back, it lifted the body and settled it across its lap, sitting it up so that its head wouldn't hang over the end of the basket.

There was a long, sustained silence after that, broken only by the occasional sob-like squeak.

Inside the basket Dominic tried not to move, knowing the slightest sound might give him away.

After a while drops dripped onto Dominic's head. He thought at first that they were the monster's tears, but they kept on coming. Even a beast this size couldn't produce tears that heavy and warm and...

Dominic grimaced. *Blood.* No fresh blood had flowed while the dead monster was on its back, but now that it had been moved into an upright position, the red stuff was oozing out. It must have trickled down its father's legs, pooled on top of the basket, and was now seeping through.

Dominic wanted to brush away the drops. He shivered, hating this baptism of blood, worried that the monster's foul liquid might infect his open wounds and the places where blisters had popped. (He had forgotten that he was already heavily smeared from their fight.) But if he moved, the living monster might hear. He had to keep still, not make a noise, and hope that...

His stomach rumbled.

Dominic's face paled beneath its layers of burnt skin. He held his breath and listened for any change in the monster's breathing. But if it had heard, it had dismissed the noise as a creaking of the boards or a settling of the earth. He'd got away with it. No harm done. All was well.

His stomach rumbled again. Louder this time.

Dominic thought he heard the monster grunt, but it was hard to tell over the suddenly increased beating of his heart.

He had to stop his stomach rumbling, but how? He was parched, starving and cramped. He could control his fingers and toes, stop them from trembling. But his stomach wasn't under his control. He could normally hold in a fart (Martini might claim otherwise), but how could he make the rumbling noises go away? It wasn't like he could tuck into steak and chips, washed down with beer.

Dominic gulped drily, tongue twitching as he thought about downing a pint of lovely, cold beer. He tried to push the image from his head, sure that his stomach would rumble louder if his brain flashed a picture of a pint its way. He considered some form of meditation, hoping it might distract him.

But then he paused. The best way to settle a rumbling stomach was to fill it. As he'd already noted, he had no steak and chips to tuck into.

But there was blood.

Dominic's stomach turned – quietly, praise God – as he thought about drinking the dead monster's blood. He'd eaten black pudding in Ireland. He'd tried blood sausage in a Polish restaurant that Martini had dragged him to. And he had often tasted his own blood, when he nicked himself shaving and licked a finger to dab the cut with spit. The finger always came away bloody, and rather than muddy the shaving water, he would suck on it until it was clean, then carry on shaving.

But he'd never drunk the crimson liquid. He didn't know anyone who had, or where you might get a cup if you fancied it — he doubted butchers were licensed to sell such goods.

Even if he'd been a seasoned connoisseur of all things blood-related, there was no way of knowing if the monster's blood was safe to drink. It might be poisonous. Hell, for all he knew it was acidic, like in the *Alien* movies. It might burn a hole through his throat and finish him off before

Daddy even knew that he was there.

Best not to chance it. He'd just struggle on and…

His stomach rumbled again. Dominic squeezed his eyes shut and swore loudly inside his head. Then, since fate seemed determined to put him ever further through the wringer, he turned his chin up, moved his head around until he felt drops on his nose, shifted slightly, opened his mouth, and lay there like a baby as blood dripped between his lips.

When his tongue was heavily soaked, he closed his mouth, clenched his fingers into fists and swallowed. He felt himself gag and forced himself not to. For a second he thought the blood was burning, but then decided that was just his dried-out oesophagus tightening as he got it working again.

Shaking his head glumly – but lightly, wary of making any noise – Dominic leant back again, opened wide and carried on drinking, growing fat on the spilled blood of the monster he had killed.

## SEVENTY-THREE

The blood stopped flowing eventually, but the monster didn't seem to notice. It sat there, cradling its lost child, moaning and weeping.

The last of the candles flickered out. Dominic expected the room to descend into darkness, but to his surprise he found that he could still see fairly well. That was when he realised that night had passed. It was day outside.

The night had lasted an eternity. Dominic wanted to stumble into the open air, spread his arms wide, turn his face up to the sun and cry with joy. No matter that the sun had burnt him so deeply, that it would hurt to stretch, that the rays might set off a chain reaction of itching across his flesh. The darkness had tormented him far worse than the light had. He couldn't wait to put it behind him.

But he would have to, because the monster gave no sign that it planned to move. It sat there like a rock, occasionally shifting a leg or arm, maybe to ward off pins and needles, but otherwise motionless.

Dominic concentrated on staying awake. If he fell asleep, a single snore could prove his undoing. But it was hard. He was exhausted. It was stuffy and gloomy in the basket. His body craved slumber.

He played mental games to focus. He did his twelve times tables up to twenty-three times twelve, which was where he lost the run of things. Then thirteen, fourteen, fifteen – that was easy, and he stopped in the end purely out of boredom – and sixteen. He started on seventeen, but the numbers were starting to blur in his head and he quit almost immediately.

He thought of odd words and tried to define their meaning. He recalled poems and songs he had learnt as a child. Replayed scenes from some of his favourite movies and TV shows, worked at them until they were word-perfect.

Still the monster didn't budge. Dominic couldn't understand why it just sat there. It must be uncomfortable, having borne the weight of its dead son for so long. Wouldn't it be happier if it shifted to what was left of the bedding and lay down with the corpse? It might even doze off in that position, clearing the way for Dominic to sneak away to freedom.

He thought of all the things he would do if he got out of here. He'd never made many long-term plans before, but that was going to change. He'd seen that life was short and precious. Before you knew it, you could be brown bread like Curran. He wasn't going to waste any more time. He'd build a career for himself when he got home, return to uni and study hard, or set up a business of his own.

Maybe he'd marry Martini, make an honest woman of her, start knocking out kids. Despite their arguments, he loved her, and was confident that she loved him. Children hadn't crossed his mind before. He'd always thought he'd deal with those in his thirties, when he was getting too old to party. But now he decided he didn't want to be alone like poor Curran at the end. He wanted heirs to look out for him, to help him when he was old, to mourn him when he was gone.

If he had a son, he'd call him Jerome in honour of his fallen friend. Although Curran had hated that name. Perhaps it would be best not to lumber the child with the handle. But he couldn't call the kid Curran, could he? Maybe he could sneak it in as a middle name. William Curran Newton, or David Curran Newton, something like that. Yeah, that might work. That... might...

Dominic yawned and, before he could catch himself, his eyelids fluttered shut and he fell asleep.

## SEVENTY-FOUR

He snapped awake and knew instantly where he was, that he had to keep quiet, that he shouldn't move a muscle. He didn't know how long he'd been asleep, but he felt much fresher, so it might have been a few hours, maybe longer. It certainly seemed a lot brighter outside.

He could see the monster's legs through the mesh of the wicker basket. If it had abandoned its perch, it was back in place now. But Dominic didn't think that it had moved. He was pretty sure he would have stirred if it had shifted.

He offered up a quick prayer of thanks for not having snored or grunted in his sleep. Martini often complained about the noises he made in bed. He'd taken her at her word, but now he was starting to think that she'd accused him unjustly.

He adjusted his limbs, shuddering and muffling pained yelps. The sunburn scorched through him every time he moved. His head was still pounding, and there was no telling if he might suffer long-term brain damage. His skin was covered in blood and filth — surely some of his wounds would get infected, if they hadn't already.

On top of all that, he was worried about being curled up for such a long time. He might end up with deep vein thrombosis. Curran had lived in fear of DVT. He'd grow nervous if he had to sit still for more than half an hour. He claimed that was why he'd stopped going to mass, for fear a long-winded priest might prove the end of him.

Dominic smiled sadly, wincing as daggers of pain swept across his cheeks. Poor Curran. What a waste. If only he could go back in time and warn him not to leer over the teenage girl.

Then again, Curran would have been tickled if he'd been told that lust would prove his downfall. Not a bad way to go, in the Curran scheme of things. Dominic had warned him that a jealous boyfriend or husband would stab him in the back one day. Curran had always shrugged and said, "Better to die young, chasing the scent of damp knickers, than live a long life as a celibate."

Dominic hoped it hadn't been too painful. Perhaps the monster had killed Curran before dragging him back to its lair. Maybe the ruination of his body came later, when Curran was unaware of what was being done to him. Dominic doubted that, but he could hope.

Then, as he was morbidly dwelling on Curran's last moments, Dominic's eyes widened with panic. A stabbing sensation in his groin made him realise why he'd woken. It wasn't because he was ready to rise and face the world. His brain had roused him early, as it often did on nights when he'd been pubbing or clubbing, in response to a distress signal sent by his bladder.

He needed to piss.

Sweat broke out across his forehead and he clenched his teeth. This was bad. With those wide nostrils, he assumed the monster had an advanced sense of smell. If Dominic let rip, surely it would catch the scent and open the lid to investigate. He had to hold it in, but that was easier said than done.

He tried the tricks that he usually employed if he got caught short on a long car or bus journey. He thought of sex to begin with — if he got an erection, that would cut off the flow for a while. It normally worked a treat, but today he couldn't find a single erotic nerve within himself. It didn't matter what sultry actress or model he settled on, or what kind of kinky set-up he devised. As soon as the jiggy-jiggy began, he'd recall the rats in Curran's ribcage, his empty eye sockets, the way the monster had thrashed feebly as life left its limbs.

When sex failed to distract him, Dominic focused on his finances. He tried to recall his bank balance, then estimated what his bills would be this month. The holiday meant he'd have to tighten his belt. Bulgaria was a cheap place to visit, but the costs would still add up. He'd have to spend a few quiet weekends in with Martini before he could go out on the lash again.

He thought about things he wanted, a new TV, video games, a jacket. He hadn't updated his wardrobe recently. Maybe it was time to go shopping for replacement T-shirts, a few pairs of trousers. No new sweaters or hoodies though, not until the weather changed. He didn't like to buy too far ahead, otherwise he ended up looking like last season's man, and Martini complained when he lagged behind in the fashion stakes.

He wished she'd buy his clothes for him. Liz had bought most of Curran's gear, the bulk of it with her own money. Dominic wouldn't have minded giving Martini money to shop for him – unlike Curran, he didn't take advantage – just as long as she let him have a few drinks in the pub while she went off and spent it.

But Martini made him buy his own clothes. "What am I, your mother?" she'd snort whenever he raised the subject. "Go buy your own stinking jeans, but choose wisely. I'll dump you if you start looking frumpy."

Dominic grinned as he pictured her chastising him, her Mexican accent breaking through. Sometimes he wound her up on purpose, just to hear the sexy accent.

To his delight he started to get hard, and his smile spread. That proved it was true love. The thought of threesomes with actresses didn't move him, but the memory of Martini's accent did. He was definitely going to propose to her if he got out of this alive. She deserved her dream walk down the aisle, even if only for the hard-on which had sustained him in this most troubling of times.

## SEVENTY-FIVE

Dominic held in the piss. And held it in. And held it in.

He was trying not to breathe, as even the slightest movement brought drops of urine to the tip of his penis. Some had already leaked and smeared across his inner thigh, not enough to alert the monster, but he feared letting go of any more.

He kept balling his hands up into fists, eyes squeezed shut, forcing back the flow of piss by strength of will alone. He'd grabbed his penis several times, when the battle had seemed lost, physically plugging the gap. But the pain had been excruciating the last time he'd done that, and he doubted he could stand it again.

As he lay there, shivering feebly, contemplating his awful fate when the floodgates opened, there was a heavy drumming sound above him. At first he thought it was rain, and he stared at the lid of the basket with confusion.

Then, while his face was turned upwards, the liquid dripped through the wicker strands and hit his lips. He knew instantly from the salty taste that this was no rainwater. The monster was pissing.

Dominic gagged and turned his head away, worried only about trying to avoid the stream of piss. Then he realised that this was a golden opportunity (he was too tired to appreciate the pun). If he acted quickly, the monster wouldn't hear or smell him over the noise and stench of its own foul waste.

With a blissful sigh, Dominic let go and piss shot from his penis and struck the wall of the basket. A lot of it bounced back over his shins and feet, but he didn't care, any more than he cared about the monster's piss that was flowing over him, soaking into his hair and sunburnt flesh.

"Let it snow, let it snow, let it snow," he sang inside his head, imagining piss-coloured snowflakes, giggling in spite of himself. Luckily the monster didn't hear — it was still pissing and the sound masked all others.

It became a competition to finish first, although only Dominic knew about the race. Watching the monster – he could see the urine coming from the beast's flaccid penis – he urged himself to piss faster, harder. He was hellbent on stopping before the beast, so that silence would reign when it shed its last drop.

The flow above him started to die away. Dominic almost screamed, "Don't stop, you bastard!" He still had a lot of piss to void.

But then the flow strengthened again and Dominic grinned madly, not caring about the piss that was hitting his chin and splashing into his nose and eyes. He could have been a birthday boy opening his presents, he looked so happy.

He hit his own moment of pause and thought about stopping. He could have, but was worried that he might need to go again before long if he didn't clear out the decks, so he forced himself to continue, squeezing tight.

They drew to an almost simultaneous halt. The monster flicked the last few drops from the tip of its glistening penis. Dominic wanted to do the same, but didn't dare move his arm, so he settled for flexing his stomach a few times and wiggling his hips slightly.

As the sharp scent of piss filled the air of the basket around him, Dominic leant back, content to let it dry in. This was a small enough punishment. He would endure it gladly if this was the worst he had to suffer. He'd lie here, quiet as a mouse, stewing in piss, and wait for the monster to move on. He figured it would go when night fell, which hopefully wasn't more than a few hours away.

But as things turned out, he didn't have to wait that long. To his surprise the beast rose once it had finished pissing, and picked up the body of its dead child. He thought it would howl at the ceiling or start weeping again, but it only walked across the room and out through the doorway, juggling its guts around to slip through.

Dominic felt aggrieved at first. If the monster had planned to leave, why the hell hadn't it waited to piss outside?

But that feeling swiftly passed as he realised what this meant. The monster had left the cottage and taken its son's corpse with it. Dominic had no idea whether the beast was intelligent or how it operated emotionally. But it had wept for its murdered child, and now it had carted off the body rather than leave it behind to rot.

That made him suspect that the beast planned to bury the dead creature, or at least dispose of its remains in a fitting way. Perhaps it would simply lay the body to rest in the cellar and let the rats chew on it. Or maybe it would take the corpse to a sacred place deep in the forest.

Either way, the chance to escape had come. The coward within him wanted to stay in the basket until he could be certain that the monster wasn't coming back. But what if it did, sooner than he expected, and holed up for a week of mourning, trapping a starving Dominic, ending all hope of him skittering away to freedom? No, he had to be brave, and it had to be now.

Pushing the lid of the basket open, he clambered out, groaning softly as yet more blisters popped and his skin scraped against the basket and then the floor. He lay there in a pool of blood, piss and pus, flexing his arms and legs, gasping and gritting his teeth against the pain, as well as the pins and needles which had temporarily crippled him.

Then, like some primordial, red-skinned, yellow-stained slug, he lurched to his feet, stumbled across the room, and practically threw himself through the doorway into sunlight.

## SEVENTY-SIX

Dominic hadn't anticipated how bright the sun would appear after such a long time in darkness. He felt as if he was being blinded, and he pulled up short with a startled cry. As he stood there, blinking stupidly, he was a helpless target. If the monster had paused nearby and spotted him, it could have turned and taken him down before he was even aware of the threat.

But nothing attacked him, and when he looked around a minute later, shielding his watering eyes with an arm, there was no sign of the beast or its dead offspring.

He thought of returning to the cellar to retrieve Curran's corpse and stash it somewhere safe in case the monster decided to get rid of it to remove the evidence. But he was in no fit state to climb down the tree trunk, never mind back up again with a skeleton slung across his shoulders.

"*Get the fuck out of here, Newt,*" he muttered in Curran's voice. "*I'm dead. There's nothing you can do for me now. Save yourself, fool.*"

"Sure thing, boss," Dominic sighed, his heart aching. "But I'll come back for you. I swear."

He looked for the start of the path and shuffled towards it. He expected the monster to leap out of the bushes at the last instant, screeching jubilantly, but he made it out of the glade without incident and was soon hobbling back to the lake.

He was pleased to be in the shade. Sunlight should have been delightful after being in the basket for so long, but his skin stung every time a ray danced across it. Like a pustule-dotted vampire, he would need to avoid the daytime world as much as possible over the coming days and weeks.

He studied his ruined body as he made slow but steady progress. The red sheen had darkened over the course of the night and day, and more blisters had formed. A lot of those had burst while he was climbing out of the basket, and more burst now as he dragged himself forward, leaving him pus-slick all over.

He wasn't sure if the monster's piss was a danger or a boon. While he was concerned that it might infect his open wounds, he had a vague memory that urine was an antiseptic. Hadn't he read that the Romans used it on their injuries, and even as mouthwash?

"I won't go that far," he wheezed. "I'll shower in the stuff, but I won't gargle with it."

He grinned crookedly at the disgusting thought, then focused on keeping his legs moving. It wasn't easy. This was the hardest physical thing he had ever attempted. He was in so much pain. Every step was a torment. He just wanted to crawl into the bushes, rest up for a few days, try again when it didn't feel as if he was driving nails into himself every time he twitched.

"*Stop*," he pleaded as Curran. "*Lie down. Relax. Recover.*"

"No," he grunted in response. "Can't. The monster might find me."

As well as that, he was aware that he would need water soon, and food. "Man cannot live on blood alone," he mumbled, wincing at the memory. Also his wounds needed to be dressed or his limbs might start to rot. He'd seen countless films and TV shows where gangrene set in and legs had to be amputated. (It was always a leg, never an arm. He supposed losing a leg made for better drama.)

The only time he stopped was when he came to the stream. Seen by daylight, it was no more than a trickle across the forest floor, but Dominic didn't care. As he'd done on his way to the cottage, he knelt, then lay down and lowered his face into the water, lips pressed against the pebbles as he sucked.

He saw movement reflected in the stream as he drank, and was sure the monster had found him. It would snatch him up now and tear into him. He closed his eyes, groaned – sending a flurry of bubbles flying out to either side of his mouth – then carried on drinking, determined to enjoy this final draught.

But it must have simply been the trees swaying in a breeze, because nothing disturbed him and he was able to sit up and blink dumbly a few minutes later as he glanced around and found himself still alone on the path.

"Seeing things," he scowled. "Got to stop. Mustn't let my imagination run riot."

Maybe it was the blood. It hadn't done him any harm when he'd drunk it, but perhaps it was kicking in now, like a hallucinogen.

"*No matter what you think you see, take no notice,*" he warned himself, mimicking Curran's voice again. "*Stick to the path. Don't freak out. Do like Dorothy and follow the yellow brick road.*"

"The only yellow round these parts is my pissy, pus-stained back," he noted.

"*Touché,*" he murmured drily. Then he stood, took a steadying breath, let his eyes readjust, and carried on back along the path.

## SEVENTY-SEVEN

The trek was endless, but Dominic was prepared for that. Last night it had been virgin territory, but today he knew what to expect, so he didn't lose heart. He kept his gaze on his feet, willing them forward, knowing it was going to take a long time, and that it would feel even longer. He was ready. Bring the fucker on!

He kept quiet as he limped along. He wanted to whistle or voice his thoughts out loud to pass the time, but he was wary of giving his position away — he had no idea where the monster had taken the body, and while it was unlikely that it had come this way, he couldn't rule it out.

The forest was full of noises, the rustle of trees, birds and small animals. The wind sometimes whispered as it blew through the leaves, sounding like the cry of the monster, at least to Dominic's addled brain. There were times when he was sure that the beast was clinging to a tree ahead of him, waiting to drop on him as he passed. But he never looked up and he never stopped. If he was to die on this path, so be it, but he refused to let fear unhinge him.

He thought a lot about Martini, and the vow he'd made to propose to her. She was a lovely girl, good for him in so many ways. She'd worked hard to put this holiday together, and he felt bad for the way he and Curran had mocked her, all the arguments they'd had, going off drinking instead of devoting his attention to her.

"Then again," he noted silently, "the holiday didn't turn out to be the best trip ever. Curran wouldn't be lying dead in a rat-infested cellar if we'd gone to Ibiza."

But that was hardly Martini's fault. She hadn't planned for them to fall in with a crowd of boisterous teenagers, to let themselves be driven out to the middle of nowhere and abandoned. If they'd stuck to her schedule, none of this…

His eyes narrowed as he followed the thought in another direction.

So far Dominic had written this off as a stroke of misfortune. Curran made a pass at a girl, her companions over-reacted, the pair of stranded tourists just happened to chance across the monsters.

But what if it had been intentional?

Could monsters like these live in anonymity so close to civilisation? The cottage wasn't much more than several kilometres from the nearest village. People didn't come along these paths often, but hunters must be at large, along with lumberjacks, people who made maps, all sorts of others. How could they be unaware of a couple of flesh-eating monsters in their midst?

Maybe they weren't. Maybe the locals knew about the monsters and tolerated them. Hell, maybe they worshipped the demonic-looking creatures. They might see the beasts as a proud Bulgarian secret, part of their heritage, something the rest of the world knew nothing about, an endangered species to be cherished, protected and... fed.

Dominic shook his head softly. His imagination was running wild again. This wasn't a creaky old Hammer movie, where swarthy-looking, mountain-dwelling locals smiled sinisterly as they directed dumb visitors towards Count Dracula's castle.

"Let the vampire kill the outsiders," Dominic pictured one of the characters saying in a thick Transylvanian accent. "It means he won't come after *us*."

Ridiculous. Absurd. Laughable.

And yet...

They *were* in the mountains. A pack of locals *had* taken him and Curran off into the middle of nowhere and left them there. And a monster most certainly *had* torn Curran to pieces and tried to rip Dominic apart too.

Maybe Curran hadn't wandered down this path by accident. Maybe the monster had been waiting for prey to be delivered to it. Maybe this was a regular treat for the forest-dwelling beasts, home delivery Bulgaria-style.

"No," Dominic croaked. It was insane. Too many people would have to keep quiet. Somebody would talk. It wasn't like it was years ago. Even a tiny town like Laki was connected to the outside world. The villagers had mobile phones and computers. They wouldn't be able to resist the riches on offer if they could present evidence of a Yeti to those who'd been looking for decades. One of them would make contact, seek a reward, sell the others out.

It had been dumb luck, that was all, bad timing for him and Curran, a gift from the gods as far as the monsters were concerned.

And yet, as he shuffled along the path, his thoughts all over the place, he couldn't dismiss the possibility that they'd been dropped in the shit by cunning, self-preserving villagers who had done this sort of thing before.

"Martini," he whispered, thinking of her alone in Laki, searching for him and Curran, a witness to their disappearance, a liability in the eyes of the locals. No, more than a liability — a *snack*.

If he wasn't going crazy… if his suspicions weren't unfounded… then getting out of this forest might not be the end of the matter. Worse might yet await.

## SEVENTY-EIGHT

Night was falling again. He felt cold and had been shivering for a long time. He was worried about the monster, the locals sacrificing Martini, being hauled back out here if he turned up in Laki and was discovered by the teenagers.

Then he came to a T-junction and all his fears were momentarily forgotten.

He stared at it for a long, stupid moment, not remembering this from the night before, wondering if he'd taken the wrong path from the cottage, heart dropping at the thought of having to backtrack.

Then he realised that he'd come to the end of the secondary path, and was back at the one which ran from the lake to the road.

Dominic wanted to sink to his knees and weep with joy, but he was drained and doubted he'd be able to get up again, so he simply stepped on to the path, looked left, right, then left again, trying to decide which direction to take.

If he turned right, the path would lead him to the road. He could hitch a lift or stumble along until he hit that village they'd passed on their way up. Maybe he'd ask the villagers for help, say nothing about the monster, get them to drive him to a hospital in a city — Asenovgrad wasn't far away, he mused, surprised and impressed that he could recall its name — then involve the police, tell them where Martini was staying, let them deal with the locals and run whatever risks that might entail.

But he was filthy, covered in blood, piss and pus. He was thirsty too, worried that he might faint from dehydration. The lake was a lot closer than the road. If he went back to it, he could drink, slip in and cool down, wash off the muck, so at least he'd look halfway human when he turned up in the village. It would also clean out his wounds.

"What if the piss is an antiseptic?" he asked himself. "I might end up doing more harm than good."

"*Yeah,*" he added in Curran's voice. "*And maybe the monster will come trotting along while you're bathing. Wade on in and drag you under.*"

He started to chew his lip, but that hurt, so he just stood and mulled over his options. The village was his ultimate destination, but he still wasn't sure how to play his hand. If he hung around here, the monster might find him, but it could just as easily run into him on the path too.

He glanced at the sky, which was darkening by the minute, as if the answer lay up there somewhere.

Then he sighed, shook his head feebly, and turned left. He was anxious to get out of the forest, but a half-hour one way or the other probably wouldn't make any difference, and the call of the lake was hard to ignore. He had a long night ahead of him. Better to go through it in a half-dignified state than turn up in the village looking and smelling like a wildman. Hell, if they caught sight of him in his current shape, they might think he was a wicked spirit and shoot him.

He had to admit that was unlikely, but…

"…in Bulgaria," he muttered darkly as he tramped towards the lake, "anything is possible."

## SEVENTY-NINE

He studied the clearing from the relative safety of the path before stepping out into the open. He felt vulnerable as he hobbled closer to the lake. The moon had filled out completely. There was some cloud cover, so it wasn't as bright as it had been the night before, but it was still bright enough for Dominic to see — and to be seen, if the monster was lurking in any of the bushes around the area.

"You should get out of here," he told himself. "This is bad news."

But he kept going, determined to clean himself, quench his thirst and formulate a plan of action. This way he felt in control of the situation, for the first time since he'd recovered consciousness by the edge of the lake and gone stumbling off down the path.

The water felt icy when he stuck in a foot, but it didn't hurt as much as it had the day before. He figured that was because of all the grime he was caked in. It would probably sting more when he was getting out.

He hesitated, not looking forward to that pain. But it would have to come at some point, and better to get it out of the way now rather than wait for a nurse to swab him clean, which would surely be a more drawn-out, painful process.

He stumbled forward, weeping softly as pus and blood were washed away, opening up fresh wounds. When he got to a point where he could crouch, he slid underwater with barely a pause, eyes fixed on the moon, not stopping until the water was to his chin.

"Now that's what I'm talking about," he sighed through his tears, feeling for a few delicious seconds as if he was in Nirvana.

Then he shivered and that set off a chain reaction. More pain kicked in. A wave of cold swept through him. And suddenly he was crying for real, remembering Curran in the cellar, killing the monster, hiding in the basket. He felt small and alone. He had come through so much, survived more than he ever thought he could, but now he felt lost and out of his depth. He wanted someone else to take the burden from him, set him free, give him back the last forty-eight hours.

He started rubbing his hands together, then scrubbing at the blood on his arms, trying to free himself of the stains and memories. He almost howled with anguish, but stopped himself at the last second. The monster was still out there, and surely it would soon come looking for the one who had murdered its child.

He waited for the sobs to die away, then took a breath and ducked his head beneath the water. He stayed under as long as he could, brushing at his hair with his fingers, trying to scrub himself clean of the smell of the monster's piss.

He was smiling weakly when he came up. Wiping tears away, he carried on rubbing, but slowly now, gently, working his fingers up and down his body, trying to clean out all the open sores. Every move brought a grimace or gasp to his lips, but he worked in surprisingly high spirits. It was good to have a job to focus on. He was making progress. After this he'd get out and start walking, not wait to dry, knowing it was going to be chilly. The exercise would help him fight off the cold. He might even manage a short jog on the downhill stretch.

Then, in the middle of his ministrations, he heard rustling in the bushes.

He froze and waited for the sound to be repeated, praying that it wouldn't, that he'd imagined it, or that it had just been the wind.

But it came again, the noise of a large creature moving. And while he couldn't tell for sure, it seemed to be coming from the direction of the path.

Dominic hung in the water, head showing, the rest of his body submerged, hoping that the monster wouldn't see him, that clouds would scud across the face of the moon and plunge the area into darkness, that the monster would trot on by without noticing him.

But the moon was unobstructed at the moment. The monster couldn't fail to clock his head sticking out of the middle of the lake, even with its poor eyesight. Perhaps he should hold his breath and duck, wait for the beast to move on, hope it had left by the time he came up for air.

On the other hand, motion might draw its attention. Maybe it wouldn't spot him with its weak eyes, the way the beast in the cellar hadn't seen him when he'd been clinging silently to the trunk. Perhaps movement tipped them off. If he held still and toughed it out, maybe he'd be as good as invisible.

While he was trying to decide, not sure which option offered his best chance of survival, the bushes parted and a shadowy beast emerged. Dominic bit down on a scream as the creature advanced, then gawped with disbelief as it came forward into the moonlight and was revealed as...

...a deer.

"You've got to be shitting me," Dominic bleated, then laughed lightly, tears coming to his eyes yet again, but tears of happiness this time. He didn't even care that he had pissed himself when he'd thought the deer was the monster. What did that matter when he was immersed in the lake, with no one to bear witness?

"A deer," Dominic chuckled, and then, as the deer stepped up to the lake and lowered its head to drink, Dominic moved to one side – slowly, so as not to spook the animal – lowered his head and drank too, feeling at one with the deer, the lake and the night, afraid no longer, just a beast of the wilds, as free and careless as any other creature of the forest.

## EIGHTY

As he'd anticipated, getting out of the lake was more of an ordeal than climbing in had been, but he endured the pain without complaint. He was lucky to be alive and anything was tolerable after his encounter with the monsters. If he'd been told he had to live with the agony of sunburn for the rest of his life, he would have accepted it with barely a shrug.

He'd waited for the deer to move on before striking for land, in case the monster was tracking it and closing in for the kill. When the deer had drunk its fill and trotted off, with no hint of anything monstrous in the air, Dominic washed his hair one last time – he could still smell the monster's piss, but it was less pungent now – and waded out.

Although he started walking as soon as he exited the lake, to fight off the cold, he paused before leaving the clearing to look around and up at the rising moon. He didn't believe he was going to make it out of the forest alive. The pessimist within him thought he'd bump into the monster, or that it would be waiting for him at the end of the path, knowing he had to pass this way.

He stared at the moon for a long time, fearing this was the last clear view he'd ever have of it, wanting to be able to remember it when his time came, so that he could at least die with a recent, pleasant memory. He didn't want Curran's stripped remains to be the last thing he thought of.

"Might be seeing you soon," he whispered to Curran's departed spirit.

"*Hurry up,*" he answered in Curran's voice. "*It's rammed with minge up here. Or down here. Heaven or hell — who cares? It's a sex factory, and that's all I'm worried about.*"

Dominic smiled and shook his head. He wanted to believe in an afterlife, but couldn't. Sure, he'd prayed to God a lot over the last twenty-four hours, and he was willing to believe that there *might* be some sort of a supreme being, that *maybe* all the worlds of the universe were the work of design rather than a quirk of evolution.

But if that was the case, he thought God had created humans because He wanted to study them. "We're like lab rats," Dominic whispered. "God's looking for the equivalent of the cure for cancer by lobbing shit our way and studying how it impacts on us."

The troubling thing was, Dominic had yet to see a monument to the brave little lab rat. Nobody (hardcore animal rights activists excepted) spared rodents a second thought. The scientist who found the cure for cancer would be feted, but who'd remember the millions of rats which had been sacrificed along the way?

If humans were like lab rats to God, it was crazy for anyone to think there might be a reward or punishment lying in wait for them. They'd simply be tossed in the great white bin bag in the sky, along with all the other redundant carcasses.

"*When did you get so cynical?*" Dominic muttered in Curran's voice.

"When I found your corpse hanging to a cross and infested with rats," he said.

"*Fair point,*" he chuckled.

Then, with one last wistful look at the moon, he turned, set foot on the path, and shuffled off into the gloom.

## EIGHTY-ONE

He made better progress than anticipated on the path. It was almost all downhill and he found himself stumbling along at a fair pace, not far off what he would have managed without any injuries. He'd found a way to live with the pain. It was going to torment him whether he went slowly or quickly, so he pushed things as much as he could, easing up only when the waves of suffering got close to peaking and threatened to drag a scream from his lips.

He ignored any rustling noises or shifting shadows. He was convinced that he was going to cross paths with the monster, so he saw no reason to worry about it. In an almost Zen-like state he figured, "What will be, will be. If I'm destined to die here, I'll die. I'm not going to whimper and whine about it."

He didn't feel particularly proud of his brave front. He was simply resigned to a horrible end. Curran would have kicked him up the arse and told him to get a grip, but without his friend on hand, there was no one to snap him out of his depression.

He thought about nothing in particular while huffing along. He didn't fret about what would happen when he got to the village, or if Martini was safe, or if his wounds were life-threatening. All of that seemed to be the baggage of a person in a parallel universe. Here, he was fated to run into the monster and it would tear him apart. End of story.

He was so sure he was doomed that when he came to the road he started across it without thinking and would have carried on if the path had continued on the other side. But when it didn't, and he came face to face with a wall of trees and bushes, he was forced to stop, look around and consider.

That was when he realised he was back on the road where they'd hopped out of the Whore of Babylon before starting their climb to the lake.

He stared at the start of the path, frowning, wondering why the monster hadn't attacked him yet. "Come on," he shouted, losing his temper. "I'm here.

Don't drag this out. Come and get me, you ugly, motherless son of a…"

He stopped before finishing the insult. A thought had struck him. It seemed preposterous, but he felt compelled to voice it regardless.

"What if the monster isn't here?"

He mulled that over, then took it even further.

"What if it went down the cellar and never came out? What if it's back there, weeping over its dead son, or off in the depths of the forest, digging a grave?"

He blinked stupidly.

"What if I've escaped? What if I'm free?"

It was too good to be true. But if not, where was the monster? He glanced left, then right. He'd forgotten how rough the road was, not much more than a dirt track, but he could see quite a distance in both directions, and it was monster-free.

He stared at the path again, then at the moon which he thought he'd bid farewell to forever up at the lake.

"Maybe someone's looking down on me and helping me out," he whispered.

"*Or maybe it's sheer luck,*" he grunted as Curran. "*In fact it's not even that. What are the odds, in a forest this size, of you bumping into anything at all?*"

"But it will want revenge," he noted. "It wasn't thinking clearly in the cottage, or it would have left the corpse until later and come looking for me straight away. Once its head clears, it'll return, sniff around for my scent, come lumbering up the path."

"*All the more reason to get your arse in gear and MOVE IT!*" he replied, raising his voice to a shout at the end, as Curran would have.

He winced as the echoes died away, certain that he'd pushed his luck too far, that the roar would tip off the monster, which would come bursting out of the bushes any second now.

When silence returned and nothing stirred in the undergrowth, he started to believe for the first time that maybe he'd made it. He knew he wasn't out of the woods. (This time he did grin briefly at the pun.) He had to deal with the possibly malevolent villagers, or the gang in Laki if he went to rescue Martini.

This could still turn on its head. He might end up crawling into the village, begging for help, only for a sneering local to stand over him and drawl mockingly, "Well, well, what have we here? Looks like the big, bad monsters let one slip through their fingers. No problem. We'll deal with you ourselves, gringo." Or whatever the Bulgarian version of *gringo* was.

But he'd made it further than expected. He'd cleared the path and there was no sign of the monster. Hope was his to clutch again.

Suddenly, as that hope flared in his sunburnt, blistered, battered chest, he spun on his heels and set off at the nearest he could get to a gallop. He lurched so wildly that he looked like a demented, naked, sunburnt Long John Silver, but that didn't bother him. He was off the path and on the road. No monster was blocking his way. It was absurd, given where he was, but a thought shot through his head and brought a warm smile to his cracked, bleeding lips. *I'm coming home!*

## EIGHTY-TWO

No cars passed as he was jogging along. That didn't surprise him. He'd be waiting an awful long time for a lift on this dirt road. He smiled, remembering how he had hoped to hitch a lift back to the village.

He was confident now, no longer wary of an attack, paying little notice to the trees and bushes on either side. He felt safe. The monster was out of the equation. That didn't mean he was home and dry by any stretch, but he could look forward and start planning ahead.

He played with the idea of avoiding the nearby villages, hiking across the countryside until he came to a large town, but dismissed the notion. He was in no physical state to attempt such a trek. Besides, he wouldn't have been able to find his way around without a map — and he might even struggle with one. He was a creature of the city, not an expert of the wilds.

No, he would have to turn himself in locally, but should he do that in Laki or the tiny village they'd passed on their way up? His first instinct was to do it at the nearer village. If Iliya and his crew had taken the tourists to the lake intending to leave them as a sacrifice, then he definitely had foes to fear in Laki.

Then again, since the village was closer to the cottage, maybe the locals were more of a threat. In Laki, with its industrial mine and workers who'd transferred in from other parts of the country, the monsters might be a secret to most people, guarded by a close-knit circle of those in the know. Up here in the mountains, in a smaller settlement, maybe everyone knew about them.

"Madness," Dominic muttered. "Paranoia. They don't know. They'd have hunted the beasts and killed them if they did. What sort of maniacs would worship a pair of human-killing monsters?"

"*Bulgarian maniacs*," he said in Curran's voice, then scowled.

"I've got to stop doing that," he told himself. "Curran's gone. It's creepy, pretending to be him."

"*Couldn't have said it better myself,*" he laughed as Curran, then made up his mind not to do it again.

As clouds temporarily obscured the moonlight, he asked himself if it was likely that the locals were part of a conspiracy. The logical answer was of course they weren't. But logically monsters shouldn't exist in the first place, so he wasn't sure that he was on safe ground with that train of thought.

He decided it would be best not to say anything about what had transpired in the cottage, act as if he had no idea that the hills were alive with the sounds of monsters. Even if the locals were innocent, *he* wasn't. He'd killed one of the creatures. It had struck first and slaughtered Curran, but could he convince a court of that?

He slowed down. What *were* the legal ramifications? You could be prosecuted for butchering an animal, but with a wolf or bear you'd surely be pardoned if you could prove that it had been self-defence. But where would the law stand on a sentient creature? Maybe these were the only two of their kind in existence. Would a court forgive him so readily for ridding the world of half its supply of a natural wonder?

He imagined himself on the witness stand, being interrogated by a young lawyer keen to make a name for himself.

"Did you try to reason with the *infant* before you stabbed it, Mr Newton?" the prosecutor might ask icily.

"How the hell do you reason with a monster that wants to rip your head off?" Dominic would respond hotly.

"Just answer the question, please," would come the calm retort, and the eyes of every member of the jury would narrow accusingly.

Once word of the monster's slaying got out, this would become a media circus. Every news crew in the world would want a piece of the action. Plenty of people would be willing to take the monster's side, to condemn Dominic regardless of what he said. His face might end up on a T-shirt with a slogan emblazoned across the front — THIS MAN KILLS WONDERS.

Even if he escaped prosecution, did he want to go through the rest of his life known worldwide as the man who'd killed the world's first verified Yeti? Hell, there had been movies about these bastards in which they'd been portrayed as big, loveable fur balls. He could imagine scores of children weeping into their pillows at night and crying out, "Mummy, why did Dominic Newton kill Bigfoot?"

"Say nothing," he growled, picking up speed again. "Play dumb, hook up with Martini, get out and don't look back. If you say anything about what went down, you'll stir up a shit storm."

"*So what will you say instead?*" he asked, accidentally slipping back into Curran mode.

"That's what I need to think about," he murmured, and spent the rest of the march considering his tactics.

## EIGHTY-THREE

It was late when Dominic reached the end of the dirt road and turned into the tiny, sleepy village. By the position of the moon he figured it was somewhere around midnight.

"Yeah," he grunted. "Like I'm a lunar expert now."

Most of the lights were out in the houses, but a few were still shining in the building that Dominic had previously clocked as a pub, and it was to this that he made his slow, weary way. He'd anticipated an adrenalin boost when he hit the village, but instead it was as if all of the life was draining from his bones.

He paused at the door of the pub, listening to the noises within. He could hear several voices, laughter, the reassuring smell of beer and smoke.

He stepped back and stared at the sign. He couldn't read the name, as it was written in Bulgarian, no English translation. There wasn't a picture either. He was nervous, not sure if he should go in. Maybe it would be better if he rested in a barn and announced his presence in the morning.

"No," he whispered, glancing over his shoulder. If he slept in a barn, he'd spend the night worrying that the monster would find him. These people could offer him sanctuary — assuming they didn't cart him back to the lake and summon the monster to accept their humble offering.

"*Got to trust them, Newt,*" he said, unconsciously slipping back into Curran's voice. "*What sort of a horrible world would this be without trust?*"

"Right then," he muttered, squaring his shoulders, wincing as his sunburn flared and fresh pus oozed from a few ripening blisters. "Here we go." And, trying to ignore the sick feeling in his gut, he pushed the door open and stepped inside.

## EIGHTY-FOUR

Eight people were in the pub, six men and a couple of women. Most were older than Dominic, middle-aged and upwards. Five lounged in comfortable-looking chairs, while two stood at the bar chatting to the barman.

All eight looked around when the door opened, curious to see which of their neighbours had come to join them at such an advanced hour. When a naked, sunburnt, blister-pocked stranger stumbled forward into the light, every one of the locals fell mute, staring at him with wide-eyed astonishment.

"Help," Dominic croaked.

Nobody reacted.

He was covering his genitals with both hands, but when his plea met with stunned silence, he risked extending one of them.

"Help," he bleated again. "Help me. Please."

For another long moment nobody responded, and Dominic began to think they were as hostile to outsiders as he'd feared.

Then one of the women exclaimed in Bulgarian, rose in a rush and hurried towards him. Dominic flinched and almost retreated, but she hugged him before he could flee, patting the back of his head as if he was a baby, making cooing noises, and he knew in an instant that he would be OK. These were good people. He had been wrong to mistrust them.

"Thank you," he sobbed, beginning to cry with relief. His flesh stung where she was holding him but he didn't care.

One of the men snapped at the woman and she released him. She said something that Dominic gathered was an apology – the man had obviously told her to let him go, that the red-skinned stranger must be in pain – then asked him a question.

"I don't speak Bulgarian," Dominic moaned, waving his fingers in front of his mouth as if that would make everything clear.

"English?" one of the men at the bar asked.

"Yes."

"I speak some," the man said, coming forward, delighted to be taking centre stage but trying not to show it. He was broad running to fat, fighting off baldness, with a long handlebar moustache. Like most of the other men, he was wearing a shirt with the sleeves rolled up, but his was bright blue, where the rest were various shades of white. "I Anastas. What your name?"

"Dominic Newton."

"Hail, Dominic Newton," Anastas beamed, the ends of his moustache lifting as he smiled. "This Donka." The woman nodded politely and Anastas started pointing to everyone else and naming them. "Irina," he began with the other woman. "Gavrail. Vasil. Mladen. Plamen. Stanimir."

Dominic nodded vaguely as if he'd absorbed all that.

One of the other men – Dominic thought it was the one called Plamen – said something critical to Anastas, which Dominic interpreted as, "How do you expect him to remember all those names, you fool?"

Anastas responded with an angry tirade of his own, and for a moment Dominic thought they were going to come to blows over it. But then the other woman – Irina – made a comment and laughed, and everybody else laughed too.

"Apology," Anastas chuckled, leading Dominic forward. "Bit drunk. Not used to naked man coming middle of night."

"That's OK," Dominic sniffed, smiling gratefully as Anastas fluffed up the pillow on one of the chairs and gestured for him to sit.

The woman who had hugged him asked a question and Anastas whistled. "Ach! Donka right. I should ask first. Are you able sit? Not too pain?"

"No, I'm fine," Dominic smiled. "I mean, it'll be painful, but I'd rather sit than stand. It seems like a long time since…"

The rest of his sentence was a long sigh of contentment as he lowered himself into the chair. It hurt when he leant back, but he soon adjusted. It would be fine as long as he didn't move.

The barman came out from behind the bar. He was short, with a beard grown to cover pockmarks from when he was a teenager. He was a sour-looking man, but he smiled awkwardly as he produced a clean dish towel and draped it over Dominic's privates. Then he put a hand on his chest. "Vasil."

"Thank you, Vasil," Dominic said.

Vasil started a conversation with Anastas and the others chipped in. They spoke quickly and loudly, pointing to Dominic as they did.

"Vasil say he can get better thing for you," Anastas finally said. "But we not sure good. Jacket or shirt might stick and hurt, yes?"

Dominic nodded. "The towel's fine. I'm worried about infection. I think we should leave it for the medics to decide how to dress me."

Anastas didn't get all of that, but he understood that Dominic was happy with the cloth.

"So, what happen?" Anastas asked, sitting down in the chair next to Dominic's. Everyone leant forward, curious to hear the answer.

"I was trekking with my girlfriend," Dominic said, having thought through his answer in detail on his way down the dirt road. "We found a lake and sunbathed nude. We had an argument, a big fight. I went for a swim to calm down. While I was in the water, she stormed off and took my clothes. I…"

Anastas held up a hand to stop him, so that he could translate for the others. A couple of the men laughed, but the others shushed them with frowns and sharp comments. Donka leant across to pat the back of Dominic's head again. She looked like a kindly granny, with a warm, tanned, wrinkled face. If he hadn't been in so much pain he would have loved to cuddle up to her.

"I should have stayed by the lake," Dominic went on, "but I was angry. I decided to head off by myself to the place we'd planned to visit next, to show that I could do better by myself, even without any clothes or equipment."

There was lots of tutting when Anastas translated that.

"I know," Dominic groaned before Anastas could reprimand him. "It was stupid. I got lost. I tried to backtrack but it grew dark and I panicked. I found a clearing in the forest and stayed there for the night."

Irina interrupted to ask a question.

"Where clearing?" Anastas translated.

"I'm not sure," Dominic said. "Somewhere that way." He pointed to a spot in the opposite direction of the place he'd come from. "I was awake all night, worrying about bears and wolves. I meant to leave at dawn, but I was so tired, I fell asleep. When I woke it was evening and…" He waved an arm at himself.

One of the heavier men shook his head and started to speak.

"Gavrail say bad to walk through forest at night," Anastas said. "Can't see paths. Dangerous animals. Could have ended very bad."

"I know," Dominic said, "but I wasn't thinking clearly. My head…" He crossed his eyes and wobbled his head to indicate delirium.

Anastas laughed. "Mad from sun?"

"Yes. I wandered aimlessly. I could have ended up anywhere. But then my mind cleared. I wanted to rest up for the night, but I was thirsty and hungry, cold and confused. I thought it would be better to keep moving. I was afraid I'd die of hypothermia and shock."

Anastas translated and the others muttered approvingly. Irina laid a hand on his knee and squeezed. She was younger than Donka, attractive in her own rough way. Dominic might have found himself stirring at the intimate contact another time.

Irina asked Anastas something and he said, "Brave." She squeezed Dominic's knee again and repeated, "Brave."

Dominic smiled weakly. "No. Just desperate. Luckily I saw lights and aimed for them and…" He shrugged. "Here I am."

"Lucky," Anastas said, making a sucking noise. "Could be dead."

"Tell me about it," Dominic whispered, remembering Curran.

"What you want we do?" Anastas asked. "Telephone doctor? Not in village, but not far away. Can get here soon."

"That would be wonderful," Dominic smiled. "But can I call my girlfriend first? I'm sure she's worried sick. I want to let her know that I'm OK."

The women smiled when Anastas translated. Donka fluttered her eyelids and said something that no doubt meant, "He's a true lover."

Everyone laughed, even Dominic, then Vasil produced a mobile phone and handed it to Anastas, who passed it to Dominic.

"You know number?" Anastas asked.

"Hell yes," Dominic said wryly. He wasn't good at remembering numbers – there was no real reason why anyone had to in this age of mobiles – but Martini had forced him to learn hers, because he'd gone through a phase of losing his own phone, and she wanted him to be able to contact her at all times. She'd withheld sexual favours until he was able to recite it by heart.

He couldn't recall the numbers when he tried to picture them, but when he let himself relax, his fingers moved confidently across the buttons, typing them in after he'd first added the country code.

He paused before pressing the call button. If Iliya and his gang were in league with the monsters, they would have targeted Martini to stop her raising the alarm. This could be the most distressing call of Dominic's life. He almost didn't want to make it. As long as he delayed, he could hope that she was alive. But if he dialled and there was no answer, or Iliya replied, or there was a dead tone…

"Be brave," he whispered, catching Irina's eye. She didn't know what he meant, but she smiled and nodded. Taking courage from that, he pulled his lips tight with determination, and pressed.

## EIGHTY-FIVE

The phone rang once. Twice. Then it clicked halfway through the third dial tone.

"Hello?" a confused-sounding Martini said.

Tears came to Dominic's eyes and his fingers loosened on the phone.

"Hello?" Martini said again, sounding more alert this time. And worried.

"It's me," Dominic croaked.

"Dominic!" she cried, and the relief in her voice sent him into a full-on sobbing fit. "Dominic?" he heard her ask over the sound of his sobs. "What's wrong? Where are you? Are you all right?"

"I'm OK," he gasped. "Just... hard to... talk. Give me... a moment..."

He turned away from the phone and wept. Anastas shared a bewildered look with the others. Donka stood and opened her arms wide, meaning to hug Dominic again, but Vasil shook his head at her, said something softly, and she sat.

When the tears eased, Dominic lifted the phone and whispered, "I love you, M."

"I love you too," she replied automatically, but not without feeling. "Where are you? What happened? I was so worried..."

"It's bad," he said. "I got sunburnt."

"What?" He could sense her frown even from here.

"Really bad," he laughed. "I'm red as a fire engine."

"You idiot," she snapped. "What did I tell you about being careful in the sun?"

"I was drunk," he explained. "Fell asleep by... in a clearing," he said, deciding not to mention the lake. Best if he stuck to the story that he'd fed the locals.

"Were you drinking with that gang of louts?" she growled.

"Yes."

"Were they nice, those girls?" she pressed angrily.

"No one's as nice as you, M," he smiled.

"I tried to track them down," she said. "When you didn't turn up, I went to the pub, but they weren't there and nobody would tell me where they lived. I waited all day. When night came, I tried the police. They only laughed, said you'd turn up drunk, advised me to carry on with my holiday rather than sit around waiting for you, promised to call me when you showed."

"Yeah?" Dominic scowled, wondering if the police had been trying to get rid of her, if they knew something was wrong.

"I was scared," Martini went on, quietly now. "I thought something dreadful had happened. Why didn't you call?"

"My phone's in my bag in the hotel," Dominic reminded her.

"You could have borrowed someone else's."

"Whose?" he snorted, then shielded his mouth with a hand and lowered his voice. "They beat us up, took our clothes, left us in the middle of nowhere."

"The kids?" Martini asked sceptically.

"Kids from hell," Dominic snarled.

"So whose phone are you using now?"

He shook his head. "It's a long story. I'll tell you when you get here."

"Where?"

"A village about a twenty-minute drive away. I'll ask one of the locals to give you directions."

"Maybe I'll leave you there," she said frostily. "The grief you've put me through, I'm not sure you're worth bothering with."

"I know," Dominic said miserably. "I'll understand if you can't trust me, if you want nothing to do with me. But you have to come get me, M. I don't know if you're in danger or not, but we can't take chances. You have to –"

"In danger?" she interrupted sharply. "In danger of what?"

"I'll tell you later. First you need to leave. Don't pack your bag or check out. Just grab your passport and anything else essential. Get in the car. Make sure no one follows you. If you think someone's behind you, drive to Asenovgrad and go to the police, then ring me back on this number and I'll tell them my story."

"You're trying to scare me," she said, but he could tell she was uneasy.

"If you're certain you're not being followed," he continued, "come pick me up. Bring my passport, clothes, anything else you think I'll need."

"Afterburn?" she suggested.

He glanced down at his skin, which was starting to look as if it had been flayed. "We're beyond that," he muttered. "But painkillers would be good. I'll need to go to a hospital, but it will be a long drive in my condition."

"You're not making sense," Martini said softly. "Put Curran on the phone."

"He's not with me," Dominic said dully.

"What do you mean?" she asked, and he could picture her blinking.

"It's bad, M," Dominic whispered.

There was a long silence.

"Am I really in danger?" she finally asked.

"I don't think so, but maybe."

"Dominic," she said, and there was a catch in her throat, as if she was about to start crying. "What the hell happened up there?"

"I'll tell you later," he promised. "You probably won't believe me, but I'll tell you anyway. I think you're the only one I will tell, but maybe you can convince me otherwise if you feel we should report it to the police."

"Is Curran…" she started to ask but couldn't finish.

"Just come get me, M," he said as sweetly as he could. "I need you more than I've ever needed you before. I'm lost. Come lead me home. Please. I love you."

There was another pause. Then, instead of saying she loved him too, she said in a business-like tone, "Put the guy on the phone who can tell me how to get there."

"That's my girl," Dominic chuckled weakly. Then he held the phone out to an uncertain-looking Anastas and said brightly, "It's for you."

## EIGHTY-SIX

"You want me call doctor now?" Anastas asked after he'd hung up.

"No thanks," Dominic said. "Martini's going to take me to a hospital."

Anastas stared at the stranger's disfigured skin and nodded. "Good plan. But doctor might be able help while waiting."

Dominic shook his head. "It's late. I don't want to get him out of bed."

"She," Anastas corrected him. "Woman. Good doctor."

"I'm sure she is," Dominic said. "But I want to go as soon as Martini gets here. It would be different if the doctor was in the village, but if we summon her, and Martini gets here first, I'll have to wait, to be polite."

"As you like," Anastas shrugged, and translated for the others.

There was a short silence, then Irina asked a question.

"She want know if girlfriend called after drink," Anastas said.

Dominic grinned and started to tell them about the three generations of Isabella Martinezes, and the visiting cousin whose pet name for the girl stuck. Then one of the men – Mladen, a well-dressed man in his forties who was handsome except for a veined, bulging right eyelid – asked what Dominic and his girlfriend did for a living.

Vasil was delighted when he heard that the pair worked in bars. "Come work me," he boomed once Anastas told him how to say it in English. "Very good pay."

The others jeered and told Vasil he was a crook who would underpay a slave. He scowled and retired to his post behind the bar, but Dominic could tell by his smile that he'd enjoyed the ribbing.

Stanimir and Gavrail, feeling as if they should be contributing more, asked Dominic about life in London. Plamen was the only one who didn't say much. He had drunk more than his friends and was beaming off into space.

Dominic wished he could get drunk like Plamen and just stare at the wall until Martini arrived to whisk him away from this land of friend-killing monsters. But he guessed that alcohol would do him more harm than good in his current state.

"Could I have some water?" he asked after a while, as he continued to do his best to answer all of the questions that were coming his way. He didn't mind, even though it hurt to talk. It helped pass the time and distract him from the pain.

Donka asked if he'd been to Harrods. He told her that he'd been there a few times, and described the Egyptian-themed sections.

Gavrail asked about Buckingham Palace and the Tower of London. The Bulgarian had been to both on a tour of the UK many years ago, with his ex-wife. He wanted to go back, mainly to see the Cabinet War Rooms, "but I no wife now," he said through Anastas. "No one see it with. No fun going holiday on own."

A giggling Irina jokingly asked if he'd been to any fashion shows. She was surprised when he answered positively. Martini had dragged him to a few. In truth he'd gone willingly, Curran too. They hadn't cared about the clothes, but near-naked models were a different matter.

Mladen wanted to know what team Dominic supported. He was disappointed when Dominic said he wasn't into football, but cheered up when he added that an uncle had taken him to some Tottenham Hotspur games when he was a kid.

"White Hart Lane," Mladen beamed. "Cockerel. Gazza. Jimmy Greaves. Bill Nicholson. But best — Berbatov."

"Berbatov a giant," Anastas agreed. "See him play?"

"No," Dominic said, his smile fading. He remembered Curran talking about the ex-Spurs player earlier in their holiday. His eyes filled with tears as he recalled his friend, tied to that cross in the cellar, a food source and plaything for rats now.

"What wrong?" Anastas asked, staring at Dominic with concern.

"Nothing," Dominic said, trying to stop the tears but failing.

"Hey," Anastas said, clumsily patting Dominic's knee. "Not that bad. You OK."

Donka tutted at Anastas and nudged him aside. She sat beside Dominic and hugged him, whispering soothingly in Bulgarian, stroking the back of his head. Dominic turned into her and wept. As Donka murmured in his ear, the tears abated and he relaxed into her, cuddling up to the elderly woman as he had wanted to earlier, burying his face in her bosom as if he was a child being comforted by his mother. He felt better now, safe in her arms, and he remained in that position for a long, warm time, until he was disturbed by an incredulous shriek.

"You're putting the moves on fucking grannies now?"

With a guilty jerk, a startled Dominic pulled away, looked up and saw a glowering Martini standing just inside the door of the pub, livid with jealous rage.

## EIGHTY-SEVEN

"I don't believe this," Martini snarled as Dominic and the others gawped at her. "I come all this way at top speed, freaked out of my mind because I thought you were in trouble, and I find you getting it on with a granny."

"M," Dominic moaned. "It's not what you think."

"What are you talking about?" Martini yelled. "You were nuzzling her tit!"

Dominic blinked dumbly, not sure how to respond, but Donka smiled thinly. She stood and faced Martini. Martini's back stiffened and she prepared for combat. Donka started to speak, softly and calmly, and Anastas quickly translated, stumbling on his words as he tried to keep up.

"I not interest in your man, Martinez. He come to us bad way and we try help. Look him, his red, fear in eyes. He crying before you come. I try cheer. Hug him, that all. Just try to…" Anastas paused, searching for the right words. "Try to make black in head go white," he ended, scowling as he knew that didn't quite capture what Donka had said.

Martini considered that in silence. If the apparent cougar had been younger, no argument in the world would have stalled her — she'd have torn into the viper like a lioness defending her cub. But this woman was *really* old. And there were the men. If it had just been Dominic and the old biddy, she might have suspected the worst. But Dominic was no exhibitionist. He wasn't the sort to seek pleasure in front of a pack of middle-aged voyeurs.

When a distraught Martini had stepped in out of the night, all she'd focused on was her boyfriend's face buried between another woman's breasts. Now she studied Dominic and was shocked.

He'd told her on the phone about his sunburn, but she hadn't imagined anything like this. He looked too red to be real. It was the sort of impossibly scarlet colour a child might use if asked to paint Santa Claus. And the blisters! They were huge and swollen, like pale slugs clinging to his flesh. He'd also been scratched in many places, his face was puffed up from where someone had hit him hard, and there were various dark bruises dotted around his body.

But worse than all that was the look in his eyes. The older woman had said it was fear, but this went beyond normal terror. Martini had seen Dominic when he was afraid. Not often – a couple of times on the streets late at night when he'd thought they were going to be mugged, once when she missed her period and they had to contemplate the possibility of an unwanted pregnancy – but enough to know what he looked like scared. This wasn't fear as any ordinary person understood it. She'd no idea what had happened to him up here, but this wasn't the same man Martini had stormed away from in the pub in Laki.

"D?" she whispered, taking a hesitant step forward, not sure she wanted to know what he'd witnessed that could have torn him up so agonisingly.

Dominic pushed himself to his feet, groaning as he rose. He wanted to reach out to her, but that would have meant letting go of the dish towel. So instead he just smiled shakily.

"Hey, M," he croaked. "How do I look?"

Martini's eyes filled with tears. Dominic had known since he first recovered his senses by the lake that he'd been severely burnt, but it was only now, seeing the horror and pity in Martini's expression, that he realised how serious the damage must be.

"That bad?" he said lightly, trying to joke about it.

Martini shook her head silently, eyes wide.

"Hey, come on," he tried again. "It's not the end of me. I won't die from a bit of sunburn."

"The pain…" Martini whispered.

"Thanks for reminding me," he grimaced.

As they stood, staring at one another, neither able to take the next step, Donka murmured something to Anastas. He frowned at her, but she said it again, firmly this time. With a sigh, he slipped up beside Dominic and passed on the message softly, so that only he could hear.

Dominic stared at Anastas sceptically.

"Not my idea," Anastas said. "Donka."

Dominic caught Donka's eye and she nodded at him.

"What the hell," Dominic sniffed. "It's not like you guys haven't seen all of me already." Then, since he could think of nothing better to try, he followed Donka's advice, dropped the dish towel and spread his arms wide. "Come get me, M," he croaked.

Martini stared at her naked boyfriend for a long second, as he stood exposed for all to see and laugh at. But nobody laughed. Instead the locals politely turned their heads aside, though Irina did sneak one quick glance before doing so.

Just as Dominic thought that Martini was simply going to stare at him all night, a pitying moan escaped her lips. The first tears dripped from her eyes. And then, crying out his name, she hurled herself forward, into his arms, to kiss and hold and claim him once again, and forever after, as her own.

## EIGHTY-EIGHT

It hurt to hold her but Dominic didn't care. He buried his face in her hair and wept. Martini was crying too. They stood, joined, clutching one another, sobbing like lonely children.

Martini eventually broke the lock. Pushing herself away from him but holding on to his hands, she studied his burnt, battered, blistered face. She wanted to kiss him, but his lips were cracked and bloody, and she feared adding to his pain.

"What happened to you?" she sobbed.

Dominic shook his head. "I'll tell you later."

"Why not now?" she pressed.

"I might be in trouble. I don't know what to do. I need to talk it through with you before I decide. Right now it's safer not to say anything, until we've had a chance to discuss it privately."

Martini knew he wasn't being overly dramatic. She could see it in his eyes. This was no minor matter. Something terrible had happened up here in the mountains.

"Come," Anastas interrupted, prompted by Donka. "Sit. Have drink before go. Anything we get you?"

A smiling Martini and Dominic let themselves be guided to a couple of chairs. As they sat, the others formed a semi-circle around them. For a paranoid moment Dominic thought they were going to attack, that they'd been waiting for him to summon any associates that he might have been travelling with, so that they could finish off his partners as well as him.

But then he saw the locals beaming. They were happy that the young lovers had been reunited. They only wanted to enjoy this pleasant time with their visitors.

"What get?" Vasil barked from behind the bar. He made a drinking motion with his right hand, to be sure she understood.

"That's OK," Dominic said. "We need to be going."

"No pay," Vasil said, now shaking his hand from side to side.

The others whistled and made catcalls. This was obviously a rare event in the pub. Vasil swore at them, then laughed and repeated the drinking gesture.

"It would be impolite not to accept," Martini murmured.

Dominic hesitated. These people had been good to him and he didn't want to refuse their hospitality. On the other hand he was keen to move on, not just to admit himself for treatment as soon as possible, but to put the nightmare of the forest behind him.

"Oh, go on then," he decided, good manners ultimately winning out over his desire to flee. "But just a quick one. Water will be fine."

"A small beer for me, please," Martini said.

Vasil nodded approvingly and turned to his taps.

"Drinking and driving?" Dominic teased.

"Just this once," Martini said, and cast an eye over his tortured form again. "These are exceptional circumstances."

She reached out and brushed his cheek gently with her fingers. The locals cleared their throats and shuffled back a bit, affording the pair some privacy. Donka was the only one who paused, to pick up the dish towel and replace it on Dominic's lap.

Vasil returned with the beer, handing it to Martini as if it was a glass of champagne, before passing a mug of water to a grateful Dominic.

"They're nice people," Martini said.

"Yes," Dominic nodded. "They helped me when I most needed it. I won't ever forget that."

"You sound like a bad actor in a true-life TV movie," Martini noted.

"Sorry," Dominic said. "I'm too fucked to be witty."

They shared another smile. Dominic loved her so much. He couldn't believe how poorly he'd treated her. He promised himself that he would never do that again. She deserved better. She deserved his very best.

Martini's smile faded as she studied Dominic's eyes. "I know you don't want to tell me the whole story yet, but I've got to ask. Curran?"

Dominic's throat tightened and he shook his head.

Martini frowned. "What does that mean?"

Dominic took a sip of water, licked his lips, then mouthed the word, "Dead."

"*Ted?*" Martini said uncertainly.

Dominic rolled his eyes and almost snapped at her. Then he recalled the promise he'd just made. Taking her hands, he said softly, "Curran is dead, M."

She stared at him, shocked. Although he'd hinted at this on the phone, she hadn't been able to realistically contemplate such a scenario. She thought the irritating loudmouth had been arrested, or badly beaten up, or got lost. "He can't be," she moaned.

Dominic squeezed her hands. "Careful. Don't give anything away. I don't want these people to know."

"Why the hell not?" she growled.

Dominic shook his head. "I'll explain it all later."

Something about the hard twist of his lips made Martini pause. She thought about what he'd said a while ago, that he might be in trouble. She started to wonder if his hands were red not just with sunburn but with blood.

"No one followed you up from Laki?" Dominic asked.

"No," she said.

"You're sure?"

She nodded. "I kept a close watch on the rearview mirror."

"Good. What about the teenagers? Have you seen any of them?"

"No. I searched for them, like I told you, but couldn't find them. It didn't help that I only vaguely remembered what they looked like. I could barely describe them to the people in the bar." She gulped. "Was it one of those who…?"

"No," Dominic said. "They might have set us up, but I doubt it. Still, I don't want to take any chances. We'll head to Asenovgrad and check me into a hospital — I'm sure these guys can direct us to one. I'll tell you what happened as you're driving. Based on what you think, we'll either alert the police or say nothing."

"Say nothing?" Martini echoed. "But if Curran's dead, we can't just leave him here. We have to…"

She stopped when Dominic firmly squeezed her hands again.

"Your voice was starting to rise. Hold it in, M. Wait until we're in the car. This is a fucked-up situation. I don't want to abandon Curran, but if I lead the police to his body, they might think I killed him."

"Why would they think that?" Martini asked, bewildered.

"Because when I tell them who really did it, I'll sound like a madman." Dominic snorted. "Hell, in a week or two, when we're back in London, I might even start doubting myself. Maybe I'll think I imagined it all, that my brain was fried and the monsters were only in my head."

"*Monsters?*"

He smiled wearily. "Crazy or not, I know this much for sure — I love you, Isabella Martinez."

As she smiled coquettishly – he knew that sounded like another bad line from a TV film, but he didn't care, that *was* how she'd smiled – he leant forward and kissed her, not caring that it stung. As she returned the kiss, he reached up, caught the back of her head and pulled her in closer, pressing his lips hard against hers, happily taking the pain along with the pleasure.

Donka, Anastas and the others cheered. Plamen, who had barely spoken since Dominic entered, raised his glass and started to shout something. But before he could give voice to the toast, a high-pitched, piercing noise cut through the air. It came from outside the window, where a creature had been watching, waiting, until it was sure that the woman who'd come in the machine with wheels was the red man's heart-linked partner.

The eight locals and Martini frowned as the noise died away, wondering what could have made such an unusual sound. But Dominic knew. He tried to lurch to his feet, to warn them, to urge them to block all entry points, to search for a weapon, to prepare for the hell that was about to be unleashed upon them.

But Dominic was slow and the beast was swift. Before he could rise from his chair, the door of the pub was thrown open and the monster from the cottage stepped inside and leered viciously at the humans it had come to kill.

## EIGHTY-NINE

It was clear from their shocked expressions that the locals had never seen anything like this before. Dominic doubted that many living humans ever had.

The top of the monster's head scraped the ceiling as it pushed forward. It could have stooped, but it seemed to enjoy the scraping sound. Its penis was erect and protruding angrily beneath its bulging stomach.

Gavrail was first in the monster's path. The elderly, thickset man stared up at the creature as it towered over him. He was a large man, but looked like a child next to the intruder.

Gavrail didn't move as the monster lowered its head to return his stare with its vertically-set eyes. The horn-like bone jutting out of the beast's forehead poked into the side of his face. He flinched but still didn't budge. Nobody had moved.

The monster's eyes didn't narrow, but its red pupils expanded as it sniffed Gavrail's scent. When he trembled but had no other reaction, it turned its head and glanced at the other humans. Its short, stout legs were rooted close together, and the guts within its near-translucent skin seemed to slither round with excitement.

Irina was close to the monster. It lifted its stomach so that its penis extended in her direction. She moaned softly and shook her head, but still stood frozen like the rest of them.

The monster pulled an expression that might have been a scowl. Then it focused on Martini, the youngest of the women. To provoke a response, the creature raised its head, then opened its mouth wide and made a loud screeching noise, similar to the one it had emitted outside.

When the monster opened its mouth, Martini was able to see the rows of fangs. Dominic saw them too. He dully noted that it had more than its child, three or four rows, and they were longer and sharper.

Martini gasped when she saw the shark-like fangs, but didn't cry out with fear. Instead, the drunk Plamen did, shouting something that Anastas didn't need to translate as, "Fuck me!" Then he doubled over and threw up much of the beer that he'd spent the night lining his stomach with.

The monster made a pleased gurgling noise, then licked its lips with a long dark tongue as the stench of the vomit wafted to it. This was what it craved — true terror.

While Plamen was still vomiting, the monster spun and locked its teeth around Gavrail's face. It could have squeezed the whole of the man's head into its open maw, but was content to settle for his face.

Gavrail realised the danger he was in, and with a startled shout tried to tear free of the creature's embrace. Before he could, the monster bore down and drove its teeth into the bone framing Gavrail's cheeks. It jerked its head a few times. There was a snapping sound. Then the beast ripped half of Gavrail's face away, leaving only a bit of his jaw and the top of his right ear behind.

Blood spurted from deep within Gavrail's exposed brain. He fell away from his killer, arms shaking wildly, like a decapitated chicken.

The monster turned again and spat the remains of Gavrail's face at the still vomiting Plamen. As the flesh stuck to the back of his head, like a grotesque mask that an especially disturbed child might wear at Halloween, the rest of the humans snapped out of their strange spell and screamed and gibbered with horror.

It was what the monster had been waiting for. With a howl of wicked delight it spread its arms wide, gnashed its teeth playfully, and closed in on the next of its victims.

The slaughter had commenced.

## NINETY

The well-dressed, handsome Mladen tried to dodge the monster's grasp as it lumbered towards him, but he'd reacted too slowly. The beast caught him and pulled him in tight. As Mladen yelled for help or mercy, the monster opened its mouth wide. It looked like it was going to rip off his face, as it had Gavrail's, but then it spotted his odd, bulging right eyelid, and paused.

While Mladen kicked at his captor, the monster closed its mouth until only the first few fangs at the front were showing. Then it leant forward and carefully bit through the eyelid, sucking out the juice within the eye.

Mladen's screams of agony set Dominic crying again. He cringed in his chair and shook his head, trying to make the madness go away. He wanted to shut his eyes and wait for the end in darkness, but he couldn't. Instead he had to watch as the monster released the wounded Mladen, who staggered around, screaming, the remains of the liquid from his punctured eyeball dripping down his cheek.

Martini went wild and threw herself out of her chair. Landing on the floor, she scrabbled away from the monster, shrieking at the top of her voice.

The monster ignored Martini and went after Irina. She had fallen to her knees and clasped her hands in prayer. Her eyes were raised to the ceiling and she was praying frantically, lips racing to form the words that she hoped would save her.

If the monster knew anything of gods or religion, it didn't show that now, as it grabbed Irina's chin with one hand, then swept the fingernails of the other across the soft flesh of her throat, sawing at it until the folds parted and blood erupted. Irina fell aside once she was released, to spasm on the floor and die, eyes wide, lips still moving in prayer until the last of the life left her twitching form.

There was a roar of rage and Dominic saw Vasil climb on to his bar and launch himself across the room at the monster.

Vasil landed on the surprised creature's back and hammered its head with his fists. If he'd thought to pick up a knife, he might have brought down the father of the beast which Dominic had killed the night before in a similar way. But Vasil had boxed in his youth, bare-knuckle bouts with gypsies who'd been passing through. He'd won most of his fights, earning the respect of the travelling folk. He didn't think he needed a knife, even against a foe as unlikely and fierce as this.

Vasil grabbed the monster's left ear and tugged its head aside, drawing a satisfying squeal of pain. He threw a series of jabs at the creature's neck with his free hand, hoping to crush its windpipe and leave it gasping for breath.

The monster reeled around, knocking over Stanimir and Donka, who'd swept forward to help the roaring Vasil. It thumped into a wall. Vasil grunted but didn't let go. Turning, it spun again, and this time one of its elbows smashed a small window.

The monster glanced at the window, then came to a stop. It was a tiny opening, big enough for a child to squeeze through, but only if they stretched out flat and weren't too fat. With a gurgling, chuckling sound, the monster adjusted its stance and backed up against the window, so that Vasil was pressed against it.

Vasil carried on punching the monster. He didn't think he had anything to fear. He thought the monster would try to crush him against the wall, but he was confident that he could destroy its throat before it suffocated him.

But the monster had something else in mind. Dominic recalled the younger beast and how it had oozed through the window in the shack. He realised what the father of the slain creature had in mind, and started to shout a warning, but it was far too late, even if he'd been able to warn Vasil in his natural tongue.

The monster sucked in. The guts which had been hanging in a bulge over its groin suddenly shifted to the rear of the beast's body, forcing the shocked Vasil back through the window frame. Since he was too big to pass through in one piece, his spine snapped and he doubled over with a short-lived cry of shock and pain.

When the monster stepped away from the window and let its guts slip back into their natural resting place, Vasil remained lodged in the frame, bent in two as if folded in half. His fingers were shaking, but not for long, and soon they fell as still as the rest of his limbs.

The action moved on.

## NINETY-ONE

The monster looked around and spotted Anastas racing for the open door. He had seen his chance to break free.

The monster started after Anastas, then realised it wouldn't catch up with him before he made it out into the open. Rather than give chase, it stooped, picked up a heavy glass and threw it at the fleeing Anastas as it snapped upright.

The glass flew through the air and slammed into the back of Anastas's head. He went down without a whimper, hitting the floor so heavily that Dominic was sure he'd been instantly killed.

The monster took little notice of its achievement, making Dominic assume that it was all too aware of its prowess. It had expected to hit the running human when it launched the glass after him, no big deal.

Stanimir and Donka were back on their feet and they closed on the monster again. It caught them by the throat, one in each hand, and lifted them from the floor. It made what sounded like a savage laughing noise as their feet writhed and they slapped feverishly but futilely at its massive arms.

Before it could finish them off, the monster spotted Martini tracing the dead Anastas's steps. She was heading for the door, to raise the alarm and bring the rest of the village down upon the killer.

The monster had designs on the young woman. With an angry snort it dropped the other pair and darted after her, not wanting to throw an object and risk killing her.

Martini was almost at the door, scrabbling across the floor, when the monster grabbed her heels and dragged her back into the middle of the pub. She screamed as it turned her over.

"No!" Dominic cried, reaching out to her, horrified but unable to push himself out of the chair into which he'd sunk.

The monster glanced at him and sneered – at least that was how it seemed – then tore Martini's sweater from her. As she squealed, it swiftly tied her arms by her sides with the sweater. Then it tugged open the buttons on her jeans and pulled those off too, knotting them around her legs.

As Martini carried on screaming, the monster studied its handiwork and nodded. It took hold of her knickers and peeled them down to her knees, before ripping them free. Dominic's stomach flipped — he thought the beast meant to rape her in front of him. But the monster only wanted to silence her, which it did by balling up the knickers and sticking them into her mouth, before lifting her up and laying her across the bar.

A gasping Donka picked up a bottle, smashed it over the arm of a chair, then waved the jagged glass at the advancing monster, roaring a challenge.

Stanimir was on the ground, struggling for air, shaking his head. The monster paused as it drew abreast of him, then lifted a foot and slammed it down on the man's head, which popped beneath it, bits of brain shooting across the floor like poorly-cast ball bearings.

The fight drained from Donka when she saw how easily the monster had dispatched Stanimir. The bottle dropped from her hand and she fell back into the chair. She stared up silently at the beast as it came forward. The monster returned her stare, then slid a couple of fingers into her mouth.

Donka's eyes widened and she sucked on the fingers, thinking that maybe the beast had taken a shine to her, that this was foreplay. Perhaps she could use the monster's lustful feelings to bend it to her will.

But the monster hadn't been bewitched by the elderly Donka. As she sucked hopefully, it drove the fingers further into her mouth, jamming the rest of its hand in too, to rip at her tongue and the inside of her throat. Donka choked and spasmed, slapped at the monster some more, then slumped and slid lifelessly from the beast's fingers when it released her.

Plamen was still bent over the pool of vomit. He'd shut his eyes and was rocking back and forth on his knees. Dominic got the feeling that Plamen thought this was a bad dream and was trying to wake himself from it.

The monster circled the moaning man, then switched its attention to Mladen, who was still staggering around, both hands covering the gap where his right eye should be, crying out senselessly, able to focus on nothing except his pain.

The beast picked up the broken bottle that Donka had dropped, then crossed the room and pinned Mladen to the wall. As his remaining eye fixed on the monster, it pulled his hands away from the empty eye socket, then drove the bottle through it, into Mladen's brain, twisting and turning the bottle like a screw.

Mladen didn't last long, which was a mercy, and was dead before the beast pressed its snout up close to the jagged end of the bottle and sucked out a hefty chunk of his brain, nibbling on the scraps as if they were a caviar-like delicacy.

Leaving the dead Mladen to collapse in a heap, the monster returned to where Plamen was rocking and moaning. It touched the top of his skull and he instantly stopped moving and bleating. The monster nodded approvingly, then spread its hands wide and clapped them solidly to the sides of Plamen's head.

There was a sharp cracking noise. The monster struck the sides of Plamen's head again. And again, until the cracking noise was replaced by a softer, juicier noise. It moved aside as he toppled and fell forward, eyes still shut. They would never open again.

That was the end of the locals. The monster cast its gaze around the pub one last time, to be sure they were all dead.

Then it set its sights on Dominic.

## NINETY-TWO

The monster waddled across the room, taking its time, until it was standing over Dominic, who was rigid in his chair, wanting the beast to strike quickly, for this to be over.

The monster leant down until its face was level with Dominic's. He stared at its bloodied snout, the tiny red pupils in the eyes above it, the balls of white around them, the horn that was pressed almost to his nose.

Then the creature made a deep sniffing noise and moved back slightly. It cocked its head and smirked at Dominic. He gazed at it blankly.

The monster frowned and sniffed again. When Dominic still looked blank, it took a step away, hefted up its stomach, and forced a thin stream of piss from its almost fully-erect penis. It grimaced as it did that, making Dominic guess that monsters struggled as much as men when it came to pissing with a hard-on.

The urine hit the floor and splattered. The monster stopped, let its stomach fall back into place, then pointed to the pool of acrid liquid and made a long sniffing sound. Then it pointed to Dominic and sniffed again. And his eyes finally widened with understanding.

"You could smell your piss on me," he croaked.

The monster nodded, understanding the man's words even though it couldn't comprehend any of the human languages.

"You knew I was in the basket all along," he whispered, realising his escape had never been more than an illusion. "You pissed on me to mark me, so that you could follow me, to gain revenge for what I did to your son." He frowned. "But if you knew I was there, why not just…"

He stopped and his eyes flickered to where Martini lay straddled across the bar counter, naked except for her bra.

"Oh no," Dominic moaned.

The monster chuckled darkly. It could see that he understood. The death of the man who'd killed its child wasn't enough. It had suffered a horrible loss, and it meant to inflict a similar loss on him. So it had sat there all day, mourning and plotting. Having marked its prey, it set him loose, figuring there was someone out there that he would run to, someone he loved as much as the monster had loved its son.

Of course it couldn't have been sure. Maybe the human was alone in the world, or maybe the corpse in the cellar had been his lover. (Did the monster even know about the dead man in the cellar? Dominic could only speculate.) But it had been prepared to let him wander, to test its theory that it could hurt him the same way that he had hurt it. If not, it could butcher him further down the line and nothing would be lost.

Thinking he was free, Dominic had called for Martini. He could imagine the monster waiting patiently, watching them through the window that was now filled with the broken Vasil. It hadn't moved until it was certain, until it saw them kiss. Then, when it was sure that this was the man's lover, it struck.

All this flashed through Dominic's mind in a matter of seconds, and the beast saw the penny drop as clearly as it had seen the moon rising on so many delicious nights. When it knew that he was up to speed, it pressed its snout against his left cheek, cynically planting a kiss on him, the way it had seen scores of humans kiss over the years, as it had watched from deep within the shadows from which it dared only rarely emerge.

Releasing Dominic, the monster strode across the room and picked up the bound and struggling Martini. It slung her body over its right shoulder, casually, as if she weighed nothing. She screeched into the folds of her knickers and kicked out as hard as she could, to no avail.

The monster turned and pointed at Dominic. Then it pointed out the open door, up towards the mountains beyond. As he shook his head numbly and stared at the creature, it lifted the folds of its stomach again and stroked its penis, letting Dominic see that it was hard, that it was ready, that it would soon be put to use...

...unless he stopped it.

Then the monster made a high-pitched noise, bent and ducked through the door, sucking in its guts in order not to jam against the sides.

"No!" Dominic shouted after it. "Come back. Don't..."

He stopped. There was no point yelling. The monster had made its position clear. It was going to take Martini back to its shack, to fuck, torture and kill her. Dominic could either stay here and let that happen, or set off through the darkness and try to stop it.

The monster was incapable of human speech, but it had spoken to Dominic as clearly as any man or woman ever had, and what it had said was simple.

*"Abandon her and live, or come after her and die. The choice is yours."*

## NINETY-THREE

A numb Dominic stared around at the corpses. The pub was silent except for the buzzing of insects which had already started to stream in through the open door, attracted to the light and the blood.

It wasn't fair. These people had been kind to him. They'd done nothing to the monster. It should have let them be, waited until Dominic and Martini came out by themselves. He could understand the bereaved beast wanting to make it personal, but killing Anastas, Donka and the rest was a pointless, savage waste.

Then he remembered Curran, the rats, the other bones in the cellar. He figured these creatures, whatever they were, didn't place much value on the average human life.

Slowly he pushed himself out of his chair and stood. His legs were trembling. A wave of dizziness rushed through him and he thought he was going to faint. But it passed a moment later, and though he felt lightheaded, he didn't lose control of his senses.

Swaying sickly, he considered his options. He could do nothing, wait here until the massacre was discovered in the morning, act spaced-out (it wouldn't require much acting), let himself be bundled off somewhere to be interrogated and cared for.

Or he could slip away, carry on down the road, put as much distance as he could between himself and the charnel house, try to lose himself in the wilds of Bulgaria.

Or he could rouse the rest of the villagers, lead them through the forest to the monster's shack. Scenes from old *Frankenstein* movies flashed through his head. They could burn out the killer, maybe rescue Martini. Except he didn't think the monster would be there when they arrived. It surely wouldn't have left him alive if it thought he posed a genuine threat. Dominic had a feeling that it would know if a mob came after it. Perhaps it would hear or smell them from a distance and slip away into the forest, never to be seen again, either killing Martini before it left or taking her with it.

Or…

Dominic sighed miserably. This was the first option he'd thought of, but the last that he'd wanted to mull over.

*Or* he could follow the monster and face it directly, one on one.

That was what the monster was challenging him to do. It had taken Martini as a dare, to see if he had the guts to react as it had. By coming here, far from the safety of its forest base, it had proven its fearlessness, shown it would take any risk in pursuit of revenge for one it had loved.

Did Dominic dare do the same?

He knew there was virtually no way that he could get the better of the monster in a fight. And he doubted it would nobly release Martini if he went up there and offered to take her place — from what he'd seen, nobility didn't have much of a place in the world of the savage beasts.

But if he stood up as the monster had, it would wait for him and accept his challenge or his sacrifice, and there was a chance, slim as it was, that he could defeat the beast, or that it would show mercy and let Martini go. If it didn't know about Curran, maybe it would find his corpse when it returned, realise Dominic had only reacted to the threat of its son, decide he'd suffered enough and let both him and Martini walk away unharmed.

"*Yeah*," Dominic snorted, lapsing back into his mimicry of Curran. "*Like* that's *gonna happen.*"

"It might," he whimpered.

"*Get a fucking grip, Newt,*" he snarled. "*If you go up there, you're marching to your death, and the best you can hope for is that the fucker lets Martini go. Which, I must add, is about as likely as it is that I'll bounce back from the dead and run for political office on a pro-zombie platform.*"

Dominic chuckled weakly. Zombies had been a thing of Curran's when they were younger. He'd often dreamt aloud of becoming one and doing great things as a member of the undead. He felt that zombies had an undeserved bad rep, that resurrected people could be just as useful in death as they'd been in life. He'd often boasted of becoming the first zombie brain surgeon, or the first zombie to climb Everest, or the first zombie prime minister.

Dominic hadn't thought about that in years. He took a few moments to revisit those teenage times, the stupid things he and Curran had talked about, the absurd dreams they'd had for the future.

Then he gathered himself and scowled. This wasn't the time for a trip down memory lane. It was time to choose. He accepted the monster's dare and took it on at its own game, in which case Martini might live to see another sunset. Or he ran like a coward and ensured his own life, at the expense of his girlfriend's.

"What would you have done?" he asked the ghost of Jerome Curran.

"*Ran like a whipped dog,*" he answered in Curran's voice.

"Really?" he whispered.

This time there was no answer.

With a heavy sigh, Dominic took a step towards the door.

Then he stopped and grinned crookedly.

"On an empty stomach?" he murmured. "I don't think so."

Shuffling to the bar, Dominic studied the bottles stacked behind it, then leant across and picked one up. Opening it, he took a whiff of the noxious fumes, then upended it and tossed back a mouthful. He gagged as it hit his throat, then gasped as it struck his stomach. It had been like swallowing a shot of fire.

"Fuck me," he wheezed, eyes watering. "How did they live so long drinking devil's piss?" He grimaced and saluted the corpses. "No offence intended."

Dominic forced himself to down another shot. As a fiery glow spread through him, matching the radioactive glow of his sunburnt skin, he slipped around to the other side of the bar and searched for a knife. To his surprise he couldn't find any, although he did come across a small hammer.

"A lot of good this will do," he muttered, but since there was nothing better within easy reach, he held on to it.

Dominic decided to take the bottle too. He wasn't going to get drunk – he'd need to be in command of his senses – but a few more shots might give him the strength to proceed if he wavered.

"Who wants to go to their death sober?" he sniffed.

Coming back around the bar, he paused and stared at the dead locals one last time. He wanted to say something stirring, along the lines of, "I'll get the bastard for you guys." But the truth was that he was going up there to die, and while he could lie to himself and act as if he had the proverbial snowball's chance in hell, he couldn't lie to these people. For what he had brought upon them, they deserved better than that.

"Sorry," he croaked, and while he knew that wasn't enough, it was all he could find in himself to offer.

Then, with a terrified sob, clutching the hammer in one hand and the bottle of alcohol in the other, he staggered to the doorway, slipped through and stood shivering for a moment in the moonlight, before starting back up the road into the forest.

# PART SIX

*"it's a rat trap and you've been caught"*

*The beast marched through the forest, the female slung over its shoulder, ignoring her muted cries and occasional attempts to tear free of its grip. It could smell the fear on her, and that excited it.*

*The beast felt no sexual attraction to these two-legged creatures, and had never mated with one for enjoyment, only to procreate.*

*Females of its species were so rare that they might as well be non-existent, maybe one born every third or fourth generation. That should have signalled the race's extinction long ago, except they'd discovered that they could breed with their enemies.*

*When one of the beasts felt compelled to sire a child, it kidnapped a female in heat (the beasts could sniff them out), took her deep into the wilds, ravaged her and held her captive. If its seed failed to take root, it killed the woman and tried again when the mood next took it. If successful, it kept her close at hand for the thirteen months that it took the child to incubate.*

*Although the women could bear a beast's child, their bodies were not built to give birth to such over-sized creatures, and they always died during the birthing process, the infant literally ripping and chewing its way out of the womb. It was a dreadful, agonising death, but the beasts didn't care. They felt no more for the mothers than they did for any of the others that they killed, and they usually let their babies feed on the remains of the dead women, treating them to their first bloody feed of many.*

*The beast was in no mood to procreate, but knew that it would eventually feel driven to replace its slaughtered child. The easiest thing would be to kill this woman when it was done with her man, and find another when the time was right. But it wanted to hurt the killer of its son in ways that went beyond mere torment of the flesh. It had some ideas about what it would put him through if he followed it to the shack — and the beast was confident that he would — but it wanted to mock him beyond that. It had no sense of an afterlife, no concept of souls or spirits, but still it wanted to strike at him after he was dead.*

*As the woman struggled, the beast inhaled her scent again and made a dark, gurgling, chuckling sound. If things worked out the way it anticipated, it would keep the woman alive and make off with her when its work here was finished. Take her deep into the forest. Wait for its grief to pass, for its sexual fires to ignite, for the woman to come into heat. And then…*

*The beast would extract a revenge worse than any the man could dream of, and it would be more than the woman could bear. It had suffered a great loss, one that would scar it for many years to come, but it was already looking forward to the future, planning for the night when it would redistribute the pain and make the female pay a most equitable price.*

*A life taken, a life given.*

*What could be fairer than that?*

## NINETY-FOUR

Dominic drank more of the liquor than he'd planned, but it was the only way he could keep going.

The climb back up the mountain was hellish. Coming downhill had been hard, but every step in the opposite direction pushed him to his limits and beyond. He'd long passed the point of total exhaustion. He didn't know what it was inside him that kept him going, but somehow he seemed to find an extra sliver of energy every time he slowed and thought that he'd hit the last of his reserves.

But for all his natural resources, he needed a helping hand, and that was where the firewater came in. Whenever Dominic drew to a halt and couldn't go on, he took a slug from the bottle. The alcohol fired him back into action, and on he'd crawl for another five or ten minutes, before running out of steam again.

"Forget about the dwindling supplies of oil," he muttered. "You could run the world forever on a few barrels of this stuff."

He laughed, but it was barely a sound. He didn't dare waste the last few cells of his internal battery on anything as meaningless as a laugh.

"Not much further now," he kept telling himself, occasionally speaking the words aloud, more often than not just repeating them inside his head. It was a lie – he knew how long the path was, having clocked every step of it on the way down – but it sustained him. If he'd stopped to consider the length of the trek, he'd have collapsed into a weeping heap, and that would have been the end of it all.

Part of him longed for that end. That craven part didn't care about Martini. It didn't even care about what happened to him. It simply demanded rest, sleep, escape from the pain and weariness of the conscious world.

Dominic turned a deaf ear to that treacherous voice. He focused on

Martini's face, the taste of her lips when they kissed, the movements of her body beneath (or on top) of him as they made love. He remembered the first time she'd slid a hand into his pants, on their third date, when he'd taken her to see a movie. The way she'd giggled sexily as she jerked, then sucked him off. It had taken him a long time to come, because he was worried they'd be spotted by another customer or a member of staff.

"This is what happens to naughty little girls," he whispered as he trudged along the path, looking more like a zombie than a living human.

They'd argued that night, on their way home. He couldn't remember what it had been about, only that it had been the first of many, swiftly forgotten, as most of their arguments were. Why did they have to snap at each other so regularly? He loved her. She loved him. Why weren't they happy all the time?

He figured they just weren't cut out for that sort of a relationship. If they pulled through this (he knew that was a virtual impossibility, but had to hope) and stayed together, maybe they'd still be bickering fifty or sixty years down the line.

He wouldn't mind. He was starting to see their arguments as a kind of glue. In the past the fighting had annoyed him, and he'd kept thinking about breaking up with her, most recently in the pub in Laki. But now it didn't bother him. It was their way of communicating. As long as they continued to make up, he didn't care if they argued over stupid, silly stuff for the rest of their lives.

And they *would* make up. He'd see to that. He knew now how much Martini meant to him. Every step he took was an assertion of the love he felt for her. She was more important to him than his own life, literally. In the unlikely event that they came out of this alive, he'd do whatever it took to make things right with her, change if she needed him to, be whatever she wanted him to be.

"I love you, M," he groaned, coming to another standstill. He swayed from side to side, eyes squeezed shut against the tiredness and the pain. Then he took a swig from the bottle, shuddered wildly, and pushed on.

## NINETY-FIVE

When he came to the turning for the path to the cottage, he paused and thought about the lake. He'd like to be buried there. It would be a fitting final resting place. He wouldn't mind dying in the cellar or the cottage, as long as his corpse could be brought back to the lake, floated out into the centre and left to sink, his gradually stripped-bare bones dimly illuminated by the sunlight and moonlight for all the days and nights to come.

But of course that wouldn't happen. The monster would either drag his remains off into the forest and scatter them wherever they fell, or leave them in the cellar for the rats to gnaw. Maybe it would keep one or two scraps of him, to remind it of the man who'd killed its son, but Dominic didn't think so. He'd seen nothing to suggest that monsters were nostalgic.

He took another sip from the bottle and considered going back for one last look at the lake. The world was starting to brighten and dawn couldn't be far off. It would be sweet to cherish one final sunrise before he embraced the eternal night. He could even treat himself to a refreshing dip, as he had on the way back from the cottage.

But he was worried that the monster wouldn't wait. While he had no idea how intelligent it was, it hadn't survived this long by dumb luck. Whether it was intellect or instinct, it knew how to hide.

The monster had killed eight people in the pub. There would be consequences. Teams would be sent to scour the mountains, find the killer and see justice done. The monster would surely be aware of the danger it was in, and would know it had to move on ahead of the hunters.

Dominic had a feeling that the monsters had covered a lot of ground in their time. He didn't think such creatures could remain in one spot too long. He pictured them as nomads, forever wandering, holing up in caves or abandoned shacks like the one in this forest, killing to feed their dark appetites, then gliding on through the night before vengeful humans could track them down and punish them.

He didn't wonder how such beings might have evolved. All he was concerned about was the ticking clock inside his head. The sun was creeping up on them and Dominic was pretty sure that the monster would abandon its base and take off for forests new before the day was far advanced. If he didn't get to the cottage within the first few hours of daybreak, the beast would kill Martini or take her with it.

Dominic only had a small window of time to play with, and he was determined not to waste the opportunity that the monster had granted him.

"I'm coming, M," he whispered, and on he staggered, wincing every time his scalded flesh was struck by one of the penetrating rays of light of the dawning day.

## NINETY-SIX

It was day for real by the time Dominic came to the clearing in the forest and set his sights on the small log cottage. When he'd first spotted it, he'd thought of it as a fairy tale dwelling. Now he knew it was more suited to a horror story.

He couldn't see the monster or Martini. Dominic had a good idea where they would be waiting, but shuffled towards the cottage first, in case he was wrong.

He had to pause for breath on each of the three steps up to the planks where the porch had once stood. He was glad there weren't more of them. He didn't think he could have climbed a full staircase.

No candles burned inside the cottage now, but light streamed in through the windows. The room looked much smaller than it had when he'd last been here. He stared around silently at the evidence of the battle that had taken place, the scattered bedding, the splashes and smears of fresh blood across the layers of old dried-in blood and shit. He spent a long time looking at the wicker basket on which he'd killed the younger monster, and in which he'd later hidden from its father.

There was still a strong, acidic stench from when the older monster had pissed over the basket and Dominic. And was there some of his own scent mixed in with it, or was he imagining that? He grimaced as he recalled how clever he thought he was being, pissing at the same time as the beast, thinking he had fooled it.

Dominic felt a strong urge to crawl back into the basket and pull the lid closed over himself. It could serve as a coffin. He'd lie in the familiar gloom, shut his eyes, smile as he drifted off to sleep and later death. He didn't think it would take him long to die. Maybe the monster wouldn't check for him there. If he didn't show, it might assume that he'd decided not to come. Cursing him as a coward, it would set off through the forest, leaving him behind to perish and calcify. Maybe hunters would discover him if they found the cottage, or perhaps he'd lie undisturbed for years until the monster swung back this way again.

He liked the thought of a soothing fade away to black, but he'd come here to try and save Martini. What sort of grand lover would he be if he gave up on her now, having forced himself through the pain barrier all this way? Comfort wasn't his for the taking. He didn't deserve that sweet release.

Dominic looked around listlessly for a weapon that might prove more effective than the hammer, but there was nothing. He could have looked in the ditch, where he'd found the rusty knife, but he was afraid that if he crawled down into it, he wouldn't be able to crawl back out again.

"Fuck it," he whispered and took another swig from the bottle. To his surprise, it was three-quarters full — he was sure he'd drunk more than that. He thought about taking a longer draught, but as bleary as he was, he was still in control of his senses. He didn't want to get drunk. He'd definitely be no good to Martini if he was cross-eyed and legless.

One last sip, then he carefully set the bottle aside, shuffled to the doorway, across the plank and down the steps. A deep breath. A short stretch to loosen his stiff, aching limbs. Then he made his slow and solemn way to where he was sure the monster was waiting for him — in the cellar.

## NINETY-SEVEN

The doors of the box around the entrance hung open. Dominic could see light from within, much stronger than it had been the last time he'd approached. The monster must have lit more candles. Maybe it needed the light because of its poor eyesight, or maybe it just wanted Dominic to be able to see clearly, to render him even more scared than he would have been otherwise.

"No need for that," he whispered. "You'd have been every bit as menacing in the dark."

Dominic stepped over the lip of the box, on to the hard earth around the hole. He noted that the monster had replaced the trunk which its son had torn loose. It wasn't set as neatly as it had been, but it was upright. The monster must have taken the time to do that, to make it easier for him to climb down.

"Thoughtful," he muttered wryly, then turned, bent and stretched out his left foot, searching for the first toehold on his descent into Hell.

He didn't look down as he climbed, trying to blank out thoughts of what was to come, afraid he might lose his nerve and bolt for freedom if he dwelt on what he was doing. But he couldn't block out the scurrying sounds of the rats or the heavy breathing of the monster. He figured the breathing was for his benefit. The monster had deftly proved when it followed him to the pub that it could be as quiet as a mouse when it wanted.

When he came to the base of the trunks, he stepped off and stood in the zone where the monsters had pissed repeatedly to repel the rats. His back was to the bulk of the cellar. For a few seconds he stood in the piss-soaked clearing, staring up at the hole in the ceiling and the sky beyond, savouring what would almost surely be his final glimpse of it. He dully noted that clouds had swept in and obscured what had been a clear blue sky on every other day of their holiday. If only that cover had been around when it mattered. If he hadn't been sunburnt, he probably never would have come this way in the first place.

But it was too late to change what had passed, and he'd only torment himself if he started playing with notions of what might have been. Sighing with resignation, he turned his back on the world of daylight and mankind, and gave himself over entirely to the dark, flickering, underworld domain of the monster and its murdered son.

## NINETY-EIGHT

The first thing he noticed was that the cross was still upright, but Curran's corpse had been replaced with the wriggling figure of Martini. She was completely naked now. The monster had removed her bra and tied it around her eyes. Her mouth was still stuffed with her knickers and she was whimpering through the thin material.

Her feet were clear of the floor, and the monster must have pissed on the base of the cross, because although the rats were packed tight around it, none of them tried to scale the crucifix to nibble Martini's flesh.

Dominic couldn't see any marks on her, not even a bruise, and he was relieved to note no semen stains around her crotch. If it was in the monster's mind to rape her, as it had indicated in the bar, it didn't seem to have got round to that yet.

Dominic wanted to rush to Martini, pull her from the cross and lead her to safety, but he could see the monster standing behind her, crouched low, its snout hidden, peering malevolently at Dominic over her shoulder. Some of the rats were skittering across its feet but it paid them no heed.

As Dominic composed his opening statement, a nearby rat was knocked into the no-go area around the trunks. It crashed into his ankle with a startled squeak. He yelped louder than the rat and kicked it across the cellar. The monster laughed cruelly, relishing the human's fear.

Dominic ignored the chuckling beast. He'd spotted something close to where he stood — the bony remains of Jerome Curran. There wasn't much left of his butchered friend, but rats were still gnawing his corpse, burrowing their way through the last scraps of his flesh, searching for titbits of his guts and brain.

Dominic would have wept for Curran under different circumstances, but he knew he was better off saving his tears for himself and Martini. They'd most likely be corpses too soon enough, playthings for the monster, then fodder for the rats.

Raising his gaze, Dominic steeled himself and called out, "M? I came."

Martini struggled violently when she heard his voice, shrieking into the folds of her gag. The monster snorted, reached round with one hand and flicked her right nipple, before pinching the breast. She screamed mutedly.

"There's no need for that," Dominic snapped. As the creature glared at him, he added weakly, "Stop. Please."

The monster made one of its high-pitched noises, but released the breast. Dominic nodded gratefully, then focused on the blindfolded Martini.

"I've come for you, M. I'll do whatever I can to save you. Don't struggle. Keep quiet. Let me talk with this thing. I love you. Trust me. OK?"

Martini shook her head, tried to say something, then slumped and fell silent.

Dominic focused on the monster. He could see its dead son behind it, hanging upright on the wall. Its father must have hung it from a nail or hook, where the rats couldn't get at it, until it could take the body off into the forest and treat it to whatever sort of a burial was common among its foul kind. Or maybe it would leave its child here, pinned to the wall like the world's biggest butterfly.

"That was self-defence," Dominic said, pointing at the suspended beast with his hammer. Then he pointed at the corpse near his feet. "It killed my friend, then attacked me. I had no choice."

The monster hissed and brought its head up, opening its mouth so that Dominic could see its rows of fangs. It leant forward and licked the side of Martini's neck. She squealed and pulled away.

"Easy," Dominic barked, afraid she'd excite the beast and goad it into action.

Martini tried to bark something back at him, probably along the lines of, "Take it easy yourself, you bastard."

Dominic grinned sickly. If this was to be where they died, at least they'd perish as they'd spent so much of their time together — arguing.

Taking a deep breath, Dominic stepped clear of the trunks, closer to the monster. The rats parted before him. Some bared their teeth as the monster had moments before, but they didn't attack.

The monster stepped out from behind Martini and took a half-step forward. Its penis was erect and its fingers were curled into fists. When Dominic saw the size of the beast's arms, he knew he stood no chance of bettering it in a fight. One blow would knock his head clear from his neck.

"Please," Dominic said again, letting his hammer drop — it was useless anyway, so he might as well make a show of throwing it away. He extended his hands out to the sides, to show his peaceful intent. "Let us go. I know I've hurt you, but your son hurt me first, and you hurt me even more when you killed all those people in the pub. A life for several lives, his for all of my friends. Let it end there."

The monster cocked its head. It seemed to Dominic as if it was frowning reflectively, but he couldn't be sure. He didn't know how much of this it understood, if anything.

With a snort, the monster reached across and placed a hand over Martini's crotch. It wriggled a finger menacingly.

"No!" Dominic shouted, dropping to his knees, frightening the rats, which parted in a hissing, spitting mob around him. "I'm begging you. Take me. If my friends weren't enough, have me too. Just let her go. She did nothing to you. Show her mercy. You're capable of that, aren't you? If you can love your child, you must be able to respect the feelings that other people have for their loved ones."

In response, the monster's snout parted again and it leered at him, then rubbed its hand over Martini's flesh.

"*Me*," Dominic moaned, pressing both hands against his chest, grimacing as his flaking flesh flared. "Take me, not her. I'm the one you want. *Me*."

The monster paused and studied the kneeling human. It let its hand fall away as it considered what to do with him. Then, as he gazed at it hopefully, it grinned and pushed against the cross, which toppled to one side, throwing Martini towards the crush of rats on the floor.

"No!" Dominic screamed, reaching out to her, even though he knew it was hopeless.

Martini struck the floor hard. The force of the fall sent the balled-up knickers flying from her mouth and she cried out with pain, shock and fear. The rats darted out of her way as she landed among them, but almost instantly began to close on her, smelling the blood where she'd cut herself.

Before the rats could dig in, the monster hauled the cross upright. Martini was screaming with all her might, cursing the monster, crying out to Dominic to save her, begging God to intervene.

"M!" Dominic howled. "Stop. You need to be quiet."

"Fuck you!" she hollered.

"I can't help you if you anger it," he protested.

"What the fuck are you gonna do anyway?" she retorted.

"Trade myself for you, if I can," Dominic said quietly, and that settled Martini down.

The bra over her eyes had shifted during the fall, and she could half-see him out of her left eye. "Dominic?" she wept, horrified and desperate.

"We're in trouble, M," he said, not trying to stop his own tears, which were flowing freely. "I don't know if I can get you out of this, but I'll try. I need your help, OK? Maybe we can appeal to it, but only if we keep calm."

"You really think...?" she asked.

"No," he smiled. "But you're my girl, so I've got to try."

Martini managed a sick laugh, then fell silent as he'd requested.

Dominic turned his attention back to the monster. It had watched the interplay with interest, like an audience member at the theatre.

"Me for her," Dominic said, pointing to himself, then Martini, trying to make the monster understand. "If you let her go, she'll mourn me. She'll feel terrible. You'll hurt me more that way than if you kill her."

The monster stared at him blankly. Dominic figured words weren't getting him anywhere, so he pointed instead, repeating the gestures, hoping the monster would understand what he was offering.

The monster sniffed and its eyes narrowed. It could tell what the human wanted. It had no intention of letting the woman go, and the man knew that, but he didn't want to believe. He wanted to hope. It was a curious thing that the beast had noted in others of his type. They didn't always dare face the truth. That was a failing the monster had taken advantage of before, and it planned to do so again.

Taking a step away from the bound Martini, the monster lifted its guts-packed stomach to reveal its erection in all its menacing glory. Mimicking Dominic's gestures, it stroked its hard penis, then pointed at him, then at the penis.

Beneath his layers of pus and sunburn, Dominic paled. "You've got to be fucking joking," he croaked, but he could see the monster was serious. Someone was going to get raped and killed in the cellar today. Probably both of them. But the beast was telling him that if he surrendered voluntarily, if he opened wide and took the monster's rampant member in his mouth, maybe it would spare Martini.

It wasn't the way he wanted to go, but his choice was clear. If this proved the saving of Martini, so be it. A guy could do worse for the life of the woman he loved than offer himself up as a sexual slave on her behalf.

"I only wish I had an ST-fucking-D that I could pass on to you," Dominic growled, then spat with disgust and shuffled across the floor of the cellar on his knees, towards where the horny monster was eagerly awaiting its blowjob.

## NINETY-NINE

Dominic's throat was dry. He wished now that he'd finished off the rest of the liquor, so that this humiliating act could pass in a dazed blur. Instead he'd have to bear conscious witness to it all.

He wondered where it would end. Once he'd pleasured the monster with his mouth, would it turn him over and cornhole him until he bled from his arse? He suspected that was probably on the cards.

Maybe he'd die from his anal raping, given the size of the beast's cock, but he doubted it. More likely the monster would make him give head again, to clean it off, before ripping him apart the way its son had done with Curran.

Dominic paused, frozen with horror by the scene playing out in his mind's eye. The monster grunted impatiently and beckoned him forward, but he couldn't move.

*It isn't worth it*, he thought, gaze flicking to Martini, hanging helplessly on the cross. *It won't let her go. This will just give her a preview of what lies in store for her. I should piss off the fucker, try to get it so mad that it'll kill us both quickly.*

The monster grunted again and stamped the floor. The rats around it squealed and shied away.

Martini was staring at him, half horrified, half hopeful. She didn't think he could save her, but she wanted to believe, the same way he wanted to believe that the monster would relent, decide the offer of submission was as valid as the act itself, relax and smile softly, set the pair of them free and stay behind in the cellar to grieve for its lost son.

But *want* didn't matter. Dominic could see by the beast's hungry expression that it had no intention of letting him go. It wouldn't let Martini go either, not until it had ravaged her too, not until it had killed them both and left their carcasses for the rats to devour. He was a fool to have dared believe any differently.

Dominic looked around for the hammer that he'd dropped. If he could strike the monster, it might lash out and kill him instantly without meaning to. In a rage at having lost its chance to make the killer of its son suffer, it might lay into Martini, finish her off before she knew what was happening. That wouldn't be much of a relief, but it was the best they could hope for.

The trouble was, Dominic couldn't spot the hammer. It was lost beneath the ever-moving sea of rats. A few of them were sniffing him, but none had attacked yet. All of his cuts had scabbed over, so there was no scent of blood to egg them on, and the pus from his boils seemed to be acting as a deterrent. But if he went rooting among them, one was bound to bite and draw blood, which might set off the others.

The monster crooked a finger at him. Then it pointed at Martini, letting him know it would target her if he didn't honour his obligations.

Dominic whimpered, not sure what to do. Back up and search for the hammer, or shuffle forward and give the creature its blowjob? He could bite down hard on the penis, maybe enrage the beast that way. But its cock was so long and thick that if it stuffed it fully into his mouth, he probably wouldn't be able to bite, like when a bully at school had once jammed the edge of his hand between Dominic's lips, wedging them apart, rendering his teeth useless.

As the monster growled and stepped towards him, Dominic spotted something close to where he was kneeling. An arm. It had been stripped bare of most of its flesh and sinews, and rats were chewing on the bones, trying to clean them of every last bit of gristle.

It was Curran's arm. It must have come free and fallen when the monster was moving it from the cross. Dominic knew it was Curran's because of the ring on the middle finger, the odd ring that he'd picked up earlier in their travels, with the five-centimetre spike sticking out of it.

The spike was a pitiful weapon. He might scratch the monster with it, but doubted he could wreak any substantial damage. Still, maybe a scratch would be enough to draw its wrath down fully upon himself and the quaking Martini.

But even if that feeble plan worked, and Dominic could drive the beast wild by jabbing it with the spike, the ring was wedged on Curran's finger. The monster wouldn't wait for Dominic to twist it off and arm himself. It would move in to block him as soon as it saw what he was doing.

Thinking quickly, Dominic raised a hand to stop the advancing monster. As it squinted, he smiled weakly and wet his lips with his tongue to show that he was willing to proceed, then made a *Come on, big boy* gesture. The monster chuckled lustily and moved forward until its cock was within touching distance of his lips. The smell of it made his nose wrinkle. Personal hygiene clearly wasn't high on the monster's list of priorities, and there was a dark yellow crust around the foreskin of the beast's penis that made Dominic's eyes water.

Dominic glanced up at the monster's face. He had to lean back to lock gazes, looking up past the folds of its massive stomach at its leering mouth and tightly focused eyes. It nodded firmly, the lips at the end of its snout twitching, its cock quivering ahead of Dominic's mouth as it tightened with anticipation.

"For what I am about to receive…" Dominic muttered, lamely trying to crack a joke and relieve his misery. Then he lowered his head and opened wide.

## ONE HUNDRED

Dominic pulled back just before his lips brushed the tip of the monster's engorged penis. With a scowl, it reached for him, to tug him in tight. But then he gagged and heaved as if he was about to get sick. The monster paused. As vile as it was, it didn't like the idea of the human vomiting over its crotch.

Dominic twisted aside and doubled over, making a retching noise. The monster snickered and decided to wait until he was done throwing up. It scratched its bulging testicles while it waited, so as not to lose the mood.

But Dominic was faking, dry heaving to stall the monster. While it laughed and scratched, he tugged at the ring on the finger of the severed arm, which was now shielded from the beast by the bulk of Dominic's hunched-over body.

The rats that had been clinging to the arm hissed at Dominic, but they were sated and pulled back rather than fight him for it. They'd seen plenty of their kin squashed by the monsters, and saw no need to risk their lives when they weren't overly hungry.

The ring should have slid off smoothly, since there was little flesh left on the finger. But Dominic's hands were trembling, with fear and because he had to keep up the pretence that he was getting sick. His fingers were also slippery with sweat. He scrabbled for the ring, tried tugging it from the bone, but it stuck, and his fingers came away even slippier than before.

There was no time to get a proper grip on the finger and try again. Instead he bent over further, closed his eyes to the horror of what he was about to do, and set his teeth around the ring on his dead friend's finger. With one violent motion he tore it free, the bone of the finger snapping and coming away with the ring.

Dominic jammed his tongue through the centre of the ring and poked out the bit of bone that was dangling from it. As the bone fell to the floor,

Dominic slid the ring on to his own middle finger, so that the tip of the spike jutted out of the top of his hand.

Turning sharply, Dominic let himself collapse on to his back so that he was directly beneath the monster. It realised something was wrong and started to react, but before it could, Dominic swept his hand up and forward.

Dominic had been hoping to puncture the monster's testicles – if that didn't piss off the beast, nothing would – but seeing the danger, it let its stomach fall protectively over its manhood and pushed its guts forward automatically, the way it had when it manoeuvred through the doorways of the cottage and pub.

As the monster's stomach bulged, Dominic's arm was driven down while continuing forward. The tip of the spike caught on the creature's flesh and dug in, easily slicing through its translucent skin, then carried on to gouge out a thin channel, ten centimetres long, before tearing free of the beast's stomach wall.

The monster screeched, more with surprise than pain, and took a quick step back from where Dominic lay sprawled. As it did, he saw some tendrils of gut ooze out of the hole, almost like sausages poking through, and hope flared within him again. If he could carve open more gouges like that one, maybe the monster's stomach would rip into shreds. He hadn't thought the flesh would split so easily. The battle could yet be his.

But as Dominic prepared to strike again, the monster lashed out with a huge, gnarly foot. The toes caught him beneath his ribs and sent him flying across the room. He smashed into the tree trunks down which he'd earlier climbed, and fell to the floor in a stunned, broken heap. His right arm landed beneath him and snapped. It should have brought a scream to his lips, but all the air had been driven from his lungs.

As he lay on his back, spasming helplessly, right arm useless, Dominic could only watch through his tears as the monster screamed hatefully, then stormed across the cellar, kicking rats out of its way, determined to make him pay tenfold for his act of defiance.

## ONE HUNDRED AND ONE

If the monster had paused to tend to its wound, things might have played out very differently. It could have gently pushed the strands of gut back inside, bound the injury with a strip of cloth, then set about finishing what it had started with the incapacitated humans. It would have been a simple matter for it to mop up the loose ends and take its time torturing and killing the man, before making off with the woman.

But it could tell that the injury wasn't life-threatening, so in its rush to punish the man, the monster ignored the gash in its stomach and pushed on, crashing across the room like a nightmare come to life, bearing down on the wheezing, terrified, stricken Dominic.

Its stomach rocked up and down as it surged forward, and a few more tendrils of gut were thrust out of the narrow gap. The beast was unaware of this, but some of the rodents took note.

The rats were indiscriminate feeders. The monsters had supplied them with fresh meat during their visits here – humans and animals that they'd culled while creeping through the mountainous forests – but as Dominic had seen when he first explored the cellar, they had no objection to eating one of their own. They were simple creatures. Once they caught sight or scent of food, they zoned in on it.

Most of the rats in the monster's path scattered, but a few spotted the loops sticking out of the hole in its undercarriage and paused. They sniffed the air, tensed with hungry anticipation, then swarmed forward, mouths opening as Dominic's had mere moments before.

The monster came to an abrupt standstill when the first rat bit into its guts. With a high-pitched squeal, it yanked its stomach into the air and jerked it from side to side, instantly alert to the threat, looking to throw the rat clear.

The monster succeeded in ridding itself of the rat, which went zipping across the room, to smash into a wall and perish instantly, but lost its balance doing so. Its arms cartwheeled wildly as it tried to steady itself, but it was too late, and it fell backwards with a fearful cry, landing with a resounding crash.

Before the monster could rise above the cloud of dust and dirt which had been sent shooting into the air, more rats darted forward and seized the exposed guts. The monster shrieked and slapped at them, but they were not to be swatted away so easily. While several were knocked back, others dug in, fangs sinking into the soft flesh of the enticing intestines.

One of the rats backpedalled and ended up pulling out a longer strand of the monster's guts. It roared with pain and tried to get to its feet, but the rats refused to be thwarted. More drove forward, ripping at the guts and the thin flesh around them, widening the hole in the monster's stomach.

The monster rolled around in a mad circle, seeking to crush its tormentors. Lots were caught beneath it, but others swept in to replace them, wave after wave, the rats reacting with excited viciousness to whatever sharp pheromones the terrified monster was excreting.

The bruised, battered, immobile Dominic watched with disbelief as a rat shoved its entire head into the widening hole, then slipped inside the monster's stomach, to root through the layers of guts.

Others followed that first pioneer, and soon dozens of rats had forced their way into the beast, visible through the translucent flesh of its stomach. The hole was now a gaping chasm through which a stream of rats could freely flood. Those who'd been first in emerged with glistening, grisly trophies – bits of gut and inner organs – which they scurried off with to devour. Each was replaced by several more as all of the rats in the cellar converged on the screeching, writhing monster, eager to make hay while the bloodred sun shined.

The monster didn't go down without a fight. It smashed scores of rats to a pulp with its massive fists, and bit the heads off several more. But there were too many of them. No creature could have turned back the scurrying, snapping rodents, even if it had been three times the monster's size.

A few minutes after Dominic had torn what should have been an insignificant strip of flesh out of the monster's stomach, its limbs fell still and its massive head toppled backwards. It stared at the ceiling, blinking like a human, feeling the last of its lifeforce leaving its body, perhaps wondering how so mighty a beast had fallen to so insignificant a foe.

The monster's head shifted as it looked for the hanging carcass of its son, wanting that to be the last thing it saw. But blood had pumped from its lips and the rats seized on that, forcing their way into the creature's mouth, ripping at its tongue, swarming across its face.

The monster died covered by the rats, blind in a seething, sharp-fanged, multi-legged shroud, wishing in its final moments that it could have met its death in the open, beneath the light of the moon, not in an enclosed space like this, discovering only at the very end of its time that even monsters, in their loneliest, weakest moments, could find themselves afraid of the dark.

## ONE HUNDRED AND TWO

Dominic didn't want to move. He just wanted to lie there and black out, so that he couldn't feel the pain. But he was worried that the rats would target him once they'd finished picking clean the monster's carcass. The thought of them sniffing him, nibbling at his lips and eyelids while he was unconscious, then digging in, spurred him into action.

With a groan of agony he sat up and took some explorative breaths, feeling his ribs to check if any were broken. Martini was crying on the cross, calling out his name, begging him to free her. But for a minute he ignored her, waiting for the fireworks inside his head to fade, for his stomach to settle, for the world to stop spinning around him.

When he dared stand, he pushed himself to his knees, then his feet, using his left hand, cradling the broken right arm to his chest, holding it as still as he could.

"Dominic," Martini screamed. "Stop standing there like a dummy. Come over here and get me down."

Dominic scowled and thought about leaving her here for an hour or two, to teach her a lesson. Then he laughed at himself. How quickly he could swing from total love to savage pettiness!

"You're fucking *laughing* at me?" Martini shrieked.

"Hush, M," Dominic grimaced. "Don't disturb the rats while they're feeding or they might attack you."

That shut her up, and she hung in silence after that, trying not to whimper.

Dominic limped across the cellar, gaze fixed on the cross, ignoring the rats cavorting round the monster's corpse. He didn't stop to gloat. He was too weary for that. He felt a dull sense of relief to be alive, but he didn't feel triumphant. Maybe that would come later. Or maybe it wouldn't. This hadn't been a contest in which bragging rights were at stake. He'd been fighting for his life, and mere survival was all that mattered in such a situation.

He stopped when he reached Martini and leant into her, burying his face between her breasts, not sexually, but like a child cuddling up to its mother. She almost snapped at him, but when she felt him sobbing, she realised how drained and distraught he was.

"It's OK," she whispered, wishing she could hold him. "You did brilliantly. You saved me. You saved both of us. You came back for me." She started to cry again, heaving sobs. "I didn't... think... you'd come. I thought... I was going... to die here... alone."

"I love you, M," Dominic wept, throwing his left arm around her and hugging her tightly.

"I love you too," she cried, then searched for his lips with hers. Dominic sensed what she wanted, and he lifted his head slowly, painfully. They stared at each other with bloodshot, tear-filled eyes. Then, without saying anything, their lips came together, and in the horror of the cellar, with the rats still gnawing on the bones of the monster and stripping it of its flesh and inner organs, the pair of lovers closed their eyes, drowned out everything else in the world, and kissed.

## ONE HUNDRED AND THREE

Getting Martini down with just one functioning arm was harder than Dominic had anticipated. She was strapped to the posts with old, fraying strands of rope. He tried picking at the knots but they were far too tight. He looked around for a knife but couldn't find any. In the end he eased the ring from his right hand – crying out loud with pain as he did so – and slipped it on to the middle finger of his left, before slicing at the ropes with it, targeting the most frayed areas.

"I bet Curran never thought his ring would be put to so many uses," Martini murmured as he worked on the ropes, slowly sawing through them.

"If he was alive, I'm sure he'd claim the credit," Dominic sniffed. "He'd say he had a hunch we were going to get into trouble, claim it was part of a master plan."

"Yeah," Martini smiled. Then she sighed. "I'll miss him."

Dominic didn't respond to that. He didn't need to. They both knew the loss of Curran would leave a massive hole in his life.

Martini started asking him what had happened before she'd found him in the pub, how he'd been so badly sunburnt, how he'd wound up here, if he knew anything about the monster's origins.

"Hush," he said again, smiling to show he meant it lovingly, that he didn't want to start an argument. "I'll tell you all about it later. Just let me work on the ropes for now. I'm so tired, M. I'm worried I might faint. Let me concentrate and, once we're out of here, I'll answer every question you throw at me."

Martini frowned, but she could see how exhausted and battered he was, and she realised this wasn't the time to take him to task. In fact, as she studied him hard at work on the ropes, face knotted seriously, determined to release her regardless of the agony he must be in, she wondered if she would ever go for his jugular again.

Dominic had done something monumental for her tonight (she wasn't aware that day had broken). She didn't think there were many men in the world who would have offered all for the life of a loved one.

She adored her boyfriend more than ever, and she didn't want that feeling to fade. She'd enjoyed their arguments in the past but it was time to put the bickering behind them. How could she ever snap at him heatedly again, knowing that he loved her completely, that he'd risked everything to win her freedom? No, the arguments were a thing of the past, she was sure of that.

Then he accidentally nicked the flesh of her arm while sawing at the ropes.

"Watch what you're doing, fucknuts!" she shrieked.

"You try it, if you think it's so easy," he muttered.

"That better not scar," she growled.

"I hope it does," he retorted.

They glowered at each other, then burst out laughing.

"Prick," she smiled.

"Bitch," he beamed.

And they both felt far more relaxed after that.

## ONE HUNDRED AND FOUR

Eventually he managed to free her right arm, which allowed her to help him with the rest of the ropes. She took the ring from him and they alternated sawing at the strands. Not long after that, she slipped free of her shackles and he supported her as she stepped down from the cross and waited for the pins and needles to pass.

She teared up as she studied the broken-armed, bruised, bloodied, burnt and blistered Dominic. She noted the way he fought to stop her noticing his discomfort as she leant on him. He was in so much pain, but he was trying to hide it for her sake, so that she wouldn't feel bad.

"I'm fine now," she said, before she truly felt steady on her feet.

"Are you sure?" he asked as she swayed, ready to catch her if she toppled.

"Dandy," she smiled thinly, then fell silent as she stared at the mass of rats spread across the floor between them and the tree trunks.

"It's OK," he told her, not entirely sure that it was. "They won't touch us."

"What about my cuts?" she asked, studying herself for any fresh blood.

"All scabbed over."

"But they might open again when I move. Maybe we should wait until…"

He shook his head. "We need to get out of here, M. A lot of the rats have fed or are feeding. We're of no interest to them at the moment. But they'll get hungry again, and quickly, I bet."

She shivered, then nodded firmly and took a trembling step forward.

"Do you want to lean on me?" Dominic asked.

"No," she said, then looked back at him. "Do *you* want to lean on *me*?"

He smiled. "I'm not sure that *lean* is the right word." He wriggled his hips slightly, so that his penis shook in a mock show of lust.

"Filthbag," she smirked, then the pair of them hobbled across the room, nudging rats out of their way, each ready to grab the other if either of them stumbled and needed a helping hand.

## ONE HUNDRED AND FIVE

The rats parted obligingly ahead of the humans – there was enough meat on the monster's bones to last them a few full and happy days – and they made it across the room without incident.

Dominic paused as they grew near the trunks, to stare glumly at Curran's remains. When Martini saw what he was looking at, she gasped and looked away. "Poor Jerome," she moaned.

"He didn't deserve this," Dominic whispered.

"Of course not," Martini said.

"I hope it was quick, but I don't think…"

"Shh," she stopped him. "We'll never know, so don't torment yourself imagining the worst. Hell, maybe he fell and cracked his head on a rock. He might have been dead before the monster found him."

Dominic arched an eyebrow, even though it hurt.

"It's unlikely," Martini laughed. "But wouldn't you rather picture that than him tied to the cross like I was, alive and struggling while the monster tortured him?"

Dominic almost told her that Curran *had* been strapped to the cross before her, but decided that would only make her feel worse. She was right. This wasn't the time to discuss the dead. Nothing good could come of it.

"The younger one killed Curran," Dominic said instead. "At least I think it did. There was no sign of the father when I first came."

"There were two of them?" Martini asked shrilly.

Dominic pointed at the monster hanging from the wall. It was the first time she'd seen it and she cried out with fear.

"What's wrong?" Dominic asked.

"If there were two," she whimpered, "why not three?" As Dominic stared at her, his eyes widening, she added, "If there was a son, there must be a mother, right?"

"Not necessarily," he croaked. "She might be long dead."

"Or she might be waiting for us up top," Martini pointed out.

Dominic considered that, then forced a shaky smile. "Fuck it. We've killed two of the bastards already. If we've got to deal with Mummy Monster too, bring her on."

Martini blinked, then laughed, but softly. "You killed the son by yourself?"

"Yeah."

"You've turned into an action hero."

Dominic looked down at his naked, shivering, sunburnt wreck of a body. "I don't think Hollywood's gonna come calling for me just yet," he remarked drily.

The pair shared a short smile, then Martini forced herself to look at Curran's corpse. "What are we going to do with him?" she asked.

Dominic winced. "We'll have to leave him here."

"You don't want to bring his body with us?"

He cringed. "I'm not sure I'm going to be able to drag my own bones up the trunk, never mind Curran's. We can come back for him later, or tell others where to find him, depending on how we decide to play this."

"Do you think we should…" Martini began, but Dominic stopped her with a soft shake of his head.

"We'll discuss it later. We need to get out of here, M, while I can still haul myself forward, because believe me, I won't be able to for much longer."

She nodded sombrely, then tapped the trunks. "Up you go then. I'll follow."

"Ladies first," he protested.

"Not this time," she said. "You've done a lot for me tonight. It's my turn to look out for you. Scoot on up and don't worry if you slip. I'll be there to catch you."

More tears came to Dominic's eyes, but this time they were tears of joy. He wanted to kiss her, but thought he might faint in her arms if he did. Instead he turned, grabbed the trunks, told himself he could do this, fixed on the daylight in the world above that he had never thought to see again, and started to climb.

## ONE HUNDRED AND SIX

If he'd been by himself, he doubted he would have managed it. He had endured more than anyone should ever be forced to over the last couple of days, and this was one obstacle too many. Alone, he would almost certainly have slid back, spread out on the floor, and let sleep claim him. And if the rats had devoured him while he was unconscious, so be it. Anything would have been preferable to the agony of the climb.

But Martini gently coaxed him on, telling him she loved him, he was doing great, there wasn't much further to go. His own inner voice – the one that had driven him so far when his body seemed drained of energy – had fallen silent, but Martini replaced it. He couldn't let her down, not when she was showering this much love and faith upon him.

Dominic lost track of time. He slipped into a fugue-like state, where there was only the light above and the sound of Martini's voice in his ears. He regularly stopped and clung motionlessly to the trunks, only moving again when Martini poked him and urged him to continue.

Eventually he reached the top and slid into the world like a newborn, scraping his stomach on the rim of the box around the hole as he had done the last time he passed this way, crying out, but more with laughter than pain. If this was the worst the world could now throw at him, he'd take it in a heartbeat.

Martini slithered out beside him and the pair sprawled across the grass, soaking up the rays of the sun. Though it was cloudy again, the clouds weren't as thick as they'd been earlier, and sunlight burst through the gaps. Dominic knew he shouldn't be lying in the sun in his condition, but it was so wonderful that he didn't care.

Martini roused him, worried about his scalded flesh. Murmuring in his ear, she got him back on his feet, holding his left hand to help him rise, staring with concern at his right arm, which was hanging limply by his side.

"How's the arm?" she asked.

Dominic shook his head. He didn't know how to answer that.

"Was it OK when you were climbing?" she pressed.

"I can't remember," he said, the ascent already a distant memory, barely able to recall how he'd made it up the trunks with just one working arm.

Martini pressed a couple of fingers to his right cheek and smiled warmly at him. "You're going to be fine," she promised. "I'll get you out of here. Trust me, like I trusted you."

"I do," he said, then laughed at the phrase, though he wasn't sure why.

Martini turned and looked round the glade. "Is that the path?" she asked.

Dominic forced himself to focus. "I think so," he mumbled.

"You need to be sure," she sweetly admonished him. "We can't afford to get lost in the forest."

He stared until he was certain. "Yes. That takes us towards the lake. If we turn right when we get to the wider path, it'll lead us to the road."

Martini nodded and started ahead, calling him after her, figuring he'd make better time if he was following her rather than trailing along beside her.

"Wait," Dominic stopped her. "Inside the cottage. There's a bottle."

"Water?"

He smirked. "Booze."

Martini shook her head. "You don't need that now."

"But it gave me strength," he muttered.

She retraced her steps, stood on her toes and kissed him again. "I'll give you strength now," she whispered as they parted.

"More likely you'll give me a hard-on," he giggled.

"That too," she smiled and pecked him again. "Catch me if you can, Casanova," she purred, then set off down the path, calling to her sunburnt, weary lover, enticing him on with the sound of her voice and the promise of delights to come.

## ONE HUNDRED AND SEVEN

It was a long, slow march along the path, but although Dominic stumbled often, he never fell. Martini was worried that they might be attacked by another of the monsters, but that thought never crossed Dominic's mind. It wasn't that he'd dismissed the possibility that there might be a third, as yet unseen member of the beastly family. He was just too exhausted to care.

When they came to the end of the path, Martini turned right, as Dominic had directed, but he called her back and said he wanted to sit by the edge of the lake a while.

"I don't think that's a good idea," Martini said. "We should keep moving."

"We're fine," he said. "We'll have daylight for a long time yet."

"But if you stop, you might not be able to start again."

"With you to nag me?" he smiled.

She laughed, then looked at him seriously. "I really don't think we should delay. If there's another of those creatures at large…"

"We can't think that way," he said. "You were right when you told me not to consider what happened to Curran. And I'm right about this. If we don't stop and show that we're not afraid, we'll always be looking back and worrying about monsters."

"You think we can drive away the fear by resting next to a lake?" Martini asked sceptically.

"Maybe, maybe not," Dominic said. "Either way, it can't do us any harm." He hesitated, then amended that statement. "Probably."

Martini was dubious, but she could see that this mattered to Dominic, so she nodded warily and followed him as he took the lead, staggering back to the lake where all of this, as far as he was concerned, had truly begun.

## ONE HUNDRED AND EIGHT

The lake looked as pretty as it had the first time he'd seen it, on that moonlit night when he'd felt so young and alive, when the world had been a realm of seemingly harmless wonders.

He started to hobble towards the edge of the lake, wanting to sit by the water and feel the breeze blow off it. But the clouds had parted and the sun was beating down. When he felt his ruined skin prickling dangerously, he knew it would be wise not to aggravate matters. So, with a sigh, he retreated into the shade, before lowering himself and sitting on the grass beneath the trees.

Martini sat beside him. She felt uneasy with her back to the possibly monster-infested forest, but she did her best to shake that thought from her head.

"What now?" she asked.

Dominic sniffed. "I don't know."

"The bodies will have been discovered in the pub," she noted. "Search teams will be scouring the mountains. We could sit here and wait for them to find us."

He didn't need to think about that for long. "No. I don't want to be up here when night falls. A short rest, then we'll push on. If you can get me something to drink from the lake – carry it to me in leaves or your hands or whatever – that would be a bonus."

"No problem," she said, getting to her feet.

"Not yet," he stopped her. "Sit with me for a bit first. I don't want to be alone."

They stared at the lake in silence. Dominic noticed he was wearing Curran's ring, which he must have slipped on after freeing Martini. He held up his left hand and squinted at the spiked bit of jewellery. "Do you think I should have left this with Curran?"

"No," Martini said. "It will be your only memento of him. I don't think you should ever take it off."

He looked at her, surprised. "I thought you didn't like the ring."

"I don't. But if you ever disrespect it, I'll thump you."

He smiled, tears coming yet again to his eyes. He wondered if they would ever truly stop.

"It's going to be hard," he warned Martini. "A lot of people have been killed, and we're outsiders, so the police might treat us as suspects. On top of that, the monster angle will attract reporters from all over the world. We'll be at the centre of a media shitstorm, and I don't think it will die down any time soon."

"I know," she sighed. "I'd slip away quietly if I could. But we can't. We have to stay and see this through, for Curran and those people in the bar."

Dominic nodded soberly. "They were kind to me. They wanted to help."

They fell silent, remembering what had happened in the bar, Dominic reflecting on the hours leading up to that, his trip up from Laki, stripping naked, falling asleep by the side of the lake, all that had followed.

"You know what I keep hoping?" he said shortly before they rose and set off down the path back to the real world.

"What?" Martini asked.

"That an angry Curran will poke through the bushes and roar something like, *'Where the hell have you fuckers been? I've been looking for you for ages.'* And then he'll spot the ring on my finger and hold up his own hand, and there'll be a ring just like mine on it, and he'll say, *'I guess this wasn't the only one of its kind after all. Where did you find yours, Newt?'*"

Dominic had started to weep midway through his impression of Curran. Martini was weeping too, but laughing sickly at the same time. "That would be wonderful," she sobbed. "But it won't happen, will it?"

"No," Dominic said softly. "But that doesn't mean we can't hope. As dark as things got the last couple of nights, I never completely abandoned hope. Even the lowest of us deserves at least that much to cling to."

Martini leant across and wrapped an arm around him, to comfort him as best she could. Then she remembered his scorched skin and released him. "Sorry," she said. "I didn't mean to hurt you."

"That's OK," he said, smiling through his tears. He reached out and pulled her in close, snuggling up to her and kissing the top of her head. "The pain isn't that bad."

"You're sure?" she asked.

"Yeah," he said, hugging her tight and taking the discomfort gladly. "There are worse things in life than sunburn."

*SUNBURN*

*was written between 6th february 2012 and 24th march 2015*

Printed in Poland
by Amazon Fulfillment
Poland Sp. z o.o., Wrocław